**Todd McEwen** was born in California in 1953 and now lives in Edinburgh. His previous novels are *Fisher's Hornpipe*, *McX* and *Arithmetic*.

'A laugh-aloud and bittersweet threnody . . . an exquisite Joycean prayer to the daily Gods of New York' Alan Warner

'McEwen's unconditional affection for New York is awe-inspiring. Flashes of steely wit conspire with melancholy insights to provide a stirring, thoroughly absorbing portrait of a man at his grave's edge' *Time Out*

'*Who Sleeps With Katz* is not a cancer-ridden day-in-the-death-of gloomfest but a defence of the city that extends beyond New York, beyond America, and a warning not to let gentrification – the real cancer – asphalt over your town's character. McEwen is a writer alive to the sound of the city, its pulse, its velocity' *Sunday Herald*

'A dizzying, compelling novel that throws humour, pathos and crudeness up from the page in equal measures from start to finish. The language McEwen uses is rich and colourful . . . his punchy style peppered with hyphenated dialogue, capital letters and headings becomes addictive . . . raw, immediate, funny and leaving no emotion unexplored, a strong original voice' *Scotland on Sunday*

D1434211

Also by Todd McEwen

*Fisher's Hornpipe*

*McX*

*Arithmetic*

# Who Sleeps with Katz

Todd McEwen

**Granta Books**
London

Granta Publications, 2/3 Hanover Yard,
Noel Road, London N1 8BE

First published in Great Britain by Granta Books 2003
This edition published by Granta Books 2004

A CIP catalogue record for this book is available
from the British Library.

1 3 5 7 9 10 8 6 4 2

Typeset by M Rules

Printed and bound in Great Britain by
Mackays of Chatham PLC

To Lucy Ellmann

*This girl is almost awkward, carrying off*
*The lintel of convention on her shoulders,*
*A Doric river-goddess with a pitcher*
*of ice-cold wild emotions*

—Louis MacNeice, *The Kingdom*

*You've got to think of everything.*

—Louis-Ferdinand Céline

*A guy can't always be thinking.*

—Tom Kromer

# The Old Mental Capital

*Well, I am often taken for a Yale man, by Yale men. That pleases me*
*a little, because I like Yale best of all the colleges.*

—John O'Hara, *BUtterfield 8*

—have you ever heard anything so stupid? said MacK. You know
what I mean—the whole problem in this god damned town was
never hippies, yippies, yiddies, dippies, nimbies, dinkies, darkies,
dorkies, chinkies, hunkies, yuppies, eyeties or The Yankees—the
problem has always been *Yalies*. If only they would stay in New
Haven, and hadn't been led to believe they have any need or ability
to poke their pusses into New York's affairs, or a *duty*, yes a duty to
jump into their J. Press pajamas and run the Stock Exchange, some
God-given seat awaiting them . . . —You don't have to shout, said
Isidor, I know what you're . . . —I mean this is the pernicious thing,
said MacK, perhaps really the only pernicious thing in New
York—I'm really not kidding—Yale. *Yale* and its *foreign insistence* on
maintaining whiteness at the altars of, in the citadels of power—I'm
telling you it's the one thing which prevents New York from running
*utterly smoothly*, man, the dream of polyglot democracy that it is and
must become.

—Polyglot! said Isidor. Pretty big word for a guy who hadda be
excused from his foreign language requirement. —Yes, which it *must
become*, said MacK, his famous vocal cords hitting the perfect res-
onating frequency of the carbon diaphragm in the telephone on the
marble table—the achievement that must mock the rest of this
country for what it is—that *does* mock. It. —Why are you quoting
John O'Hara to me at eight o'clock in the morning? said Isidor.
—Well, there is a point, said MacK, I was looking at it last night.

1

He's part of this White Culture which I'm just completely at the end of my—I'm flabbergasted and unable to comprehend any longer why and how anyone can continue to defend it, celebrate it, re-invent it—what does this great white culture, this white civilization, which all the idiots want to cherish, to keep pristine from the blacks and the Japanese and the Europeans and the gays and the Jews and the women—of what does it consist? I mean, let's really think—John O'Hara? Pearl Jam? Lawrence Welk? Elementary school book and Bible watercolor depictions of the past? CBS?
—Not leaving out *your* great employer, said Isidor.

—The Carpenters, said MacK, Fenimore Cooper, John Grisham? Red Skelton? Hallmark, Microsoft? Mobil? Bill Clinton? Jane Fonda, Walt Disney, American Gladiators? Pat Robertson, Gene Scott? John Willie? Loni Anderson? Jaclyn Smith? The AFL? I'm asking you, man, said MacK, I mean I'm asking all of the religionists and cross-burners and anti-abortionists and professional athletes and cheerleaders and militiamen prancing through the woods in camo, waving Bowie knives and their third grade spelling, I'm *asking* the gymnastic child-abuse coaches—*this* is what you've got? THIS?

—Yeah, yeah, I know, said Isidor. What *I* got is a gut with no coffee in it. Whadda you got? —Oh, well, he called . . . —You mean the doctor called? —Yeah. —Yes and? —Hm. News for you. —So! Gee Whizz, it . . . —Let's meet up about six. —Where? —The Hour? —Okay. All right.

—Aside from my rambling and now, for me, useless analysis of the ills of New York, that call was an absolute *hymn* to male brevity, said MacK. He looked out the window in abstraction. —This music is not blending with the traffic, he said. —*What's* the matter? said the Non-Anglophone.

The jazz wasn't working with his view of the Drive. Rain dark-ened the pavement and tail-lights shone on it in a way which usually pleased him. There were still bright trees in the park. All his life he

2

had been pursuing a soundtrack, yet he balked at the *literal* application of it, those things you stick in your ears that go sss! sss! sss! sss! until you think you must go mad. He just liked looking out of the window and playing the correct record, or to carry the music in his head. What do you think is the meaning of this? Is it composition of a new sort? —You could make a piece, he mused aloud, for pre-recorded Bach, low-angle sunlight and falling leaves. And the stagehands have a script so that the leaves fall the same way each time. —Très arty, she said. —Would you cut that out? said MacK, you're not from France. —You don't know where I'm from. —Yes I do. —What's going on out there? —'Light rain', as we say on the radio. —Untie me? I want to see.

This recalled him to himself and his surroundings. His small pink 'music' room, the only one in his apartment which faced Riverside Drive. The marble café table from Paris and the inguinal hernia it represented. Coffee and bread and butter. The cat in the chair opposite the one she was bound to. The cat adored her. It jumped down and rubbed against her restricted ankles. —Sorry, he said. He loosened the ropes round her ankles, and calves, and thighs, and wrists. He wore his usual black shoes and trousers, white shirt, black waistcoat and long white apron. She hadn't spent the night but had only just come upstairs for breakfast, which he'd fed her. —Can I get you something else? he said. —No, she smiled. Just the check. She stood in her high shoes and looked out the window.

For rain and snow you need brushwork. That or Bach. You need cool jazz if nothing else is to hand. You need Ed Thigpen. *There are moments when you need Ed Thigpen*. But where *was* Ed Thigpen when you needed him? Mr Taste. But today of all days . . . —Do you know what was funny about jazz? said she. The explosion of people named Benny. Blowing into things. Was that not a surprise to everyone? The Bennies? Suddenly thousands of pieces of the shellacs and hundreds of people named Benny exist. No? Formerly an outré name, a name of a man with a gun. Also, later, Oscar.

He found some Bill Evans in which there were brushes.

—What's the *exact* relationship of jazz to traffic? he said. —Of course I do not know, and neither do you, she said, but if you get the right music it will always look right. I love it best for the evening cocktail this month, and all winter long. You always balance the lights with the outside. And the martini. The sushi. And dear cat, she said, tickling it. For breakfast I think it a little nicer in the summer, I like that, the coffee with the window open so you keep discovering the aroma maybe in the breeze?

This music reminded MacK of West 58th Street, the old studios there. How the nightly iterations of the show's orchestra fused with the slim traffic and particular lights of that street. West 58th felt like a *New Yorker* cover in the Seventies, or maybe the *New Yorker* imposed that. They impose so much.

Cars left colors behind them like leaves; the rain shaped them. Music will stop time in the city occasionally. But always there is duty.

He looked at the taxis especially, yellow against the black road and green and red of the park. He put on Lester Young's 'I Didn't Know What Time it Was'. —Bye bye, she said. She kissed him on the neck and tickled the cat, put her coat on over her lurid, unbreakfast attire and went out through the kitchen and down the back stairs chez elle.

The usual folderol extricating himself from the doorman before he heard something utterly stupid. He was sure that he caught something damaging out of the corner of his ear as he fled up the side street towards Broadway.

# Upper Broadway

It's about my first love, he said, looking up at the traffic light—it changed and he stepped off the curb. When he first came to this neighborhood the stop lights were old, with only red and green

4

lamps—no yellow—they trusted you back then. They thought you were an adult who could make up your mind. When he discovered the stop lights, he had immediately wished them older again, of the type which gonged and put out a little flag STOP or GO. Never had been much to say about these few blocks, the incredible merchants who surround a university, selling knock-offs of fashionable shoes, roach traps for twice what anyone pays in the rest of the world or even below 110th Street. It is likely, MacK thought, that a sandwich costs fifty dollars here now.

The bar where he and Isidor learned to drink gone for years, replaced by the hamburger chain where no one learns anything, though they study misery. Here is the hardware store where he did buy his first roach trap, here still the small grocery where a wild-haired man caressed your hand in giving change, baggy eyes shifting. All in all a gentle introduction to town, one roach and one pervert.

Paused a block south. Had thought there wasn't much to do with him and Isidor here, had thought that for a long while, but how? It hadn't been the university neighborhood to MacK for years, not till today. That was where the bar had been, and here was where we learned to smoke, where we took it up seriously for good and all, MacK thought—ruing it, and ruing that he had drawn Isidor into it.

### THE CITY SPEAKS:
### OF COURSE WE SELL TOBACCO SIR.

Their first purchases here at Ben and Nat's—the yellow pouches of 'Teddy', MacK's calabash with a porcelain bowl—ah, later Nat and Phil's after Ben *succumbed* to his self-prescribed ten imitation Habanas i.d., which they all thought ironic and even—funny.

Now that my lung cancer is here, has *finally arrived*, MacK thought, tipping his proverbial hat to those who had predicted proverbially it would—including himself and his loving, paranoid parents, whom he would now precede in death—he set himself the task, on this walk, of deciding, as a poetic and furious concept, which cigarette in the whole world had given it to him.

**30 cigarettes per day × 365 days × 25 years
= 273,750 cigarettes,**

of which how many might you recall? But it is axiomatic among tumor-ologists that it is not 273,750 cigarettes that you puffed away to nothing, rain or shine, yours or someone else's—and what does *that* matter? —you going to go find them? Blame them? They won't even remember, you, Bud—filter or no, happy or sad—but *just one*, a single speck of a fleck of smoke from one mean-minded piece of horticulture.

*Really, quite a lot has to do with the old neighborhood.* MacK thought that it could have been the *first* cigarette he ever really smoked, a 'True' (Blue) in the resonant, tiled bathroom his sophomore year, where he declaimed Chaucer on advice, and became an Announcer—but *smoked* in imitation of his Renaissance professor, who exhaled the pure thought which killed scholasticism oddly and ironically in this smoke. *Ass Hole (Blue). Ass Hole (Green).* But what bad luck that would be—it wasn't fun enough for MacK's poetic and furious concept.

He'd told the doctor he wouldn't want to fight it, and with some repugnance, an attitude which seemed to be left over from the national treatment of *conscientious objectors*, the doctor agreed to send MacK to another who 'sympathized' with patients who, *inexplicably*, believed that when your number is up, it is up. A physician who would help MacK manage, at least experience, if not enjoy, his dying, rather than frustrate it, filling his last months with a lot of morpheated *pep talk*. (You read the papers.)

—*You want a doctor that sympathizes.* —Yeah—scuse *me*.

When he was twenty-five, his hated long-time family doctor told MacK he would contract it, just as *he* had. Good news! It was his last appointment with the man—and in fact MacK was his last patient. Good! —Why do you think I should get this too? said MacK —*Because you're a bitter little shit just like I am.*

Cold breath of the river up 114th Street; a wink of frost bright on the stones of the park, which MacK could see beyond the building on the north corner down there, where he'd lived for a year. It is remarkable how you cannot remember your personal history of every thing and every place in town—you'd go nuts—even though you touch upon these every day. The cold burnt-coffee smell of the West Side in winter. The airshaft apartment he'd thought grand, and the depressing fact that the girl he would spend ten years getting over had moved into the *next building*, that he could actually see her fluorescent desk lamp—which he had loved—far below his kitchen window. The many wind-cooled hopes of Riverside Drive.

But it *was* with her that he'd smoked one of the first. An endless, cried-over salad of the 1970s—you remember them. You know the feeling of the new-democratic gourmet foods sticking in your throat—*quiche lorraine, guacamole, Mateus*—all this crap jamming up your gullet was why everyone constantly burst into tears between 1970 and 1980. In a dark steak and ale emporium—Lincoln Center, to his dismay. —Buy us some cigarettes, she suddenly said, I could do with some raunch—as if she'd awakened to the fact that she was playing a part—the Breakup Scene—they were suddenly to be adult, *to wallow in their own disaster*. Always good news. But how had their tenderness become raunchy, he thought—his tears, though splashed on a lot of turkey and Swiss cheese, were *genuine*.

She looked cute with the 'Kent' and it tortured his sense of loss. 'Kents' from a machine! —which he never smoked again because of that deep, turbulent scene in that dark stupid place—also because 'Kents' smell of the shit-heaps in burning termite nests.

'*The* Broadway?' someone'd written him when first MacK came to town—how seldom you think of Broadway with the name ringing; just a long street with an intense multiple personality disorder. Was Broadway, in midtown even, ever conceived to be glamorous any more? Who has stranger ideas, SAILORS or PEOPLE FROM OHIO? All anyone *thunderstruck* by the word Broadway needs for the disabusement of magic—and they do need this—is a stroll down Broadway in the 100s, thought MacK, as he waded through discount shops, bales of socks, misspellings: Shot of *Whisey* 50¢. But having not walked in the 100s since returning to the neighborhood he was a little surprised that the university had managed to drive wedges of pretense into the place—now there was *espresso for white people*; before there was merely Cuban coffee—for everybody.

At 103rd Street MacK looked again toward the river; halfway down the block on the left was an apartment he and Izzy shared during the Bitterly Cold Winter of 1977, as the newspapers were calling it in November already. Their bankrupt landlord rasped at them through the mouth of the receiver—the Official Receiver—they wouldn't get any heating oil unless they paid their rent—and they said they weren't going to pay any rent unless they got heating oil RIGHT NOW; also the ceiling of MacK's room was like unto a sieve. —That's no reason not to pay, said the Official Receiver. —I can't think of a better one, said MacK. Isidor grabbed the phone and announced he had begun to 'chop up', as he put it, the Mission style oak furniture in the living-room and was burning it in the massive Hugh M Hefner exposed brick hearth of the place—it seemed a Playboy Mansion for cockroaches. —I'm freezing, he said to the Receiver, and that is the sound of your client's dining ensemble warming me up—the oil truck arrived within the hour; the stains of the guy's heaving splattering rush are on the sidewalk still.

MacK had smoked some 'Camels' in that apartment when he and Isidor had the idea of taking Broadway by storm. The theater district, not the 100s. Remembered a number of snow afternoons with the 'Camels' in a holder—which always outraged Iz.

—I'll tell you right now, said MacK to himself, but aloud, in a conscious nod to Isidor, perhaps, today—which cigarette it had better *not* be—any of the damp cigarettes offered me by any god damned drunk *Brit*. Those are the people to get you really smoking, not *play* smoking. Of *course* I'm blaming them! he said to a woman coming out of the smallest laundromat in the world—he remembered it well—they smoke all the time, no sense of STYLE, they call their cigarettes *hairy rags* and to set seal on themselves as the *ashtrays of Europe*, they will actually *talk about death*, thus courting it, while handing them around—not in the *Think on this when ye smoak tobacco*, cut-down-at-eve sense but in grunting through their 'arses' about everything being out of your control so you might as well just 'top' yourself! 'MATE!'—the whole United Kingdom one lost, blurry empire of cut silk.

Fuming now, approaching 96th—the familiar large street tube poured out clouds like a big 'True' (Blue). The big idiot off whom MacK had taken literally a hundred 'Marlboros' in the McAnn's near Herald Square always said the same thing as he, smiling, opened the flap, politely pulled one cigarette an inch up from its fellows, and pointed the pack at MacK like a Luger: *I'm not going to go alone*. Well, said MacK, you haven't. But it would be better if you had. For me.

—But what about every stunk-out bar where I *haven't* smoked? he said. What of that? And what about those who have bored the crap out of me, offering me thousands of cigarettes late into the nights I was loveless—and now your filthy 'pretty smokes' have killed me, what of that? And stopped to get his breath, leaning on the stone ledge at the entrance to the IRT, seeing himself doing it at the same moment—seeing a man who couldn't walk, who couldn't get his breath—*such as you might see*. Implored the god of the IRT—here it was, for worship, succor, or at least for transport off this scene.

# The Gods of Town

*Most dreadfully sorry* but we don't care, do we, what is going on out there in that god damn country. We got our own problems in this our town—we have needs; *'People have NEEDS!'*—we want to LIVE—whereas nobody out *there* can sound a solitary *fart* about being alive—that god damn country is only about death, living death. Consequently we have our own systems of belief. Where is 'Jesus' and that crowd, we would like to know, when you are twenty minutes late for a meeting, it has just begun to hail, *painful* big stones, there are no cabs and no public telephones, there is no scarf, no UMBRELLA maybe! This is *important*. This is your *life*. Well—he is not there. But here are these little telephones, the new guardians of our existence—in shape so like the lares and penates of old—they even cradle themselves, benign and observant, in their own altar in the home. Here is the IRT. Here is the doorman.

How *not* to worship as gods, that is the question, the lady who brings you coffee, the delicatessen with the most reliable head cheese in the world, the sturdy humming motor of the elevator which lands you with a soft kiss on the floor where your meeting is? What of the utility and lovable, dependable stimulus of the Non-Anglophone's goatskin boots? We don't *take for granted* the egg cream, the smell of roasting chestnuts, the umbrella-vendor, fresh shellfish, the No. 1 train, the many Restaurant Martinis of quality, the surpassing fresh cigars—we *worship them here* because THESE ARE THE GODS THAT DELIVER.

Modern life demands flexibility, does it not? Even the *Romans*, a people hardly renowned for their *tolerance*, were happy to take on a new god that seemed useful, wherever they went. They looked into the local religion, gathered its gods to them, and worshipped them with enthusiasm and respect right away! OK they enslaved and murdered the *people*, but they liked all kinds gods!

Of course there are some gods which are simply too exalted for the men and women who crawl like dogs, like *bugs on the street*, to petition directly: the IRT, City Hall, the gas company, the guy who brings seltzer, what the hell is his problem anyway? But in New York, *and only in New York*, you have the freedom to order your pantheon as you will. You like George Bellows better than the man with the THING under his eye at the deli, FINE. And you can mass your gods in order to petition the big boys—there may *be* a way of contacting the gas company through George Bellows and bourbon on the rocks. Set up your altar and do it. We don't bother with CHURCHES.

Like the guy said, in mythic thinking 'distinctions between natural forces and social conventions are not clearly perceived'. Oh, BUDDY! Isn't that your life in New York in a f***ing NUT SHELL? We need more of this fine mythic thinking.

MacK's patient attention to the gods of town had spawned a renascence of painting and sculpture—you see he *suits himself*—which he assigned conveniently to pre-existing public works of art: the monument to the martyrs of the *Maine* at Columbus Circle was for him a kind of ancestor screen, the little gold guys various uncles, aunts, teachers and cartoon characters in decreasing order of favor. He could in Central Park delight in a blindfold *William Powell* [the chief god of Manhattan life] *Riding the Porpoise of Gin*. *Bette Davis* [his female counterpart] *Crowns Johnny Carson with the Wreath of Morpheus*. And the great tableau beloved of us all, near the boat basin, *The Polizei Welcome Mass Transit to Brooklyn with Eros and a Pomeranian while Abe Beame Beckons to Dionysus behind a Cheeseburger Wrapper.*

In classic and agreeable fashion, Central Park is a god and also the *abode* of the god.

Hundreds and thousands of TREES connect our island with the heavens.

We got complicated gods: the Chrysler Building, the Metropolitan Opera, the Board of Estimate, the Port Authority (Gee Whizz!). We got simple: eggs scrambled with calf brains by Hungarians on a winter morning, drums, *toupees* (the garment district their HQ). We got subterranean rivers from the old Underworld.

'The altar or the inscription could be carved with the figure of the god or with the symbols of the god's powers.' Take a look at your COCKTAIL NAPKIN!

We got the all-seeing sun and the moon which peeks at you when you're doing something you shouldn't maybe. We got all kinds statues replete with divinity.

We have our Mayors: divine kingship is a form of polytheism.

And—sadly—our gods are countered by demonic forces. The IRT wrestles with quite a few—no names need be named but there is sometimes a powerful demon at work in the token-booth at 50th Street. Wears a dirty blue shirt. The weather, in February, is a demon—or at least a bitch. There is Asbestos. There is the guy who lived upstairs from Isidor with the dogs. The dogs themselves. F***—*all dogs.* AND, as a kind of Miltonian-size *counter* to all the striving, scheming, smoking, buying, selling, thinking, stinking, drinking and LOVING in this our town, there is, across the river, NEW JERSEY. So it's a struggle—what isn't?

We *believe* in the power of objects—why else would we cut up our credit cards, remove the license plates from the car we abandon at 128th Street and the West Side Highway, throw *pennies*—malign, time-wasting demons—into the GARBAGE, if not to quell their powers when we no longer need or want them?

Why do you take a complimentary ballpoint pen from one restaurateur and not the other?

*Some* people place their cheeseburger wrapper in the gutter rather than the litter bin—they believe, obviously, that there in the gutter its magic will be sapped, rather than amassing new, rebellious and rowdy powers in the confined space of the bin with its *partners in chaos*.

If you will take a moment to observe us, with charity, you will see that we are indeed all of us a-worshipping these gods. In this our town. The stern old gods are gone. They got 'mono'—then they died!

In the RCA Building, one of MacK's gods, lived many of his others: microphones, light bulbs, the mischievous god which hovered for him around things made of stone. The great god Radio of course and her nemesis Television. Under Nancy Schwartz's little suits, the gods of silk and night and just-possible orgasm. But of the thousand reasons MacK loved the RCA Building, the proud container of his little struggle to exist, the most salient and wonderful was that Rockefeller Center celebrated, perpetuated the great, meaning gods of the ancient world, Prometheus, Poseidon, Atlas—and others of recent memory, Washington and Lincoln (both deified to the point of unreachability), the steam locomotive, burly-armed linotype operators on the altar of the Associated Press Building . . . even the glory of the American Girl in a skating skirt.

Defy you to identify a glossier chamber of the HEART OF CAPITALISM, and smack dab in the middle of it is an ecstatic swirl of the best of gods. What theism could the capitalists promote other than a wild, rich, doomed, FUN, multifarious one? So *please*—enough of this 'partnership' of 'Christ' and corporation. They *can't* go along with 'Jesus'—there's no PERCENTAGE in it.

Any other line of thinking is

**BALONEY*!***

# Upper Broadway

The breathlessness was panic—nothing had changed in his chest in the three days since he'd got the *real* good news for modern man. There hadn't been much pain yet and he didn't wheeze—the whole thing had cropped up as *back pain*—he was still thinking of going back to work *for as long as his lungs didn't make noise*, he'd said to Shelby Stein, *production noise*, that was a good one, and as long as he didn't spatter his beloved microphone with mucus. Yes, the good news—you're going to croak, you've *got* to. More people have got to die, and faster, and many must die by cigarette. Do your bit, MacK said to himself, so.

He was sitting on the steps now—*in people's way*—and leaned against the low granite wall, his head far down enough that there was no escaping the idea he was in distress—though escape it the people of Broadway and 96th would for a few moments longer, he thought. He had trained himself through years of coffee, tobacco and hangover-induced panic (*Change your life*, his hated family doctor said. —Change *this*, MacK replied lamely, though the method is a sound one) to think of DESTINATION, of Isidor. A tear escaped his dream-eye, the lazy one filled with sand after an imagist night—though perhaps that was the cindery wind of the subway—and fell on a perfect circle of ancient black gum at the same moment a hand in a glove came into his field of vision and a man asked if he were all right—if he needed help? *Contact* can break that cycle, even if everything seems compressed and malevolent, terribly near; even if he only thought of the man as his glove and couldn't remember his face in the following days. —No, said MacK, it's just some bad news, thank you. The helping hand of New York—which never doubt—may quickly be withdrawn if it expects you are wasting its time. —You think *you* got bad news! said the hand, in walking away, it seemed to MacK, who still hadn't sought the hand or face of the voice.


Only a few blocks from home, he reflected, but the IRT roared and filled its mouth and lips with old electricity—you could hear the express coming from WAY away—the distances of Manhattan seem doubled in that dark. On cold days the rails sing rather than whine or grate, sing, rush like a river—MacK sat halfway down the steps to the totem-booth and its massive priest, listened to the rushing as if to that of his western river, where, it struck him, he had smoked one of the great cigarettes of his existence, and that he owed it to himself and to humanity that he *decide* on which cigarette he'd *like* to have done him in, perhaps more than selecting the most craven one for *blame*. It was a 'Camel' bought in a lodge shop, thrilling with the odor of inbreeding, on his way up through the mountains. The sort of place which deals only in cigarettes, chewing tobacco, jerky, bait, beer that tastes of trout, and pocket watches on a faded card by the cash register. Remembered all this with the fond painterly clarity which all trips away from Manhattan acquire—it was true that although MacK had grown up only a hundred miles from that river, it had never meant a god damned thing to him until he had gone to New York and got perverted, as his mother said, started smoking—and later got in the habit of returning to the river for *romantic purposes.* —*Jetting around?* Isidor had said, invading yet *another* life?

The first 'Camel' he'd had out of that pack was one of the most ennobling—*the bite of tobacco beside a river* being one of the sublime manly moments. Though how many manly moments like that can you take till you wind up in this predicament, completely *unmanned? The bite of tobacco beside a river*—not in the sense of advertisement, but really—get your yenidje into that pipe and flame it yellow, yellow as the yenidje and the aspens around you at altitude—the smoke rich and white as fresh birch bark—and you begin to wonder, MacK said to himself, but out loud, what this plant is put on earth for, if not our consolation? You can't make shoes out of it.

*The bite of tobacco beside a river*, the stones under the water made silver by the moon seen closer and specially from the Sierra, and, so he thought, Red waiting for him in the tent, all woman (make *seething* noise between teeth), though while MacK had been having these male epiphanies one after another she had taken her credit card up to the hotel and got herself a room—having thought not much of this four-day exit from Manhattan—especially after slipping on something in the camp's washy toilet block—with this guy who after all had a top job, of sorts, even if it bored the crap out of him—she thought the tent unspecial and wanted to be closer to the bar and room service and the little shop selling not bait but designer resort wear. *Here?*

The rest of that pack of 'Camels', MacK reflected, were among the worst he ever smoked, creating an ulcerish BILE which ultimately led him to need to get away from Red and—quite possibly one of these, subsequent to the great first one, was It, *the* one, gave him his bad news, his good news, along the lines of the theory that calf-headed babies are born to rape victims and Republicans after congress with escaped mental patients—*congress*. Smoke a cigarette when you're miserable, *eating yourself up inside* as the saying goes, and that'll kill you. That was the Red story in a nut—transcendent at the beginning and very soon he'd found himself alone with his petty 'realizations' on the bridge; the silver and all that turned to tar.

Panic and all this scum from the past aside, MacK felt happy for a moment, on the steps of the 1, 2 and 3 trains, realizing he had two jolly lists to make, the cigarettes he *wanted* to have killed him, and the ones he would *despise* for doing so.


People walked around him grumbling—a little. You're always sorry to see someone sitting on the subway steps, aren't you, because they're going to ask you for money maybe or—this is the distressing thing—they've *given up*. And you that close yourself. But, MacK thought, should I despise the cigarettes I *didn't* enjoy for killing me, or assign a nobility in doing so to the ones I *did*? What about all those *airport misery cigarettes*? Or the little cigarettes they sell in France—no bigger than a roll-up—which he stood smoking one after another, much as one may discover one has absently eaten a ONE LB bag of candy—looking out at a much rainier version of Montmartre than had been predicted by . . . anyone, especially MacK and Red. Man was she fed up this time. 'Gravités', they called them, the little cigarettes sold by weight and not number—what an idea, like you were stuffing handfuls of shag into your chest. But come on, every cigarette is a misery cigarette. You make fun of 'True' (Blue) for being the ass hole's cigarette? Come, they're *all* ass hole's cigarettes, the lot of them—the holiday exotics, the *papirocii* of Moscow, the 'Gitanes', 'Sher Bidis', 'Turkish State Monopolies', 'Gold Flake' for God's sake—thought they didn't count, eh! What about down on your hands and knees digging in the waste basket for flu cigarettes, the ones you tried to eliminate from your life forever by running them under the tap? The Sobranie 'Cocktails' in little milk-glass cups at weddings—what if it were one of those? *Damn* you'd feel an idiot. The *brands* you found yourself unwrapping—you caught yourself once in a while in a dim acknowledgement that you really did need to smoke *anything*. —*You're some smoker, eh?* said the man in the bar in Cork, who'd only been sitting next you for an hour, through several small cigars, three 'Major Extra Size' and now a pipeful of 'Erinmore' bought up the road—and for *them* to remark on it . . . Of course the same guy approaches you on the way home. —*Any fags?* and you proudly hold out your closing-time purchase, a new pack of 'Carroll's'—and he turns up his nose. —*No 'Majors'?*

—The most delicious cigarettes in the world, said MacK out loud on the steps of the IRT, I say it who shouldn't. —Crazy one, said a guy with a little boy coming down and avoiding MacK.

The irony is that you smoke most when you're unhappy, because of the illusion of happiness. But what if life suddenly worked out? Or you roused yourself and made yourself happy in some way—or it happened by accident—what else are you propitiating these gods for?—and there you are, with this mine of phlegm inside you, waiting for your *happy* self to breezily tread on it and blow you a hundred feet in the air and scatter you all over town. Well *then* you've got something to worry about, so there you are the same old miserable bastard; but isn't that the same reasoning that *keeps everyone smoking: Ah, pal, ah'm f\*\*\*ed awready*—yes, but are you? When the doctor looks at you as he did me the other day, said MacK, *that's* when you're f\*\*\*ed, and it hurts, and it would have been a moment to avoid.

—Here, said someone—here. And pressed a five on MacK and hurried down the steps, do you think anyone has time to wait for thanks in this our town? They're all very modest. MacK looked down at his clothes, which were very nice, and felt his chin, which was smooth, and in feeling his chin recalled the recent haircut and the morning's shampoo (he'd started crying when the water came on—*the shampooing* as they say in France—what the Hell do *they* know about '-ing' anyway?)—but he had to take stock of himself in this way—there being no mirror—to be reassured he didn't look awful and that it *was* odd that the lady had given him five bucks—proof he'd been speaking aloud, he guessed. Proof that to sit on the steps of the 1, 2 and 3 and *say* something assures everyone you've *lost your senses* and that you should be given money to go away—but what do they know, you could have been reciting the *Aeneid*—which would only shore up their case—oh you can play music or even SING, like that *ass* on the steps at 14th Street, *Sa-ha-hahm-hm whay-ay-aeayeare o-ho-ho-o-verr the ray-ee-ay-ee-hain-hain-hain-boww*—etc—and everyone's comfortable but SAY something, talk, declaim, and you're suddenly much closer to arrest than you ever have been. Imagine yourself a Demosthenes, why not, strutting up and down the platform, your mouth stuffed with tokens—wouldn't work so well with twenty Metrocards—though 'twould be more hygienic.

Now the thing about talking out loud in public, or talking to yourself, which are not the same thing, although everyone thinks they are, is that you OUGHT TO DO IT. Everyone *does* do it, in the office pod or cubicle, at home, during the shampooing, MacK thought, again recalling the morning's shower, he'd cried in it, but *had also talked a deal of good sense*, planning out today—the walk, hitting the street—a brave act, face town with what you know, hit The Hour with Iz at the end of the day. There's a basic dishonesty in society today about talking 'to yourself'. Who does not say, *aloud*, to himself or herself, when stepping into the shower for the shampooing, 'my brother in law is an incredible weasel', or 'the next time I see Sid Herkenhoff I ought to pop him in the nose'—or 'if only I could get S—W— 's trousers down, what a picnic that would be'? Don't *kid* yourself, people are saying stuff like that 'to themselves' (though that's erroneous), something like that about *YOU* right now! They're saying it to people they *wish were there*, people they wish they had the gumbo to say it to—or people they wish they *were*—all over town—NOW!

—Why should saying something aloud brand you as insane, MacK said, why should *that* be the index of what is mad, of mad behavior —compared to running for office, being a lawyer, working on Pine Street, going on Outward Bound, or to church, buying a new house, 'deciding' your partner is not attractive, moving to the South or the West, neglecting your education, or thinking something on TELEVISION was really pretty interesting? HAH? '*Yes, they're making some marvelous programs these days*—' If anything, said MacK, coming very close to the theories of Isidor at this point, Izzy who truly *cannot* stop himself speaking aloud in public any longer, which is part of the reason he confines himself increasingly to his tower—there've been a few run-ins with the police—it really ought to be ENCOURAGED BY CITY HALL—it's a good way of getting to meet people and promoting HARMONY—relationships wouldn't be based on physical attraction, but in *mutual understanding*. If everyone talked about her crap, his crap aloud, all the time, then you'd move seamlessly from your own preoccupations into someone else's—or, say on the 96th Street downtown platform, into everyone else's—and then back into your own—like jazz—it would be jazz—you'd stop looking at everybody's hair and legs and chin clefts and tits and briefcases and suits and you'd really know what they're about. —It *isn't* mad, he said, it makes perfect sense—it isn't talking to yourself, it's merely a conversation with someone you haven't *quite met*, MacK said, WHAT'S WRONG WITH IT! The big priest in his bullet-proof Plexiglas shrine glanced at MacK wearily, heaved a sigh—reached for the phone.

MacK stood and went back up to the street; none of that crap today. Merely a man who looked fine, with some bad news under his belt, and a mission. No picaresque veerings into small hells—at least not until you get to Isidor—just a guy with a problem and a couple days off. A love of town on a bright day. Why not?

Why not place under arrest all these people talking 'to themselves', into these *little phones* . . . they really *are* insane.

# That's Laughs Tonight

Spiritual journeys are hugely dull—they sell—but if you're reading one you ain't having one. MacK tried to think of his journey downtown as something other. A *celebration*, he thought, and began to laugh—it was a word they used at work. To the Presentation Department over in TELEVISION, *celebration* meant cutting up all the segments of a hit series into bits and linking them with bullshit espoused by someone who'd never had a hit series, either because the original star had just died of a drug overdose or because someone on the 15th floor saw a hole in the schedule (usually in the summer) and by drinking extra hard devised some sort of anniversary relating to the series, the master copies of which were COSTING THE COMPANY MONEY by sitting on a shelf in Burbank or over in Lyndhurst.

But a *celebration* involves work by editors, thought MacK, and so is much more the mark of respect than the *tribute*, which is the simple re-running of one episode, because some ass hole has definitely died—all a tribute involves is the Traffic Department clearing air time, with sponsors getting bumped, perhaps rounding up some of the original sponsors (a 'special tribute')—and Presentation affixing a solemn logo or freeze-frame to the head or tail of the episode:

### IN MEMORY OF SO-AND-SO
### 1947–1999

with something nauseating like *Still Laughing* or *We Hear You* underneath, *gods* is television depraved. MacK remembered a Production Standards meeting he'd attended three or four years before, something they had twice a year—the president had said they needed to 'ensure that there was *continuity of recognizability* between all networks'—and a fight broke out between the Presentation Department and the Video Department—strictly a matter of opinions, and morals, and money—over what *was* a respectful amount of time to display such a memorial shot. Presentation said you could cut to it before the production logos but after the network logo, hold it for three seconds, and fade it out in two, thus making it an easily-handled five extra seconds, which could be dealt with as they usually did, by speeding up and chopping the production logos, and by dropping network into the locals' laps three or four seconds late, let *them* take up the slack, tell their idiot anchors to lay off five seconds of drool with the weather girl. Guy from Video—older hand after all, probably thinking of JFK's and even FDR's funerals—rose up out of his chair all Cavendish and ruffled Brooks Brothers offense at this: —Why it's an outrage, which was the first time MacK had heard *why* used as an interjection in years—let alone the word *outrage* in the RCA Building—you've got to *fade up* at least in four, give people enough time to read it a couple of times—*Read* it?! said someone in the back—let it *sink in* for Christ's sake, and fade to grey scale in four or five and *then* to black! Anything else looks like playing pin the tail on the donkey, the guy said, slightly overtriumphantly.

Of course it didn't end there—Programming stepped in and ordered Research to come up with a *numerical value* to be assigned to every network personality, past and present, news, sports and entertainment, based on their peak numbers (to aid decision-making they also requested a value based on each personality's *mean* numbers), which would be used to compute the length of hold on memorial messages in the future. —Damned if I'm going to lose *over two seconds of prime time* on someone who didn't really pull viewers, looking at the big picture, you know, over all, said the guy from Programming—he was a deputy. Then a fresh fight broke out over *tributes* which Video said ought to be more or less the same but Programming and Presentation quickly decided could be forced on to voice-over if time was tight—and when was it not?

So that got dumped on MacK's counterpart, Shelby Stein, Chief Announcer of the TELEVISION network, who had to go write a memo to the announcers about being 'solemn and quick' in such a situation—when no memorial tag would be displayed and the network's grief would have to be demonstrated purely by voice-over with the end credits before hitting the promos for later shows—*Solemn, yes, and God damn quick*, Shelby wrote. *You must move quickly back to a normal promo tone, which may be difficult in the case of upcoming comedy.* Presentation made a half-assed commitment to providing more serious promos if there was to be a memorial v.o., pushing a news special or an upcoming documentary, except that there weren't any any more, and everyone knew they wouldn't do it—Presentation doesn't do jack shit. *Tapes showing your ability to do this to my office by January 23rd—they will as usual be cleared by Programming and if not satisfactory I will assign you a coach.*

[SAMPLE ANNOUNCE]
THIS EPISODE OF *PET TRAUMA WARD* HAS BEEN SHOWN AS A MEMORIAL TO SO-AND-SO—OUR FRIEND. !TONIGHT ON *BONACKER*—! SEEDHEAD FINDS A PIECE OF WOOD—[CLIP :07] —AND BONACKER CAN'T BELIEVE IT! —[CLIP :04] —THAT'S LAUGHS TONIGHT ON *BONACKER*! —[LAUGH TRACK TO STING & LOGO—NETWORK I.D. —TO AFFILIATES.]

Shelby could write a memo that made you think; the veeps thought it was all simple how-to. The *veeps* cleared the *memos*—you believe that? After meetings like this MacK often went down to the lobby and walked under *Sert's great mural, 'Time'*—as it said in the souvenir book and as you heard the tourist guides bleat—looking at the clouds and noble machines. Those were the days maybe, he thought, when airplanes didn't smell like businessmen's crap warm with coffee and artificial creamer—the workers, the vision, everyone *reaching*, for *something*, I don't know . . . But MacK often imagined that *Sert*, Rivera's replacement, might have left a little *space* for Lenin, even though they'd literally kicked Rivera's *huge ass* out onto 49th Street, thrown his brushes, palette and beret after him—*Get lost, pendejo!*—thought the *invisible Lenin* might be near this big nude, perhaps a relative of Prometheus, the big gold guy taking a bath outside—since Lenin had a *beard* he might have wanted to stand near the *locomotive*. At times, say on a dark winter afternoon, the lights in the lobby gave a vibrancy to the mural, a real lift and swirl to all that black and brown old capitalism.

—But you know, said Shelby one day when MacK had taken *him* down to the lobby too, after a meeting about which letter, N, B, or C, was supposed to sound the grandest and most proud—if you were really looking up through these clouds, up through the building, you wouldn't see the sky or the sun, said Shelby. The sky is out *there*, he said, and gestured toward the skating rink—what you'd see is *fifty stories of asses sitting on chairs.* Some people in the lobby took note of this, partly because Shelby's voice was loud and famous, whatever he did with it . . . when he was buying a round at Hurley's he often said joyfully *This is on me!*—he had nothing to spend his money on, Shelby—which sounded so much like *This is NBC* that people looked and one of the duty announcers who was having a highball in the back choked on a rock and ran upstairs, thinking he was hearing a cue. —*And some of them ain't bad looking*, said Shelby, who was one of those who use quaint contractions to state something at once risqué and beneath him—but which in fact he was thinking about all the time.

There are three cool entrances to the RCA Building, and MacK always came in the one designated 50 West 50th Street because he was usually coming from the 50th Street subway, and liked to walk by the Music Hall; Shelby preferred 49 West 49th Street because he was coming from some big-spenders' garage and it was closer to the bank of elevators for the TELEVISION floors. For smoking Shelby liked to stand outside the 30 Rockefeller Plaza door—*There's a canopy and sometimes GOILS*, he said—he thought people might recognize him—though who would have recognized him unless he were speaking?—he simply looked like somebody hanging around smoking. If he and MacK agreed to have a drink at Hurley's, they each took their favorite exit and met at the door of the bar on Sixth Avenue and sneered at each other.


Bored at work, often left profoundly alone on the twentieth floor for hours with nothing to do except wait for the red light to come on, speak his piece, mark his log sheet (☐ FED TO KEY STATIONS ☐ FED TO NETWORK ☐ FED TO LIVE NETWORK ☐ CONTINUITY NO.___ AUTH N SCHWARTZ) —at times it seemed odd to him he should be entombed in this electrically live though acoustically dead casket on the twentieth floor—a little live cancer cell in the grey dead tissue of the RCA Building, using this great apparatus, this swelling organ of vacuum tubes, granite, lamps, diorite, elevators, carpeting, of *power*—just to open the microphone and say things like 'This—is NBC' or 'Stations, promo feed T-5-B will be sent three minutes early today, at 14:24:30'—when he could have been offering a few of his own opinions—at any rate, began a hobby of lists and charts, where most would be happy with acrostics, or JUMBLE—a double-entry day-book of his modest erotic life. Bought a solid accountant's book for this, full of appealing graph patterns and columns— decided to add up the particular talents of each lover and arrive at an over-all, logarithmic rating—talk about raising the next power—which was bound to depress him, since whoever got the highest value would still be unavailable, and still no doubt pissed off as Hell—ye *gods* he'd broken it off miserably with them all— there'd be no going back and declaring *You are everything on this chart!* and reflaming bed-time by dint of statistical analysis.

Of course a lot of the more refined tastes had to belong to the conjecture of nostalgia, since he hadn't known about the uses of string, many of the useful portals of the body, &c, &c, *until he moved to New York and got perverted*, as Isidor used to say. The chart was

| Mlle. | Levres. | Talons. | Ficelles. | Toucher. | Jeu. |
|---|---|---|---|---|---|
| Eliza | As if she had once known how. | I. Miller. | Wouldn't hear of it. | Dreamy. | Laughed in face. |
| Nadia II | Like a SOLAR FLARE! | Hauts! | Worrisome night of her green garden twine. | Velvet, or poss. chowder. | ! 'You be a Hungarian impresario and I'll be girl w/ three-hand piano act' ! |
| Girl from BMT | The little octopus! | C. Jourdan, but kept taking them off; played w/ them when she was in shower. | Refused to be released. Lost sleep. | Somehow, sand got in. | Cowboys—again. Had to buy toy 6-shooter. $ 7.95 |
| Pegeen | A tad gloppy. | Wore flats contr. to instr. | Lost half-hitch somewhere. | Perfect. | Asked me to talk like Lloyd Bridges. Refused. |

becoming more complicated with regard to the *fourth* dimension, as he was extrapolating and deducing the possible erotic aspects of women he had had and others he had not had, from their business and weekend attires and attitudes. Nancy Schwartz, for instance, he was almost positive must own smalls of maroon satin, a projection based upon the qualities of several blouses she wore when visiting Master Control. Maroon was going out of style—it held an unremarkable but assumed place in his erotic pantheon—much as in the delicatessen you *assume* there to be mayonnaise on your sandwich. He was sure, looking at the chart, that Francine Buzza would have enjoyed climbing on top of him, if he had only known such *filthy pleasure* five years before, and whenever he would open this *f\*\*\*ing* book he achingly, sobbingly wished he had asked to see Bunny Watanabe's shoe closet.

### BUT IT WAS ONLY A HOBBY—*!*

Gods the *office*, thought MacK, who hadn't decided when to go back to work really or if at all. Why not go down and stand on Fulton Street for the rest of the time? Rest of your *life*. *Your life*, after all. What's going back to the office going to do but remind you of the good news? But *Lenin* turned MacK's thoughts of the lobby funereal—he'd never been able to bear the very dark, back part of the lobby—where they sell the tat—he had a horror of the black marble well leading to the lower level—do you hear me? *he hated the lower level* (he hated the lower level of Grant's Tomb, too) hated the way the brass squares set in the black stone curved down there—and was bothered every morning when he walked past the security desk by the thought that there had been a huge, possibly eternal staircase there at one time, walled up quickly in the Fifties when the whole building was trashed for TELEVISION in an absolute panic—they'd needed a scene dock. Hated the idea of *walled up*. When MacK was in a bad mood the black lobby seemed a mausoleum, now perhaps forever. He felt the same way at a cash machine, just off Madison

Square, a special one, as he thought, designed for bankers, surrounded by *too much granite in a soft shape*; it was too creepy to get your money out of a little tomb anyway. So: a CELEBRATION, this walk, MacK thought—at least the five seconds—and grey scale would be nice.

New York is a good place to die. You have your St Vincent's. You have your elegant Madison Avenue mortuaries.

The air seemed to have cleared—or the smog that panic is maybe. Who needs the subway? Gods—the office!

# That Day

He thought: a snow day ten years before, ten *years*, the kind of idea which makes Isidor squirm and profane. There they were leaving Isidor's tower, bundled up, MacK on a visit from one of his god damn network outpostings, joyful in an inadequate overcoat from some stupid part of the country where these things are a matter of form and not of keeping warm. The discreet, the usual sidelong glance from Isidor at what MacK was wearing. Grey snow, not yet slush, snow determined to stay a while and make you cold. And some falling, just enough to speed you the couple of blocks. There were these Irish joints they'd never been, over beyond Third, which needed enumerating. Came out of the tower just to 'walk around'—the porage underfoot was their Enabler as if they needed one.

Out of the tower, past the doorman who was wearing *his* snow day face—a combination of the child and soldier in each of us. —Going to be mighty cold later, Gentlemen. Doormen always try to tell you what to think about the weather. This doorman was known to wear dresses in his time off, so Isidor, *sotto voce*: —Hardly a day for chiffon, Frank.

It is pleasant to have to put the struggle of a snow and noise walk into the conversation. The snow excusing you from the judgement of the city and giving always that sense of holiday. Even on Pine Street it is said they enjoy snow.

It was one of those places that appears ready to serve Guinness at an early hour. Down some steps from the street and through an oddly suburban door, past neon signs. Already some wet patches on the floor. But pool tables . . . ——How can you pay attention to your beer, asked Iz, making a face at the sour pasteboard of his pint, if you have to do stuff with a lot of BALLS? Drives me nuts. The bartender, a man of degraded affability, could tell they had come not for the pool but for the drink and they did not care for the drink——these bartenders *should* be nervous at eleven o'clock in the morning——but why are we embarrassed when we do not like our drink, when we do not love the environment in which we drink our drink? Why is it not OK to put down our drink, or ask for another, or simply, Americanly leave? But perhaps to leave is European——what one wants to avoid is an abuse of self, even though in beer with the distinct taste of last night one has been insulted and impugned. To have to put down the glass and leave under the dull smirk of billiard players——! But their footing in the vortex of the day was established.

It was not so many minutes to McSorley's, where Isidor broke with history and had two darks, so as to stay in the *stout spectrum*——MacK fortified himself with two-and-two, gods but they get smaller every year, and for his *petit déjeuner* the liverwurst and onion sandwich *avec la moutarde de old maison at home*, which are too well known to admit description. Isidor never eats before dinner. The snow fell and they wished the fire had been lit, but the history of the stove and the broad backs of other men kept them insulated from the world, truly, at their table. This is why you come out into the world in snow——to be professionally repackaged against it. And to hear nothing——but the infrequent car on 7th Street. With lunch-cool stomachs they emerged in an hour, having discussed that branch of history which dealt with the two of them at that table——the day was now surely styled

**That Day**

in MacK's mind—and faced into the snow and the secretive destination of Wally's, a very old bar in an unmarked courtyard in the West Village. One never knows, do one, is Wally's going to be open for business but as they were together and MacK was wearing the needy talisman of a pathetic coat this was a day of luck, of significance. And if Wally's were open it would be the quiet chapel of the hours of afternoon, a family of aloof dogs napping by the fire. And it was not inconceivable, given the flakes which sketched HOLIDAY outside, that it was not too early for a martini, on a day like today when MacK was visiting town in a *gauche overcoat*—he'd gotten *looks* from people he knew on a brief stop at the RCA Building—a Wally's martini, which were more *décor* than anything. MacK took off the inappropriate coat and felt himself slipping on an invisible garment of the past, sitting in Wally's—a comfortable cultural mackinaw sewed for him by the Wilbur Sisters or Irma Rombauer—felt all the streets they'd traversed return to the way he and Isidor had always wanted to see them, how they looked in 1945. Out of pre-addled bonhomie he'd said the word *Gibson*.

The thing arrived in a wet glass of pure patina, it tasted as if made wholly of onion pickle juice. MacK had sipped at it and though initially overwhelmed, felt he should react with optimism and so pretended he was driving through one of the many *Onion Capitals* of his youth, father saying *Hold on, there, you've never had one of these before have you?* So maybe this is what it's supposed to taste like—though I don't recall, MacK thought, Cary Grant making any one of the faces I would now like to be making. —This tastes a little . . . is it supposed to b-hee . . . , he said explosively and handed the glass to Isidor who took a mouthful and rose up crying no No NO!, rushed for the bar and collared the soft hippie with the red beard. —This is *onion juice*, man, said Iz, are you insane? Guy hick-blinked and then revealed he'd used the last onion in the jar and had simply upended it into the ice and the gin. —But this is *madness*, said Isidor, don't you have a strainer? Bring my friend a martini right away and use an olive. I could have your license for this. (Isidor, for some wild reason, believed that barbers and bartenders were still all issued with *licenses* by the State of New York—therefore that there was some kind of Masculine Amenity Authority that would haul into JAIL the asses of those who would make with a sloppy drink or cut your hair into peculiar *shelf-like formations*.) The fellow meekly obeyed. *It was quite possibly the only martini mixed at that moment in town by a feller in BIB OVERALLS*. One of the dogs opened a contented eye but that was as far as Isidor's ripples went. And so another, then on to a brief sample of an ale or two and it was time for to meet Sylvie at Sevilla for dinner. That Day.

The streets were quite dark and there were lots of people coming TOWARD the boys many of whom no doubt had Wally's in mind. But a Wally's full of custom which was the only way *they* had ever seen it. And it was not so many blocks to Sevilla, which is located, I tell you now, AT THE CORNER OF BEDFORD AND CHARLES.

And here was Sylvie, muse and nurse, in the window, waiting for MacK and Isidor, looking rather decorative, Christmassy the year round she was, like Celeste Holm, the goddess of nice New York girlfriends. —Can this girl perch on a bar stool and look expectantly festive, said Isidor, or what? Even though she's just come from therapy . . . —*Therapy!?*, MacK recoiled, what kind of therapy! —Search me, said Isidor.

Heaven has a specific address; and there they always address you specifically. They're all from Galicia, these *angeles*, and so they twang at you, solicitous *guitarrons*. Roberto the bartender's *O.Y.U.?* as he slides the Isidoronic martinis toward the boys; Sylvie looks on with her iced Xeres. No fool she. None of this *What have you done to me!?* for her. These were among the best Restaurant Martinis in town because Iz had trained Roberto over months. He had *trained Roberto*. True to the phlegmatic spirit of his native village Roberto took this penetrating customer's instruction without rancor, including it in the ups and downs of life which he suffered in their totality, in every glance at the world through his sad blue eyes—truth to tell a color remarkably similar to Isidor's.

It is not known whether on That Day Sylvie found the boys merely gay company, a bit the worse for wear, or completely nuts and strong in their disbelieving. But she played along as though life was merry and it was. What had been slowly taken through the afternoon was readily absorbed by the planet *mariscada*—its orbiting moons of frozen beer. When not waiting on them with *short-jacketed alacrity*, as MacK had characterized it in his index of waitering, Antonio stood by the table and exchanged ideas about the latest films. —The guy's mad for them, said Izzy, and I like hearing his point of view because it is always, elegantly, 100% wrong. Not because he's from Spain, but because he lives in Queens.

MacK leaned back cautiously at one point—the carpentry of the booths was untrustworthy—and observed

### ISIDOR & SYLVIE: A TABLEAU

Iz perspiring, digging for clams at the bottom of the pot : Sylvie dabbing her mouth and looking at him in a way that was at first monitory but ascended to loving : reflective surfaces of the bottles and glassware and Isidor's spectacles : Sylvie's necklace : soft sweet wools of their clothes : the co-incidence of their flesh tones and the general ease of their being together : a city love made of companionship and romantic feeling for this our town.

How could *this* be? : out into the wet snow for a look-in at the Minetta, to which Sylvie agreed, she always agreed to let the boys have their fun, unlike some women in some chapters we could name, frantically trying to *pull them apart* at eleven o'clock in the cold!

Discussion and then experiment ensued on the subject of the martini as *digestif*. If Sylvie objected she held her peace as sense of a sort was still being made, and anyway she could easily flee the several blocks to home.

The Minetta was bright and Isidor took up the command of the bar, inspecting the bartender's equipment, holding his glass up to the light, MacK felt suddenly he was back under the glaring copper frontier-style *kitchen lamp of childhood*, father showing MacK some simple chemistry experiment. The science MacK never understood, but the *effect*, such as turning a clear fluid violet, was certainly something known to the early religious japesters—mess around with people's drinks and *man* you have their attention. Sylvie still looked at Isidor with something like love, and MacK, still partly in his chemistry lesson, recognized, as he did from time to time, the similarities between Isidor and MacK's own father, the slightly drooping moustaches, the restrained 'aviator' frames which emphasized the sadness of the eyes which MacK had spent his life trying to animate—when you think about it.

But rather than stay and stay and make fools, away from the bright light and across the chilly park to the tower. Sinking into the leather chairs in front of the sharp-smelling fireplace, stroking the cat who watches the humidor being brought out—it had oft thought of taking up smoking; Sylvie excusing herself and going for bed; the lights of downtown for the seeing and jazz brushwork underscoring the blatter of wet snow on the window. The cigar. Quiet descends. Some talk of the past.

The armagnac. The calvados.

But *then*, the rising of a new idea. A clean, reasonable, sane idea! Up and out, like youth itself, to the Knickerbocker, just up the street, really—why not just one or two? —After all, not every day a guy brings a coat like *that* to New York, said Isidor—you'd love to be outside *using it*, wouldn't you?

So they drifted like snow as you do in happy dreams, the short-subjects before the nightly monster movie—up the little street and on to the big street—watched over by the god of late errands, making them deaf to the entreaties of 8th Street and invisible to the malcontents of University Place.

One or two, a whiskey, a beer in the pleasant Knickerbocker —guys playing music in the rear in an open-handed spirit—men appreciating the pretty women who would come out on a night like this—the people of this our town enjoying themselves—and truly, with the minimum of urbane distance—*liking each other*.

# *This Again*, or,
# the Routine of the Empty

In the cold months, Washington Square seems in suspended animation, it glistens and suggests birth later, like some icky pod or *sac* in a biology film. MacK, rambly on his way to the IRT, often avoided University Place as he might again be ensnared in his awful ROUTINE OF THE EMPTY:

At the all-night grocery on 10th he would buy a large can of beer, for taking uptown, which was unnecessary; it was often too cold to pronounce *Oranjeboom*—he felt it a trap. Then across the street to the news-stand to plant himself defiant, bleary and nervous in front of the rack, searching for *Bulletin of the Leg Scientists* (THE LEG STANDS AT THREE MINUTES TO MIDNIGHT!), would mumble and then had laboriously to enunciate because of the suggested humping *Pack of plain 'Camels' please* and fumble fumble with f\*\*\*ing money, which seemed an inappropriately real element in these repetitious, bulldozed codas of evenings, of which Isidor and Sylvie were ever unaware—*fumbling* in front of the genial news vendor. Out to the street with all this *silly booty*—a magazine he disdained.

Always recognized he was doing it again. *You're doing this again* he said on many nights, out loud like Iz. He felt his eyes to be as wide open as searchlights, though they were puffy and nearly shut; thought he could take in the wonderful human sounds of this our town through his gigantic radio-telescopic ears. So he would gradually get to the IRT at 14th and Seventh, having journeyed blotto through this, one of the sleepiest parts of town there is. St Vincent scatters sand in your eyes around one-thirty. It is frightening to recall, the next morning in your bed of acute pain, the city in such a deranged state, everything so hysterically slow, so stretched and zinging. Indeed it is remarkable that a person in such a blasted and forlorn condition can make himself understood, to the genial news vendor, to the priest of the tokens, make himself presentable enough to his own doorman to be let in the building (Boris has standards after all). It is, in fact, *a tribute to New York*.

On the coldest night of the previous year, when it was foolish to drink at Isidor's tower, equally foolish to go out into the cold, he had *found himself doing it again*; the can of beer stuck to the flesh of his hand even in the grocery. It seemed madness to search the magazines (*Frozen Gams, Lap Land, Leg-Cicle*). Crazy to think of drawing his hand out of his coat to light one of the oddly stiff 'Camels'.

On Fifth Avenue, a man and his dog in front of the Forbes Magazine building—possibly frozen to it. Guy *sitting on the pavement*, it was too much to bear, *the cold floor of New York*. Was there not a room of any sort, anywhere in town where he could be inside, even the IRT? The dog was too cold to sit down, it wasn't going to *lay its nipples* on the cold stoop of the Forbes Magazine building, f*** that, it thought. It stood and panted and gave MacK a look doubtful of its master—the *dog* knew, or at least believed, *hoped* that the guy was being a little theatrical. MacK felt propelled toward the man and the dog, by what in the Oyster Bar or Hurley's would have been martini-fuelled bonhomie, but out here at this temperature and because of this squalid scene, the near frozen beings, the cold-hearted Forbes Magazine building, was a story of survival, an *arctic adventure*. MacK thought he had to *keep the man talking* in order to keep him alive. The man's polyester yarn hat, his beard, his coat seemed to indicate he was going to sit there all night, on *Fifth*, where hardly anyone would come by. Though he was in this state, he started to look a little bored and worried by MacK's going on and on. Now the dog gave MacK the same look: *Okay buddy see you later*. MacK gave the man twenty dollars, the cigarettes, the matches. And the can of beer, though he later thought it might have been medically wrong. Kept the magazine—not that many people into the leg stuff—guy's got a dog.

MacK made the IRT without incident. But here on the uptown platform was the guy singing *Sa-ha-hahm whay-eay-air-air-air o-ho-ho-ver the reay-ee-ay-ay-hain-hain-hain beauwww*—but on the downtown platform he had lo and behold a HECKLER who turned out to be his own FATHER: —Hey why don't you take that shit back to Detroit? —*hain-hain-hain . . . whaaa?* —I SAID, why don't you take that shit back to Detroit? —*Man, I'm FROM Detroit. You know I'm from Detroit, why you tell me to take it back to Detroit?* —Nobody wants 'at around here. [Arrival of uptown No. 3.] —*I see YOUR ass TOMORROW*.

# The Smoking Hero

The apartment buildings of Broadway in the 90s look heroic in a certain light—or perhaps if you are being heroic. There are vistas toward midtown which can be inspiring, or at least they hint of its lure. Sometimes at least in the past Broadway looked as though it might curve down (or up) toward your future—not that it is the only avenue that can suggest things to a young guy or gal. MacK faced south—let the CELEBRATION begin. Guy next to a key shop—one of these guys who just stands there—looking at you as if to say, this IS my employment, motherF***ER, lit up a 'Camel' filter—with its faint aroma of *actual* 'Camels'—funny how one's attention will be caught by the lighting of one particular ciga-rette—how many were being lit at this very moment—how many loves desires and tempers flaring like matches and lighters all over town? Is New York the only place where you may smoke freely in North America? Thought so. Go ahead! Blow your brains out! —Now that I'm 'not smoking' any more, thought MacK—or amn't I? Funny—they get you in there and tell you a thing like that, and they don't say *I'd cut down if I were you—ought to knock it off you know*—it must really be over for me, he thought, and suddenly Broadway looked very sad, as if it led *nowhere*. There was a dark patch, not of panic this time, only of—not loneliness—already missing every-one, already having said goodbye—though he was still standing there, facing downtown. Had it been precipitated by anything other than itself, MacK would have gone for a pack of 'Camels' now, perhaps gone back home and looked out at the Drive, the marble table, the appropriate drink, the cat, a girl. I'm walking into the sunset? he thought—but there was Isidor at the end of the day, so.

But now here's a fellow *asking* for one—and MacK reached automatically as always into the jacket pocket—it still not being cold enough for a MacKENZIE to wear—or buy even—this year's overcoat. There were some. —Thanks, my man. You're a hero, man. You're a smokin' hero. *Me?* thought MacK, walking away from the pleasant transaction—it always is, unless the request for nicotia is a blind and what's really wanted is money or love. Now *I'm* a smoking hero, thought MacK, who'd had his own, he'd worshipped them as fervently as he did the gods of the city:

*Smoking Hero* Mr Playfair himself, the courtly antiquarian bookseller who Izzy'd bought Bibulo & Schenkler from—still around when Izzy started working there in the mid Seventies and MacK had come regularly in and out of the shop. The shop smelled *eloquent*, MacK thought, of latakia and perique. Stained goatee. Mr Playfair used to roll his cigarettes out of pipe tobacco, using some ancient device he picked up in France, a thick metal wallet with mysterious rubber rollers which looked like something that might be harboring *polio*—smoked these with great relish, luxuriously, knowledgeably, in a patent 'ejector' holder—at the memory of which MacK smiled—remembering a summer upstate when, out of sheer boredom and heat oppression, MacK had purchased the selfsame holder from a small inbred store at the crossroads—and began rolling Playfairish smokes from his can of 'Forest'. He put these slug-shaped, overly damp cigarettes in the holder and pointedly smoked them on the balcony, to get attention. —Why don't you cut that out? called Isidor from far in the woods, where he was standing with his oboe—don't you know you look exactly like Lillian Hellman?

Alone for a winter month in Vermont—again at the mercy of country-store-as-entertainment, he took up 'Pall Malls', the constant medicament of *S. Hero* Shelby Stein—until he fainted a week later, having snowshoed energetically to the store to buy some more, and back—and in the faintly cinematographic process of fainting he recalled Shelby's manicured but stained fingernails, his large yellow teeth. He never went to the dentist, Shelby, *never*—he was afraid maybe that it would affect his voice—the forced removal of all that vibrating tar—but NBC *made* him go several years later—after craning his neck and scraping around for an hour, with a lamp on his head, the dentist says, *Well, Mr Stein, I'm glad to say you don't have any cavities—OF COURSE WHAT COULD LIVE IN A MOUTH LIKE THAT?* Recalled Shelby's brown, scummy laugh—a good thing he never had to laugh on the air. When he came to, MacK found he'd banged his eye on the corner of the coffee table and went back to 'Camels'.

His distant *S. Hero* cousin, the most glamorous of smokers, who MacK never met till he was thirty—already a barrister in London, though he was several years younger than MacK—he affected at that time a cape, a stick, a limp. He was the first British person of either sex to have designer stubble. Integral to his flourishes of cape, stick, stubble-rub and Romantic Cough was the charming sleight-of-hand he performed with his brass petrol lighter and carton of 'Major Extra Size', *the most delicious cigarettes in the world*, said MacK aloud at 86th and Broadway, *I say it who shouldn't.* He was very well spoken and quickly became an impossibly romantic figure to MacK. The girls thought so too and they lay down by hundreds to help him go over his cases; each wanted to help him up the stairs. (His limp seemed somehow virile—there was never the implication that he was physically weak—the impression he gave was that of man who limped due to exquisite *mental* suffering, on behalf of humanity.) During his month in the London bureau MacK got some of his cousin's cast-offs, though most, when they found MacK could not approach the Queen's Bench, and was American, would only lip him, and British fellation only drives you crazy for a fag while it's going on.

## Upper Broadway

Although on the surface stuck, MacK thought, like those trains possibly sitting below him at the very moment, those trains which arrive in the station briskly, *march in*, to which your mood may correspond, some mornings—they snap open their doors militarily and you think here is hope—the lights are bright and the *precise moments of enticement* this train offers you (maybe it is even a new train!) remind you of the morning's shampooing, deodorant soap—and so on—so you get on, along with the other bushy tails and then the train just *f\*\*\*ing* sits there—you're willing to give it a minute or two—but there is no announcement, you begin to look at each other—you've read everybody's front page by now—and then the compressor switches off, which means you'll be sitting there a while—and when you realize the doors have been open long enough for the whole car to lose its heat (or in summer its cool), lose its *heart*, really, you see some nonbushy tails have had time to get in now, like rats—they think it's a *regular* train—no no no!—but since they're in, people who just walked down the stairs without purpose, who bought a token without thinking, they have now *made* it an ordinary train and it seems all your good intent is stupid, meaningless bullshit—it seems NEUROTIC. Doesn't it?

He'd decided against the IRT but was standing twenty feet above this god, thinking hard about it—feeling *nostalgic* for all that, if you will, reminded that he might not really be going back to work, which he did usually by walking up to Broadway from Riverside—if he wanted to look at girls he went to 116th and if he wanted to feel a part of the city, to 110th. MacK was never late, but daily gave himself the choice of riding the local to 50th—this on 'humanity' days—and walking over to Sixth; or if he felt architectural and spaced he'd change to the express at 96th—feeling newspapery, overcoaty and busy—and go down to 42nd, walk over to Sixth and up—to look up Sixth toward the Park, especially on a wet morning. He liked discerning the silver and red of the Music Hall marquee, signally when the sun lit that against a dark sky—liked it in the morning or at night, as it mirrored the NBC canopy on 50th where he went into work, and the gun grey sky was close to the color of the metal and this reminds you the city is put together nicely, actually is a living thing, even though architects are always trying to take credit for it—crap-asses. Can you believe they have anything to do with such a place? Up there in their offices, with their manicures and *very neat clothing*; all architects blow imaginary dust off everything all the time—they're sick. They blow.

Standing there stuck like a train, or as if struck by one, tottering, about to die, he thought, though the immediate and imminent end he'd been sure of half an hour before was forgotten—he imagined the usual trip to work, wondered if he'd ever actually be up there again, ever see Shelby, the grey carpeting and the pillars oddly placed in his little wired box? Nancy Schwartz? But now it seemed it hadn't been panic or disease or death but a sweep of nostalgia for his apartment building, which he'd left, what, thirty minutes ago?—and for the warmth, the *possibility* of warmth, of Olive, perhaps only that of contemplating her, which now—

I must call her Olive, because that really is her name and I want all of her to be in this—I can't bear to change it, to see another name here.

# Theo MacKenzie His Building

FIREPROOF CONSTRUCTION THROUGHOUT, said proudly the original prospectus for 407 Riverside Drive—The Wynd—nobody calls it that old sandstone name up there, they call it 407: *You going back to 407?* MacK had seen the prospectus in Olive's apartment—she was on the Residents' Committee and had written a graceful guide for new dwellers in The Wynd—which had gone largely condominium in the Seventies and Eighties—the frankly terrified middle classes massing on their rock poking out of the hydrosphere of racism—not her fault. She'd grown up there. She loved 407. Olive drifted through the building in perfect skirts, thought MacK—how could everyone not have fallen in love with her? To have a spirit like that in your apartment building? Why you didn't even feel that way about the most beautiful guard at the Museum of Modern Art; the Rockettes; the redhead at Rocco, the only (turned out to be from New Paltz, screw it) woman you ever followed down the street even half a BLOCK.

Although MacK made a good living he was still privileged—if that word may be used any more to mean ANYTHING in this our town—and grateful to have got his apartment, its view up the Drive and across the river—or properly, down into the park, as MacK was on a lower floor and could discern New Jersey only through the trees of *winter*. He liked this level and would have felt guilty in one of the more *commanding*—as the ugly phrase has it—upper joints. He had achieved this as a loyal and skilful lover of The Wynd, and many of its occupants, in several ways.

He had known for over twenty years the lovely Mrs Leninsky, Olive's auntie, who'd put in a good word and practically willed the thing to him after she gave up housekeeping by spray cleaner and sensibly went to spend her last years with her brother and his enlarged heart on the ground floor of New Jersey. MacK had known her son Sidney since university and despite many practical jokes upon him in a vain attempt *to get back at Sidney for his personality*—once gluing Sidney's hand to his face (as he slept) with a proprietary adhesive the strength of which was cause for a brutal lecturing of MacK by the emergency room doctor—they remained friends. Sidney even gave me my first job in New York, thought MacK, thinking over his great lusts and little loves for many of the females of The Wynd, not least Mrs Leninsky herself, the kindest, most magnanimous woman in New York—she lived right here, folks—whose spirit of giving and communality never wavered, he supposed, from the night the Nazis kicked down the door of her family home in Vienna. My *crushes*, he thought, on Sidney's sister, on musical girls visiting the Leninskys' over the years, why is desire so extensive in this our town? The surprising tonguing by the cook during preparation for a Thanksgiving dinner years ago, why yes I've always been a member of the family, he thought.

For years he had pictured his triumphs as occurring in the Leninskys' apartment, even in his dreams. Imaginary things, accompanying dazzlingly-dressed Olive in an evening of Bernstein songs on Sidney's Bechstein which MacK can't even *play*.

And now not to survive even most of them. Here I'm to die only recently having got the apartment I wanted? Almost *inheriting* it really—doesn't the word imply immortality? Hell.

Mrs Leninsky was a nice lady. And being a nice lady she spent all her time being nice; she had a job being nice to crippled people and when she wasn't doing that she was out being nice to a lot of other people to whom the Nazis also hadn't been nice and who had great need of people being nice to them even though they were pissed off and crabby, and when Mrs Leninsky wasn't being nice to *them* she was sitting nicely in the Metropolitan and being very nice to the Beaux Arts Trio by understanding what they were doing. Or she was being nice to Sidney *by ignoring his personality*, and being nice to his sister, to the point of practically killing them, or being nice to her niece Olive, MacK's romantic light.

Three years ago, MacK thought ruefully as he passed the notable and oppressive bagel establishments of the low 80s, Mrs Leninsky had managed to sell him her apartment, and at the same time his fitful 'long-term' (*Ha!*) 'relationship' (*double H!*) with Red came to an end—you can only protest your love so long—and your essential innocence—to someone who does not want to hear it. So philosophically and luckily MacK thought, several days after he moved in: HENCEFORTH I CONFINE MY LOVE LIFE TO 407 RIVERSIDE DRIVE.

The cook stopped coming when Mrs Leninsky left—much as I

entreated her, he thought—and it quickly came obvious that this left the Non-Anglophone (real name Olga Ennhopona, from —Romania?). She lived several floors below, with her mother, who wore a headscarf and looked for all the world like the women engaged in that very serious conversation they're having in the rolling fields of tobacco on the 'Balkan Sobranie' label, the carts rumbling away. MacK gave the Non-Anglophone flowers to see what would happen and to return the favor immediately which must be the thing in—Romania?—she shyly sent her mother upstairs with a *sack of dried corn*, which threw things for several months, yet now the Non-Anglophone is often to be found being fed snacks and drinks in my high-backed chair and talking quite witty, he thought. There was too a snooty Pine Street bulless in one of the penthouses, and there was Judy Picklewicz, *Picklewicz of Piscataway*, on the third floor, a tiny blonde who wrote comedy for a living—and this was very appealing was it not? —and whose metallic black legs and very high heels had MacK following her down the tiled hall—but she worked for CBS. For the real purposes of love, Olive.

Only Olive.

Everyone else in the building used a walker and needed HELP ALL THE TIME. *You're such a nice young man.* But he stuck with his decizh, banished even were the many thoughts of Nancy Schwartz at work and the women Shelby Stein literally pushed at him in Hurley's. Mr Polite.

Mrs Leninsky was a very nice lady with no time for doing anything in her house except in what she considered the most convenient MODERN way. She had bought all her furniture in 1965 from Consolidated Modern Art, a tangled emporium on 72nd Street, world headquarters at the time for 'Danish' sofas with alarming fabrics which could not be matched with anything, little blond tables with metallic black legs, which seemed to MacK like tables he ought to follow around, *hassocks*, who really is supposed to sit for an evening of Schubert on a hassock? But they turned out to be useful for certain Non-Anglophonic rites. MacK was satisfied to swallow Mrs Leninsky's furniture whole, had thrown out his own in fact. With few changes Mrs Leninsky's apartment had now some kind of hip, at least as far as MacK had accomplished by 'consolidating' the weirdest Sixties furniture in the pink room with his hernia table and record collection. As Sixties homemaker Mrs Leninsky was a great believer in self-adhesive objects—paper cup dispensers, dish towel holders, shelves even, clocks—*a paper cup dispenser in every room*—I always meant to get the sandblasters in to eliminate the remnant crusts of these, thought MacK, and now too late. What micro-archeology of the Leninskys, he wondered, was left upon the wall?

But he still religiously bought the cups, as a kind of memorial to the generosity of Mrs Leninsky—who'd given him a view—and who'd bequeathed him Olive—he'd hoped. He had to travel some distance to get the little cups but what of it. Man sometimes they were HANDY.


Who knows from fireproof? But The Wynd was solid, replete with things MacK looked for in a building, indicators and providers of stability and oldness: the service elevator, which had to have frosted glass doors on each landing—you *must* be able to see the bright boxes ascend and descend, the friendly uniformed silhouettes—this is city drama and the smooth-running Twenties and Thirties on a *plate*, Busby Berkeley and the lick of expressionism all in one. The inner door has to be opened with a very worn brass handle. The shaft must give off the smell of cared-for old motors, the lovely oils of generations, but never smell of *hot motor*. The service corridors and back stairs, where MacK liked to spend much of his time, on his stoop as it were, smoking and reading the *Daily News*, he required to be painted in grey enamel to two-thirds the height of the walls, then crème. They had to be lit by incandescent bulbs—working in the RCA Building and its cradling warmth, lacking fluorescent fixtures except on the television floors, had convinced MacK for all time—as if anyone needed convincing —that *the extra expense of incandescent light* is the only way forward, the only decent thing, the only light that is inclusive and brings all men and women into civilization itself. As it was perfectly expressed in 1935. Incandescent light IS 'the light of civilization'. Fluorescent light alienates us, ruins our city, our society and our nation. It makes pizza look a fright.

O you ought to have seen MacK before he moved in, prowling the corridors with the Super, though of course he knew the building well already, even some of its recesses, thanks to the cook—MacK approached the Granolithic floor of the lobby with real reverence (so like going to work, though he did not recognize that)—o happy was he that all the light bulbs in the basement were of 25 watts. —How I came to know so many of those people before I moved in, he said to himself, all these weighty West Side Polish and Viennese families. Their altruism and dependability, cohesive like the Granolithic floor of the lobby of The Wynd, the thousand dimly lit polished lobbies of the West Side. And now he rose early, especially on summer mornings, made dark coffee and opened the windows onto the Drive, letting the night's smoky air-conditioning out into the city. He sat in the pink room in any season. Now he thought he might there pass many, or most, of the last pleasant moments that were to be his—before the nurses start showing up. *Nurses.*

Why doesn't Manhattan tip more toward New Jersey, MacK thought, with all these heavy *family buildings* on Riverside and West End? While on the East Side you just have a lot of flight attendants with wicker furniture who *aren't home*—unless Park Avenue makes up for it—but all those hi-rises on Second and Third—the stuff of magazine cartoons—must be light as feathers. Mob concrete like Hostess Twinkies, plywood where there should be sheet rock and metal. But ·here we have the University and Grant's Tomb, which must weigh a ton. MacK was not unfamiliar with certain *lurches of feeling* on the West Side, the slide and dip of hangover, even when safe in his armchair at the marble table, which he felt might be the thing beginning, New York tipping drastically into the Hudson—the *worst* would be all that East Side crap sliding across you as you went under, getting biffed by a lot of bad chef's salads and Lincoln Town Cars and bar stools from those Third Avenue places for people who're afraid of New York.

He would sit at his marble table in the mornings with coffee, he thought, bread and butter, the cat, the Non-Anglophone sweetly still. He would give up the newspapers (he read the *New York Times* in the pink room and the *Daily News* on the 'stoop') and just think about the women in the building. He heard enough 'news' just walking past the News Division on his way to work. You hear a lot of news.

Isidor would almost never visit MacK in The Wynd, even though he liked MacK's ribbon of river, the fleeting slivers of sloop sails in June, could *tolerate* he supposed a martini in the pink room, speculate on what suggestions the high-backed chairs made. Frankly, Isidor had always disapproved theoretically MacK's friendship with Mrs Leninsky, his little courtships in the building, now the infatuation with Olive, whatever went on with the prettily packaged Non-Anglophone, whom he *definitely did not wish to encounter, Sir* . . . Isidor was Downtown Man now and always fervently wished any sightings of himself on the Upper West Side to quickly pass into speculation and folk history. MacK had used his affinities with the Leninskys to BECOME one of them, Isidor felt; this was a shameless inworming, the unnecessary acts of a misguided man, an idiot really squirming and forcing himself into a place Isidor could not imagine *anyone* wanting to be:

### IN A JEWISH FAMILY!

And what's more, *he eats the f\*\*\*ing food!* And this drove Isidor bananas.

*How*, reasoned Isidor, could this proto or sub Wazp (Iz has never been sure how to categorize MacK for his own ultimate purposes), Wazp O' the West, eat matzobrei and mushroom barley soup, challah, rugelach? HAH? And MacK for his part realized this and for his own edification would say to Isidor on occasion, *in public*, that he wanted some flanken, a *good plate of flanken*—and watch Isidor hit the ceiling. How can this guy joke around like this, thought angry Isidor, it's not like he *converts*, it's like he pretends to be a Jew with a Celtic name. The brief stop-over, Sir. MacK had this way of joking around, a synthesis of comedians 1958–1971—he and Isidor did it on purpose to each other from time to time—in some ways it was MacK's real humor—but to top this with the *incredible* claim that he liked flanken, he'd *like some good flanken*, is an insult, thought Izzy, to my intelligence, to my Mama. Oops, thought of her. F***!

On this question: MacK and his ancient, desperate bid to rid himself of the attentions of his cousin Maureen, who relentlessly came at him with a bible and a lot of questions when they were supposed to be having their childhoods! Playing! Finally one day he told her, when she'd mashed him up against the wall of the laundry room of their grandmother's house, she breathing new testament all over him and the bodice of her party dress moving up and down quickly from the hide-and-seek—he finally *said*: *Don't tell anyone but I am secretly Jewish*. It seemed the only response to oppression.

An incident in MacK's disorderly spiritual life which Isidor wouldn't have been surprised to know—though he didn't—Iz too had cousins good only for to escape and revile. MacK always thought it sounded more a sex story than a bid for religious tolerance, A BREAK FOR FREEDOM. It didn't work—she kept after him until he started stealing her underwear, which resulted, in a few weeks, in the *total cessation of their relationship with one another for all time*—and it is a method to be commended. She won't even look at him at *funerals* now. So some things can work out.

—

Sidney, who unnervingly was Olive's cousin, kept *mentioning* MacK
to her in this SIDNEY WAY—one of those types of ways which
you are never sure helps—off and on MacK had been at family
dinners with Mrs Leninsky, Sidney and Olive, during the years he
was falling in love, with Olive and the building. A year before Mrs
Leninsky left, he and Olive chanced to have a conversation in private—waiting for the elevator—he thought she might take some
little interest in him—she suddenly asked *Are you Jewish, MacK?*, not
suspiciously but more as if the thought he *might* be had just struck
her—he saw it was more important to her than he had hoped. She
hadn't considered it previously, he saw, but now that he was possibly more than a guy just around the family, around The Wynd, she
needed to think it out.

And his feeble answer, which in Olive's generous spirit and love-
liness she has never mentioned to me again, says MacK to himself in
the street, and did not hold against me, was a surprised and uncomfortable

### Well SIDNEY says I am!

which was supposed to be a complex and rich remark *meaning:*
does religion matter?—I am one of the lynch-pin neurotics here
in town and something of a comedian and besides I eat a lot of
stuff from Murray's Sturgeon Shop so you needn't worry . . .
But this made him sound, of course, like a JACK ASS. And how
could the Chief Announcer of the NBC Radio Network be so
poor at ad lib?

Olive knew nothing of MacK's confinement of his animal spirits to
407 even after he moved in. An affable, curious, game woman. So of
course she agreed to see him, friend of Sidney's, what could be
wrong with it?

When you are allowed into someone's apartment in the beginning of—? —, politely allowed to look politely around—someone

you have not yet kissed—the conversation is IDIOTIC. Even if youse is a natch, even if you will marry and have six children (a tragic youngster, even)—even if you're Comden and Green, Leopold and Loeb, Anthony y Cleopatra, the talk of the first days: —fumble!

But things are happening, you *have* got to the apartment stage—the purpose of which is to allow you to examine the STUFF OF THE POSSIBLE BELOVED. To judge her, him—cruelly? —peremptorily, by it?—if need be. Many a tragic youngster has not been born into the world because her possible mother caught sight of an Al Hirt LP. MacK was quite taken with Olive's stuff—since it was hers, to begin with—and she was part of the Leninskys and 407—his own building!, he had thought with pleasure.

He was anxious to move on to the next stage—which hasn't happened—*It never happened*, he said now on Broadway. Even though they attempted it for several months during which MacK *visibly warmed* whenever the thought of Olive came to him in his electric casket of dials at 30 Rockefeller Plaza. —Our whole relationship, he said, which never occurred and now never can, consisted entirely in the introductory stage! Twenty precinema drinks. *Wine*, too, for too long—before we realized we both prefer *brown liquor*. Unfortunate love—when you make maybe a hot-house of town and try to force a bud.

The closest he had come to her was awkwardly getting up from her sofa to 'help' her (= WATCH and you know it) make coffee during long discussions which to his deep disappointment never revealed or even heralded love—were never personal enough, not at all. The kind of evening you know—how that sort of time feels—you're being *so* polite—it still isn't really apparent what sort of visit either of you thinks this really is . . . Ah, there must be more nice hope each early evening in New York than anywhere on earth. Must be so many guys in the newer jacket helpfully watching women make coffee, women who are desirable and careful, who know how to make conversation, with table lamps lit for a while—until it is time for the Belasco, Alice Tully, the Trans-Lux—hope hot in coffee pots, in tiny snapping bubbles in home-made ice cubes—warmed by pretty lamps and book-lined walls. Hopes which keep the engine of town going. —But the conversation remains that of the movie foyer, said MacK, and what have these people made of things by midnight?

—And the *picture*, he said with a bitterness which was a new and hated thing. He had leaned his shoulder on the wall of Olive's little hallway these times—it led from the front door past the kitchen, into the living-room—her bedroom was beyond—forever—while she made this coffee and they talked of the maddeningly inconsequential. *The doorman made a pass at me last year, funny, me too*. And noticed an enticingly young Olive in this school picture on the wall. Isn't it just great how at age forty you can still witness yourself suffering the torments of the damned—your skin—hair—that shirt!—let's you and I see George Eastman in HELL.

Olive was way in the back—she hadn't begun to turn into what she now was. She looked like a collection of fence palings—looking down at the floor in an embarrassment of adolescence—your shame and disgust and terror at what is happening to you forever preserved. The picture was taken so long ago it had no glamor to it, as everything seems to have now—MacK recognized the asphalt tiles which threw glare at the lens—the flooring of school and supermarket—he could smell sweeping compound. Hadn't he sat himself in the same molded beige plastic chairs which seemed briefly the harbingers of a new world in 1966 until a big dumb guy in Civilization learned to crease and fold them back like an ear? After which your school was filled with chairs without backs?

*OLIVE*, in the back row, where life has not yet started, but two bad girls in the front row ever so slightly flipping the bird, snickering *about* laughing hard, the way girls laugh, as though it's their *last chance* to laugh. So doomed and adult—their earrings and nail polish said it—bad girl, bad teeth—biker chicks at the Lycée Française? —the precocious one the closest to flipping the bird in reality—one arm across her ribbed breasts, grasping her elbow—you could see the giggle—her left hand lying palm-up as if casually on her thigh, the first third and fourth fingers curled just behind the middle finger—oh man she was GOOD—been practicing for years—and this was the picture they distributed to the class! And her friend, in classic *friend* mode, who imitates the bad girl's hair and clothes, so far as she's able in her strictured home, but in whose doughy featureless face you don't find the same *will to evil*, or much of a life coming at all—she's egged on to smoke on the way home but can't do it *at* school the way Princess Flipping Bird could. *You* know, the friend tried to make her clothes provocative, slightly illegal like the Princess's—and now she's married to a nice guy in Connecticut but they have a tragic youngster who occasionally gets write-ups in the local paper. The Princess disappeared from her life in the first car of boys, said MacK to himself still with the bitterness. And there to the left were the large grown up spectacles and pretty interesting lips of *Natalie*—MacK knew her name as she'd signed the picture to Olive—Natalie blurred a little as she was giving her black hair a toss when the shutter fired . . .

Very unfortunately from the first day he visited Olive's apartment MacK became preoccupied with this f***ing picture. It was the energy, the past maybe, not the insolence—of course the intriguing view of early Olive—and now anything seemed able, at the right moment, to make him miserably consider something, *anything* he'd never got around to. This god damned picture had so many potential stories in it—*I call them into my office*—he hires Natalie as his secretary, she was so . . . *loyal*—he runs into Princess Flipping Bird in Hurley's—the friend! —is with her! —suburb—tragic baby—he *sees* it in her *face!* —the whole thing is *ridiculous*, said MacK, they're just girls who went to a school in New York twenty years ago, *twenty,* stupid.

And wondered if Olive knew them still. By the time his romance with Olive was half not through, MacK's dream-eye had wandered on to the bad girls and Natalie so many times that he missed the picture in his own apartment and did not know what to do about it. —I should have smuggled it out of her place, said MacK, *out of respect for her*, and had it photostatted and returned it—would have been easy in overcoat weather. Would have put my copy in the same black dime-store frame—kept it by the bed—*I call them into my office*—or the bathroom. Would have been too weird to hang it in the relative place in his own apartment (he had the same short hall containing similar lost bereft and un-figured-out items).

One of the many disappointments of an early death: he wouldn't be able any more to visit this *stupid picture*.


Isidor, surprisingly, had nothing against Olive—liked her in fact—had even invited the two of them to a jazz club he liked and beamed at them across bird-bath martinis—by which I mean of considerable diameter, not 20 ml you merely flick your feathers in. —*Isidor* saw that jazz might be our bond, said MacK, facing downtown and thinking of the streets of the West Village the way you may on a remote corner. *Now* the guy tells me, after I dragged her to Carnegie Hall. *Isidor* discovered she knew all about it, that she could have shown *me* all about it! Where MacK had been feeling like Babbitt with his Beiderbecke cd, she showed him Braxton; MacK stuck in the Holland Tunnel of *nostalgie* and she shows him *Dave* Holland.

So obviously you don't do bondage cocktails with Anthony Braxton and you don't do it with the girl who's introduced him to you and you don't do it with Fletcher Henderson either!, as the Non-Anglophone often pointed out in irritation. (MacK thought she *liked* Fletcher Henderson.) Rooty toot toot.

This meant fortuitously that jazz would lose its theatrical, talismanic role in the dimmer-mellow cocktail hour. He'd indeed been using this all as a sound track for—*pffft!* Much as the ZHLUB of previous generations might buy his secretary some lamé number, fix her a *pitcher* (ugh) *of martinis*—what is *that?*—and stick on *Music for the Love Hours*. Phew!

Isidor beamed at them across the bird-baths and complained about the snacks. —What do you want? said MacK, the heaving sashimi of the Sea of Japan? *These ashtrays are plastic*. —Yeah well, said Isidor, something a little nicer than party mix, with a ten-dollar martini you expect something a little . . . perhaps you and your friend would like some flanken. Waiter? And she laughed. So prettily. But am *I* allowed to laugh at this? thought MacK. —It's funny, he said.

Down Broadway with regained equilibrium, he thought, or at least Librium. Something like that ere long. *So much to look forward to*, as Iz said in speaking of the gradual, nasty, noisy falling apart of his parents. There was a conversation he and MacK had had in the elevator a month before (Isidor will open up personally between the tenth and fifteenth floors of his tower—if the lady with the metal nose doesn't get on)—MacK was admitting he thought the doctor would soon tell him *Yes you're ill, you've had it in fact*, and said to Iz that in a strange way becoming a member of the family of the building had killed him—his immersion in family life had started death ticking. He thought that without taking on the tragic role he had in The Wynd and with the Leninskys he could have gone to and from his 'glittering catafalque' in the RCA Building, the nightly embalming martini, the pretty, immobilized girls forever. —But that was all no good, it's better this way, MacK said. Not really knowing. He didn't believe he wouldn't have died—cerebration must end or you will go mad and moldy—but he felt his aging had been arrested by static routine, as if by the heavy sound-proof walls at work—and that the Leninskys had given it a kick-start. —Yes, you've always been a great friend of the Jewish people, said Isidor.

Who somehow wanted to agree they'd killed him if that proved to be the case.

Now MacK on the street corner thought about Olive in the way dying people think, he supposed: he'd understood nothing, nothing about Olive or New York or jazz or baseball. What *are* these things about? Too late to understand New York except to walk through it several times more. If only he had got away from jazz as the silly soundtrack for looking out the window with, mornings, before going to his entirely absurd job, the very biblical definition of EPHEMERA, helping the winking blinking network hypnotize people to forget their lives were passing by and couldn't come back. Continue with that only so long as it helped him to stare out the window and take his intricate pleasures from town as he could.

But he and Olive had *come close*—that is not failure—to understanding or knowing each other maybe. —If there is to be no more time, there is today, MacK said to himself, during which she may be seen, visited, appreciated. Fixed perhaps in memory. On my way downtown I will just casually POP IN as I pass her office.

# Broadway & 79th

Since he'd stood looking out at the Drive this morning, looking down into the dark cup of coffee, the taste of which he found he paid attention to particularly—its black and astringency made poignant, somehow *pointed* by the doctor's call—the gentle talk of the Non-Anglophone—MacK had pictured the whole day as motion. Had sent his mind's eye as on a camera dolly or crane, all through Manhattan, calling in at various places, seeing people, taking in old haunts—too many actually to accomplish. But wondered, or thought, that this day might be his last day out and about—last *official* day.

MacK ruminated on the main door of 407, which on setting out on his travels he had found open, the doorman hiding in that revolting little room of his—how much the half-open door of

Lenin's tomb glimpsed at two in the morning—as I am sure you are aware—will affect you!—not only creepy that people are doing things in there at night, but the implication that a coming and going from death is possible or even likely—the thought of the *heavy ceremonial door* standing partly open. Something that oughtn't to be open standing casually ajar . . .

Of course *so much to look forward to* as Isidor said—but in picturing the busy day, with Isidor at the end, the soft lights of The Hour, it had all been movement, flight of one kind or another, and here he'd allowed himself to become mournfully sidetracked, by thoughts of Olive, whom he had slightly exuberantly determined to see. *Just popping in* would put light in the middle of the day. Would it be odd simply to walk in to her office, see her look up? But such a thing could happen, he'd been there before—the others looked at him a little knowingly, he thought—she wouldn't have said anything but they saw anyone who came to see her as a potential mate. People in offices are like that—they've no imagination. Whenever MacK had to go to the Presentation Department to see Nancy Schwartz, there was a guy, Ed Zink, who had the office next to hers and *would* wink and up-thumb MacK during his entire transaction with Nancy, which always was very pleasant but for Ed Zink's facial contortions, which as the business went on became more exaggerated and even hideous—women are right, men are predatory and evil. How dare *Ed Zink* make this burlesque semaphore while MacK rested his hand on Nancy's desk, poring over the print-outs, *Projected Continuity Television & Radio Networks 17 February 1600 - 1930 EST Confidential Not To Be Taken From Rockefeller Center—Auth N Schwartz*, looking at her dark hair, resolving to make that entry about the burgundian probability of her underwear in his semi-secret ledger? At least it was still a secret to Ed Zink he hoped.

Meanwhile heading down Broadway, its usual beck. Times Square really is magnetic, he thought—it draws you down, or up, Broadway, but *for what?* There's no point to it any more, it's like dung draws scarabs one supposes, but one does feel drawn *along* Broadway.

# Tombs

Uneasy feelings can accrue in the West 70s. The scary Pillow Bank
lives there, and to think therefore about death in a new way, which
he already was, thanks a lot. The Pillow Bank, an odd-looking thing
built in the Depression, odd that they had the money to build a
*monumental bank*. The architect must have been desperate for something to do for quite some time—you can see all his drink-fuelled
nightmares of Scottish coffering coming out. The heavy sandstone
blocks all have their edges ground down to a softer line. The main
door is set back, hiding from the Oriental copper lanterns. If you
stand across Broadway the Pillow Bank looks quilted. The absurd
soft-looking stone, the lanterns and also the proximity of the
Riverside Memorial Chapel on Amsterdam got all MacK's tomb
juices going. You can walk by a lot of icky stuff without *having* to
notice it—you must—but one stormy day he and Sidney had been
walking up Amsterdam, quickly—hoping the sky wouldn't divulge
quite its all before they could reach the *Dublin House*—when these
two stiffs unloading another stiff let him slip and flop out onto the
sidewalk—not ugly, just dead—as if a final comment on the
day—and now this IN USE 24 HOURS PER DAY loading dock
with its interior rubber curtain and frosted glass and *fluorescent light*
and *very ominous clipboards on hooks* is one of MacK's dreaded funerary whirlpools. *Mazel tov* on yer mausolea. Always drawn to, he
thought, and repulsed by, marble, stone, granite, particularly black,
black with grey, with red, folded—*pillowed* stone, as it folded around
the 'sleeping person'. Sweet, dead air. Doors recessed and stairways
flattened, the steps wide, to make them easier for—the dead?
Indirect lighting—from torchières—which was one of the things
that could give him the creeps in the RCA Building, even if he was
standing with Shelby Stein and denigrating somebody. In Grant's
Tomb the mixture of quiet, eternal stone with sinister *mechanical*

*systems* you only glimpse—ventilators, electrical closets, the feeling that the building is a little more alive than those immured in it, that you are in a slightly grim trap at the moment—the building is on its guard.

Shallow steps, particularly, always going down into a dark well; also any UNEXPLAINED RECESSES or empty, auxiliary rooms—what are they for!

Light playing on the ceiling of a dome, or seen softly in a cupola or cloister—that's what makes you think Lenin is in there. He's at home; he still exists somehow. Pop in.

*Lenin's Tomb* is MacK's name also for a cash machine set in red granite and black diorite, in the wall of an immense temple of the business of the XIX century just off Madison Square, companies that cannot die because their buildings weigh so much, which machine MacK has occasion to consult (the awful weight of the whole building forcing his paltry cash out like squished fruit).

But in his normal travels of the West Side he encounters little tomb-fear; the Pillow Bank is the worst—the soft stones remind him of Isidor's disastrous decision to carpet the sunken living-room in his apartment—there are two shallow steps leading down to it and after they had been neatly done in stone grey wool they looked so like what Mausolus, or rather *Artemisia* would have wanted that MacK could barely walk down them; he sat unsteadily on Isidor's couch with his hands on his knees and after several anguished visits had to request that Isidor have the carpet taken up. No, the Pillow Bank is the worst thing in the weekly round—aside from the back lobby at work. The lobby of the old telephone building on lower Broadway holds some complicated problems for MacK, but you'd only be going there on some sort of historical jaunt, with architects, not likely. *Field trips suck*, Isidor said.

The softness of the Pillow Bank reminds MacK of how they bury people in England. Cozily. Everybody's buried flat in America now, sleeping flat under brass or stone markers pushed down into the grass. So you can gaze at a cemetery and think only of golf. But in (ahhh) *England* they're concerned for your comfort—*after* you've died, that is—your grave is a plump, delicious little bed. For weeks after your burial it will be draped with flowers, while a quilt of thick grass grows. Then you'll sleep tight—warm under your soft blankets of loam. See the fat little headstones, like marshmallows, or toast, leaning back slightly, just like lovely little pillows propped up for reading, *watching telly*, knitting. It's too inviting, the English grave, MacK thought. What's wrong with wanting to be tucked up as if by Mummy forever?

—What's wrong is what's *happening* under there, motherf***ers, said MacK as he stepped off the curb, having come to the end of the block and the city was moving again, with relief. Many possible journeys on the day. But it was suddenly important, MacK thought, to see Olive. He'd give nothing away. Just *pop in* as anyone might have. Her office, the Fairchild Building. Madison again. Madison, Madison, *Madison* figures in everything—lots to do with Isidor, the museum, all the tobacconists. He felt suddenly tilted, like the *Fishermen's Last Supper* by Marsden Hartley in the Whitney. On Madison. And before he actually would come upon the Pillow Bank and had to deal with all of that he turned and *ran!* Straight for Amsterdam and the Park! With cancer!


Never a runner, only a talker and a smoker. F***er. MacK nonetheless was able to gather speed in a convincing way for brief episodes—though perhaps it was necessary to convince only himself today. The day was apple-cold and he might avoid that which he hated most in the world: to perspire. He kept his own bottle of spray cleaner at work to keep MARKS off the console; even though radio studios of the National Broadcasting Company are air-conditioned to 66° Fahrenheit. Up Amsterdam Avenue he ran, past its beer emporia which smell of cold in summer and the comforting fires of 'Marlboro Lites' in winter—turned east to trot nervously past Planetarium Station, the meanest Post Office in New York—and experienced once again the unreasonable depth of his disappointment at this—*Well you in the wrong f***ing line motherf***er how you feel now?*—he who so loved the Planetarium and thought you should never name anything bad after it—then things widened and then the trees and turrets of the museum of natural history and smokes in the leaves from a chestnut and hot dog man—the wiener guy checked him with the kind of look you always get when you run but not in running *clothes*—actually a look of pity and disgust—who's gotta run?—guy's gotta *run* over here—though it's often taken for suspicion—the colors of the leaves turning, the smoke which seemed theatrical—the gay *sabretto's* umbrella—his stripy shirt and MacK already felt breathless now and imagined a moment out of *musicals* where he hands MacK a hot dog and MacK would do-si-do around his cart—hold out a buck—he waves it off with a smile—CUZ I'M DYING!—they dance up and down the sidewalk together while large-eyed small animals of the Park environs gather to watch . . .

He slowed in front of the Planetarium, found himself stopping to face it to his surprise but it was the home of many gods, gods of soundproofing and of his early love of *lit controls*, ye gods he thought the Planetarium is where I stored the whole of my childhood here in town without knowing it maybe; here was a god if not *the* god of funerary lighting, and here the surprisingly graceful Projector itself, whirling its dumbbell worlds through its own hysterical night—little gods of recessed Art Deco doorways and double doors and Granolithic floors—he thought in astonishment that the various planetaria of his childhood might have propelled him directly and materially into the RCA Building—but the *sabretteur* was staring at him strangely far from dancing and if there was anything MacK disliked it was: *being regarded with suspicion by outdoor vendors* so off at a trot again toward the red and yellow foliage of the Park, nicely set off he thought by a new black paving of Central Park West just like looking out the window from the pink room at home.

Central Park is everyone's refuge, everyone goes there several times a day, at least in their thoughts——it's why we aren't London tenks gut or Los Angeles——and puffing keenly remembered his old enchantment with it——in the brave bicycle days——the first blinding explosion of autumn he'd ever experienced was here, *right here*——nothing had ever changed color in October, or ever, when he was a boy——but *these* trees were what he had been looking for all his life and to be able to stir himself *into the autumn itself* through his new found and cherished 'Owl' and 'Sobranie' with the chestnut vendors' smoke and the park department's bonfires and all that brightness——what he'd been waiting for since masturbating himself to a pulp in the feeble suburb where I constructed, he said, a little XIX century east coast of the mind, made it out of a worn green Viking edition of Thoreau, Pete Seeger, my tenor recorder, an Osmiroid italic pen, what bushes I could find that did make fall and a horse chestnut I cherished for its brown luster——tried to polish it in the pocket like the old men of the Buckeye State, ——*Is that all there is of tradition in your family?* Isidor'd asked, *keeping a piece of garbage in your pocket?*, and when he was finally reunited for that's what it was with the vibrant seasons here, with a particularly vivid pumpkin on Canal Street his first Hallowe'en in this our town he'd thought *I'm alive*, imagine a pumpkin doing *that* for you——but I am a sentimental joe, MacK thought, underneath *this tough radio announcing exterior* I am a big girl's blouse ha ha ha and say it was really time to stop running as everything hurt quite a bit and he had run all the way from Broadway and surely he hadn't run this far since running all the way across the George Washington Bridge early one morning in 1973 to convince some girl that . . . so what, all he got was the father pulling his blanko look.

So waited for the signal here at the West Drive with an affable-looking man who had a golf bag over his shoulder. MacK could not help noticing that each club had a *cover*——had never considered the need for this——imagined it was something his ancestors would eschew, possibly did eschew and were thrown out of Scotland because of it—they do everything so achingly properly, MacK lamented, and chid himself for this too—and then with a start he saw that each tight-fitting leather cover displayed an enameled face—like a little family crowding out of the bag to look friendly out at MacK—and *then* he took a close look at the face on the cover of the——?—driver, he supposed—and realized it was but exactly the face of *Abraham D Beame*, and then in a nanosecond experienced the conviction that the set of golf club covers represented the mayors of this our town and in a flash this was dispelled by the positively *creepy* discovery that they *all* had the likeness of Beame, eleven little Abe Beames! *Abe Beame's face!* So he had to say to the affable-looking man, natch: —Amazing covers. —*Thanks man.* They were still waiting for the light to change—the affable-looking man looked only straight ahead. —They're all Beame, is that right? said MacK. —*I wouldn't know*, the affable-looking man said, still looking ahead. —But where did you, who do you think they, ah . . . MacK trailed off, seeing now the affable-looking man had stolen them only a minute or two before. —*I really don't know*, said the affable-looking man striding off now with the green light, the little mayors joggling for position and smiling goodbye from their bag at MacK who remained still for a moment. And then MacK crossed the West Drive onto a different trail from the affable-looking man and made across the bridle path toward the Sheep Meadow and he saw he was moving like a marionette on a familiar journey—he hadn't intended to visit this old part of life but here were the children of metal, what the Hell is it with this Park, some days there are more statues of kids than kids—perhaps the mayor's idea of safety. The bronze kids glinted through the foliage and now here he was at *SHAKESPEARE IN THE PARK!*

# The Pursuit of Actresses

## WHEN YOU ARE TWENTY-TWO-YEARS OLD
## YOU WILL DO ANYTHING FOR A LIVING

Sidney has a way with waiters: torture. With banter. The busier they are, the more Sidney banters. He drives them mad with increasingly stupid asides until their eyes are so glazed and their jaws so set their teeth begin to crack. What's more, not only is it a chore just getting Sidney's order out from between his idiotic jokes, but Sidney keeps *changing* his order. The waiter can't see that Sidney's orders are throw-away lines. The waiter scribbles on page after page of his pad, he's confused, he's red in the face, he's even starting to write down some of the jokes . . . Then Sidney ambushes the waiter. He's just given his real order, that was his stomach talking, he suddenly *slams* his menu shut and loudly says *And can we have that right away please!* Once when MacK was dining with Sidney and he pulled this, the waiter abruptly wet himself. But that was an extreme case.

MacK is usually embarrassed by Sidney's behavior, but he's happy to be eating with him, on the sort of day in early summer you can enjoy before the very streets swell with perspiration. MacK needs a new job. He wants money, excitement, *l'art*. So Sidney's offered him the first job that has come along at the theater.

Conclusion of enchiladas. MacK bunches up his napkin and burps into its absorbency. Startled from a reverie by this noise, the waiter comes. —Dessert and coffee, says he. —Whole cheese-cake, says Sidney. Yet more charm, thinks the waiter. A shameful scene follows: more banter, frustration, and a lot of cake if not a whole.

To walk off almost a whole cake takes almost a whole after-noon, almost the whole of Third Avenue, north to south. In the

30s, Sidney draws MacK aside. By gesturing he indicates a woman on a bicycle. She wears very short whites. Her hair is cut in a bob; sunglasses of the day. Although MacK notices a particular speckle, a ring-around-the-nightclub look under the eyes, Sidney does not. —That's an *actress*, boy, he says, watch this. Sidney fills his lungs to capacity and pronounces the name *Mlle South Carolina Java*. The bicycle woman turns, peers through her shades at Sidney while remaining in admirable traffic light pose on her machine. A smile impossible to evaluate plays on her lips. —Mamzel, says Sidney, of course you remember me. —Of course, she replies. You put your hand in my bodice. Every night cept Mondies. A taxi driver takes this in and honks urgently. —Huh! says MacK. Sidney starts pulling him up the street. —Her microphone she means, he says, it must of course be placed exactly. MacK follows Sidney round a corner. They stand bent over and panting on the threshold of a luncheon-ette. —I think she likes me, says Sidney. This is the first time the Mamzel notices me to talk to. —There was, says MacK, an element of . . . wryness? —Could go either way, says Sidney, but listen, you ought to hear her sing. In her celebrated role, in her hooped cos-tume she drifts about the stage like a feather from the pillow of our lord.

—What will it be, buddy? says the luncheonetteer. For Sidney has staggered in and sat. —Champagne, says Sidney. —Egg cream for me, says MacK. Guy says to his sublunchary:

**Gimme two egg creams out.**

Several nights later. MacK and Sidney in the control room, fondling knobs. Their job. —She's coming on soon, Sidney whispers, wait until you get a load. —Warning electric 29, croons Lampedusa, stage manager and meddling he-bitch. —Just wait, says Sidney. —Stand by electric 29, says Lampedusa. Sidney's eyes widen slowly in thrill. —Electric 29 go, says Lampedusa. On stage, the entrance of Mlle South Carolina Java: whole nations of audience spontaneously applaud. MacK is transfixed by Sidney's transfixment: it's amusing to see a familiar organism come to a complete halt. —29 bloody go, yells Lampedusa. —You mean me? says MacK. Sidney snaps out of it and cuffs him. —Certainly he means you! What are you doing? Go! Go! MacK tweaks the appropriate knob. —Little late I guess, he says. —A little! fumes the Lamp, listen you have a great future, of course it's not in the theater. —Ba-dum-bump, says Sidney. Over the headphones titters of the crew arrive from various dark points. —Don't worry, says Sidney, I'm the shop steward. Only I can fire you. —Good, says MacK, go and get knotted, Lampedusa. —You're fired! says Sidney, that's insubordination.

But on stage something is happening besides the play. In the heat of the summer Park hundreds of bugs are drawn to the gaily lit tableau. Every time Mlle Carolina opens up for breath, tons of 'em fly down her throat. They swarm over her authentic snood. But the Mlle thinks she has the solution: she stops the play.

—Could we have the lights lower please? The Mlle casts heart-breaking looks at the control room. —What's she saying? hisses Lampedusa. He's off book, the swine. —We're on page fifty, says Sidney helpfully. —But what . . . ? —She wants the level down, because of insects, says MacK. —Oh no, says Lampedusa, 33 through 37 are bumps!

Sidney goes crazy. His big chance. In MacK's ear he booms: Master down one and one-half! Ahead one-third, clang of distant telegraph. Outside, things get dimmer. The audience applauds again. Mlle Carolina sweetly bows in the direction of the control room. Inside, Sidney is meltingly in love. MacK and the Lamp are just melting. Throughout history, air-conditioning is too expensive for the likes of them.

After the performance, Sidney bolts headlong from the room and rushes backstage. He hurls himself against the door of the Mlle's dressing-room, scratching with his nails and biting at the paper star. Under this assault the door gives way and we find the Mlle désha-billée. —Mamzel, Mamzel, cries Sidney, it's me, what turned down

the lights for you. He blushes modest. O you can't have forgot.
—Oh. Thanks. And goes back to demaquillating herself. Now
Sidney blushes fulsome to recognize beneath a bulging drape the
winged tips of Signore Bastinetto, leading cad and man. Sidney's
heart breaks dully; he retreats mumbling *Remember me, remember me.*

Several hours later, in the Freesia. Sidney slams down his empty
glass. —Dag nabbum, he says, each and every one ovum.


It is like falling in love with the subject of a painting. You don't, can't
take *Woman Drying Herself* to lunch. You mustn't!


MacK at the fly gallery, throwing levers, helped in the hoisting of
booms by Mouie, vivacious dark and small. MacK's sort really, looking
at history. But he is blind to everything but Mlle Weisswurst, star of the
new play. —What's she got I ain't? whines Mouie. MacK can't hear. He
subconsciously feels Mouie's vivacious dark small presence, her developed little forearms appearing from the rolled slightly up sleeves of a
notorious black sweater. But MacK thinks only of the Mlle.

Lampedusa assumes the role of matchmaker, the cow. —You can't
fool me, he drizzles in the privacy of the control room, the
Mademoiselle! You ache for her. Ah it is ze oldest story in ze world, is
it not? MacK is alarmed lest others perceive his pain. —Why are you
talking like that, he says. —But listen, says Lampedusa, she is, I can
reveal, involved with Signore Mandelbaum. —What! says MacK, that
no-talent! —Ah yes it is sad but true is it not? oozes Lampedusa, he has
an extensive loft and he can seem boyish and sincere, so said the papers.
(Snorts from MacK.) —But I, says the Lamp, subtly will undertake to
apprise the Mademoiselle of your . . . sentiments. —Under the cir-
cumstances, says MacK. —Exactly, says Lampedusa. How's that for *la*
buddy-buddy? —And in return? says suddenly suspicious MacK.
—Why in return, says the Lamp confidentially, *stop cocking up my show!*

—

Mouie deserts MacK in her affections, taking up for lack of anything else with Canopa, heaviest stagehand in the world. There are fears for her safety. Sidney and MacK indolently while away rehearsals in the control room. —Our job begins on opening night, says Sidney, just give them work light, anything else is criminal.

They while away intermissions in the Freesia. Sidney grips his rimy glass, he discourses hotly. —She is vivacious dark and small, he says, o those forearms. Her teeth are little candies without the wrappers. —Forearmed is forewarned, says MacK. He makes bubbles in his drink, brooding about Signore Mandelbaum. —Why are they always named Jack? he says. —Who? —Other men.

Sidney is cast down, he suddenly thinks Mouie has a Jack somewhere, a Jack searching for her, although Canopa is a stone anyone would leave unturned.

In the control room as in rooms all the world round, men dream at their jobs. MacK and Sidney's job is to aid the dreams of the pit. MacK dreams of Mlle Weisswurst. Sidney devotes himself to making banter on the headphones with Mouie, crouched up far away in the flies. She seems responsive. Once a night she has to pull a string and make a special effect. —This headphone system is not for frivolity let me remind you? says Lampedusa, warning electric 44, fly gallery 9. MacK's eyes are on Mlle Weisswurst's stunning performance. She is a rare English rose beset by war and brass bands. Tell the truth, the Mlle looks like old photographs of MacK's ma.

Mlle Jo-Ann Weisswurst, Ohio originally, leads a life something between her own and representations of the lives of actresses in jolly old movies. The lineaments of her face seem against her wishes to cast her in inconclusive roles in life as well as on the stage. The Mlle has an expressively wide though dainty mouth, ripe eyelids, a fine forehead. While photographable, her cheekbones are not those of high art. Her eyebrows are of prairie stock. She is petite but not petite enough to play a believably petite person. So she toils in the

English theater's gift to the ages, comedy that is never funny. The Mlle finds no satisfaction in her wobbly paychecks nor in her minuscule apartment which is sometimes hard to find.

Signore Mandelbaum is a lanky rebel. His family of moneyed paleontologists wildly disapprove of his theatrical career even though they send him money. And occasional boxes of bones, meant to entice. Thus the Signore has a welcoming extensive loft and can be, when not shampooed in gin, boyish and sincere. So said the papers.

Lying in the *L* of the loft, the Mlle thinks: any actress secure enough in the hideous insecurity of her profession would never consort with a member of the crew, lackaday! What a dirty bunch of plaid-shirt-wearing drunks. Whew! Perhaps a night with a burly scenic carpenter. But no.

But Mlle Jo-Ann has noticed that MacK's eyebrows are of the hinterland. And so when Lampedusa begins fussing round her dressing-room she takes an unwise interest in his prying, rude, weighted questions. It's not his job but the Lamp is attractively retying the flounces on one of the Mlle's gowns. The Mlle brushes her hair, her black and white heroines smile back at her from the mirror.

—May I say how much I enjoy your performance, says Lampedusa, and your scenes with the Signore, divine! No doubt some of this triumph is due to your relationship with the Signore, which I hope is lovely and interpersonal? —His loft is extensive, says the Mlle. There is a view of Soho and the bridges. He is often boyish and sincere. —But how marvellous! intones Lampedusa like an overgreased trombone, yet, Mademoiselle Jo-Ann, there is another in our happy company on whom your charms they have not been lost. No?

The Mlle searches a drawer for her Japanese fan, for to add the extra coyness. —Why, what do you mean, Lampie? she flutters.

—I mean the worthy MacK, electrician! cries Lampedusa, triumphantly leaving off the flounces although he is in love with them. O Mademoiselle he is smitten, he drools on the knob panel during your scenes. Not the drool of stupidity, Mademoiselle, but the *authentic slobber of love*. He asked me personally to feel you on the matter—I am his ambassador. Since he is a lowly artisan and you a bejewelled glistering thing.

—Yeah, sure, why not? says the Mlle from beneath the panchro sponge. He's got eyebrows from Ohio.

In the middle of the show, Lampedusa starts throwing weird hand-signals at MacK. MacK scrutinizes the rheostats in his purview. —Whassamatta? —You'll find out, says the Lamp, stand by electric 68. —Am I going to be fired? says MacK. —Only I can fire you, says Sidney. —Electric 68 go, says Lampedusa. —Look, what is up? says MacK. —Electric 68 go! says Lampedusa. —You're fired! shouts Sidney, pulling the lever for MacK the distracted.

The need of drama is often strangely met. Lampedusa's errand is it. Is enough for MacK. Over several weeks he begins to dream and drip at his glowing meters, dysfunctional in the knowledge that Mlle Jo-Ann is not insensitive to his finer aspects. It is his distraction from his leaking roof, all the perverts of the BMT, the Bud Abbott demeanor of Sidney, the problematic liquids of the Freesia. Doesn't actually have to approach the object of love—and then—*of course!*

The show closes, for a move to the Belasco, it is said, but some guy named Bernie torpedoes it about 38th Street. Mlle Jo-Ann enters MacK's soul only as a glow, like a distant recalled barbecue. It is easy to think love of those who never arrive.

MacK stares at a blank ream of yellow news, soon to be a smash role for the Mlle, so recently arrived on the stage of this country and MacK's heart. The hour is late. Guy works in the theater for . . . a year? *The theater is a discipline, young man, it is a whole life and you need lots of vague training at state colleges.* And yet he says to himself, *only I can write for her, only I could ever make her really and truly happy.* But this play smells; it is about two fat men MacK has never met. He telephones to Sidney for advice. —Hello? —Ya think the two guys could stand litotes in a scene already charged with paronomasia? —You've awakened me. You're fired.


—Once they told us Indians killed bison only out of need, that when the things were dead they'd go over and *pat 'em*, on the shoulder, and say *I'm sorry*, says MacK. Isn't that breathtakingly swell? I bet they never did any such thing. But say they did, what does it suggest for those who eschew flesh on humanitarian grounds? Might get 'em back on the meat wagon with the I'm Sorry brand of franks. Do ya think? Are you listening to me?

MacK reflects it is curious that he is drinking cup of café-au-lait after cup with Sidney. Normally Sidney abjures stimulants, he cannot be relied upon for dissipation of any kind. He is afraid his dinky but undeniable *chin cleft* will just melt away. Yet Sidney grabbed at MacK in 50th Street, dragged him down to Shubert Alley, into the Petit-Four and started pouring gallons of coffee down the both of them. MacK's trachea is seared and he doesn't know what to make of this new Sidney who wolfs coffee and frantically examines everyone up and down. —See h h here, what's up? MacK's starting to stutter and bark his words he's had so much Sumatra. —Nothing nothing nothing, I'm fine fine fine, says Sidney. —Have I done something to offend you? says MacK, you hardly can look me in the mug. —No no no, says Sidney. His eyes go round his head like the rings of Saturn. Suddenly he crushes MacK's biceps. —*She's here*, growls Sidney, burning with the gemlike. MacK twists in his chair. All he can see is the ugly double-vent of a big-ass businessman behind him.

But then it all makes sense. Why Sidney would want to sit in a little hell like the Petit-Four. Why he would take an afternoon away from his fresnels, the fresnels that he loves like a woman. Why feign enjoyment of what to him had always been poison. The Great

Doppo! Even though MacK can scarcely make her out he turns to Sidney and laughs. Might've known!

The Great Doppo appears numinous and nightly in—let us be frank—the great play of our time in the theater across the street. She brings to her role not only her beauty over which men and critics have duelled and gone mad, but insight and a talent that have earned her slavering notices in the papers. Every night the audience is swallowed whole, screaming, into the infinity of History and Meaning by her gigantic . . . green eyes. The Great Doppo chews 'em up and spits 'em out. And they love it.

Sidney is the most spat-out of all, he sees the thing almost every night and on weekends the matinées. Around the Great Doppo is an admiring crowd and her keeper.

Now the strange thing happens, does it not? Sidney begins trying on battle-plans like summer suits. Looking into Sidney's eyes, MacK sees them spin from idea to idea, on the wise of a slot machine. —Do you have a pencil, says Sidney. These management type guys they never write anything down. MacK lends him a No. 2 pencil, ruminating on the former glory of coffee-houses for writing things in, not that the Petit-Four is anything but a drain for waste money. Sidney's being vibrates with the nerve of the hunt, he scrawls with intensity. —Waiter! he calls, take this and a large Venezia i Napoli, double clotted cream, to the Great Doppo. *Avec mes compliments.* Toot the suit!

Departure of penguinlike being. Sidney starts flamadiddling his fingers on the table. He squirms in his chair. Rearranges the sit of his spectacles on his schnozz. Remarshals scarf between jacket and arran, styles his hair with his right hand, un and re buttons his shirt. Advances socks up legs, reties shoe. His pupils are very small. He stares rigidly ahead, his every nerve searches for some molecule of his being or things that orbit it which might be out of place. —What did you write? says MacK. —Oh, merely that we'd met before, says Sidney. I suggested some dimensionalities.

A shadow falls across MacK's brown froth. MacK looks up and

behold! an obviously angry obviously actress, holding a Venezia i Napoli. With deftness and dignity she swirls it into his lap. It's rather hot. —What is the meaning of this, cries Sidney, jumping to his gallant's feet. —This worm sent me this note, says the Great Doppo, I suppose he is your friend. She hands the note *his own note* to Sidney. He reads it laboriously and looks panicked from the Great Doppo to MacK. —There must be some mistake, says Sidney, I've never seen this man before in my life.

—Turds, says the Great Doppo. —Don't talk to him that way, says MacK, he is a member of the General Public. Then, inspiration! as the Great Doppo turns to recommence semicanoodle with her thuggish minder. —By the way, says MacK, that play you're in is drivel. —F*** me, Sidney groans. —O is that so, says the Great Doppo pirouetting. She makes fisties and stores them on her hips. —Yes I'm afraid it's entirely wrong for you. —Perhaps you would care to explain that, say, in my rooms, at eleven o'clock tonight with a bottle of pink champagne. —I guess I have a few opinions. —Well then.


—I was only trying to help you, says MacK in the IRT. —This is my stop, says Sidney, fuming, I'm getting out. Out, please! —What *dimensionalities?* MacK calls after him.


At the door of the rooms of the Great Doppo a knock comes. Hushing her enthusiastically responding hound, the Great Doppo opens up to find atop two legs a quivering pile of flowers, heart-shaped boxes and protrudingly embarrassing bottles of brut. —Ah, do come in, she says. Indicates the way with a waft of Chinese silk, spirals of incense, fractals of parfum and 'Sobranie'. —Charmed, says MacK, trying to avoid the hound, which has a real talent for the underfoot. The Great Doppo excuses herself to ice up. MacK puts himself on the sofa. He and the hound look deeply into each other's eyes and MacK clears his throat a lot.

Tick, tock.

—Well well, says the Great Doppo, arranging her clouds on the far end of the sofa. So you have a conception of the theater. —I . . . —Get over here.

Two bottles of champagne float empty and upended in their bucket. The sampler has been trashed, its various ribbons and pretty papers in disarray all around the room. The flowers droop, mute.

## On the Avenue

—Affairs with actresses? Whose pictures are on buses yet? How different life turned out to be, mercy. It pointedly lacks this sort of thing now, MacK said, emerging from the Park—Manhattan turned out to be strangely quiet in that way, the 1930s can never really happen to you no matter how much you want them—worse still I'd be sleeping under a bridge, not a tuxed smartie macassaring his microphone. O MacK knew the history of his own company's suavity; it was required. Something caught in his throat and he thought *There's a romance to my company . . . there was something exciting and thrilling about NBC that CBS never had. Very cold hearted over there in their cow shed.*

He inhaled the clean but complex airs of the East Side.

But there's never one of a thing in New York. There's the Schmancy East Side, these old towers of granite and brass and iron and velvet, and the glassy ones, the curious squares, defended private streets, no story, even though MacK's larynx is a frequent visitor to the smartest homes. The Quiet East Side, down Second and Third, where hangs Sunday repose. The Crap East Side, spreading nincompoop burgers and teenwear, on a mission from the malevolent gods of Hackensack. The Nibelungen of Nada. What of the Dumb-Ass East Side, a floating world of niteries where some of the 'pages' from NBC demonstrate *yes they can sing*, they make nice—a tiny *nation of yearning struggle* no one ever sees—it plays only to itself and all this sebaceous energy never emerges ever from the pages of *Show Business*—MacK had put in time in these joints years ago when some of his friends were trying to Break In, first you'll have to break out of these sour Michelob mills he thought. How many bacon cheeseburgers could he have eaten watching these crazy kids—they're in their twenties but the head shots made them look fifty, as if they'd just realized nothing was going to happen, like they lived in a TRAILER. Guy who took all the head shots had a camera that did that, a *predicting camera*. If only he had used it for good rather than evil.

—Must get off Fifth, he said, Fifth just doesn't have the humanity of Central Park West, the only real choices are Madison or Fifth and much as it is nice to have the Park on your right as you go downtown, there are a lot of weird people here, people who don't understand anything they see outside their apartments—such as . . . *me*. There really are very old ladies bent almost double by jewelry and there really are pink poodles. —Madison almost always the obvious choice, said MacK as he started across Fifth and got honked at. —Yeah, if you ever make it, snorted a guy who was paid to walk a *dog*. —Wise ass. See this always happens over here right away.

At Madison looked around, always wondering where the *Madison Bar* was—it could only be found on rainy nights when the bus never came—physically it disappeared during the day but no, here it was, its front door a gathered, sleeping face at eleven in the morning . . . a portal to one of the New Yorks that ghosted in and out of Manhattan, the Crap East Side maybe, which like Non New York has no fixed location and can jump out at you anywhere, right when you think you're in the middle of the OK East Side or the Pretty East Side . . .

## The Madison Bar

Last time in the Madison Bar MacK had been stunned, *stunned*, firstly by basketball, which he could never quite believe, that people will watch others sweat in a big stuffy room; men's legs (he recalled the 1962 shorts of Rick Barry and gagged)—secondly by a guy who had brought the Dumb-Ass East Side with him through the door like a fug—it was wrapped around him like an Afghan—talking to two Irish girls through a thick cloud of misunderstanding built of 'Winston Lights' (come *on*) and 'Stoli' martinis—'Stoli' he kept saying, '*Stoli*'—his speech was clear but he must have been blootered as the girls rolled their eyes so—ostentatiously right at each other in the middle of his sentences—you could practically hear their eyeballs plop in their highballs. —*How do you like living in New York?*—he came up with that one, suddenly, several times—*Have you been to any clubs? Have ya been to that new club on 85th?* (Roll, roll: Nah, na yet like)—*Do you know there are more cars in New York than in Ireland?* Guy sounded like reading the left-hand page of a Berlitz. —*Stoli martini Frank, Stoli—where do you live?* They didn't answer that one but for some reason they gave him their names and thus having conquered—?—something, triumphed in some small way he got up unsteadily and excused himself—they scampered for the street door while he checked his hair and congratulated himself and smoked and vomited all at the same time in the mens.

Ah poor MacK caught between basketball and this guy whilst trying to put his thoughts of Olive in order; he'd just taken her to the movies. He thought he might write it on a napkin. *She is intelligent, kind, the wearer of experience in life. She looks sweetly tired. Very stylish, looks a humdinger in the rain with her deep red lipstick and delicate skin. Radiates a real beauty of soul.* Here the napkin had run out—and rather than have to ask the bartender whose name might likely be Mort Rushmore for any *favors* he allowed himself to be driven out into the rain by rue and the zoo of the sweaty old Knickerbockers and this guy, the Madison Bore in the Madison Bar, driven out to follow Olive over to the West Side and into her building which after all was his own now, thinking he would never know her and couldn't even get her fine points down on a *napkin*, which one might keep as a souvenir.

—

It isn't only what is *on* Madison as you walk down it. It is the knowledge of *what* you walk through, the miasms of several cultures which can fatigue and enrage. Upper Madison has a homely, family feel to it, what with the Madison Restaurant, snow day cream of chicken and its many saltines. The old people who don't know what to do with themselves all day but go backwards and forwards between two Soup Burgs with a doggie in a little coat. *So much to look forward to*. Hello there. Hello. Walk south and you're in gallery and antique land, or first you're in antique land and then you're in gallery land and there is barely a cup of coffee to be found, *forget* cream of chicken!, *man* how they can treat you from block to block. Then an eddy of glories of semi-civic life, the neighborhood of historical societies, various Leagues, tooth-minders and twisters, tiny private schools and Japanese confectioners who are always empty because everyone is STILL LOOKING FOR THAT CREAM OF CHICKEN, said MacK at a good clip.

Around the 60s you start your descent into Little Tokyo as Iz calls it as it's hard to walk without getting pushed and shoved and having to avoid these people from New Jersey all dressed in *skins*, who have cataracts, who are each carrying something like a kilogram of waste *inside their bodies*, at any rate the big specs so dark they never step aside. WHY AREN'T THESE PEOPLE IN THEIR OFFICES? HAH?

But of course, Sherry-Lehmann, and in the odd pause in all the activity, down around 48th, the Wilbur Sisters themselves. And then of course he felt nauseous about this. Walking down Madison on an autumn afternoon can be pleasing but Madison on the wrong sort of day will drive you mad, you keep getting *glimpses of Fifth*, you think *should I be over there maybe?*, sometimes it looks festive, so *shoot* me. But when you're on Fifth it can seem you're a thousand miles from anything you know . . . the stone wall of the Park presents an unbroken sedulous grey statement of account for blocks and blocks without variation, repeating itself and the corners and cars ad nauseam like the endless background in a cartoon chase; perhaps the whole of Fifth Avenue is a Möbius strip. MacK had always felt upper Fifth to be an 'artist's impression' in wash, a matte suspended in front of the brain's Panaflex. —Of course some people have managed a better grasp of Upper Fifth, he said—they live there, enough of this *Fifth* jazz—

## Madison & 53rd

A little confused and afraid. —Oh yeah, the Fairchild Building, let's see, dat's at . . . fiffy toid and Madison, the guy in the hat said—friendly enough. MacK felt he had somehow forgotten—five blocks north of the Wilbur Sisters—ought to've clocked *that* when he visited Olive before—but isn't it true that sometimes you just don't know where you are in this our town?—it only lasts a few minutes. Sun on the many panes—you could see how the glen-plaid steel-cut suits of the early Sixties worked in harmony with the buildings and the haircuts—Madison at work; Madison comes out to play; crisp piano and very precise brushwork. Jazz like lamps—Ed Thigpen coming and going through revolving doors of magazine buildings, his brushes in an attaché case. The Fairchild is one of the old *gentlemanly* buildings—and there was something related to the aspect of the RCA Building which offered a kind of communal warmth—not just expressed in *murals*—but in 1930 Rockefeller Center was supposed to be a model for the whole city—which frankly, said MacK, is enough to make you guffaw, given what happened to the whole *country* since then—as MacK and Shelby Stein frequently *did* guffaw, after breathing in Sert's great mural, *Time*. But still there was something to cherish in humanism you find here and there in this our town, stuck like gum on the under sides of things—an ember—*some*body, at *some* time in history, must have had a beneficent feeling toward *some*one. Look at the directory in the lobby of the Fairchild Building: are these not all people, my people, your people, pulling together? Making and selling things? —*What's* *wrong with the world of 1957 anyway*, said MacK under his breath, and felt a stab of guilt, betraying the Sixties and their necessary destruction of all that post-war refrigerator horse shit—which of course has been completely *ineffectual*—as we're back to BIG refrigerators and BIG cars, BACK TO BIG IN A BIG WAY—but the security guy frowned.

O pleasing elevators of the Fairchild Building. Actually icky—the cabs remodeled, but the smooth old motors—an excellent, shipshape basement, half-grey walls, 25-watt bulbs to be sure. You know, whatever the *Christian Coalition* may think, there are a lot of plain old offices in New York, offices not made of marble, many offices which lack deep carpeting with secretaries writhing in, thought MacK, even the RCA Building, functional, beautiful, never luxurious—even the Music Hall, which is grand, but its grandeur is for *you*, in 1930. You were wearing a hat. Everything in New York was for you.

In a minute the doors would open on the 18th floor and he'd walk along, as he had several times, down the plain corridor to the door of

## KAM-ART BROS., INC.

where Olive worked every day in the company her father had started. Running it now, really, her father tired and puffing in the city, taking the day off more and more. His hat, suit, overcoat, car—the old routine—but visiting the building something like a former owner or even a ghost. What became important was the still alive hat and journey—he ceased to look into the accounts. MacK loved Olive the more for this, her love for her father and his modest accomplishment, she had picked it up, dealt with the clients in a forthright, honest, lovely way. He liked to see her working along with everyone else, coming out of her father's glassed-in office for MacK's moony visits. Is there anything more attractive to us town boys than competence, assurance? Sign of survival after all—not to veer into that New-York-is-a-jungle, DNA twaddle. But MacK loved her, loved the look of her in her understated and slightly arty suits, her lipstick, her quiet stride.

Kam-Art Bros., Inc., dealt daily with the design of paddy-to-the-touch corrugated boxes for light bulbs, the ones which, once squeezed——. The design for their major client hadn't changed since Olive's father made it in 1964. But! So many things like squeezy boxes have to be worried through the decades, in plain offices like this.

He thought again, as the elevator doors opened and a bell rang, of their movie date, which was both open and closed, and inconclusive; of her inquiry as to his religion. Never thought he would be obliged to answer such a question in New York——but where else? ——And now I'm going to die and New York never got around to allowing me to be Jewish——right at the end here when I most need to, he said.

At the office he reached out for the knob——the door with combed-look frosted glass in it, *Kam-Art Bros., Inc.* painted there the day they moved in, in 1959, and never retouched——it did strike him as odd——what was he doing just *showing up*, in the *middle of a business day!?*, he could hear his father——I'm *popping in*, is what I'm doing, said MacK——he'd opened the door and he saw the carpet and the receptionist and there might be a smile when he asked to see Olive.


She was looking at a computerized schema of light-bulb boxes——what else?——the 25-watt, in blue and yellow and white. If only she had known of MacK's fondness for 25-watt bulbs she'd have got him a few from the rep, who always tried to give her bulbs——but are you hearing this, a guy has to *represent light bulbs*. What the——? Even though the package designs were old-fashioned and stark and immutable, Olive had a nostalgia for the days of two-color printing——it reminded her of her childhood——and her moment of reminiscing was confused and then atomized when in a small sequence of flashes through the office—the main door opening, confusion of the office lights, sun light and hallway light—she saw in these lights MacK's face, coming in, smiling at the receptionist—he's always polite and pleasant, Olive thought in the flashes, MacK's *concise head*—he told her the NBC barber said once *Very concise head Sir*—being directed by the receptionist's pinknailed hand—now he was looking in her direction. But his eyes weren't his own, were very dark in the slow-moving prism of the outer door whirring on its closer—and Olive was on her feet and going over to him—she didn't run, though she might have, so plain was the news on his face.

The way she looked as she came toward him, the corner of her mouth, her tongue peeping out and preparing her, the *recognizable poignancy of her freckles* shocked him into the realization that she knew, had instantly known why he was there. This hurt MacK because it ruined the pretense he had allowed himself—that he was just saying hello. Merely *popping in* . . . He couldn't say anything. Now I'm a *tragic sick person*, he thought, roaming a building where I don't have an office—could be a matter for SECURITY.

*In the middle of a business day!?*

He was a disquieting sight; he could only mean one thing.


For her part: Olive found MacK stern about things, irascible in his opinions of paintings and movies; not one of those men who turn every organ of New York to their own use—drinking up the Modern like a martini and making the *New York Review of Books* their dripping brunch waffle and staying with a woman just through the current pack of 'Marlboro Lites'—but in keeping to himself, in making time to THINK in his apartment, Olive thought MacK might in fact have New York by a better handle.

She found him nice. She found him confused. She found him ignorant of the simplest intellectually arresting points of jazz and baseball (why *did* he live in New York? —for Isidor). She found him eager and funny and lost in the career of disembodiment he had at NBC and wondered what it meant to him.

Their last conversation had been in her apartment, on the other side of the building from his own—he looking at the picture of the girls from the Lycée—Olive was making coffee in preparation, they thought, for another *inconclusive visit to the Modern*—he'd stopped bothering to keep track of these goddamn visits and he thought standing there looking at the bad girls that there are entirely too many museums in New York—and none of them was going to do the trick with Olive, offer her a glimpse into what might be their romance, show her something eerie and recognizable, tragic or old that stimulates the orgone, eros, the romantic—what is the point of *dragging* these women around museums, Mr New York?

—You know, screw it, said MacK, they *wrecked the lobby you know*. So the Modern was bagged and they sat at Olive's table with wine and her little coffee pot from Naples. She was talking about her poor father's gradual debility and MacK suddenly found the entire great hairy go-round with his doctor spilling out of him, a litany, the way *semen* comes out once it starts—surprised at the thought—pointedly, he noticed himself thinking, because he hated all those people who will top one disease with another:

—*I've got a bum knee.*

—*Yes . . . oh but my BRAIN!*

So here was Olive saying *my father's heart disease*—which he'd every right to have at the age of eighty—and MacK blurting out *I probably have lung cancer,* then trying to trail off, soften it for himself as much as for Olive—*they aren't quite sure*—. His face heated by actually saying these words. Thought he'd know what they would sound like but hadn't really.

She expressed her shock and concern so sweetly. She did not take his hand as he hoped she might. MacK just sat there wondering that he was still outside; outside the family, the building, Jewry,

Olive. And indeed how close was she going to come now to someone who might DIE? Someone who treated her religion as something which could be *assigned* to him, as a cultural whim, or a joke of *Sidney*? Where is my anger? It boiled up that night, MacK thought, I was very angry at this probable cancer right there because before my eyes it was eliminating my chances of love *that evening*.

*Guess I better go*—that's what you say. *Let me know what happens*, she said at the door—he couldn't figure what she meant—he was so full of stupid self-pity, ignoring the complicated reality of their interest in each other. Pondered, in the hall, the biological injustices of the present age which prevented Olive from taking him to her bed for solace—but you're SCREWY, even without these bugs on the loose she'd never f*** him out of 'sympathy'.


But Olive had not been so disinterested in MacK as it pleased him—you know—on some level to suppose. But the EGG TIMER: this expensive plastic clam brooding in the grotto of the bedside drawer, the tyrannical little magistrate of the pockabook—occasionally you allow it a taste of you that few men can have experienced—it gets to know you hideously, thoroughly—a digital incubus you have *paid* for—and when you do think you would quite like to make love you open up the thing and it blinks, in *red*,

NO!

NO!

NO!

The simple disagreement of electronics and desire—she'd figured it would come right in a week or two. Meanwhile, the museums.


After pensively leaving Olive and going down to the ground floor and crossing to his side of the building, he discovered the Non-Anglophone having trouble as always with her door key—he helped her in—her Yale lock (you see what happens?) was installed upside down for some idiotic reason of *supers*. She stood looking at him with her very large eyes. She searched his face, which must have held anguish beyond the usual New York five o'clock shadow of death. Let's face it, whatever's happened to you, by the end of the day you're sick of it. She sat him down and gave him a serving of a goat dish of her people, whoever they exactly were. A large glass of red wine and f***ed him against the old refrigerator in her boots which smacked, he imagined, of ENVER HOXHA. And the irony is: with crazy goat-driven sex you don't worry about The Bugs like you just did out there in the hall.

This morning Olive had been thinking about MacK on the subway. Olive remained beautiful on the subway, remote from the subway, even on hot days, even though she used the No. 1 and even though she went through the impossible rigmarole of going to Grand Central and getting the *f***ing* F at Rockefeller Center—and even thought in a mode you might associate with *him*, that sometimes she might be beneath the RCA Building, when she was down in that scarily shitty station—and that he was up there in it.

There are plenty of people who are mighty impressed with themselves in this our town, but they still have to go to work—it never struck Olive that she lived in an exciting place even though almost every morning she saw a character from Sesame Street buying a breakfast of hot dogs and cigarettes—no one has time to stop and think that what they're doing would seem impossibly glamorous in that terrible big country out there.

Olive had been a few places and in a few romances which had great unsuitability as her parents thought—Mrs Leninsky's sister and her husband—who of course lived in The Wynd. Ten years ago they'd got one of the penthouses—yes, yes—but like all penthouses it was a mixed blessing—the guy in the other one kept coming out in the foyer in his underpants, raving about forgotten or obscure doughnuts.

But was this part of Olive's reluctance about MacK—that her parents would instantly find out if anything were to 'go on'?—quotation marks like that are the drawback of *buildings*. Where MacK quietly treasured the idea of 'marrying' *into* the family of the building, the building of the family—Olive was wary of making trouble, now that her fate in the firm seemed as sealed as a door in Thebes—as she'd made trouble (for *herself*—her mother and father were confident they'd stop almost anything) with her Italian, her Celt, her Dane, her Fireman, her Orthodox Labor Lawyer already (he chewed with his mouth open)—in her attempts to get *out*.

She talked quietly to MacK now in her father's office, assuring him no one had sensed anything *tragic* or of emergency about his coming—although MacK hadn't heard it, she'd spoken to him and invited him in as normally as if he'd had a suitcase full of light bulbs—what'd *they* know anyway? —*Why did you come to see me?* —I had a call from the . . . —*I know. But why did you come to see ME?* —I was on a walk. I was thinking about the, our building. —*407?* She talked with him in such tones of understanding you could scarcely believe quite such a conversation was happening in an office. Because it was Olive there was a quiet saxophone ballad behind everything, he thought—maybe jazz leaks out of all the glass boxes of Madison Avenue long before the cocktail hour—from when things were largely grey and brown.

If you have a problem in New York, someone will help you. Almost anyone will.

Her quietness and composure and level beauty made him want to weep—but he was exhilarated too, by the city, by the odd feeling of *holiday*, the thought of Isidor at the end of the day. He felt inarticulate—and happy to be with her—and embarrassed about that; still felt he was a visual and sociological problem within the confines of the Fairchild Building.

But now Olive was saying that *she* had had a fright the year before.

Her breast. And now MacK did begin to weep—for the *word breast*—the signals about tissues they were exchanging!—for the pain she might have had, for the worry she suffered—and because her breast he imagined as something ineffably sweet—and he had never seen it.

He choked on all this, seeing she was worried about him but was she also worried about what kind of scene might develop here maybe—was this a moment which demanded rationalism? So be it—rational guy, after all. Degree. Apartment. Place to go in RCA Building. Wanted to say *I'll miss our little chats*—but that was cruel—or *remember me, memento mori*—but why saddle OLIVE with that crap, truly *why* break into her life and dump your possible end in her lap and expect her to do something about it? Horse shit!

At the elevator bank, she kissed him, with a meaningful tenderness he'd never have imagined, even his romantic fantasies having only to do with the surfaces of things, the taste of a cigarette at a moment of declaration. First words, never last words. You could say it was because she had been through the 'same thing'—all these doctors, all this coffee and thinking about the end of life—wishing you could call all your life to you at one moment, at your desk—but that had ended and she was going to live—was living—her life become the usual question mark—the downward curve of which toward that **dot** we choose to ignore.

# 50 West 50th Street

> *Four-thirty Sunday afternoon in New York, and the RCA Building stands up tall and respectfully removes its hat.*
>
> —Introduction to an NBC program, 1940s

With MacK it was always radio—he stood across the street from his favored entrance to the RCA Building—attempting not to think about the blackest portion of the lobby—gold squares, who cares. Watched people coming and going under the coffered lamps which no one but himself ever bothered to look up and love, or be loved by the old gentler city there. Here comes Nancy Schwartz. —Radio, he said aloud, in his *known voice*. In the same gawp's way he was now looking at the metal awning and the red NBC, he'd used to gaze at the bronze lettering *KGO-810* at the old ABC building in San Francisco—the scenario, if you will have it, was: a bleak, pitted adolescent took the train into the city to stand in fog or rain and stare through heavy plate glass at various hip AM personalities—if you can accept AM as hip in 1968—three layers of glass which made something only a few feet away very remote, remote as the network, teeming away just behind the meter glow and red keys on the engineer's panel—the network, which swept the station up into its arms for five minutes every hour with a mighty drum roll—and kissed its tush, Shelby would have said. Discovered something about suavity from watching the sometimes surprising embodiments of the area's best-loved voices coming and going from this rather elegant studio—what snazzy dressers—fell in love with the Electro-Voice microphone in its suspensory—noticed that someone had taped a typewritten sign under the Simplex clock at the announcers' desk—*I CHOOSE NOT TO SMOKE*—and set himself for a career like that of the duty announcer—a hero the unions have had to give up—who came into the studio twice an hour, leaned into the microphone and gave a station break rather perfectly making almost all the radios in northern California throb—the rest of the time he sat around eating oranges. MacK *peering in* at these guys just making a living who certainly found most repellent the idea of being worshipped by a *pockmarked monster*—but being a Californian with *by law* no religious training what so ever, he worshipped what plain gods were available.

When MacK got in the cab to come to 50 West 50th Street for his first day of work, it throbbed in the same way as he *over-pronounced* 'NBC at Radio City!' as Isidor was always accusing him of slipping into work mode. Ignoring MacK's several *years of struggle*, in the wilderness of gabble, doing ads, reading the news to millions who didn't care, not only what the news *was*, but didn't care what it *sounded* like, bastards—and I did achieve it, MacK suddenly thought, but hadn't for years, that his job *was* like the one he had coveted peering into that old radio station in the rain (a little ashamed of this, company man now)—sitting in his studio, the directors in his head-phones—*'Standby announce'*—the red lights tick down—*'And . . . announce!'*—and after all there was not much to say these days.

—Radio is hooey, let's admit it, said MacK looking at the 50th Street entrance, there goes Nancy Schwartz back in, worse than hooey, it's *guano*, but at least there is still such a thing as the NBC Radio Network and my studio and the old elevators and I've been able to preserve the illusion of polish and romance if not exactly *meaning*. Radio began verily as the new tribune of the people in the twentieth century, prac-tically in this very building. And now it only mocks and undermines them. Can you believe that disk jockeys *still exist*?

Radio is adolescence, rejection, revenge. One is always hidden. There are meters. KNOBS.

He still felt something electric in the atmosphere of the older stu-dios on his floor—ye gods five years ago they came up from Engineering with plans for a technical renovation, some digital board with sliding pots and MacK had flipped: —You are *not* going to put *sliding potentiometers* in my studio, he said, this is the *RCA Building*.

He imagined some kind of similarly charged sacred air around altars—and it occurred to him that he felt about all these places the way he did about the TOMBS collecting in his head, which were now becoming more of a preoccupation, because of . . . —So, work will kill you, said MacK, nothing prophetic in that idea.


Last year, standing outside the Rockefeller Plaza entrance with Shelby, who was smoking one of his legion 'Pall Malls': MacK looked up at the sculpted beardy above them, *'Wisdom and Knowledge Shall Be The Stability Of Thy Times'*, and said: —Wait a minute, is this Zeus or Prometheus? —Beats me, said Shelby, I always thought it was Santa. MacK ignored this. But you have to get the pantheon straight. —So *that's* Prometheus, he said, looking out at the gold rink hunk. Shelby hissed his last lungful between his teeth and threw the butt so that it landed just behind the heel of the real door man, a character in a top hat who had been trained to wait for celebrities with an umbrella. Shelby always tried to flip it right there, perhaps hoping for some kind of hot foot. He was under pressures that those in radio could only dream about. He looked out at Prometheus with his slightly yellow eyes. —Yeah well *my* liver ain't so good either, and stalked off under Sert's great mural, *Time*, to the elevators to go upstairs and do promos for *Bonacker*, which was then at number three, and Promotions was pressing so *hard*.

—My years of struggle, smiled MacK, which in fact were not, involving only long shifts on the local station as well. The Seventies and Eighties were not overly difficult at work, but what did make them years of struggle, said MacK, suddenly chilled, was Tumbleson, *she* was the struggle.

Since he was working weird shifts he could often, around four o'clock, walk down to where she worked on Vanderbilt Avenue—filling himself with what he thought of as the *copper feeling* of midtown in an autumn evening, a romantic compound he made for himself of the early street lights, the sun going down on the side of the RCA Building maybe, smoke from the vendors' carts, a pipe of 'Owl'. He would walk her home, to the Upper West Side, where she kept a pewter beer goblet for him in her freezer—a nice gesture to her man—frequently his lips would freeze to it and shred.

He would make grand statements, looking out from her apartment at a large but mundane panorama of the West 70s.

### I LOVE THIS CITY. I LOVE YOU.

What the Hell was he talking about? But Tumbleson was not a romantic girl, she had no little god of New York romance to worship, no James Cagney to MacK's Celeste Holm, and concerned only with the hackneyed epic of Business, she was experiencing the slow disillusionment and sedimentation of time which only working in a midtown office can provide.

Did YOU never make any sartorial mistakes 1970–1980? He bought some shoes near Lincoln Center which seemed *reasonable facsimiles* of tasseled loafers but after he walked in them for several days they became oddly shaped and depressing—they made Tumbleson furious. (Shelby kindly pointed out that tasseled loafers aren't for walking in. —Look at me, he said, I *drive* in—from *Larchmont*. His were tan.)

After a time MacK and Tumbleson began each to believe the other was trapped in *the wrong New York*; and there is nothing you can do about that.


You may think that your face is just you, or how you look. What you put food in and talk out of—but in New York it is a tool, a weapon maybe, said MacK, crossing to the ice rink. You have to hone it, push it through the streets of people, and if you have a sharp, an amazing, a frightening *ferocious face* like *Tumbleson*, you'll get where you're going a lot quicker.


## 44th & Vanderbilt

Which always sounds like something that isn't in Manhattan—ought to be in Brooklyn or on the Monopoly board. *Almighty*, he'd never noticed that the Yale Club was designed by the Pillow Bank guy—must have been—even sneakily tried to make it look like *Columbia*, to *justify* somehow the presence of Yale in New York—as if buggering everything in Pine Street isn't enough. Built this new haven for themselves a few tottering steps from the tracks to New Haven—where is your *courage?*—'We need it right by the train.' F*** you! Remembered the look of these lanterns on copper evenings when he was 'dating' Tumbleson—isn't it fatuous to use the innocent rectangles of the calendar to mean *penetration?*—in the mid Seventies, when no one gave a damn about New York except Isidor and Jackie Onassis. Tumbleson was at a complete loss about all the charms he went on about—never liked Isidor anyway—MacK thought she'd ruined her ability to understand New York at all, working for Yalies, like foreign ground, a consulate.

Today the lobby was even more tomb-like than he remembered it—the tiny sensations you could glean of Vanderbilt Avenue, which after all was *immediately outside*, in bright sunshine, made it and the whole city seem, yes, something to be disparaged and belittled—that *could* be manipulated from in here. Guy in a uniform. —*May* I help you, Sir? —Yes. I wish to book the New Haven Room for the Tie Appreciation Group, thought MacK, as I do every October. But this guy's eyebrow, which ought to be taxidermied and mounted over the marble hearth upon his death, he should *drop dead* as soon as possible, MacK thought—was clearly a thing to avoid stimulating. —Tumbleson, said MacK to the Frank Morgan look-alike.

You expect a Pierpont Morgan look-alike and they have a *Frank* Morgan look-alike.

—Is Miss Tumbleson expecting you, Sir? —She was expecting me for dinner at her small apartment in the mid 70s in the mid Seventies, said MacK. *The guy's eyebrow.* —So no, not in her wildest dreams. The guy phones . . .

MacK used to try to find some warmth or even a welcome in this place—to convince himself that sleeping with Tumbleson made life light and gay, that he was an honorary part of the Yale family—though it was some dysfunctional family—drunk at lunch and staggering around, peering bleary at cabinets of trophies and funerary sweaters . . . *Have you seen the display? Have you seen the display?* this guy Charlie would always say—after his first martini—Tumbleson worked for him—when MacK showed up every other day to share his *truly innocent* NBC vending machine sandwich with her. —*Carter—tryna get rid of martinis, at lunch anyhow—on the attack, isn't he?* Charlie went on and on—*James EARL Carter, a peanut farmer, can you—credit cards too, he hates 'em. Have you seen the display?* But Carter has the right idea, thought MacK, at least prevent CHARLIE from getting his mitts on unlimited credit and the lunch hour martinis. But of course MacK had been a big problem in Tumbleson's life—saw that now. She probably worried for months how to get rid of him. —*You know what they used to tell us in the war?* said Charlie after his third. —What? —*Keep a tight asshole!* —Oh . . . you're it?


Discovered her, composed and presentable behind a large desk in the FUNCTIONS DEPARTMENT, which she responsibly ran now.

—*Look who's here.* She seemed all right. Pretty. —Sorry I'm late. —*Ha.* Looked about the same as before, as *twenty years before*, the kind of thing that drives Izzy . . . —*What have you been doing?* —Well, I've been stuck in the RCA Building for the last twelve years. —*What you always wanted.* —But in the elevator? **Ba-dum-bump!** She smiled; became a little wary. —*What are you doing here?* —I was on a walk and . . . realized the Club looks like my bank. —*!*— —Just thought you might be in. —*Oh I'm in. I've been in.* She paused for a moment in which they both traveled a bit and then grew older. —*Care for a cocktail? I'm the housekeeper, you might say.* Twirled a key on the end of a fine gold chain—just as she used to make provoking gestures out of *Cosmopolitan*, MacK thought.

She led him through blank serving corridors to a bar—the Members' Bar—which wasn't in use. Smelled of chlorine and wool. —*This doesn't open till five—they can get crocked in the dining room at lunch. Still abusing the bottle?* —I'm shocked. Rather it me. —*Martini?*

In an obscure, plentifully stocked bar with Tumbleson!—the stuff of rather desperate phantasy during Redless weekends of the past—now shut sudden away and perhaps cruel from the brightness and inappropriate optimism he'd felt for the last hours, leaving the West Side and wandering happily in midtown which may be thought never to end—always hope and well-being to be found between 59th and 34th—even if but provisionally your own. Her body remembered in her dark suit beneath the darkness that is Yale and its pillowed stone, shuttered against the eyes of Manhattan which would be annoyed to see everyone staggering around in here. In those ties.

—Incredibly, I accede. —*Good for you*. She sounded suddenly tired, like a kick-ass Chandler broad—which she could have been, maybe—if she'd been taller. She had filed down her sweet voice with twenty years of 'Marlboro Lites'. He saw as she lit one and then started up with the glass and metal. MacK leaned on the bar, which was stone and chilly, imagined reclining on it, thought of the cornerstone of the Riverside Memorial Chapel—what an annoying obstacle-course of crypts was Manhattan become.

They raised their glasses to each other silently, almost in the dark.

Isn't it awful to remember what it is like to consciously convince yourself you are in love? Such a huge lie makes every movement painful, every decision agony. For both. MacK was falling in love with the city and supposed he was, or could, with Tumbleson at the same time, or assumed it would happen, *natch*—much as he had *presumed*, when a child, that intercourse occurs when both parties are asleep. Or had *hoped*. He would drift around midtown and rejoice in the tobacconists and shirt stores as evening descended—the copper point of balance between the rapidly deepening sky and the wakening street lamps. Smoke. Prized Autumn, and therefore of course he must be in love with this girl, taking her home most days to the appalling West 70s and that *god awful cop bar*, so that she could shuck her Yale exoskeleton and get her therapeutic helping of violence and sleaze.

Tumbleson turned, with the Yale Club Rubber Martini Olive ($24.95 at Club shop) in her teeth. —*They think this is funny*, she said. *We sell a lot of these.* She squeezed it and it squeaked. —*It's for their dogs.* —That I can well believe. Where do you live now? —*Hartsdale.* —!— —*I'm married, MacK . . . surprised?* —Oddly, I—no. He now learned all about Hartsdale, and about her *doubly tragic youngster*, which had *cysts* and—ironically—could not pronounce its *Ss*—nothing to be done, *but then she suddenly found him out and caressed him*—kneeling, replaced the dog's toy with himself for some moments—got up and turned against the bar—somehow representing the receding aspects of herself and Yale—into which she had never quite disappeared—at least not ideologically, wholly—and they began to move as they used . . . This could be, he thought, one of the last times, *the* last time, and it's with—but what the Hell, she has needs!—that's what she used to say when she'd been with someone else—*people have needs.* MacK felt himself fall back from the city for a moment and observe it—the cycle of fidelity and infidelity, wished or not, worried or not—the Ferris wheel of New York privilege he'd never ridden properly—nor even seen the view. The Yale Club is solidly built, he thought, as her noise came—he started on his—she pushed him back with a small, impatient, yet recognizable hand. Took a mouthful of the cold grey silver, which she had made with real style, he noticed—if only Isidor were here—of course you have to deal with high-octane to get these guys disoriented and down to their ties and sock garters in daylight hours—and put it to him. The old days! He remembered their past funs—which never led to love, no matter how intense—and thought of the beautiful, possible Olive.

Arrived, in Tumbleson's pillowed, stony mouth. Infinite stack of Yale Club napkins.

—Why did you do that? asked MacK, touching her upper arm with . . . *something* strong he was feeling—she didn't know the edge of the world was something he could glimpse readily from the poop of his *Niña*—which seemed the absolute limit of what he might touch—even though she was leaning, relaxed, against the bar, one leg crossed over the other.

—Because we're going to die some day.

Goodbye, all the warmth of Yale.

Had told himself: nothing today—not one—he'd save the capacity for *wonderment* for Isidor and The Hour—but out the big door and around a corner or two to McAnn's, the one where you go way WAY down the stairs and the old bar huddles against the wall in the big dark place—still embarrassed to have usurped the cafeteria of decent office girls of 1950 in the name of the needs of the honestly confused men of midtown. But a glass of beer, a cheeseburger?—a jolly dollop of quotidian smirch after that vivid, chilly twenty minutes in the Roost of the Big Shots—sometimes, Mom, it is just a coolant. Have to remind you that cleanliness and order belong to the land of the imagination. And I am probably the only fellow in the whole joint with lipstick on him, though who can know, he thought, with the first untroubled smile of the day—he caught this himself—it is two o'clock and after all is said and done

**THIS IS A HAPPY TOWN.**

# Why I Hate Food

At the mention of food, thought MacK, it always gradually breaks out a fight. Something has happened to the way people eat; there are too many TRIBES about it. There is the tribe of those who eat only at home, their tiny kitchens stuffed with cookbooks. If they have space they have built kitchen *islands*, under spotlights, grand opera kitchens where the dinner guest drowses drunkly and slowly starves while watching his fat, obsessed host prepare the meal—there is a man on Thompson Street who has an APPLAUSE sign over his island. Its burners in the night. You see it from the imagined safety of your ship. The drums.

Some will only eat in restaurants—they can't, *won't* make you coffee or a drink, even in *anticipation* of the restaurant. But the largest tribe are those who cannot eat the GOOD FOOD WHICH IS FREELY AVAILABLE ON EVERY CORNER IN THIS OUR TOWN. It's right in front of them—but if *sustenance* is mentioned, so is a *taxi*. You could be walking past the GRAND CENTRAL OYSTER BAR even, but no, *NO,* being *proximate* to a place *rules it out*; complicated negotiations must be entered into between every one in the party and you are then forced into a taxi—*the forcemeat stuffing of a taxi*—and hurtled somewhere far uptown, far down-town, and preferably across town from where you realized you were hungry. So hungry. Or *thought* you were hungry! Hasn't your appetite disappeared after one of these *contretemps* asserted of course in the friendliest possible way? HAH?

As we go about town, we encounter a number of altercations, hold-ups, confrontations—it's inevitable—what *look like crimes*—we step around them in the street, on the subway steps, people locked in combat, yes—we observe little tussles out the window of our office or the bus. A has B by the lapels; C uses her stilettos unfairly. But most of these contests aren't crimes—they are people *arguing about where to eat*. It really has come to this. Our town is so disconnected from its sources of supply that where to dine has become a life-and-death struggle—it seems nothing has changed since the Neolithic (excepting perhaps napery). Arguing about where to eat is just as exhausting as chipping your arrow-head and going out to try and kill capybara ancestor; eventually in surprise succeeding and hauling it home, chopping it up and heating it in some unimaginable way.

And supermarkets are all run by JACK ASSES. They take even more time than capybara ancestor.

—

—I truly hate food, MacK said to Isidor recently, I just can't take it any more. F*** food! Of course, *f***food,* he thought immediately—not Bob Guccione spilling Bosco on the rattan, you idiot—but the bachelor picking up little snacks to salt the appetite of his intended—carbohydrates and *rounded* things that might be popped between red lips—things that are slimy—f***food. Isidor became very uneasy when MacK said f***food as it sounded like a put-down of food, which he could not bear, for *food* to be denigrated—F*** FRUIT especially, MacK loudly said in a bad mood one day in Union Square. It's really just sugar and water in a suspiciously plasticky wrapping. Really bad for you. My teeth always ache at the thought of biting apples. *I hate food!*

Isidor's eyes became a wide, morose blue at this. —Keep your voice down, he said under his breath. —It's all the preparation, MacK said, the horrible amount of time—even as a child it drove me MAD to watch people making food, my poor mother, the gas, father raging at his brazier, trying to make it fun, trying to make it—MANLY? Every moment I've spent shopping, cooking, eating and washing dishes I've wished I were smoking, reading, drinking or screwing. Don't you see how important it is to recognize the restaurant, the delicatessen, the pretzel-and-chestnut man as THE ONLY SOURCES OF FOOD? Otherwise you'll end up crying in the street. *Sanctify* the delicatessen, said MacK, the restaurant and their waiters which are closest to your front door, no matter how bad. What better example of the American spirit, of cooperation? Of the primal transaction? I give you something of value, shells or cigarettes, and you feed me. —But why are you fetishizing it? said Izzy, that holy transaction takes place at McDonalds 2,000 times per hour. —Ach, that doesn't count.

—Your argument is a good one, said Isidor, except I happen to know it places you at the mercy of Mary Jo's Deli. I know I know and all the feebleness of upper Broadway, MacK thought, and yes I am made sick with fear standing in Mary Jo's watching flies buzzing in the fittings, how never a single one finds its way even by accident to its blue electric Zing Zing. —Yes I EAT CARDBOARD he said and greeny baloneys because I'm sticking to my theory and it's a good one. Mine is the only theory that helps the ecology of the city and saves me time. Provides jobs. And what is the point of living in a city unless you want to save time? If you want to *waste* time go to Larchmont or Vermont or Montana—where you may pay handsomely to waste your time, waiting in line to buy gasoline or having children—or better, *you can pay people to waste your time FOR you*. Out there. Isn't this the essence of the city? You live in town because you want someone to make your morning coffee for you. Don't you think it's CHEATING to prepare food in your own home? It is only drink that nourishes and ennobles, he said. Admit it! If everyone would *just admit* that then we could send all our wheat overseas to those hungry people—they're not allowed to drink, anyway. We get what we need, they get what they need. —I don't know, said Isidor.

# Bump Bump

Look what happened to the idea of food, MacK said to himself, when, years ago, you were allowed to run your fingers over the prominent contours of the vulva—nothing more—of this girl from Hunter College for three or four hours on a rainy afternoon—in the shower you could still see the dull mark on your wrist the elastic of her underwear incised there. Your poor hand in the exact same position for three hours. You withdrew it from her jeans, bloodgorged numb and purple—if only it had been another extremity—and suggested dinner, which she took as calmly as she had the mauly diddling since three o'clock. —*I'm a vegetarian*, she breathed, doing up the many buttons.

In the old neighborhood, *vegetarian* meant either a muenster cheese sandwich or that Chinese food which had been most boiled in the world—it was losing its molecular integrity. In a state ricocheting between guilt and largesse you took this two-bump beauty (thinking all evening of the pronounced quality of her labia, bump-bump, bump-bump under your fingers) to The Farmyard—*New York's Old-Established Vegetarian Restaurant*, here, in the West 40s. Bump bump, the taxi on potholes outside a garage—rain had come on while you lay on your bed, she staring at the ceiling and you wondering what the hell was happening with your life—nothing. The driver pointed out a modest door and a dingy lighted stair—the taxi went off in a series of puddles and bangs and you took the bored girl's arm out of rocketing chivalry of all sorts. Thunder, suddenly, musically, insistently; lightning across the front of the building, which took on a sinister look thanks to the crenellations of a hamburger joint on the corner. At the same moment this restaurant's venerable sign faltered and—bzzzt—The Farmyard—went out. Bump-Bump went up the stairs, you following, observing with vexation the nautical lacing at the back of her jeans—your recent prison; the scene which greeted you in the dining-room robbed you of air and drew you together—*at last she grabbed you*, in horror movie uncertainty. The shabby peanut-oiled maître d' indicated a SEA beyond of the truly distressed and decrepit; the lame, the halt dining as best they could. Here a man with a growth on his cheek *twice* the size of the growth on the ham and salad tub man at Mary Jo's Deli—hell, twice the size of what he was having for dinner; there a family of hunchbacks in their seventies or eighties *having their food cut up for them* by a waiter with a glass eye. No one a recognizable morphic type, shape, or color, and—you know—that's saying something in this our town. But Bump-Bump rushed to sit down—you lost interest in her body entirely at this point except for beginning to SCOUR HER COUNTENANCE for incipient pallor, growths, twistings—to affirm your moral insertion of her into this menagerie.

The food was classical Vegetarian with a stultifyingly capital *V*—everything vegetal fungal and udderal chopped up and molded at ferocious industrial temperature and pressure to *resemble meat*—only despite these extreme processes the semblance was but slim; each

97

dish with a sickly dairy taste—cold *moussaka* run over by the dog-catcher. Bump-Bump ordered diffidently and seemed determined to notice nothing. When the limping waiter snatched the cover from the platter you stared in fury at your cool parsnipwursts—a shocking reiteration of the late afternoon and its rain—the girl's vulva that of a public monument—and you could barely resist fingering the depression between the two—.

Lump lump, going down. Nothing to be said, apparently, the stuff did require a lot of chewing—it was dawning on you that far from coming to The Farmyard to improve their lot, these wretches, whom you were more likely to have encountered in a fun-house—had in this place, from this food—GOT that way.

No proper ending, thought MacK—New York never lets anything die off completely between two people—but a sequel—several months later in Mary Jo's, Bump-Bump, with bigger eyes and smile, faced him off near the potato chips. *Accosted* him just as he was staggering and feeling ill at the sight of the growth on the ham and salad tub man's face, wondering if he dined at The Farmyard. And she incredulously said, *You're buying baloney!?* Above his ranged fluorescent furrows of browning caking salads, bump bump bump, the ham and salad tub man salivated at her.

## The Little Plate of Childhood

Let us take a trip down Alimentary Lane—before our food moved to New York and became perverted. Here, on a winter evening, is your plate—a jolly Georgian coaching scene—the plate is *brown and white*—and here is just *enough* juice from your little chop pleasantly to obscure the scene ('Catching the Mail')—your little chop is half an inch thick—not insignificant you might say, after all an animal has been sacrificed in your honor—but there is no suggestion of pride or plumpness or luxury in your little chop—there is something insistent about its quality as *fuel*—it is a piece of coal for your engine and since this is a WEEK NIGHT, a SCHOOL NIGHT, it's to be regarded as nothing more—there is a sterility, a NURSE-LIKE quality about mother's kitchen, is there not? Is the little chop itself your nurse? You think about it on the street corner, it is a smell you can conjure anywhere (and have done, even to put yourself to sleep in lonely rooms), your little chop, the broiler, the hood, the kitchen, the hot handles of the pots and pans, the clock, the light, the beans, the rice. Down with potatoes, the role of carbohydrate will this evening ladies and gentlemen be played by White Rice, not sticky together like school rice from a scoop but not of the featheriest and most disparate. Difficult to photograph, a circumspect mound, a tussock of rice with a pat of butter upon it—the butter photographs distinctly and the rice is as always a white shape with disturbing points or shadows. For all New York's claims to cover the waterfront of gastronomy, this is a smell you will never find here, not in the most ordinary corner luncheon-ette or the plainest Sixth Avenue hotel serving the biggest dumbest hicks: the little plate of childhood.

—Ye gods This is all *in* me now, said MacK, these poorly rotogravured and pastel molecules, *inside* and perhaps nourishing something still, some idea of what dinner might be like for someone of RECTITUDE, someone with *character*. I still don't know what half the stuff was that I ate!

—Sure, you *lachrymose schlemazl*, all you eat now or all you tell everyone at the bar you eat is brown rice and vegetables delicately sautéed or oven roasted—how you stay in good trim for a city boy or girl, the balance, god's own roughage slicing all the gin and nicotine out of you. But as Isidor points out, that's all a pathetic throw-back to the little plate of childhood—except for the boring little piece of meat jumping up and down, *begging* to be carried away by the postilions of the mail.

# Destroy All Monsters

In Our Years in Yorkville, there was a battle going on between the epic and the romantic, particularly in MacK's stomach, in his belief in, his loyalty to *two foods* he had decided it was all right to be preoccupied with—but just *screw* everybody and their restaurant neuroses—*really*, yes. The heavenly GUMBO of Mary-Ann, which he was invited to eat once a month, usually on the 27th, though he could think of no explanation for this—must have been some kind of Catholic reason, a *shrove* thing? $2 + 7 = 9$ so OK maybe that adds up to gumbo, hell if he was going to *ask* her, that'd be rude—VS the hot yellow and brown MATZOBREI of Dave and Leo at the D&L Dairy which he could have had every day if he wanted—some weeks he did. Even though it was on the same level as the gumbo, speaking of a little bit of heaven here, it took quite a few matzobreis to balance the monthly gumbo *so in a sense* everything was all right. But the more MacK thought about the gumbo and the matzobrei they seemed to be engaged in a contest with each other, one of those end-of-the-world things—the gumbo the world as man has known it with all its and his imperfections and the matzobrei the hot *searing* from the gods that will come on the very last minute . . . that you can still order from the *lunch* menu. Usually two-thirty, three o'clock.

Or more specifically in terms of romance and epic, the gumbo and the matzobrei were playing out a war of the city—the gumbo has *been around*, it *is* romance, the Caribbean, the wonderful polyglot hemisphere; it gathered its flavors subtly many places—it simmers, smolders, seethes, pouts, teases—and you give in, it seduces you, takes you over. The matzobrei is the simplicity and persistent dignity of the proletariat—some days it doesn't taste very good, actually—once MacK even made a face at Dave about it, *what* a f***ing mistake—but one has to eat—so they *say*. One is always basing one's life on the plain things that have gone before, the fish of Scotland, the yogurt of Georgia, cardboard of England; the *matzobrei* is the compressed and slightly tired though still human life of Europe; the matzobrei has been through the grinder, pal, through the f***ing mill—but it picks itself up out of the gutter and is *still being served*. (The particular one Leo'd given MacK seemed to have been through both world wars—but you *expect* it to taste like that, all suffering and sweat—some days in New York that's a rather unpalatable lunch—but everyone has to have it.)

Isidor was a staunch defender of the gumbo—since Mary-Ann would make it for him almost any time he wanted it, natch—so what gave MacK indigestion about the whole idea was that if the gumbo was romantic (and of course Izzy and Mary-Ann had romance, sure, are allowed it) then what food was going to satisfy Isidor's constant defense of the EPIC? (Unless it was the catholicity of what he consumed—anything in any neighborhood at any time—the only food Izzy had ever directly rejected was *funnel cake* at the Ninth Avenue Festival, though he claimed it was the silly *sound* of it, he didn't particularly care that it was *doughnuts* that had been through a *centrifuge*. —It sounds stupid as *bundt cake*, said Izzy—although perhaps the cake is the problem there and not its name. But there are many professional boxers, from places like *Pennsylvania*, who owe their early bulkings-up, that quintessential *luggishness* which pushed them away from life and into the ring, to *funnel cake* and its whole family of frankly unbelievable carbohydrates. You wonder what those from other planets—and they had better get here soon—would make of these things: *Why are they squeezing this glop into hot fat just like waste falls from their asses!* —HOW COULD IZZY EAT GUMBO, KNOWING IT WAS ROMANTIC AND NOT EPIC?, said MacK, who to this day has not been able to figure it out. —Unless he regarded the New World as an *epic romance*, but—pffft! What happens then? The gumbo and the matzobrei *become each other* on a teleological Ninth Avenue and—*voilà*—you have nothing to argue about.

If MacK could have but known it, at just this moment was a new giant come on the horizon to battle the towering MATZOBREI and the antediluvian GUMBO, to knock over some skyscrapers in what might admittedly be a rubber suit, kick some model cars around—fake smoke—little planes swooping on nylon wire. Its name was NAGA. *Huh!*

But he wouldn't be around to witness this ultimate destruction of the city. *Huh!*

# Canned Pears and You

One day last year in Isidor's bookshop MacK discovered the source of all this iniquity. He unearthed, from many overlays and corruptions of the need for food and drink in this our town, the color, texture, temperature, the proteins ('building blocks'—*sheesh!*), the nourishment, the MEANING of his, and Izzy's, youth. Iz stocks tons of ephemera which can make you very uncomfortable about your country and your birthright. In the dark cookery aisle MacK beheld a thing from the antique land we *all* came from, where, woe, mother would get hold of the recipe page in the local paper: *Serving Butter Attractively. Chipped Beef, an Introduction. Cottage Cheese—What Is It?* To wit:

**Down East Clam Dunk:** *Oh, great,* thought MacK, *the* verbe-comme-nom *school of cuisine.* **Blue Cheese Bologna Wedges:** *Bologna—is this spelling supposed to dignify it? 'The FUN staple meat', according to the book. It goes on to describe in surprising detail where it may be wedged.* **Cream of Baked Bean Soup:** *Are you kidding?* **Frank-Topped Zesty Succotash:** *Yiiih!—though it was the most important meat of the period, which encouraged the eating of (canned) vegetables.* **Frank 'n Vegetable Soup:** *And what they did to the letter N! Formerly a kind and useful letter.* **Luau Barbecued Ribs:** *Ah, Hawaii! Shangri-La of the mid-Fifties imagination; now merely the headquarters of minor drug dealers and gas guzzlers.* **Waikiki Kabobs:**

*Spelling just wasn't a problem to our parents. Did you know this? Also try our Waikiki Nog.* **Fiesta Corn Pudding:** *Can you imagine real Mexicans sitting around with bowls of this? They'd hang it from a string and beat the shit out of it.* **Company Cauliflower:** *They arrive, you take their coats, all is early Kennedy jollity, and then their eyes light on . . . !* **Baked Salad of the Sea:** *There was this phrase, 'of the sea', which haunted that time and drifted all around. My uncle once took me to a 'Car Wash of the Sea' in McLean, Texas. And then the idea that BAKING made a thing ready for the table, that it was physically possible to BAKE ANYTHING, as per:* **Baked Cheese Sandwiches, Baked Cheese 'n Ham Sandwiches, Ham 'n Blue Cheese Old Tyme Baked Sandwiches, Baked Swedish Meatballs** *Louis*: ye *gods*, the ups, the downs, the doomed marriages. **Frank 'n Luau Cauliflower-Topped Baked Hi-Fi Party Rib Coolers of the Sea . . .**

*The bookstore had got very airless indeed; the stuffy aisle—*

MacK could bear it no longer. —Say, he called out to Isidor, as if for air, *Cheesy Ponytail Franks. Place frankfurters in roll. Place sandwiches on rectangles of aluminum foil. Seal carefully and twist ends to give ponytail look!* Izzy rushed over. There in the dark cookery aisle they cackled and wept together. As he paged through this warped book, Isidor acquired a distant, bilious expression. He teetered. —Don't you hate the word *casserole* and its associated house-filling smell, said MacK suddenly, that of a big earthenware half-glazed dish with a frightening, hollow handle? Doesn't the word *casserole* itself SMELL, of unimaginatively used onions? —Yes, Iz said, how dare they serve dollops of stuff *straight from the cooking vessel*. It strikes at the heart of sensibility. It *deprives waiters of work*.

—*Baked Tuna Ring*. —Oh, said Iz, anything that could be formed into a ring was good. You *reel* from all that post-war sloth. People *will* paint that, said Izzy, as an energetic American time, but really they wanted everything all mixed up with cheese. They wanted it all 'piping hot'. And look: by the time you got to dessert, everything had taken its toll, you'd no energy left to keep cooking: *Refrigerator Cake,*

*No-Bake Confetti Brownies*. —Yes, MacK said, even though preparing the entrées merely involved stirring onion soup mix into . . . *I feel sick.*

No wonder that Isidor and MacK, reared on this kind of thing, are conflicted in their attitudes to food—and everything else for that matter. But while MacK can hardly bear to think about food, was *driven away from it at an early age*, cuisine of the atomic era had determined Isidor on loving food. Trauma ensued—Isidor always asks people about MacK *Did he feed you?* If someone visits MacK, whether uptown or out of town, the first thing Isidor asks them is

## DID HE FEED YOU?

> *The sea is only the medium of a preternatural*
> *and wonderful existence; it is*
> *only movement and love.*
>
> —Captain Nemo, *Twenty Thousand Leagues*
> *Under the Sea*

## The Discovery of Fish and its Waiters

took place on a damp day long ago, Isidor and MacK standing half-relaxed on the prosaic rain-corner of Seventh Avenue and 34th Street. A Monday afternoon, perhaps a public holiday, though you couldn't tell due to the absence of people who *stroll*.

They had just come out of Penn Station,—*that low-ceilinged Hell*, said Isidor, of course you won't remember the old Penn Station. —No, MacK said, I won't, and I'd rather not remember this one either. —I'm telling you, said Isidor, in Hell all the ceilings will be very low, with hot spotlights which singe the acoustical tile surrounding them so it looks like someone has been cooking French toast up there. Architects have got to go.

MacK cast about for something to contrast with the present moment on the dull rain-corner, though contrast is hard won in the West 30s. They had just visited Isidor's parents by train. Isidor's mother, for reasons of her own, believed MacK was a 'Negro' and gave him special, though off-balance, treatment. Isidor's father was fairly sure MacK was not. He took it up with her after the boys had left. ——He is more or less like us, what is the matter with you? he said, picking his noonday fight. ——Hoo hah! said Mrs Katz, 'more or less'!

There was very little contrast between the Katzes' house and the Erie-Lackawanna Railroad. Sitting on the wicker seats was just as stultifying as sitting on the couch of any parent—no one's choosing *sides* here. There are days, aren't there?, rare ones, when you feel like doing, and can actually do, what normal, relaxed people do. ——Radio City, MacK said, thinking of the huge comforting dark to be found there on days such as this; the smugness *Morpheus* feels as you take your wallet out of your coat while passing under the illuminated name LEON LEONIDOFF. ——The thing is dwindling but still there, said Isidor, and I respect that. You hear me? I *respec'* that. Let's go.

Yet they remained there on the corner, cold and bleary from the Erie-Lackawanna. MacK was reminiscing over Mrs Katz's food if truth be told. Isidor was put out with him for appreciating it. ——What the hell do you mean by thanking her for her flanken? he had said. How dare you thank my murderer? ——Oh well, MacK said, I don't know, two boys without their momma. Iz spat on what turned out to be a mouse in the gutter. On MacK's mind was the silver and red marquee at the Music Hall, the warm dark, long purple lights, the smell of a thousand damp coats tidily attended to. MacK looked up and down 34th Street—half way toward Eighth MacK saw a mirroring of the neon his thoughts, a warm old sign in the middle of the block. Already Isidor and MacK were susceptible to commercial overgrowths, barnacles of this kind—*Paddy's Clam House*. As if one, without speaking, they turned in the rain and walked toward it, the orange-white-green neon promising comfort of an old and inexpensive sort. Paused at the door. —Do you eat fish? said MacK. —Well, no, said Iz. And pushed on the door and they were enveloped in the steam and scream of a Fish Restaurant; where they always should have been.

There was a bar. Right as you went in—not original, but there, a little apology for those who came during times of great uproar and had to wait for a table. The charm of small glasses of Piel's for 25¢; part of the spell was looking at the ¢. —One of the last ¢ signs, said Isidor, it must be. They felt like birdwatchers; one could keep a log. MacK looked at his printed napkin, 'Paddy's Clam House', and felt finally a part of the history of his family, all the fish they'd swallowed. —My grandfather and his derby in the clam-houses of San Francisco, MacK said to Iz. He gave me a rare tongue-lashing once, outside Alioto's, he said Chowder, surely you will eat *chowder*, everybody eats CHOWDER?! I said I would have one of the awful hamburgers they grudgingly fry you on a corner of the grill in fish restaurants, but he wouldn't let me be seen with him in Alioto's if I wasn't going to eat fish. He was always going on about eggs, eggs will *kill* you, every egg a *bullet,* yet his favorite thing was to rush into Alioto's in his raincoat and eat six dozens of fried clams. —Hypocrisy is on the rise, said Isidor.

MacK thought of his grandfather going over to a bar while waiting for the cable car to be turned at the foot of Powell Street—he liked the way the sun shone through the little clerestories at him. The bar smelt of brass and hat and glass-smear.

### DRINKS 35¢

It wasn't called a bar at all; oddly, the sign outside said *Laurel Drinks*, and the wiseguy boys of the neighborhood perpetually and freshly wrote SHE DOES? underneath this with chalk and charcoal and dog pooh. Boys like the one the grandfather once was, when he felt the height of the city dizzying, and the freedom which came with dizziness: the freedom to pull the plait of the Chinaman who sold his mother vitriol, the freedom to tie a dog to the California Street cable by its tail, the freedom to hop on and hop off any moving conveyance for any reason. No conductor or Confucian or mother had ever caught him.

The bartender gave the boys big menus. —I don't, uh, said Isidor, what do you—. You should have seen them, side by side, in the mirror behind the bar, perusing their first Fish Restaurant menu, two small worried fellas, perusing it like it'd never been perused. The bartender thought they might be FOREIGNERS who COULDN'T READ.

—I gotta table for you guys, said a waiter, this way. They followed him into the din, into the SEA of white cloths, chairs, coats, people and their fingers, people talking about their ties, their stomachs, businesses—some spoke of cars, f*** *cars*. Being at 34th and Seventh, there was a bit of talk of drapery. —My parents are afraid of fish, said Isidor. —Yeah well that's very tough, said the waiter. —It's the sensuality, MacK offered, as they sat. —No, it isn't, said the waiter. —They're from Poland, said Isidor. —What do you want from me, MacK said, I'm afraid too. My dad used to take me to a *trout farm*—we floated on a lot of slimy water and caught fish who were drugged and hypnotized to OBEY. The whole thing made me very apprehensive. These fish tongued up their own silt all day which was scraped off the bottom of the pond and made into pellets which became their suppers. —*They ate their own defaeces?* said Isidor. How'd they avoid scraping up mud too from the bottom? —It was lined with cement, MacK said, blushing with awareness that he was unworthy of sitting here—what truck had he with fish—save the truck which came and emptied the brainwashed trout into that hideous basin in the semidesert? MacK leaned toward Iz. —I used to throw up at the end, he said, it was the quality of the water we were floating on and this orange pop out of this cooler-which-didn't-cool-it. I'd had no contact with a fish and no expectation of eating one, but *blugggh!* —Pretty funny, said Isidor, looking around, nervous. He felt the conversation was inappropriate for other tables.

It is odd of me, always to have despised the very idea of fish, thought MacK, considering that when young my favorite place was a tidal pool; at night after perusing *The Illustrated Book of the Sea* I often dreamt of a life under the waves, swimming effortlessly with my special friends the giant sun fish and the nautilus . . . That is until things got complicated and *they all turned into dreams of suffocation.* —My mother would boil a king crab all day, MacK said to Iz. The smell filled the house, even the *sofa cushions.* We had to brain her with the pot lid to get her to quit.

—It's extensive, I almost said universal, said Isidor, the child's hatred of fish; it's sex of course—salty, raw, pungent, inflamed, raving, pervading, a mystery to which they are not admitted. They are excluded from fish and from the rites of the parental bedroom and so they hate and fear both. —Thank you, MacK said, after a pause during which they both thought they *had* been a wee bit audible. —Where anyway is all this *salty pervading* sex you've been having? You're skating, you know, awful close to the old fishpussy thing. We are not men like that, men who think that pussy is fish and fish pussy! Men who work for a living! —Would you *stop* talking about this? said a man at the next table. —See, I have problems with, continued Isidor, red, low—I could never get past the affinity cats have for fish and couldn't sort the metaphor. —What metaphor, MacK said, it isn't a—

—Ha ha ha!, what do *you* guys know about *pussy?*, said the waiter, standing there; rocking on the balls of his feet. Big smile, greying hair combed back, short white jacket, beneath it a short white apron, black trousers and shoes. White shirt and black bow tie; towel and pad in hand—MacK could have given his description to any policeman. One's affinity for such get-ups is strong, is it not? —the orderliness of those who play *petanque.*

Smiling, engaged, affably hostile—he had taken in the conversation of these boys at the salient word and was including himself in; had already put Isidor and MacK in his 'little world'—but expressions like this are very irritating—there is only *one* world, after all, and those who would make *special worlds* usually have the purposes of capitalism in mind—'*Welcome to the World of Golf*'—or belittlement. He's in his own world, twirl finger by temple.

#### —What'll ya have today—

The menu was large and daily set in tiny Fournier. Bluefish, oysters, snapper, crackers, sauces—these things raced in arcs of ice water around their heads. Isidor was stunned by the menu and its choices, all the words he was unused to conjuring—

#### —Okay fellas what can I get yiz—

MacK too clammed up as he stared at the verification of everything he had ever encountered, in a way—the fingers of an old weird-O in his palm, the glistening of girls, the manners of the staff of the IRT. Isidor, subsumed in the menu, saw the city's past, and in the new words found poetry, found his calling: an invisible, partly Gershwin stair was built right beside him which led in several years to the door of his bookshop. You could almost hear the hammers and saws. The waiter's pad was thick; orders now being sweated in the kitchen curved round it to the back; a stripe of royal blue carbon paper; it seemed properly a quality of the waiter's plump hand, spoke richesse just like the menu—

#### —. . . fellas!—

—of a sudden they plunged and ordered, MacK a dish of steamed clams, since that was a thing Grandfather had belittled him about, and a finnan haddie, which MacK conceived looked like Grandfather in his derby. And salad—that is, iceberg lettuce and ½ small tomato under thick putty-colored Goo. *Please*. And Isidor *chowder*, New England to be sure—if he was going to eat this it ought to have the Brahmin's luxury, the surroundings of Paddy's notwithstanding. He had long coveted the hexagonal cracker. And bluefish, as it sounded clean, proper, big game. Maybe. No one is too sure of their Hemingway any more.

—*No bluefish*, said the waiter, looking off to the side and turning over a page of his pad—as if there were *never* bluefish—isn't this the kind of thing that drives you nuts—you go into a place where the menu is printed in Fournier *every day* and immediately the guy tells you *no blue fish*. That is New York, pal. —*Then snapper*, said Isidor, snapping his menu shut like he came there always maybe. He hoped by doing this not to have his stock lowered in the kitchen or with the waiter. —You wanna stay with your beers there? said the waiter. Oh there must be drink with fish as surely as there must be astringent après le rasage. —White wine, Isidor fairly shouted; then he looked up at the waiter through his appealing brows—what kinds do you have, he said. —All kinds, fellas, said the waiter, moving quickly away and making a violent sign to the little bartender, yelling *TWO WINES!*

MacK goggled at the place, the black and white waiters moving with many difficulties through the autumn exhalations of the coats and the energetic, ordinary talk in the air like knives for icy pats of butter. Here a whole realm to share with Isidor! —When I was but a babe, in front of the motherf***ing television, MacK said, there were vast restaurants under the sea—the waiters were penguins and lobsters played castanets in the floor show. —Yeah, I know, said Izzy—the orchestra was all trayf. As usual after visiting New Jersey, Isidor was feeling tinges of guilt. —But there's nothing wrong with this! I think we have *got* to have more and more restaurants and waiters and glassware and fish and white wine for everyone, said Isidor looking around excitedly, or everything is going to EXPLODE. Civilization *really will be lost* in slips between pizza box, computer keyboard and drooly lips.

—A Fish Restaurant, clamorous yet efficient, is the obvious model for government! MacK said to Isidor. For how is anything going to get *sorted out*, out there in that god damn country, unless everyone can get together? That's how the country was *founded*, people *got together*, in a room, a Fish Restaurant . . . ! Iz suddenly blotted his mouth and then leaned over toward the tank of lobsters. One of them seemed to approach him, waving its claws with some kind of vague message or greeting. —PREPARE FOR GOVERN-MENT! shouted Isidor.

MacK felt he understood the city for the first time—how it actually works, how it is the engine of civilization and liberation—saw the place of delicatessens, waiters and restaurants in a great scheme, and of the FISHES themselves. It really couldn't have been planned better by Moses himself. (Robt.) I give you something of value and you feed me. What could be . . . greater? More historic? It generates an energy which runs the city along ineluctable lines. It explains *everything* that our town is a Fish Restaurant, that it raves and pervades, that there is noise and rudeness, rudeness which is salt spray, the pungent flesh of things which get done. Paddy's was so like life . . . everyone was being mistreated. O God they loved it. The source of all rudeness, or bracing American character, may be the flesh of fish, which TANGS, and keeps us in mind of the old city, the old mental capital, keeps us on the old cold streets of sunsets and harsh ideas, keeps us going back and forth across New York Bay on the *Mary Murray* and the *Cornelius G. Kolff*—when taking the Staten Island ferry always wait for a boat with a *nice name*—over the fishes, our sustenance, our salvation. Would that it kept us fighting the Revolutionary War, which everybody out there in that god damn country has ceased to do.

It suddenly struck MacK that waiter panache and aplomb, a *real* waiter's, are needed to survive in town today; to preserve the forms of civilization. —Isn't the waiter's attire the ideal town wear? he said to Isidor.


*The Apron*—none of the city's dribblings, especially in spring, would get on you, the rusty water from awnings, melony sludge from disappearing ice at the fruit stand. Nor do your own spillages, unbalances of beer, pose any threat to your true costume, neither the cigarette-ash coffee and milk covered tables of the Village—pffft! —the INDUSTRIAL LAUNDRY takes care of your apron overnight at agonizingly high temperature and pressure.

*The Clean White Shirt*—a religion in itself, gentlemen, your credo to the world, you maintain; you endure. You can be as ordered, as eternal a *tabula rasa* as the white tiles, granted on which you may have lain, of the giant Mens Room of any great hotel. What we put on *over* the clean white shirt, an apron, a shop-keeper's coat, a suit sharp-cornered for to prick people turning the corner of Pine Street, doesn't matter—just for the moment.

*The Towel*—why you don't see everyone carrying a towel in New York I don't know, he thought, unless that's what they have in those plump briefcases and bags, lots of nice white towels. If it ain't money. Never *known* such a place for getting stuff on you, never *seen* so many people who need a bit of wiping before they get to the office. If each had his waiter's towel, there would never again come that moment when you must stutter obvious things to the groomed, embalmed, refrigerated receptional beauty, having just blown in off 100° Fahrenheit Street to drip and flake and *breathe* all over the frighteningly clean formica of her station. (Confidential to Mr L Bean of Freeport: *'These robust 100% Egyptian cotton Belgian waiter's fore-arm towels are the best we've seen . . .'* Missing a trick there.)

What *is* that stuff on the banister of the IRT, south stairs, 14th Street station (downtown side)? It's there every day. Again —towel—rectified.

*And the Black Trousers*, thanks to their buddy the apron, don't show cigar ash, soot, fish blood, that stuff on the IRT banister (south stairs). Sober companions of the clean white shirt, ready for *anything* after work, the quiet assertion of non-denominational faith in the possibility of people if they would *just get serious*; if they would be Scottish or Portuguese just for a little while?

———

—The waiter is the backbone of civilization, MacK said to Izzy, and ultimately its savior. —I agree, waiters are at the heart of everything, said Isidor. Let's judge everyone we know by how they treat the waiters. Before we finally and officially all *become* waiters in the city of tomorrow, the last way we will have of relating to one another. *Waiters all!* yelled Isidor. Although, he said with menace, some of us would like to think we are waited UPON. —But we all *serve something*, said MacK. There is no real neutrality, aloofness, no escape of one's streetly responsibilities in New York. There is no doing nothing. Always there is duty!

It would be an admirable goal to be the rudest fish waiter in New York; it would make you the kind of King of all this. MacK propounded a theory of waiter attire for himself and over the coming months adopted this costume for himself, black trousers and clean white shirt. Dressed this way, he thought, he could quietly show people where to sit, just anywhere, or even what to do. He would get money and tips. Pick up valuable Pine Street information from people he encountered every day. He could become

## THE CAPTAIN OF THE NEIGHBORHOOD.

—New York is the last place where the graces of waiting table are real, said Isidor. An honorable profession in decline, like those of sign-writer, street-sweeper, tobacconist, whore. Do you think anyone is paid a living wage to bring you a biscuit in *Seattle*, or even a piece of meat? Even though they nourish and sustain all those uptight people of the Northwest? —Pffft!, MacK said. —*It used to be a living*, Izzy said. Waiters raised happily disorganized families in the shadow of the hotel, their collars open on Sundays.

Imagine who comes to call when you offer a job waiting table *these* days. By the Sixties college students had all but replaced waiters from the union hall; then in the Seventies it was high school students, then in the Eighties it was Reagan and so the most unbelievable collection of retard-Os, junior high girls on drugs, pathetic PhDs, out-and-out nutcases—no one would stay more than a month or two, unionize *that* if you will. Where were all the guys with little moustaches? Imagine Reagan destroying everyone's livelihood and sense of well-being just like that! Imagine Reagan *your waiter*. He destroys practically every job that he can't do himself, then falls victim to his own obliteration of the economy and he's serving you your meal:

—*Waiter? Waiter. We also ordered some new potatoes.*

—*Well, you know . . . on new potatoes . . . a lot of people in this country . . . I've spoken with them . . . and . . . well, they think that old potatoes are . . . well . . .*

—*Shut up!*


Paddy's Clam House braced, scarified, excoriated and cajoled them. The fish they ate went down in a trance. It was a little under and over cooked—the food at Paddy's was never very good—tasted of not much except New York and ice water. What mattered were the textures and the texts of that hour. Isidor's meal was deep, MacK's horizontal. They began really to spread their proteins through the city from that day.

The waiter put the check in front of Isidor the way he had put down their plates, as if serving was not so much an intimate trans-action as it was a reminder that they were merely part of the Great Chain of Being. Now no familiarities or banter.

—Do you realize we will never again discuss genitals with that guy? said Isidor, as they moved toward the hanging coats blocking the door like a mob that might turn ugly. —We could hang around, MacK said, see when he gets off.

As usual after visiting New Jersey, Isidor was feeling the horn and wanted intoxicated. In the fine spray of indifference, brine and sarcasm of the Fish Restaurant he imagined bright legs in the Radio City Music Hall; legs like sardines. For the first time Isidor and MacK experienced that temerity for the glistening streets given by flesh of the sea.

# The Far East

A lot of this has to do with what you see walking around in the rain—the connection for instance you make between the dull grey light in the upper floors of Isidor's book shop—the smell of paper and the rain outside—the specific city you choose to live in. Each man, woman, child, dog and cat in New York has to spend all day choosing in which city to live—it's different for each.

Many years ago, thought MacK, there was an apartment. It was WAY over on the East Side, in the lower 80s, almost at the river. The city that Isidor was gradually choosing to live in radiated from his and Mary-Ann's possessions in this place—especially from their books, skeltered across three old bookcases such as any second-hand book dealer might have been happy to have—Mary-Ann had worked for one of the sea-musty antiquarian dealers of Florida. She'd long been interested, as was Izzy, in the histories of strange things and places, as well as food, and her books reflected her journey from the hot confusion of school in Boston to the unremunerative delight in sampling the seafood, salty men and ephemera of Florida, to her next, and current adventure, New York. Mary-Ann was a girl with a lot of outward poise, despite the Worcester accent, but due to the men and the salt and her reading she was a tigress: energy shone bright from her forehead. But Mary-Ann's looks, her books, her dalliances were all shut at the moment.

Her faded cookbooks: mostly from the 1940s, some very salty, from her kitchen in a sea-blue hut she rented in Coco Palms for the season and a half of her 'exuberation', her father called it. Being a policeman. Some quite moldy books on the history of Florida and its coast, some others on the South, with which she had fallen out of love—she couldn't understand it and who from Massachusetts can.

—

It was almost as if no one cared about New York between 1965 and 1975—they were just going to plunder it—although JACKIE O began trying to save Grand Central—MacK and Izzy had both gaped at the grotesque headline in the *Daily News*: FORD TO CITY: DROP DEAD. But Izzy had been buying up little bits of its past, for what real purpose he wasn't sure yet, though all this knowledge of the city—*I read what I buy, Sir*—had as much to do with how he would make himself as what he would make of New York. He had begun collecting books on the city when he was still at college. For years he haunted the pleasant, plain bookshops of Fourth Avenue, the Peacock, Sundwall's, Bibulo and Schenkler, for books and pamphlets on the japesters and thugs of all decades of the place; he had a few items on the history of the Interborough Rapid Transit Company; forensic pathology; Lenny Bruce (the thumbedest book in the joint); books on jazz as well as records.

MacK, lying on the floor of the little living-room of the apartment. He turned on a table lamp he'd put on the floor next to his 'bed', a collection of pillows and paper towels—sculpted for him by Mary-Ann. He lay square on a hard-on, trying to shock it with the full weight of his stomach—and began to study the books near the floor in the case. The jazz books seemed to have climbed up to where the Florida books lived—and the cookbooks from all over were settling in with the New York material—the books had been making love in the night, Iz's books commingling with Mary-Ann's more easily than they two, maybe.

MacK wriggled—this was the only time when he felt the red-painted floorboards to be uncomfortable—for while you can lie on your dick in bed, and, remotely, pretend the mattress cradles you as a girl might—in a shakedown you're just a stupid f\*\*\*er lying on his dick on the cold and lonely floor—the pressure confirms it—*you've no girl*.

But this wasn't a problem at the moment; certainly the only thing to worry about was: cutting off the blood supply owing to the weight of MacK's STOMACH, or snagging it on a nail, some of which now raised themselves up from the boards. MacK reveled, or would later revel, in what was becoming a delight of Isidor's and Mary-Ann's apartment, its almost solid comfort, as solid as something you may find when you are twenty-five, as welcoming as the warm windows you glimpse in apartment buildings on the West Side—to which you silently apply the word *family*—or even in midtown: the idea that from a window across the back garden, Izzy's and Mary-Ann's apartment could be glimpsed as book-lined and lit with table lamps; having a sofa. The warm low lights playing on the louvered door and the window shutters, really the wherewithal of a frugal but comfortable city life of 1945.

MacK looked carefully at the spine of a book published by the Princeton University Press in 1948. In tan cloth, it was modestly embossed with a little gold, a dark grey 'label'. From the painted floor MacK strained to reach out in the chill, and opened the book, breathing deeply of its smell, which it seemed was that of 1948: overcoats, buses, ferries, New Jersey itself maybe—also the perfect mustiness, without dank, of the better not-too-pristine used bookstores. *This is the book*, MacK mumbled, *to be seen here, in this book-comfortable room.*

The floor above (presumably) being similarly bare, the nail-heads (presumably) would raise themselves up in alarm at this time (barely *six*) each morning and two enormous dogs woke up, scratching and whimpering for their evil master, asleep in the upstairs equivalent of Izzy's and Mary-Ann's bedroom—but he might as well have come down the stairs in his unfamiliar European pajamas and asked to join them, for all Izzy could put him out of mind. And he was convinced the evil master enjoyed the dogs immorally, though it is hard to imagine doing this *absolutely first thing*.

But perhaps it was they who instigated the affair?

Even though it was early, there was a holiday cast to the light coming through the half-opened shutters as MacK lay on his hard-on on the hard floor. From previous experience he knew Les Girls across the hall would begin to squeal 'TIME TO GO TO WO-ORK!' before long, even though it was a holiday. *Les Girls*, four of them in a fit of rooming together in the way of an old film: Iz and MacK had never laid eyes on them, though Mary-Ann had—MacK pictured them all cotton peignoir and roller; Izzy pictured them boiling in oil. Between Les Girls, who woke the whole floor with their 'TIME TO GO TO WO-ORK!' giggling every morning about seven (this was the actual beginning of yups, who later ruled the earth), the Dogs of Sodom upstairs, and the brooding menace of the huge pigeons of the window-sill, Isidor lay awake half the night dreading the period between six and eight—he had begun to wake Mary-Ann with his own impression of the pigeons, *hmou hmou hmou*.

Les Girls did begin to squeal 'HAPPEE THANKSGIVEEN!' in cascades of Daytonian nasality.

# Thanksgiving Day

The Dogs of Sodom were going down the stairs and MacK could see light come from under Iz's and Mary-Ann's door and he was elated; *Thanksgiving-day*. The sun sharp across the spine of the Princeton University Press book reminded him of the orange paper band on 'Thanksgiving Day' pipe tobacco, sold only at this time of year in Boston, an old-fashioned shop with the leaves outside in Park Square almost blown away. Old-fashioned irresistible packaging, though after several years' game partaking of this heavily Virginia-based *grand old tradition*, MacK and Iz determined the following year to shred up the label and smoke *it*.

*Thanksgiving*, never very important in his orbits, which MacK recalled most profoundly experiencing at the beach with father. Leaving the poor 12-lb bird to its slow mummification they drove over the hills, MacK rejoicing in the few deciduous trees to be found in their cryogenically preserved portion of California—he was missing the East where it seemed he'd always belonged, where only comes the atomic flash of fall. The weather at the shore was dull, though not properly cold. MacK was also missing the girl who'd practically *thrown him out of the east coast*, and he tramped up and down the beach with his father and their dog, feeling too hot in his eastern jacket, feeling utterly left out of Thanksgiving, the holidays, altogether, even though here were the elements, Dad, Dog, Walk, Jacket, and Natural Forms, even though not radiantly deciduous. The holidays were coming; now they were here—but *he* was not going to get drunk on the spirit of the holidays, not stumbling, libidinous and crude on sunlight combined with the TV, the tumbling freshet of phone calls from elsewhere . . .

Looked out across the waves while the Dad described what-all machines the ancestors were hooked up to these days, looked warily into some of the green dark culverts of the waves and remembered the undersea genre of animated cartoon—lobsters and eels were lining up outside the Oyster Bar about fifty feet out and twenty feet down from where he was standing—all dressed up and being shown to their seats by penguins for their Thanksgiving dinner of—sea turkey?—is that a name for—well—polyps for cranberries.

And missing the proper atmosphere of the holiday in the home of the girl who'd thrown him out of the East Coast—*there* everyone went in for *communal leaf raking and smoldering* before hacking and eating the bird up . . . But MacK happily back in the east now, the girl somewhere unknown, he thought maybe the West Side, or Philadelphia. Happy on his hard-on with Isidor about to get up.


Izzy and Mary-Ann both the bleary type, irksome to MacK, who was from a long line of neurotic work ethic people. Very *pale* people. Saturdays father scraped outside with a *hoe* until the little MacK got up and felt guilty for not gardening. —*Oh, up already?* —Yes, my dad. Mary-Ann had a selection of slatternly bathrobes which only added to her charm, that of the open doughnut shop of New England and not its older values. Well—the girl had a selection of everything.

Her attempt? at Thanksgiving breakfast table talk—*You boys goin' out soon for that turkey?*—brought a groan from Iz, hiding from the spirit of the holidays behind the *Times*, over which he now glared at MacK and started picking his first fight of the day: —How come you never read the paper? MacK knew this was a big topic, a sore point, and was amazed and disturbed they would have to fight this fight so early on a holiday morning (he didn't care for holidays except when he was homesick), in front of Mary-Ann, on whom he was still trying to make a good impression so that he might zip over to the East Side and crash here at any time. —It's bullshit, is why. —*I'm* reading it. That make it bullshit? I read bullshit? —You know it's bullshit. What about all the people we know who work there? You yourself said they were idiots. Anyway you spend all your time reading novels, not newspapers. —How do you know? —Because your house is full of novels. And the *History of Magic and Experimental Science* by Lynn Thorndike. —Yeah well that takes up most of the space, said Isidor—but there are things going on in the world, pal. —No there aren't!

At which Mary-Ann got up for more coffee, caughey or kwoffey—as it might be spelled in her dialect, MacK thought, whose own mother's greatest fear on seeing him off for New York was not that he'd be killed in the alley of legend—but that he would come back pronouncing coffee *kwoffey* and orange *arange* and saying *take cayah* all the time—and reminded the boys the butcher was only open that morning, *which they were throwing away.*

Out the vestibule, where MacK always tried to figure the names of the evil master and of Les Girls, the common perfidy of medical tape and stained calling cards and dymo labels on the mailboxes. —This GROMEK *must* be the owner of a Hell hound, he said. —I know what you mean, said Isidor, but in fact that is not he. There was some turquoise twirly girly script hiding behind the drainflower window on one box: Maddy Brown: but neither was that the popular sleepover capitaine of Les Girls.

When they were in the vestibule, whether coming in or going out, Izzy was never in a mood good enough to tax him with questions like this.


The city muffled with holiday, though so far east it is always quiet. But they were far enough from the river the only sound they might hear from it would be a tug's horn; the usual rumble of traffic on FDR Drive was crying out, entombed below street level here, though no volume of cars set the East Side a-vibrating today, hiding as the celebrants were or would be on the Taconic Parkway, in drifts of grandmothers and food, their occupants inside, pounding against the glass, so lately alive. Families.

—Thanksgiving is cruel and can strike without warning, said MacK. —Plizz give generous, said Isidor.

Here in the Far East, thin snow turning to ice on the street and Izzy started swearing. —F***ing cold, man. I can't believe I have to go out and get this turkey, to *have* turkey, which I don't even want. I hate Thanksgiving. Do you realize that no one realizes it's all about eating shit? How does coprophagia honor the *Pilgrims?* Hah? How does my eating the most horrible food, food from *England*, which I don't want, memorialize their f***ing sacrifice, whatever it was? Why am I supposed to be thankful that *they ate shit?* —Because Indians? said MacK—I don't know.

They walked west to First Avenue and then up to 86th and west again. The Lure of the West. Izzy and MacK had 'grown up' on the West Side and had always professed to hate the East Side. They had clung to the West Side like baby opossums. Izzy had the bravery to go downtown once in a while, but for years the Far East remained unknown. The East Side was known to MacK as a boy from drawings

in *Mad* ('the dog-infested jungle of East 59th Street') so he thought
he knew it. And he was confirmed in this vision of it after visiting a
friend's older sister, recently moved into a building on Third
Avenue: the lobby was covered in something like marble, there was
a crude version of a door man, a rubber plant; all the women in the
elevator wore stretch pants and turquoise nylon turbans and talked
through their gum. The sister smoked and chewed gum, bit her
nails and poked at her crumbling mascara all at the same time, spoke
the Queens English. There were delicatessens and tailor shops which
could only be the entrances to the headquarters of international spy
networks—so there had been no need to re-examine the East Side
for many years—this, after all, is an East Side digression—and so
was Izzy's life with Mary-Ann.

The connection between East 86th Street and suburbia is profound,
thought MacK, for here at nine in the morning on Thanksgiving Day
it is practically dead. It was a morning on which you particularly
noted the small confluences of hard corny snow, dog shit and cigarette butts, because there were no souls out with their Yorkville
story-faces to look at: the very old Germans were not eating potatoes in the Ideal and the very old Irish people were not eating
potatoes in the Blarney Stone and the very old Hungarians were not
eating goulash at the Budapest. East 86th Street and Second and
Third Avenues would only partially rouse themselves this morning;
Yorkville would roll over, look at the clock and calendar of
Thanksgiving, smack its chops, and be snoring again by three
o'clock.

John the bartender, who Izzy cultivated, was still asleep in
Queens. The old lady who ran the very odd German candy store,
who had a condition which made her mouth swing in a sort of fleshy
reticule—way down *here*—wasn't to be seen standing behind her
rows of blue mice, tenks gut.

Izzy won't stay in Yorkville, MacK thought, but he's growing here somehow—we'll all acquire our first grey hairs over here one way or another. He titled their existence at this time 'Our Years in Yorkville'—but you didn't notice *him* making a move over here.

## Something from Schaller and Weber

Which was open, bright and empty. Isidor always felt the need to say something rude or sarcastic whenever he opened the door of a shop—why?—why did Sidney never use the seat of a toilet, except to slam, crouching with his ass low down in the bowl just over the surface of the water, who did he think he was?—Tarzan?—*Why?* —because these are men!

Didn't smell like Thanksgiving, smelt like bauernwurst, which was OK. But an odd feeling to look at trays of delicatessen, MacK thought, something tugged at him, prickled his waspie gonad, lit the fuse in a tiny cranberry-shaped bomb of guilt—he ought to be sitting in a frame house in Westchester, leaves in varied reds framed in the dining-room window. But that would be the Tumblesons, so f*** that.

*Jocularity*. A dangerous commodity to have or open a squat container of (in this case a hung-over Schaller and Weber counterman) around Isidor. *Used carefully it can warm and enrich our lives; used fool-ishly it can destroy them.* Guy thinks he knows Iz—may or may not—anyway acts like he does, mit the extra impetus of the barren holiday feel in the shop maybe, here they are open for bizniz and there's no pipples. So:

—Whudda *you* want? MacK can feel Iz's hangover bristle like a gorilla suit under his overcoat. —You don't know what I want! —(Smile cracks a little, but) That's why I'm asking! —Oh yeah? Well I came in here to see about a big bird I can stuff—right up my ass! How about that? Iz smiling but that steel challenge always there and MacK knows there may be no dinner in about three seconds; so does the guy. —Ah, there's no need for that, you little ****. (The word that isn't said—but the fight has happened; Izzy instantly furious, his dark blue eyes shooting sparks all over the counter and the pickle trays.) Guy turns around and goes into the back muttering what name? —K-A-T-Z, says Iz, now of course the whole show is up, the guy's won, at least on the German front. Guy broke the rules, reflects MacK, perspiring by a display of Bahlsen biscuits; he made a joke first.

From the back: —I got a lot of Katzes. But Iz relents, inexplicably, except that he nearly always does, if that is some kind of explanation. —Oh yeah? Lotza kotz? Lotzim kotzim? But how many TOIKEYS?, using the guy's *own vowel*. Guy pokes the head around. —East 83rd, says Iz. Guy grins, sort of, and walks toward the counter with it.

MacK looked down at the Bahlsen biscuits and thought of the apartments where people offered them, on thirty-year-old 'modern' plates, such as are stacked by Mrs Leninsky and stacked again in Rosenthal's mother's kitchen, unchanged since 1957—Rosenthal, several months before, trying to make *fudge* in *SoHo*.

The very idea of which.

She'd spent so many years eating nothing, the charming Rosenthal, but pulses and millet, as in rejecting her mother and all her cookery, that MacK thought it must surely be a fudge of dark lentil bubbling on the stove in the tiny apartment where he always tried to make love with her but often could not because of the size—his style was cramped. And Rosenthal was chary about access to the front door at all—she threw him down a key in an unerotic sock if she'd decided to let him in. Too, his earthy gonad had often been flooded by the Upwardly Mobile Brewing Co., Inc., around the corner. Man, she hated that brewery. *Fudge* she'd let him have! Rosenthal was, incongruously, drawing on the girl scout aspect of her upbringing—there was one—it was just too long ago for things to solidify—as MacK often noted. It could not be made to coalesce, not by boiling it for an hour beyond time, not by beating and pounding on it. But it was a domestic liquid so it could be made to freeze. Eventually. So Rosenthal hacked it into chunks which she then rolled into cylinders, wrapped in foil, and froze 'em again. She gave MacK a small one which destroyed the pocket of his beige overcoat on a hot AA train seat which was making a pounding noise. Took the larger one up to her mother in the suburbs who, on seeing the penile foil emerge from the suspect city daughter's bag, launched herself forward and exclaimed (and here is the point, you—) *Ooo! Somezing from Schaller und Weber?* Imagine the expressions on this elegant post-European mama as MacK's suspicions crossed her face: that true fudge would be hard to make below, say, 35th Street; that this was *lentils*.

But now Rosenthal eats meat and cream and lives in Montpelier! There's no escaping geographical declination! Hooray!

Woke to see Isidor at the cash register, deciding whether to take it all out on the woman—but the little gods of Thanksgiving, Cotton Mather and Elmer Fudd—available in candle form—gave Iz a tap on the head—there'd be no fight today. Get drunk on the spirit of the holidays, or—

—It's eleven, said Izzy (loudly, once again in the doorway)—let's get a beer.

It was ten.

They schlepped the turkey between them in its exciting red fishnet, as once they'd hauled a butchered sucking-pig onto the IRT, having made an offering to each god in the station beforehand —token, gum, mints, chocolate, phone . . . as long as their change held out. There was consternation among dog owners, as there followed consternation between Isidor's cats, who knew the thing was hanging in the bathroom all night to drain the last of its blood into the tub. But it was MacK's grasp of reality which had disturbed Isidor, when MacK said, *the best meat comes from kosher butchers*—though for a moment before he smacked him Iz had agreed—drunk? Quit your fooling!

# The Bavarian Inn

The Bavarian Inn, now gone. Kicked off the street, out of Yorkville and precipitating the whole neighborhood's decline into a souvenir and cheap hat shop of TAT; now all of East 86th looks and smells like the familiar pissed-upon cubbyhole in the subway where your man sells umbrellas and cigarettes. The whole joint is fluorescent-lit and yellow and black and red and the radio is on, thanks to the thug who jemmied the Bavarian Inn out of the world.

Under a very high ceiling which you took to be Bavarian (there were beams, though MacK had never examined them as he thought he should—neither he nor Isidor had ended up lying on the floor here so there wasn't that ease in looking); there was some kind of Germany that never existed, except on post cards, beer bottles and in watercolor drawings in *Holiday* magazine twenty years before. The walls were dark green and covered with cuckoo clocks and a papier-mâché alp. There was a big bar looking out onto 86th Street, where you might watch an older, more settled New York walk by, with a modest supper and the late edition in its string bag, as if the window screened out anything after 1960—

Standing one night at this corner of the bar, MacK had proudly announced a very short-lived intention to *marry Tumbleson*—it lasted most of the evening—at which Izzy visibly blanched and said *I feel as though I hardly know you*. MacK was filled with remorse—marriage was a complicated issue, they'd be parted, he'd be krazyglued to West End Avenue, or—it'd probably never stick. But bonhomie: he bought several rounds of drinks for Isidor, Mary-Ann, Pietro Arditti and the bar, for which Izzy rebuked him: —Jeez, get a couple drinks in this guy and he starts *buying* everything. Which was *his* form of remorse.

There were big steam tables between the bar and the dining area—where you ate hasenpfeffer and königsberger klopse handed you by a Yorkville hausfrau in an amazingly tightly laced Bavarian bodice; this invasive plumpness rather like the little hasen—*All up front but rather dull meat*, said Pietro Arditti; and in fact there was a man who played 'The Third Man' and 'Edelweiss' on an electric zither. But no one was going to eat here today—MacK and Iz were surprised to find the place open, the steam tables empty and cold. The bartender looked around feebly, as if he'd forgotten *not* to open. Had he passed the shuttered Ideal and whispered *gott damm* to himself? His upper lip drooped like those of the dead elks which drooped over them all from on high.

But they didn't know this guy, with his lip and polishing cloth—Iz was fresh from his confrontation with the meat head at Schaller and Weber—guy wasn't looking too friendly either, though the welcome here was often like one you get at Grand Central: *Go f\*\*\* yourself!*

—What can I get ya? (At least he speaks.)—Two Club Weisse, please. —Ja, kindl weisse is for the old ladies, eh, Ludwig, the guy says, over his shoulder, which is bad, MacK thinks, he's saying something about Isidor to someone else.

This is a guy, Izzy thinks, whose glass smearing and toothpick-lingus will not be interrupted by the finer points of pourage—and he was right—the glasses aren't cold, they aren't wet—guy pours them into the glasses like they were *Schlitz*—is surprised then alarmed by the huge amounts of foam, stares out at the street, pussyflicks his toothpick some more, finally slubs another gulp into each glass and pushes them over to the *fellas*, leaving the rest in the bottles; not a lemon in sight. Said the eyes: holiday, gof\*\*\*yaself, right? Lights a cigarette.

Isidor's head did something funny, but there was no explosion: was the holiday muffling him too, tamping him down? Was he thinking of Mary-Ann and the apartment and the low lights and the books? (One's thoughts do tend homeward when one's given a wrongful drink.) Izzy was seduced by the holiday, even though he was not going anywhere with football and raking and preturkey sandwiches and 'Prince Albert' pipe tobacco and the local LITTLE BIG game—*Yeah these kids put on a pretty good show, doing really great this year, gimme this over pro ball any day*—Just think, you could be in the suburbs today—but that would mean the Tumblesons, so f\*\*\* that. But this is what is killing our country, what has killed it, the idea that conversation can be had about anything, that you have to have an opinion, that you have in fact to AGREE with everyone any more, MacK thought, try this at the tail gate party—*I think that this school stinks and that everyone who goes to it is an idiot, I ought to know because I went here, I think this is a tremendous waste of time, it's cold, this is my only day off this year, I'd rather be inside my house with a bottle of gin reading* Moby Dick *and getting blown by my wife, I don't know why we force these kids into this, what kind of sick ambition does it instill in them, NO, I don't like sports, or you, you're all a bunch of Nazis, what I want to know is WHY IS EVERYBODY DOING EXACTLY THE SAME THING AROUND HERE?*

# The Dublin House

Was Izzy so hypnotized by the holiday's ancient inaudible cry that he was becoming philosophic? Faced with this lugubrious mug-wiper . . . —They fired John last week, said Iz, from the other place, sons of bitches, he said. (The first bartender of his personal cultivation.) Droopy glasswipe didn't pay any attention to this, aside from coming alive in some tiny way at the obscenity, which was some indication he might be more on *their side* from now on—though you can't tell—but he obviously didn't know who *John* was, though the job of Germanically dispensing bier up and down East 86th Street makes a small fraternity—screw him—Izzy could talk in comfort.

It is the weaning stage of your Manhattanhood, the cultivation of your first bartender, the stranger for these two barfellows, Isidor, belligerent and ready to talk about anything, certain that K-A-T-Z is blazoned on him, constantly bothered by this 'certainty' on the streets of Yorkville, and John, a man smelling of a one-bedroom in

Queens (evincing the attentive yet ultimately unsuccessful grooming of a fifty-seven-year-old single man), with a discernible Germanic sourness—funny that *they* should have bonded, thought MacK, while Iz's and his assiduous *West* Side attempts to become Celtic, or at least Disno-British—Holy Mother o' God what for did they spend all those hours in the Dublin House?—the ordering of pints of Guinness, the herringboning, the flat cap (Izzy looked good in it and MacK did not, another sartorio-historic riddle)—were stonewalled by Jack, the worshipful red-faced stoic who ran the place. The strongest abjuration he ever gave a customer raving in a pool of Powers: *take a rest*. And said to MacK who would suddenly (politely) blurt out of nowhere deep concern over the current physical safety of Walter Mondale: —*Don't you worry, lad, your man's all right*. But in Jack's last analysis they were still boys who smelt of that college approach to drink, the bar a library in more ways than one, not because Iz was Katz and MacK was *too* polite, not talking New York, but because you boys are too young (he never said this)—you're not part of *this* New York—why don't you move on and let West 79th Street sink away from the world, with its Woolworths around the corner and the last IRT station with those f***in' cylindrical token-eating machines—leave us alone boys in our lack of focus.

True—try to find a *cohesive idea* on Broadway between 79th and 74th—the bend, the *bend* f***s everything up!


# The Bavarian Inn

—*Fired!*, said Izzy, you believe that? —What for? —Ah, business is bad—somethin'—I don't know. Although: MacK had not thought much of John when they finally met—another sour lifetime Manhattan bartender—you let enough of these guys in and they people your dreams. But John and Isidor had bonded over the ring—perhaps the whole thing was a set-up?—and Izzy had taken to stopping by over there to watch the fights. —I went to the bathroom and there was a guy goose-stepping up and down in front of the mirror, said Iz. —*Zat's nuthink*, said MacK, did you know last summer I went in there with Alasdair MacNiel of Ugadale, a real Scot from Scotland, famous BBC announcer with a queer red face and ears bent by the no doubt one Victorian pair of iron baby forceps in Inverness—a red beard which looked like he *glued* it on—and this thoroughly inebriated Bavarian clocks us from the bar and immediately comes over and sits with us—oh he was Yorkville through and through but you could've put a little loden jacket on him showing off his big pink drunk ass and one of those pipes that looks like a toilet—he had a moustache which yearned to walrusize itself and become the cause of the First World War—sits with us and starts accusing this *Celt* of being a member of MOSSAD. —Gee Whizz, said Izzy. —You know, said MacK, you're trying to tell yourself the guy's just an early afternoon drunk you can *deflect* with amiable chat, but whatever you venture, the weather, the slightly more serious assertion that this man is a guest in our city, *buddy*—and the guy's till-like response is—again and again —*Nonetheless, you are in the Mossad; nonetheless, you are in the Mossad*—and then you get a look into the guy's eyes and you see that flame—the guy is mentally dive-bombing this Jew, he's found a Jew at lunchtime here in Yorkville! But of course Izzy saw that fire all the time around here—though the restaurants were good and so was the Paprika Shop, street life, shop life is not always great for a Jew in Yorkville . . . MacK saw he didn't need to finish. MacNiel of Ugadale's pure comment when they'd got four or five blocks down Third Avenue, away from the guy bumping around like a pinball in his little box of Naztalgia and hate:

**'Now—I wasna very comfortable wi'** *that*.**'**

Half the Club Weisse had topped up Izzy's resentment of that—that den of iniquity—*why I oughta*—here in the solemn quiet of the

Bavarian Inn, through which oddly filtered the breath of the waspy holiday from the suburbs, which discomfited Iz and perhaps thus gave him strength against this discomfiture, he headed for the old wooden phone booth. —*Back in a minute.*

# The Heidelberg

One of the last of these, with a molded seat; light, a fan that comes on as you shut the hinged door—the telephone *dings* as you drop your nickels—pretty comfortable, thought Izzy—the bastards answer, some guy who turfed John out of his job—the bastards are *open*—why?—why today? Just so the right amount of bier can be drunk to accomplish errands Germanically before Yorkville sinks under the waves of Thanksgiving and America.

—*Heidelberg.* —Hindenburg? says Izzy in his best perverted Peter Lorre. —*What!?* —Hindenburg? —(In great annoyance) *Nein, nein! Heidelberg! HEIDEL-berg!* —Well, says Iz, you're still a big gas-bag! —and hangs up, knowing the torrent of German to come just from the inspiration.

# The Bavarian Inn

Another? No, it isn't feasible, the glasses, the guy . . . —Besides, this is not *drinking* time, said Isidor, this is a *holiday*, do you hear what I'm saying? A holiday—no *drinking*—we have to *enjoy* ourselves. Disgustedly leaves a tip with *such* a *slap* from wallet already that MacK's eyebrow goes up in a *huge* demonstration of emotion and Izzy says—Hey, I have to drink here ya know. Suddenly defending the guy, thought MacK—that they were enjoying disliking so, silently, during the tall not-quite-rights.

# Thanksgiving Day

The walk back to Izzy's was less inspiring than the walk from, for now the turkey had been acquired. There was a necessary component to Izzy and MacK's walkings, alone or together: NEED, the NEEDS each conceived, or that the town, in its infiniteness, forced on you, or *conceived for you:* you NEED that THING; to live in this our town is to agree to obsessive-compulsive disorder, *gimme* it, the whole *place* is one obsessive-compulsive panic attack. Treatment for this has yet to be devised. Some of these were gourmettish needs pressed on Isidor by Mary-Ann but some errands come rattling out of the subconscious—you don't really want to know what has given rise to them. Then too Izzy's and MacK's errands had for years sometimes converged and sometimes not, on the planes of the real, the imagined, the nonsensical:

A few weeks before, a journey to the Paprika Shop was for Iz a Mary-Ann errand, so contained a bit of duress—he didn't like to be sent out for things as at that time his only conception of house-husband—though their union lacked blessing—was sadly monochromatic; but paprika pleased him as did the Paprika Shop and its astonishing *sneezing* proprietor, its many *serious drawers*—its genuine claim to be the oldest going concern in Yorkville; for MacK the same trip had the imaginary *necessity* of acquiring a recording by *Kecskes,* a Hungarian clarinetist, whose name he had been carrying on a slip of paper in his wallet *for four years*. —I'll sell you Kecskes—**hapci!**—if you want him, boy, said the proprietor, who had magyariana as well as twenty-six kinds of paprika, but he's no good—**hapci!**

People have needs.

—

132

There was a heaviness which you had to admit eventually overrode *holiday*—they'd remember it as an unusually cold one. The crusts of snow haloed with dog pee and various oils, the post Club Weisse landscape—surely Izzy was looking homeward now. Even East 83rd Street, which in Izzy and Mary-Ann's block was of blank, even idiotic aspect (*no one home?*) had acquired holiday warmth: here and there you saw a lamp lighted in a front room and people sitting around, doing—somethin'—I don't know. Tell you one thing—you saw fewer idiots slowly bloating in front of TV than you would have out on a holiday walk and looking in people's front rooms out in the suburbs—not none, but fewer—having come from a couch of pre-turkey cold cuts and little kings, rousing themselves in an effort to create room in their gigantic stomicks before the onslaught of cholesterol and relative-bagging—digest, digest, digest—the lamps, leaves, TV—but that would be the Tumblesons—so f*** that. *Course those city folks have a lot of problems too ya know. OH yeah.*

—Where are the dogs of Hell? said MacK as they entered the porch or vestibule. —Ay, where are they? said Isidor—I think they're *in* Hell. Welcome back.

To enter the Katzenmurphy apartment they . . . opened the door, which put them in the middle of the kitchen ($8' \times 8'$). It was full of smell from Thanksgiving already—Mary-Ann was cooking bitter cranberries and chopping up bread and celery—turkish and hamish smells were cuddling the floorboards and walls.

## How Describe Mary-Ann Murphy

In her element, her shape in the steam? There was a—seamless? —American energy of the past, and of now, running through the Katzenmurphy apartment, situated here on East 83rd Street, on this holiday; running through Mary-Ann's upbringing, which you took to be one of rollicking sisterly hilarity and the charm of Worcester, if New England can be said to exert a kind of 'charm' on New Yorkers—who uneasily feel that it is some kind of prettier, embryonically better version of New York, where Federalism didn't go wrong—like a painting maybe—they can think this if they want so long as they don't visit it—through Mary-Ann's past and Florida and her cookbooks right into Izzy; her cooking running into his mouth, but that was not it altogether.

## What Isidor Had Found
## What it Means to a Man to Find It
## Or—Most of It

Mary-Ann was in herself an amalgam of several ethics important or sub-consciously cherished by Isidor, admired by MacK. She embodied the careless charm you saw in that girl on the bus. In an ancient pin-up calendar—that was it—found behind boxes of nails in the garage. With very little effort you could imagine Mary-Ann's lips rouged redder—and while most girls' hairstyles of the late 1940s were hideous, the way the top looked like a *volcanic plug*, the rest of the hair empoodled around it, yi *yi*, you could imagine finding Mary-Ann while flipping guiltily through the thing—her round figure energizing the housedress of the decade; she's fanning a reluctant barbecue with the hem of it, the whole she-bang—MacK and Izzy thought, suddenly needing to lean against various walls and take her in, cooking, Mary-Ann in the steam—against this combination of innocent household economy, lipstick, the beauty parlor and other such old-fashioned ideas and pretty legs in sheer stockings peeking from under a prim apron, heels higher than necessary to the task and of an arresting color. *None of this* going on—Mary-Ann was very modest and never showed off—if Izzy enjoyed dioramas of any bygone era—Mary-Ann would be the perfect canvas for it, thought MacK, getting strangely thirsty—then it was in the privacy of their room with the paint-thick door wedged shut, only the *hmou hmou* of the pigeons to bother them. Pretend you're f***ing in Paris why dontcha?

Mary-Ann had a job of the sort you get by *neglecting your education and doing what you please*, according to her father, being a policeman. *O sure, just following your nose around the country for a few years like some kind of*—as MacK well knew—Tumbleson had told him he had to eliminate half his employment history from his curriculum vitae—*Can't you hold a job?* He had given up on his head and was just following his vocal cords around. Mary-Ann now worked dutifully with good humor if not soulfully in a TV production house of no merit—one of the many office floors one can find oneself in on Lexington Avenue in the 40s. The glamour America attaches to television is *hilarious*, thought MacK. This company post-produced, which is a technical term meaning *to f*** around with*, some rock music crap you had vaguely heard of but never seen—and amazingly employed ten or twenty people, all of the same age, who didn't look as though they lived in New York at all. Lexington is one of the avenues on which you can feel yourself slipping out of New York—perhaps Lexington and on lower Second and Third is where a lot of these people live—you find yourself walking on a block in which all the stores suddenly look naïve, suburban—the bars are fake bars, the news-stand sells the stuff of supermarket magazine racks—nobody reads this crap in New York—the pastrami has no smell—the rest of the country laps around the edge of Manhattan—just see what things look like at the other end of the Queens Midtown Tunnel—it's like a little wrong-way telescope—foreign; that god damn country.

Izzy worried about her, and about nothing more so than her job, where he thought they mustn't use her intelligence; sure they value her for her tits alone. Parallel with her Catholic modesty and good-heartedness Mary-Ann liked parties—if she got tipsy it was in the way you'd expect her pin-up to get tipsy—her cheeks went pink as champagne and she began to hiccup, giggle, flirt and bounce and flounce. (More than once MacK had felt her foot on his foreleg under the table—no matter.) Iz maintains, no doubt, thought MacK, the most ghastly fantasies of her behavior behind the scenes at rock concerts—it was the phrase 'all areas' flapping on the pass on her breast that froze him to the marrow—'all areas' indeed; it drove him mad, mad do you hear?

But do you see what he'd found? A femininity from outwith the city (he did not believe in its 'cold heart', but) and surpassing any current exemplars, a pretty, honest, voluptuous GAL as your aunt might rasp, slightly out of the concept of the generation; like taking up with a wartime fantasy of your uncle's.

It more than suited Iz. He was fond of reminding, *i.e.* scathing, MacK and Pietro Arditti and Sidney and the others with the fact they hadn't liked Mary-Ann, hadn't liked her at all when he first upped scope and spotted her—with the incredible sNobberY of one's twenties they couldn't see any farther than their own diplomas, didn't see her history, the curves she could throw (in the broad sense), hadn't tasted her GUMBO—which reeked of mature knowledge of the world, erotic adventures among old books and a few salty men of Boca Raton, just an Old Bay State girl giving life a whirl. MacK had no idea where Isidor and Mary-Ann had met but they seemed remarkably easy together—he went to her apartment with Izzy and tasted the GUMBO there—despite the glum fluorescent lobby of the little walk-up in the East 70s and the barely-there spindly furniture, still positing tropical exuberation somehow even in that dark little space—*yeah, might be something to this woman after all*—phew!

## Thanksgiving Day

Izzy dropped the turkey heavily on the floor, tried actually to bounce it on its ass—*Hope you're satisfied!*—he hated carrying things as who does not—Mary-Ann gave out with a grin born in that family, MacK thought, the kidding, absorbing the ever-changing moods of the truculent policeman, perhaps that was it, whereas in *MY* family, he thought, there was no kidding about being in a bad mood, you couldn't burlesque anything—*Why I oughta*—mother hated Abbott and Costello—MacK prevented from wearing his clip-on tie without a clasp—But LOU COSTELLO doesn't wear a tie clasp!—*Go to your room!*

You boys have been to the Bavarian Inn haven't you, said Mary-Ann. —So shoot me, said Isidor. —I ought to—why don'tcha *tell* a girl when there's fun to be had? She chopped at a stalk of celery. —You wouldna liked it, said Izzy, it was very depressing. But get this—we made a crank call, 'cause of John. —Ya did? What did ya say? —Called 'em a gas-bag, said Isidor. —A gas-bag? —'Cause of the Hindenburg. —? —, said Mary Ann. —Yeah, anyway. Want me to cut up onions? And they revolved toward preparing the dinner together and MacK felt the holiday creep over him again, like fog from the river. He offered to help *chop*, why does this word have to do with every aspect of Thanksgiving?—but you can't help a couple prepare a meal, because: that is a *fight*. On Thanksgiving the heavy weaponry comes out—MacK's eyelids had been twitching since he and Iz had arrived back at the Katzenmurphy, in anticipation of an argument over the size of the turkey. Everything in the kitchen was of reduced size—the oven looked, in comparison with the ovens out there in America, across the rivers, like some kind of toy—the turkey looked giant, something you see girls in pencil skirts screaming at on TV late at night, and bloated, like the balloons floating hideous and jovial over the very cold crowd on Fifth Avenue at this very moment—the crowd that always wonders *Is that it?* at a certain point and then rejects these looming icy grimaces in favor of *molecular motion*, a quick walk home, their ovens. The Katzenmurphy sink was really a wash-hand basin. The toilet was small, like the plentiful little toilets of kindergarten, and in order to fit the angle of the tiny bathroom it had been necessary to procure, at some time in the dim past of Yorkville, a miniature toilet that was perfectly *round*, this doesn't fit the normal anatomy and one always had an odd feeling after sitting there and emerged from the bathroom with a queer expression on one's face which Iz could recognize and laugh at.

—Where do you get little spatulas like this? So you have room in here to flip a pancake or omelette? —I got that at Hammacher Schlemmer, MacK, said Mary-Ann.

—No no, you just go f*** yourself in the front room while we do this, just relax, enjoy said Izzy. So MacK sat with several of his favorite books of theirs, one on the civilization that ANTS have, the other describing the ickier procedures of the medical examiner. The brain is encased in a bony box.

Before the queen had seen all her workers die for the season and before the thoracic cavity had been aspirated with the trochar—the page where MacK always got dizzy and gave up—the carcase of the turkey had been stuffed—with natron?—and crow-barred into the oven, having been greased to the purpose; the counter was wiped and Mary-Ann was washing her hands and hanging up her apron—Izzy came in and put on a record.

*Now the terrible waiting begins. Now you hear the Great Clock of Your Aunt begin to tick and tick and tick ever more slowly—the ticking of the Puritanical bombs in a hundred million turkeys—out THERE.*

They drowsed, in a little nap of tea, wine, the *New York Times*, gardening books. Izzy and Mary-Ann argued a little. They spoke in an old-couple way MacK had not heard before but how else can you talk on Thanksgiving, the thing *gives* you white hair. *Did you remember butter for the sprouts? When are you going to roast the potatoes?* WQXR ('*The radio station with cheese between the slices*') sounded particularly dreadful: aside from carrying a Service of Thanksgiving® from St Patrick's and playing a few Ives songs it had no way to deal with the holiday so it was reduced to playing anything that could be dragged out of its 'library' with *hunting horns* in it. So over the course of the day this created a mournful, hollow feeling in the gut—and at the back of the sense memory a desire for *schnitzel*; not poultry and berries.


—Zzz.


# The Commendatore

At four o'clock the door bell rang and Iz jumped up—f*** this! They had all forgotten Pietro Arditti. You may have looked forward to having company when an invitation was made, but when you have shared the vicissitudes of the day then he who comes *MERELY* to eat—even if he is your good friend on any other day—shows up, doesn't know the drill, hasn't heard the day's jokes—he's going to get it in the neck—at least around here, thought MacK, who still had the coroner's handbook on his stomach, and rose from under it with psychological difficulty.

—Ya *friend's* heah, said Mary-Ann, who sounded even more like Edward Kennedy when she was put out.

—Gee Whizz. Iz pressed the button on the corroded speaking device in the kitchen, into which there was no point in speaking—its bizarre appearance suggested its conduit led not to the porch where Pietro Arditti was ringing but down, down beneath the river, down into one of the dwarf-staffed engine rooms of New York. Down the stairs you could hear the inner door bang open, almost feel the cold of the late afternoon, and a lot of puffing and blowing echoed around the mosaic and enamel hall. —Hey why doesn't QXR just play those records of *whales* on Thanksgiving, said Iz, it'd be just the—HOW ARE YOU! he boomed like a foghorn at the spouting Pietro Arditti before him.

This is all going to be a strange contest in bluster, and self-parody oddly aimed at hurting one's opponent, though sometimes not. GREAT!

Pietro Arditti was weighted with little decorative paper bags from the finest stores. —You look like a Christmas tree, said Izzy, grabbing them from Pietro Arditti's sheepskinned mitts—this was Iz being charitable and jolly. —Gee, Christmas, said Pietro Arditti, tomorrow's the day it begins. The thought pierced them all and shut 'em up for as long as it took Mary-Ann to think of a wreath on a Boston door; Pietro Arditti to think of egg nog; MacK to recall the coffeeish smell in the toilets of 747s and the aroma of oranges and 'Royal Yacht' following plum pudding; and Isidor to stumble in horror over the little bags, imagining the imminent descent of grasping madness—*tomorrow*—for this our town is a reasonable place is it not, brotherhood abounds except in the days before Christmas, when a guy could get killed just trying to walk from 50th to 53rd and Fifth on December 21st 1977 at 3.35 pm, thank you very much. —Gee Whizz, he said again and yanked Pietro Arditti's coat off, having to jump up and clutch at the guy's neck to do so, his penultimate act as host for the evening as it turned out. —Come in come in, said Iz, go in—though it didn't count—as you were standing always in the kitchen you knew you had to go into the only room that wasn't bed or bog.

—Whatcha got there, Pietro Arditti? said Mary-Ann looking at the little bags the way everyone in this our town looks at little bags. —Bhh-po-ho!ho! blew faintly yulish this mighty cetacean loosed from his aquarium, nothing less than the World of Business® itself—and these were the unremodeled days of Carter when the tiled lobby of Pietro Arditti's offices looked like it was designed to be full of water, instead of shit. Sorry. Have a drink! GREAT!

Iz and Pietro Arditti puffed and blew at each other remarkably in the Sinclair Lewis style; Pietro Arditti gave Mary-Ann several kisses and squeezes—a few darts passed between her and Iz—though he knew she relished this about as much as the paper cut on her pretty lower lip she got almost every day on Lexington Avenue—the huffing was partly comedy, take-off on the genre of business cats whose subaltern Pietro Arditti was—in those days—but as they got older there was to be more bluster, panic and less parody to it——regrettably.

MacK blows too though he is out of practice, hiding from Tumbleson as he is he doesn't hear the overweening weenying of business every day. *The man works in a soundproof box.*

They carried the packages into the living-room. There were bags from Sherry-Lehmann, from Dunhill, Bonté, Zabar's and—the *Carnegie Delicatessen!?* Iz poked his puss into all of them but wouldn't use his hands.

## Working with your hands = not good!

Pietro Arditti had brought : a Chateauneuf and a bottle of the Madeira wine of St Edmund Hall, Oxford—*pretty interesting*, said Izzy, as if to convey he acknowledged the pedigree of the stuff although it was something he would have decided against himself, would have abandoned staring at the mead and rainwater shelf in the gloomy belly of Sherry-Lehmann, the dark leviathan of Madison Avenue, one of their inquisitive pomaded suits breathing in your ear—no. —This isn't dessert wine, you know, said Iz at his politest, it's the Brits, man, they sop up this crap with their f***ing tea at four-thirty—somethin', I don't know. But thanks—*in a way*. —I know that, said Pietro Arditti, who didn't. These friends—for so they were—were still a little in the dessert wine stage of life—it's touching : three 'Montecruz' cigars, a Churchill for himself, a Panetela for Izzy, since they went to work entirely in suits, and a Rothschild for MacK, who was tidy and squat and one of the RCA Building's bohemians. —Hmm, said Iz, not bad, what a guy, &c, though again his tone suggested he had discovered pastures beyond the Canaries. He'd been insulted the year before upon discovering the brown delights of 'Partagas' to see Pietro Arditti immediately take 'Partagas' up as his own, and at a grotesquely loud party at his West End Avenue brownstone refer to them as 'Party Guys' while drinking sangria and leaning on his tiny marble mantel, the one thing of interest in the place, cocking his head and winking. *Plenty of jobs in finance!* : Oh and also from the Dunhill family vault a pretty box of Sobranie 'Cocktail' cigarettes for Mary-Ann, who cooed, genuinely—though not her style: she favored tough-girl smokes like the 'Picayunes' she picked up in New Orleans or 'Home Runs' from Baltimore—Mary-Ann knew her way around lots of the uriny news stands of the East, knew how to kill time near every major train and bus depot. Isidor struggled to maintain a front of detachment, but his eyes were widening just as the others' while Pietro Arditti plundered the helpless little bags : eight *petits-fours* (Iz turned up his nose) : Madeira cake (acknowledged its place), and struggled out of the bag : a huge BRIOCHE—at which Izzy rolled his eyes and began to mouth—*Wh—th—f*—and Pietro Arditti triumphed—*For break-fast, you nuts!* Iz smiled (though his eyes weren't)—*You think you're staying for breakfast?* —and in the middle of this Mary-Ann quietly took the chic red-and-white Bonté bag for herself—: two bags of dark roast coffee (Iz grunted; coffee was like tap water to him) and : —*A pastrami sandwich!!??* cried Iz, who grabbed and hefted it accusatorily like you might weigh a baseball you were thinking of throwing deliberately at somebody's head.

—Give me a break, man, said Pietro Arditti, I been going great guns since seven, *I* didn't know what time we were gonna eat—gotta carry all this crap around over here. Over there. —I can't believe this, said Iz, here a beautiful goil's making a big bird for a guy, blowing her brain out, and he brings a big Geek-A-Roni sand-wich to ruin his dinner wit'. —With which to ruin, said MacK. —Oh Isidor, ca'am down, said Mary-Ann, the poor guy's been rushin' around. —Gee Whizz, said Iz, I suppose you want a glass of wine with that—a *fine wine*—after your tough day. What the Hell are you talking about? You didn't go to work today. —I was on the phone a lot, said Pietro Arditti. —How long till we eat? Iz asked Mary-Ann—and unceremoniously uncorked a bottle he didn't bother to show the label of.

—

Each took his booty off to a corner of the apartment. Pietro Arditti was left to wrestle the great sandwich alone on the settee—the difficulties of eating it produced lots of creaking noises—the settee was old wicker—they might have been in a little holiday boat of joy. Mary-Ann poured herself a glass of the red wine as Isidor was looking at his cigar in the opposite corner—she selected a green Sobranie 'Cocktail' and puffed at it while rinsing the sprouts. MacK stole between them and opened the miniature refrigerator for a beer—they seemed to have shrunk. Now the *sandwich noise* was over—*Jeez, you OK now?* said Iz in an exaggerated version of Pietro Arditti's own gas station accent—Iz put on some music.

What was Pietro Arditti doing in New York? —he himself sometimes wanted to know. His training had taken him from the Providence Plantations to New York and back up to Harvard and then back again to town. He was a guy who was fast developing the 'idea' that he didn't 'want' to live in New York, for various 'aesthetic' reasons: *i.e.* even with a Harvard© M.B.A.® he didn't think he was going to make enough money to live in town—and just what do you think everyone here lives on?—millions?—he did not mean enough to *live* here—but enough to *cushion* himself with Checker cabs and wine *against* this our town, which rained blows and affronts like cats and dogs down on him wherever he went. He was not a man to go with a flow. MacK and Iz, late night work: scenario for a grand opera, *Don Arditti*, in which the metal Roger Williams atop the Rhode Island State House comes to life, takes a bus to Port-of-Authority, as it is known to every taxi driver, grabs Pietro Arditti out of a meeting at the Hilton and drags him back to New England for good (forceful *operatic laughter: A Ha ha ha ha ha ha ha!*)—along with every other Ivy Leaguer in the World of Business®. But the sandwich had helped Pietro Arditti out of his townish discomfort for today.

—

Although the table was small Mary-Ann had come up with a miniaturized homey look for their spread (except for the turkey which
could barely fit)—the potatoes were in a tureen and the cranberry
sauce in a cut glass dish with a spoon representing the *'CITY WALLS
OF ST AUGUSTINE'*—something of her grandmother's—and the
holiday seeped through the windows again in the city light of late
afternoon—they felt snug and festive; the *size* of everything . . .

MacK didn't like the look of the bread basket—an affair of stout
twigs and the feel of workshops—pardon—for the unfortunate. It
looked like the home of the *Lame Squirrel*—the other animals
brought him his Thanksgiving dinner—don't *ask*—winter was
coming—his big big-eye tears—but as this book was still resting in
the natal place—he might picture where—MacK choked up. Later
in the evening he thought of opening a spot in the Village, The *Lamé*
Squirrel—sense had practically deserted him.

Pietro Arditti went for a potato first thing. It was sautéed in
butter and olive oil, a mixture of alcohols known only to Mary-Ann
and one of the tatterdemalion cook books with the little mousta-
chio'd chef again going *buon appetito!* on the cloth of the
spine—Pietro Arditti pronounced them excellent thus: OH MAN!
Mary-Ann smiled, Isidor too, proud of her, vain even. They ate,
each surprised to find themselves together, eating, on the holiday in
the city, when it always seems that everyone travels on Thanksgiving,
the helplessly stuffed families in cars, the freezing late trains, the
planes with their smell of coffee'd businessman shit—but if that is
so, why do you not end up *knocking at the door of an empty house?*

MacK took a gander at the stuffing and for a moment his
bohemian folding chair became the large hard chairs of his own
family's dining-room, it was memory of the *translucent celery*, which
he'd had a horror of, that did it, and the turkey, a thing they had only
twice a year, cooked without a lot of help by his fretting mother,
who had all the cooks of OHIO looking over her shoulder and
making *little noises* with their mouths; you can barely see over the
edge of the table and you hate nuts, cranberries, the *translucent*

*celery*——the dining-room chairs are still too large, even today, MacK thought——he and his sister were not going to get any bigger——and now his little parents were shrinking.

The conversation limped, or was desultory: Pietro Arditti had not yet caught up with the tenor of the day, though as they ate——and this is the warm, Dickensian paragraph——and felt in their bowels the warmth of TRADITIONAL AMERICAN FARE——this improved. Too, if you were eating with Mary-Ann, there was always opportunity to praise her. ——OH MAN, said Pietro Arditti again, as she and MacK rose to replenish the tureens, isn't this great, MacK? And here the Latin School raised its head, though it was buried far in the dead New England leaves of his brain: ——*These guys are a real couple of Epicureans*. MacK heard the bottom of Isidor's wine glass strike the table and a high, sharp inhalation. ——IT SO HAPPENS, said Izzy . . . ——It's starting, said MacK under his breath to Mary-Ann in the kitchen. ——Oh deah!

——YOU'RE MISUSING THAT TERM LIKE EVERY OTHER JERK OF THE PLANET (one of Isidor's most hated expressions, anything to do with *the planet*——you can see the emotion)——WHAT DO YOU MEAN I'M AN EPICUREAN?

Pietro Arditti's eyes slid back and forth——already!——looking from Isidor to the empty bohemian chairs of MacK and Mary-Ann and back again——if only they had been sitting there!——he *became pink*——with challenge, he'd had Latin and Greek after all, fat lot of good it does you, the uniform of the Latin School on an afternoon bus in downtown Providence——the motto on the escutcheon of which the rough boys translated as KICK MY ASS, might as well be painted on your back!

——You know, said Pietro Arditti, hedonism——pursuit of pleasure. C'mon, what are you——MacK and Mary-Ann brought the amazing potatoes. ——Oh what are you boys arguing about? said Mary-Ann, half-consciously becoming the mother of each.

——You think Epicurus went around telling everybody to pig out, don't you, said Isidor, just eat the Geek-A-Ronis all the time, like you? That what you think? Cause I have news for you, pal—the Epicureans lived on water and bread made from one of those near-impossible grains—barley?—bere?—*somethin'*—I don't know—and a pint of wine a day—and you can bet it wasn't like that Chateauneuf you're drinking or the other one YOU brought (there were duelling Chateauneufs) or even that Madeira you so *kindly* purchased and they weren't smoking no maduro maduro either—

—Hey—

—No, YOU hey—Epicureanism *is* a hedonistic philosophy, scumbag, but in hedonism, the pleasure—which *is* the criterion—isn't sensual. Epicurus taught us—*us,* dick head—that the *higher* pleasures are the ones to be sought—peace of mind, *ass hole,* and social justice and civilization and all that shit. You want to find someone like *you,* who thought everyone should eat huge Geek-A-Roni meatball heros all the time, *mnuh mnuh mnuh,* and burp and fart and bonk—you go back to Aristippus, he's the guy for you—the Cyrenaics, they're just like you—they can't think of anything but whatever big fat Geek-A-Roni or broad with her legs spread—*Isidor!* said Mary-Ann—is right in front of 'em, and they *told* everyone that was the only thing that could *ever* be thought about. You believe that?

—Wuh, said Pietro Arditti—

—But even *that* guy, Aristippus, finally had to admit that all this lowbrow getting, all these *Rhode Island pleasures,* chewing up tons of fat *mnuh mnuh mnuh* and getting drunk off your ass every night like a f***ing GEEK, they brought pain. PAIN! Get it, ass hole? You guzzle booze, you get sick—you screw every hole in sight and society breaks down, people go ape shit—so even the Cyrenaics in the end, the *pigs* of the philosophical world, the guys with the fanny packs and the Geek-A-Roni sandwiches and Big Gulp soft drinks and big dicks and big slurpees and BIG TITS—even *they* admitted there might be some higher pleasures to be sought—*Like the pleasures of debate?* said Pietro Arditti—which didn't cause an equal amount of PAIN, said Izzy. So that's what Epicurus built on, the pursuit of *those* pleasures, not stuffing your face like a meatball at my table and

grabbing my girl's ass when you came in the door, *BASTARDO*.
— Isidor, said Mary-Ann.

Pietro Arditti felt slightly abused. —So I suppose you're leading
a lofty life here. —Yeah! —On East 83rd Street! —Yeah!
—Pursuing high ideals. —Yeah, I *am*—cause I know all about the
*pain*. —Ho! —Yeah in fact I *am* an Epicurean, if you want to know,
in the real sense, not the shit head sense, because I am a civilized
man and I *know* my history and what the pleasures of the intellect are

1. **Jazz**
2. **Wine**
3. **Paprika**

not like YOU who seem to have forgotten everything you ever
learned. Don't you think my parents would have preferred a sane,
orderly world, filled with good feeling? What do you think the
Nazis were except a bunch of Cyrenaics? —Now, hold on a minute,
said Pietro Arditti. —*You* hold on—and Iz banged into the kitchen
as he was about to *lose his temper*.

Brought out the next bottle of wine—in fairness, they did recognize it was faintly funny to be eating their way through this
argument—in this pause they recognized that, even Isidor smiled a
little, though the moray eel of his argumentum was not going to be got
off Pietro Arditti's leg without being CHOPPED off. —The state
must go, said Iz, summing up, raising his glass, the state must go and
logic with it. It sounded suddenly like a toast so they all lifted theirs—

### The State Must Go!

—Who would like some more turkey and potatoes? said Mary-
Ann, who under stress of the argument pronounced potatoes like
*Badedas* which set MacK wondering what Edward Kennedy uses in
the shower. Old Spice soap on a rope. —F*** turkey! shouted Izzy,
expansive now that he'd conquered Pietro Arditti—cheese! *Send me
some Cythnian cheese so that should I choose I may fare sumptuously*. We
want cheese! We want cheese!

—We don't *have* cheese Isidor, said Mary-Ann, you know that. Or if we do it's that stoopid Cracka Barrel, which you hate.

# A Guy's Mother

MacK and Pietro Arditti were on thirds, Mary-Ann and Isidor decelerating. —What's the matter with you guys, said Izzy, you some kind of Stoics? —Yeah, said MacK, his mouth full of cranberry so he looked like the guy that chews betel nut in *National Geographic*, it's our duty to eat this dinner, our selfless duty to society and it doesn't matter how much we eat because pain is not an evil. (Hoping to defuse . . .) —Yeah, well, said Iz, you're a great stoic like Aristotle—Onassis. Have a cigar.

GREAT!

—But there was pumpkin pie and fruitcake first (how Dickensian *now?*). Pietro Arditti, who had after all watched the storms come and go across Isidor as much as the rest of them, opened the Madeira which they thought a cooler thing to try than port—though Izzy said ominously: —Of course you know I have armagnac for later. So what else is new? Since he finally realized no one had been doing any talking. —Perhaps Mister Argumenti will favor us . . . —That reminds me! said Pietro Arditti, get this. I changed my name. You should call me Mr *Ardent* now. —*WHAT!?* said Isidor in a very loud voice . . . *MISTER!?* —Isidor, said Mary-Ann. —Yeah I changed my name along with my religion. —MacK's turn to choke, on his fruitcake which had soft glacéed pineapple in it which did something subtle, from the past, to the walnuts—since he'd grown up in California and had no religious instruction whatsoever, believed in the gods of the city, and had to keep everyone he knew strictly categorized so as to abjure their beliefs (not to their faces)—he was afraid of being drawn into one monotheism or another. Pietro Arditti had till this moment filled the very important New England Italian Catholic niche which now gaped in

MacK's brain like a robbed grave—iron letters weeping rust down a marble surface—

—What the f*** are you *TALKING* about, said Isidor, and in a similar tone: —What have you *chosen*, said MacK, and: —What religion ARE ya, said Mary-Ann.

—I'm an Episcopalian, said Pietro Arditti, in a tone which said nothing of joy, of blessed relief, of happiness, or justified and courageous pride in finding the right way to a god, but smelt only of 'I got the car washed' or 'Honey, I'm home'—which is about right. Izzy's eyes were not so much bugged out as they had flattened themselves against the insides of his glasses—they looked as though they had been painted on, in there.

—I can't believe this, he said, looking down at his dessert plate like the pieces of cake on it had just performed a sexual act. —You eat dinner with a guy and then you find out you didn't even know who it *WAS!* I'm dumbfounded.

Of course he wasn't—he immediately went on the attack.

—Everyone have to change their name when they become an Episcopalian? —Certainly not, said Mr Ardent. I—just like the way it looks better. —*WHAT YOU MEAN*, said Isidor, is that World of F***ing Business® doesn't like names that end with a e i o u and sometimes y. That it? You're having the big vowel movement—like we need another wasp in this town. Thanks a lot!

MacK thought furiously about the demolition of Pietro Arditti's—Mr Ardent's—niche in his pantheon—this was an offense against his aesthetics as well—the wider Ardittis occupied quite a few important though contradictory slots in MacK's columbarium worldview (he used them for a number of things): pious people of the working-class; the franchisees of a major petroleum company; situation-comedy Italians; people who really know how to find a pizza pie in Providence. He was particularly upset to think that what he had imagined to be a heritage of lively debate, heated argument but at least out in the open, and the rude good nature of the Old World was now to be abandoned by Mr Ardent, whose children would be raised in an atmosphere of air-conditioning and fruit cocktail. (The two achievements of high Episcopalian civilization—air-conditioning cools ardors and prevents clothes from being stained by . . . *perspiration*; fruit cocktail is colorful and *digestible* and fits most neatly into the USDA food pyramid, a great little god which we all worship, admit it. But stay—isn't it really a *triangle*? Come on.) Any racial energy will be lost, thought MacK, becoming an Episcopalian is like taking Emily Post to bed. And isn't this just as Izzy says, part of the homogenizing terror the World of Business® is wreaking on Pietro Arditti? —on all of us? He must've changed his front name too—Pete Ardent?

The idea that everything that can possibly be a business *ought* to be a business—and that if it *is* a business then it is all right—porno, armaments, nuclear power, cigarettes, *'HEALTH FOODS'*—because business and growth are the ultimate necessity—as if it is now deemed necessary by everyone to cheat Earth of all its resources as quickly as possible, so we can *move on*, to—?, thought MacK.

—Dessert? said Mary-Ann, who would like more dessert? And, thinking of what leaving her own ostensible church would precipitate in her family (though her connection to it was as tenuous as had been her attachment to her school uniform at 3.15), she said, What does ya mother have to say about it, Pietro Arditti? —Oh, well, said Mr Ardent, chillingly casual, I'm an Episcopalian now so I guess mothers aren't very important.

—*P - h - e - w !* whistled Izzy. The guy gives up on his own mother, you believe this? All you have to do is abandon the Mother of God, not your *OWN* mother for Christ's sake.

So MacK was very sad as this seemed the dead bell of exuberation, Pietro Arditti the indefatigable *party guy* become *the party man*, a biddable apparatchik of Pine Street. *Izzy* didn't care for they were all rotten, all the Christians and their categories, denominations—as he uncorked the armagnac he said it was wrong for Mr Ardent to neglect his mother, *to say such a thing on Thanks-f\*\*\*ing-giving—all I'll say*. Except that the whole thing is *really—f\*\*\*ing—weird*. But I suppose, said Iz, you've enjoyed that holiday meal much more than ever before, now that you're practically a f***ing Pilgrim and a Daughter of the American Revolution.

Mr Ardent bristled a trifle at this increasing assault. But he was just *so much larger than Isidor* that he knew nothing could happen to him.

—Why don'tcha lay off? suddenly rose up Mary-Ann. Pietro Arditti—I mean, Mista Awdent's just tryna make his way in the world like the rest of us, *Isidor*. He can change his name if he wantsa. I think it sounds *nice*.

—That what you think? said Iz—think I should change my name to Ichabod Crane? Think MacK should get away from that creeping swart Celticness and go totally Anglo-Saxon? Mr Manning, Mr—Kenilworth?—what the f*** does your name *mean*, anyway? What's a *Kenzie?* —No idea, said MacK. —And what about you honey? said Iz, such a beautiful goil with the name of Murphy, which will keep you the scullery maid and brick-layer you so obviously are. —Oh stop it, Izzy—though she *was* bothered by the name of Murphy, which she felt at times in New York a hugely weighted, laughable hat of some kind. —Why don'tcha lay off? And he did—cuz he was five times warmed—by his friends, by the valences of debate in which he had traveled, by grand holiday fayre, by armagnac, and by the knowledge that he was at this very moment contemplating the finer things in life and had contacted high ideals—having run the history of Epicureanism from sensual pleasure right up to peace of mind in one evening—never mind how it was achieved, by kicking Mr Ardent in the bottom. This is a warm, Dickensian paragraph too. And, MacK thought, the holiday still drifted around the room, and even though important things had been stated frankly and even baldly, their group, it had to be admitted, was ever cohesive, held together, as was the little school in Epicurus's garden, by the charm of Isidor's brains and personality.

*So there are these two maggots on the edge of the sidewalk, say around Murray Hill, it's a summer morning and they're wriggling around, and one of them happens to fall into the gutter, into a dead cat. So several weeks go by and one day the maggot who stayed on the sidewalk runs into the other—his old friend. My my, he says, just look at you—I've been struggling to get a living up here but you're so sleek and fat! How'd you do it? And the other maggot says, Brains and personality, brother, brains and personality.*

Isidor had achieved what the Epicureans could only theorize—he withdrew himself each day more and more from external influences (he for one believed the gods have nothing to do with us) the IRT, the IND, Times Square, Schaller and Weber, cops, jocks, and WQXR; and therefore 'lived like a god among men'.

What happened to the Madeira cake?

Mr Ardent was not insensible to the spirit of the holiday—and while he had felt under attack, as he often did by the time dessert was finished at Izzy's and Mary-Ann's, he saw that Izzy had ascended to some higher philosophic plane—that he'd calmed—that he'd *shut up*—so he smiled while taking a paring knife to the end of his Churchill—after all, he'd done the right thing for his career in World of Business®, whatever Izzy thought—and spoke in imitation of Isidor's imitation of *his* voice. —Leave my mother out of this; your mother wears Army boots! —F*** you! So they were happy and here there was a warming scene, Mr Ardent putting on the large sheepskin coat in which he moved through the city, a thick and hardened side of meat; the soft silk scarf he had been affecting lately—the gay blue harbinger of a suit to come. Izzy slapped him on the back in a completely theatrical way, out of his conception of hale fellowship in the World of Business®, but also gave him his hand, once Mr Ardent's were in the frighteningly untanned-looking muttony gloves which matched his coat. Several kisses on the cheek from Mary-Ann, who was happy to see the boys parting so equable—the holiday night air was running up the stairwell and smelled of Christmas coming. —Well steer clear of culture, that's my advice, said Isidor. —You'll be able to do that easily, said MacK, now that you're an Episcopalian—they shook hands. Mr Ardent went down the stairs and stood for a moment adjusting his scarf and gloves in the unpainted vestibule of Isidor's apartment building. With the Churchill at full throttle Mr Ardent looked like an eye-rolling capitalist fish from the undersea night club. There was a cab on Second.

There is also holiday in washing dishes, the odors of dinner mingling with that of Joy Joy Joy and the percolator put on to help the cleaning up—a final jot of armagnac—or a bottle of beer as MacK studied the amalgamated dinnerware of Isidor and Mary-Ann while he carried it to the sink. They'd both owned plain white dishes—Isidor's were heavier, stolen from diners maybe—what after all is the purpose of diners?—Mary-Ann's thin, as from an import shop smelling like excelsior and incense—both owned three each of glasses for red and for white, a small number of pots (Mary-Ann knew exactly what she needed to make the GUMBO in the pill-box of her previous kitchen). Both had owned one corkscrew *moderne* apiece, both hated oven mitts and tea towels. So putting their kitchen together had taken no time—a sign?

Isidor began idly picking his after-dinner fight. —What the Hell are you defending that guy for? he said as Mary-Ann brought in the table cloth. —Well, I know it's ridiculous, Isidor, she said, I can see that—but he's down there with all those stuck-up basteds on Pine Street all day an' he gets nervous I guess—he's only tryna make a living ya know. —Think I'm not trying to make a living? —I didn't say that. What is wrong with you? —I think it's an outrage . . . guy changes his *name?* and his *religion?* just so he can join the Yale Club? —Well if he wantsa join the Yale Club whatsa matta with that? —You're starting to sound like a Rockette. —What's wrong with soundin' like a Rockette? My sista's a Rockette! —I know, I know—he'd forgotten. —Yeah, what is wrong with Rockettes at all, piped up MacK, recalling the sista's stems—wondering if intervention was needed and if this was it—they display 'em in old-fashioned *get-ups* to be sure, but they are the legs of today. He suddenly thought he *shouldn't* mix into this. —Remember the time we used the bathroom at the Yale Club? he said, deciding to address the subject under discussion—or its ancillary. —Yes I remember said Izzy, annoyed, there was a time when wearing any kind of tie and a stupid jacket legitimized you up the wazoo in this town . . . no more, man—now they look, they actually look at the cloth and the cut, baby—I have to go to the *Roosevelt* for a midtown squizz. —Although, said MacK, the guy in there is very friendly. —Yeah. The *black* guy is friendly. —Yeah. —No more of that public restroom shit for Mr Ardent, said Isidor—he'll be handed the key to the executive washroom before you know it—YEAH, BABY! —You boys are terrible, said Mary-Ann.

—Know what? said Izzy to MacK, I think this is a very beautiful girl, don't you? —Um, yas, said MacK. —But she's got some krezzy ideas in that head I think. —Stop it, Isidor, right now, she said. —So we're going to go a couple of rounds about it, if you don't mind. —Oh Isidor, not tonight, said Mary-Ann, it's *Thanksgiving*. —Exactly, said Izzy, in his best horror movie accent. —Full of beans aren't ya, comparing one guy to another like that? Think I don't put bread on the table? This poor schmuck and I dragged that Jesuitical turkey of yours all the way from Schaller and Weber, the empire of the franks! —*Via* the Bavarian Inn I think, said Mary-Ann. —So what, we got thirsty dragging it, said Iz from the bedroom, that OK with you? And came out with the gloves. —Those new? said MacK. —You bet they ah, said Mary-Ann. —I love her Everlastingly, said Iz.

# The Champ

There was an overhead light in the living-room, which they all hated—it destroyed the apartment's book warmth, and made the beige walls bleak, like a place in which there were only arguments, cartoon tenement parents yelling at kids—if you saw it from out-side. But Iz climbed up on the table and unscrewed the large white globe and replaced it with a reflector flood he kept under the bed,

Mary-Ann wiped her hands on her apron and tutted about having to do this after making dinner, after all. —Come on, said Iz, tomorrow's a holiday too. —Almost wish I *was* going to the office, so, she said. —Come *on*.

GREAT!

—Have a cigar, man, said Iz, sit down, enjoy yourself. Have a beer. He helped her with her gloves on and got his own laced; she with her teeth. They looked at each other and then at MacK for a moment—which was supposed to be some sort of beginning? *Ding*, thought MacK—Izzy turned off the kitchen light—they started circling—MacK lighted up.

—So, think that guy ought to've changed his name, huh? said Iz, plying her with a few inquisitive jabs. —I never said that, Isidor, and you know it, said Mary-Ann. She was lighter on her feet but obviously hadn't been studying long—mostly her guard imitated Izzy's—she was still in her cardigan—she'd taken her shoes off so as to approach his level. The upper part of Iz knew how to box, or at least how to appear to box, thought MacK, reflecting also it was ironic that Iz was now in his white shirt sleeves and dark trousers—whenever MacK wore the same Izzy screamed at him *What are you, a Portuguese waiter? Two espresso!*—and therefore looked like the referee. Iz spent two hours on a heavy bag downtown every Thursday. He wanted to hang one up in the Katzenmurphy, but it would have taken up all the remaining space, being the largest thing in there by far (saving the visits of Pietro—*Mr Ardent*). But while he'd developed quite a chest and shoulders pounding the King of Unresponse, he hadn't looked to his footwork.

—*The champ is looking a little sluggish tonight!* —*Can't agree with ya more, Ed!* —*We had reports from training camp that the champ has been hitting the armagnac as well as the heavy bag!*—*'s been skipping skipping rope!* —*Well it doesn't look like he's been skipping any bouts at the old training table!*—*He's a capacity crowd unto himself tonight, Ed!* —*The champ looks muzzy!*—*the champ looks like he's swallowed an entire toikey wit all da trimmins . . .*

—Would you **shut up?** said Isidor. —Sorry, said MacK. Izzy and Mary-Ann's eyes were bright as they circled under the flood lamp. Izzy started scoring points on Mary-Ann, but he wasn't putting anything behind it—lady after all. Mary-Ann didn't know how to block him and was getting red in the face. Izzy scored on her shoulder, her sternum, and made a little point of goading her solar plexus. —God damn it, she said, and her eye grew beady. —Oh, *god* is it, said Izzy, not something a nice Catholic goil says—course you could *change your name*—hhh! (he scored a right above her breast)—like Pietro Arditti and then God couldn't find you. —Isidor, I'm warnin' ya, said Mary-Ann, stepping back and shouldering off her sweater, dragging the sleeves over the big red gloves with her mouth, now she circled again, in her black leotard—her cheeks very red and her eyes dewy.

—Come on, ya little runt, show us what ye're made of—ya sawed-off little loudmout'. —What? I'm a loudmouth?—and he braised her chin—think I'm going to take that from a cop's daughter? —I'm warnin' ya Isidor, quit makin' personal remarks while weah boxin' or ya gonna get it. Ya little Epicurean ya. —What! I'm not an Epicurean! —C'mon, Eppy! —I told you, I'm not an Epicurean, not in the way *'MR ARDENT'* says I am—the big geek—don't you understand that? He doesn't know the—Mary-Ann almost got him in the bag. —I say you *ah*. —I am not (swings a little wild). —Oh yeah? Where were you and MacK today? I think your day began at Schalla and Weba. I think ya drank some imported beahs at the Bavarian Inn. I think ya came back here and ate a gigantic dinna, that *I* cooked, and drank two bottlesa fancy—*French*—oof—wine (she was starting to hit out crazy now; she didn't connect)—ya smoked a big fat CIGA ya friend brought ya, and ya guzzled about a quata bottla armagnac—also guess what? —What, said Izzy, starting to sweat. —Those cans of plums ya bought at Zabar's? —What about 'em? —Look at the label, Isidor—theyah called *'EPICURE'*. Iz swung a big right at her: —*I'm going to give you!* —and Mary-Ann fell, 'intentionally, without a blow'.

Izzy stared down at her on the floor, eyes wide in disbelief

—You're disqualified, he shouted, that's DISqualification. Mary-Ann lay fetchingly on the floor looking up at Izzy with her pink cheeks and moist eyes, breathing hard. He went for her—here was a brief descent into PANCRATIUM and MacK looked away briefly, not really thinking *Ding!*, before Iz realized the bout was still on—they staggered to their feet and breathed at each other like rhinoceri. —You're disqualified, he said. —I'm disqualified? she said, I'm going to bust ya Epicurean ass—I'm gonna send ya off to a higher plane where ya can canamplate the good. —Oh yeah? —Yeah! said Mary-Ann, and found *such* an uppercut some-where within her girlish interior—an uppercut you couldn't believe—that MacK rose out of his slouch on the couch and the dogs of Sodom upstairs snuffled and growled just it seemed with the hissing air immediately prior to her connection with Isidor's chin—really just hauled off and—as you could imagine people doing in these tenements fifty years before, to the tune of boiled dinners and life in the back yards; children playing in and out of the laundry—dogs—really just f***ing *flattened* the guy. He was slowly lifted in the air along with some of the furnishings, pictures, potted plants and the wicker chairs, there was a low roaring noise such as is supposed to precede earthquakes, and Isidor fell onto the floor as heavy and sack-like a thing as Mr Ardent or the big bag at the gym. Mary-Ann stepped back and calmly began unlacing her gloves with her teeth. —Wanted some cheese huh, she hotly said—dropped the gloves on a chair and went into the kitchen—looked at herself in the shaving mirror over the sink —smoothed her hair—dipped her finger in the stream of cold water—then daintily touched a few drops over each eyelid and came back in. Isidor might have had a big lily sticking out of his chest. Slapped him, without animosity, certainly none of that which had powered her uppercut, what an uppercut, you shoulda—he opened his eyes and *actually said* Where Am I? —Ya on the floor ya crazy Epicurean basted.

# Mary Ann's Mary Janes

Armagnac, the antipuritan poultice of the evening, first to float the gang slightly above and away from the holiday—now to bring Isidor firmly back down into it. His eyes were $X$s. —Come on, honey, said Mary-Ann, time for bed. Good-night, MacK—can ya make up ya bed on the floor? You know where everything is. It's more comfortable than the couch I always think. —How does she know that? wondered MacK as he dragged the cushions off the furniture to make the Mondrianic arrangement of pillows and other things on which he would lie. Faint light came through the blind and shone on a print, a dark skyscraper of the Thirties.

MacK roiled in his mosaic bed, reaching occasionally out to hug the puzzle of pillows back together—a crevasse closed on him—he sprang to fill the shape. He replayed the bout in his mind and was warmed by the idea of Mary-Ann in her black leotard, circling, feinting—Iz called her a Rockette, but here is no bad thing, a Rockette in the house would be . . . Well she sure is a curvy GAL and can she cook? Brother. And some fighter.

A number of weeks before, MacK had arranged to meet them at the Plaza Garibaldi. He decided to drop off his overcoat at Izzy's, since it had become suddenly too warm for it—don't you hate this?—or hang it up in the Bavarian Inn and see how it looked—phone Iz from there to ask if in late afternoon a Club Weisse appealed while they waited for Mary-Ann, who never got uptown before 7.30. —I'm stuck doing some stuff, said Isidor, but drop it off—we'll meet you for dinner. Izzy had a desk he prized made from the front door of his last apartment on the West Side—he'd unscrewed it from the hinges and thrown it in the van, last thing. —I need a bigger desk in the new place. —?—said MacK. —Hey, they never gave me any heat here, so what do they need a front door? He did accounts at the desk (he hated doing

158

them in the shop) though it was usually covered in cigar boxes and soaked-off wine labels—much room was taken up by the large desk lamp Izzy used to monitor the decantation of wine into his carafe.

So MacK stopped by with the awful burden of his coat—what is worse than having the wrong coat, having to labor under the thing that is making you hot?—in fact, carrying anything is crap—*it is not urban*—it ought to be country folk and suburban idiots who *carry* things, bundles of sticks, washing, designer ice cream, the bodies of girls they've had to murder because of violating the cousin laws. Theoretically you shouldn't have to carry *anything* with you *ever* in the city, thought MacK, since *everything* is available on every corner . . . But Mary-Ann was home! Late afternoon light in the living-room, only the second, short time of day that actual photons found their way into the place. Izzy had buzzed him in, but when MacK came through the kitchen and through to the living-room he found them—sitting—that is, together—Mary-Ann was on Isidor's lap, which, why not, but. Iz told MacK to put his coat down and they'd meet him in a couple of hours, with more than a breath of solemnity—*somethin'*—*I don't know*, MacK thought. It struck him that Mary-Ann looked quite autumnal, in a plaid skirt and knee socks—well—so what, she's from Massachusetts—and was probably the only woman in that whole 'television' company who wore a *blouse*. —You guys OK? said MacK. —Yah. He *backed* out of the room, away from this—Mary-Ann's mary janes, brand new and barely touching *en pointe* the floor as she sat in Izzy's lap—well interrupting anyone is the pits; ought to be a misdemeanor.

MacK rolled left to right as if sea-sick, wedging himself permanently—as he found—in its usual spot. The curvatures evinced during the bout—the mary janes—these were good things to sleep on—thanks.

—

*Muffled, from the bedroom:*
   —Whoa, say, whuddya call that?
   —Say hello to 'Mr Ardent', honey.


# Baloney: Election Day

NOVEMBER you associate with topcoats and the grim visages of
Next Presidents in black and white—*colors* are for the *powerless*—but
Primary Day in summer is always bright. Mayhap it's the only day
you have any say-so, the only day on which to *celebrate* this damnable
process, which ruins both sleep and wage-earning, and causes nothing to improve but only to get worse and worse. This business of
keeping the lorises on their toes. The last person you voted
for—should he or she even have been DOG CATCHER? *No.*

Isidor always awoke to it with relish—uncharacteristically
whipped out of bed leaving Mary-Ann behind—she was from
Massachusetts after all and had no confidence in politicians—they
kept getting shot, thrown in jail, they *lied,* they wore *helmets.* —You
are what is wrong with this country, you know, said Isidor, beginning
to shave and loudly hum. 'My Country, 'Tis of Thee.' He did this
every primary-bright morning. From under the pillow: —Oh puh-
*leeze*, Isidor—f***offwhydontcha?

Such is the breadth of opinion so charmingly allowed in this our
town. —Wake *up*, said Isidor, it's time to exercise your franchise.
—That what ya callin' it now?

MacK arose with pride from the '14-15' puzzle of his bedding.
Sunlight dribbled down into the little back yard and through the
small window of the living-room and there was that undeniable
clairvoyance you receive, from time to time, that a perfect summer
morning awaits you. He had arranged to VOTE with his FRIEND.

During Our Years in Yorkville MacK took every opportunity to
sleep on the floor of the Katzenmurphy apartment. He was living at
this time on *West* 83rd while Isidor and Mary-Ann lived on *East*

83rd. It was the only point in his existence, he thought now, on his grand north to south *victory tour*, when going *west to east* was my focus. It said much of his affection for the two of them, and not a little about his feudal loneliness.

Back-and-forth has never had the force of up-and-down, he reflected.

The familiar and frustrating hour to wait and watch Isidor drink his little gallon of joe and read the *New York Times*, which on election day he always did with *extra ferocity and flapping*. Mary-Ann primped, plumped and cooed—it was always a nervous morning for her as her patriotism, neither greater nor lesser than yours, was subject to attack.

At ten o'clock the three of them stood at what each privately thought of as the Corner of Decision, 83rd and First, not because it was election day but because at this corner one decided whether to face north and go up to 86th and apply for succor to the crosstown bus and/or the Lexington Avenue subway, or to become part of the vast particulate suspension of humanity and filter, in any way you could, toward midtown. Iz kissed Mary-Ann goodbye. —*Commie slut*, he said. As she crossed the street she waved back at the two voters: —*So long, suckers!*

Isidor made to cross the avenue but MacK swerved. —No! said Iz, no! Not another sandwich, you're going to have to get a special pocket made. But followed him into the deli. —Baloney and swiss on a roll, lettuce and mayo? said MacK. —I know, said the guy.

Isidor could do *nothing* about MacK's being very impressed with the baloney here. Or that MacK had now acquired the habit of buying a baloney and swiss on a roll whenever he passed, whether to or from Iz's—business hours permitting. Sometimes he ate them and sometimes he didn't—given the ban on breakfast at Isidor's they sometimes came in handy—though Iz would come out of his bedroom and shout if he heard the hallmark rustling of deli paper. Some nights this sandwich was one of the elements of MacK's bed on the floor—more than once his pillow. This sandwich was banned from Isidor's refrigerator—to no avail. —How can you just *walk around* with a sandwich, said Isidor, where is your briefcase? —These don't fit in my briefcase, said MacK. His was the rather slim *Briefcase of Ideas*. —Lead on if you please.

—It seems logical, said Isidor, to get a balanced view. He was always talking of this. So they spent an hour in the rather dirty Blarney Castle, while MacK watched Izzy read the *other paper*, for which Iz would never pay. He was sometimes inspired or even swayed by its brand of nutty populism—some elected offices in the land did benefit from his annual perusal of it. He affected to put it down with a dismissive plop after rubbing it in the puddle, crumb and ash of the bar. —Guess I've heard what the hairy apes have to say. —You shouldn't talk that way you know, MacK said, one of these days that wretched paper of yours is going to go out-and-out Republican, instead of *hiding* it all in the 'Living' section—and then you'll have to read this one. —Well that is a day I can stand to wait for, said Isidor, secretly wishing that the city had a newspaper worthy of the name, not just all this *prose*.

—*It is time*, he said, although every political soul in the bar considered *staying* in the bar with its air-conditioning, free newspapers and mess.

Down a side street in the beautiful city morning—there were flowers in pots on black-painted fire escapes of the brick tenements, which seemed patriotic as all get-out, thought MacK. —We go in here, said Isidor. He pushed open a door, above which were flags flying, and bunting. Inside was a linoleum-covered stair. —After you. MacK climbed the stair and found himself in what looked like a room where you might have to hang around for a long time while someone re-lined your brakes or hid and smoked before fixing your teeth. The walls were shiny wood-effect paneling, the lights, glaring on more linoleum yet, were *fluorescent* (but one makes sacrifices for democracy, he thought). There were frightening chairs and standing ashtrays filled with sand, reminiscent of the auto club or the telephone company when it served the people, and frightening magazines devoted to the male desiderata. Aggressive-looking rubber plants postured in pots with little flags stuck in the artificial soil. There was a window, with a ledge, such as you beg at for dispensations in places like this. It was very Non-New York—the two Voting Men might have been in Queens; or Columbus. —Where are the booths? said MacK. Izzy walked over to the window and pressed a button that said PRESS. —Keep your pants on, he said.

—*Who* keeping his pants on? said a voice as the window slid open. What can I do for you gentlemen? —We are here to vote of course, said Isidor. Isn't it election day? —It surely is, said the pleasant receptionist. Who you want to vote for? —Hey, she's not supposed to—, said MacK. —Would you let *me* handle this? said Izzy. We want to vote for Lily and Donna. —You in luck, said the receptionist, they waiting for you solid citizens in Voting Booth Number Seven. Now *she* pressed a buzzer and a door next to her window came ajar. Iz made for this with surety in his *shoes for a guy who walks* and held it for MacK. The receptionist watched MacK cross the floor. —What in the parcel? —It's a *sandwich*, said Isidor, you believe that? —Now I seen *everything*.

MacK followed Isidor down the hall. —I don't think I brought my sample ballot, he said. —Guy brings a sandwich and not his ballot, said Iz. He tapped at the door of Voting Booth Number Seven.

The booth was sunny and looked out on the street. A breeze came through the windows decorated with bunting, which MacK had seen from below. —What's in the package? said Donna, and MacK was immediately charmed by her. She wore a blue dress while Lily was in red and already welcoming Isidor with white gloves. —This booth suit you, said Izzy, or you want another? —I curse machine politics, said MacK. Things are so much more straightforward in California. —Are you from *California?* said Donna.

There was a large sofa. As usual Isidor got down to things quickly on the left wing of it: —Tell me, he said to Lily, as they began working together, your opinion of the Sanitation Bill. —I'm against it, Sir, she said. —The bill!? —No, silly, GARBAGE. —Good. Wow.

MacK had not studied the ballot, being from California and therefore without political training or awareness, so Donna had to draw him out. —My! And how will *you* be voting today? she said, though who or what she addressed—. —I always vote my conscience, said MacK. —Bullshit! panted Iz. —You seem eager enough, said Donna, look, Lily. —Mmm. —Tactics are important, are everything, said Isidor—so Lily took up something else with him.

The flags and bunting in the breeze behind Donna: MacK felt he was falling in love. What an impressionable guy.

The old republic reared its head.

After some martial, stirring minutes Isidor again said it was important to get all points of view. So they exchanged places. —Switch-hit voting, said Isidor, democracy, baseball and hot dogs. —I know you, don't I? said Donna.

Isidor's guidance. MacK's vigor.

The levers were pulled and the boys' intentions for the city and nation were plainly registered. It seemed the Republicans were to do badly today, as we generally hope to be the case in this our town. Lily smoothed her red outfit with her white gloves and reclined on the sofa. After tapping over to the door to receive a tray of cocktails and tea from an unseen hand, Donna draped herself nicely over MacK in an armchair. MacK opened up the baloney and swiss and offered it round. —Good god, said Isidor, but the girls tore off a morsel each and seemed to relish them. Isidor was always concerned with decorum and this was a good thing. He knotted his tie and took out his wallet. —No no, said Donna, poll taxes are always paid on departure. Someone was sneezing up a storm in the next room: —**Hapci! HAPCI!** —There there, said a girl.

Isidor paid at the sliding window. He paid in the *coin of fun*, that commodity we all work so hard for, to jingle in our trousers.

On the street, election day seemed even more beautiful than before. Iz and MacK walked toward Lexington Avenue. They were content to be silent as trotting in front of them was a girl in pretty pink shoes. Voting together as they had was perhaps the fullest expression of their friendship through another medium—though there were the supplementary media, beer and shellfish.

## The Far East

Still there in the morning—perilous near conjunction of the cuttly underside of the thing and a big nailhead—the light came in perhaps as yesterday and MacK got up and collected a few of Izzy's books and a few of Mary-Ann's—the most powerful gods in the house. The day after Thanksgiving is a nightmare to define in city terms. A few people are allowed to sleep in, but most must work, must act like they didn't jiggle their endorphins the day before and cloud the mind with sport—they have a desperate epic journey on their hands—they've got to get to the office before *THE SHOPPING* starts. The dogs—it remained to be seen how much sleeping Iz and Mary-Ann had managed.

According to Isidor, he felt calm. Very calm. Nothing like a K.O. for the effects of armagnac—hadn't he said this for many years? —where does that leave yer Ibuprofen hah? —got to hand it to the girl.

By the time the three of them hit the street the lucky ones had made it to work—there was a bustle to East 86th but this would pale. —Just think what it's like about 50th and Fifth right now, said Izzy in his over-coat. They shuddered. —But where we gonna go today? I'm freezin' already, Isidor, said Mary-Ann, let's take a bus or somethin'. Iz agreed to take a bus to Fifth because of the wind and the Bavarian Inn.

It was only four or five avenue blocks but the 86th Street crosstown carried them from the still-quiet still unexplored Far East right into the blaring zooming semi-suburb Yorkville was becoming. The snow had left the streets mostly but it clung to awnings and roofs and threw enough of the light of a pretty winter day into the bus to lighten the feeling of doom. Izzy and Mary-Ann huddled, Iz in his overcoat-as-battle-tank posture, *thrust into the masses* at the apocalyptic hour of 10.45 am. Behind the driver sat the mother of the worst-behaved kids in New York, they're screaming, they're yelling, jumping up and down on the seats, the mother is very tired, with bags under the eyes from Hell—you could imagine what Thanksgiving had been like for her—no, you couldn't—it was probably all over the walls from cranberries, from stuffing—she had a prematurely sallow face, a face not from New York—but you could tell she thought she was going to die here, maybe today. The piercing screams and craven misbehavior of these children were annoying everyone, who had of course left their houses in the best of holiday spirits—if *that* isn't enough to make you vomit—Christmas begins today—hooray—particularly the driver, who found himself the captain of a bus that couldn't move, in traffic that was becoming monumental—his bus was *failing to live up to its only purpose*, which was to go back and forth and back and forth on 86th Street driving him insane in a few short years. They were totally bogged in front of Gimbel's, where a Saint Nicholas rang a bell, which you could hear above everything, the insidious nasty high and possibly electrically amplified note of the impending holiday, even in the bus with its stuck windows and thumping heater and the engine which might only *idle* ever again. In her desperate sallowness the young mother grabbed her son's head and twisted it around so he was looking at Gimbel's—or traffic—*he* didn't know. —Look, there's Santa, she said (the *Santa* might have formed part of a prayer for release from her agony), Santa! Wave to Santa. God *damn* if this doesn't still work, as MacK observed, and saw that Izzy saw too—*Santa* and kids' mouths drop open, their movements become drugged . . . —*Santa!* said the boy to his sister, and they suddenly began banging as hard as they could on the flabby plexiglas windows of the poor old bus, *screaming* SANTAAA! SANTAAA! HI SANTAAA!, which was an even greater violation of everyone else's civil liberties—and after

two minutes of this *f\*\*\*ing* daemonium during which the bus suffered two changes of the Lexington Avenue stop-light without being
allowed to move an inch, the driver turned in his seat and spat at the
boy: —*There's no such thing as Santa Claus*, at which the entire bus
broke into HEART-WARMING APPLAUSE.

The little boy looks away from the window, stays his hand with
which he's been banging like a bitter guy in a prison movie, in
mid-swing—looks the driver over carefully, from cap aslant
sticky-outy hair to the dirty shirt, silly badge, trouser stripe
cadged from a mailman it looks like, to the *track shoes!?* and
says—F\*\*\* you. At which the entire bus breaks into HEART-
WARMING APPLAUSE.

There is nothing that delights us more than when an employee of
the MTA gets it and gets it good. Truly: *there is nothing more delightful*.


—God damn kids. Isidor hated getting off the bus on Fifth Avenue,
even if he were going to walk down Fifth Avenue—he didn't like the
way the bus had to wait, or the way it turned, its loud signal click-
ing on the dashboard, it drove him crazy—*Goin' crazy!*
—consequently he always got off at Madison. So they stood, as
many people do, shivering and knocking their hands together in
front of the Madison Restaurant, or Soup Burg, thinking they'd only
just eaten breakfast but that one of those cups of cream of chicken
soup—small pack of saltines . . .

They had to decide as usual which avenue to walk down. —Hey,
how come we never walk down *Pak?* said Mary-Ann, folding her
shoulders about her in the cold. —*Park!?* said Izzy, *Park* is where you
go to *die*. Or get shrunk and *then* die. —Aren't you completely
crushed, chimed in MacK, and annihilated by the heaviness of those
buildings? Their tomb-like suffocating weight? What they look like
under the vapor lamps? (No response.) —Are you kidding? they
both shouted, Park Avenue is DEAD MATTER.

# A Gibson Girl

The day was museum-cold, with the reflected quiet light which pulls you into the Whitney or the Metropolitan or the Modern and lets you feel cozy about being there. (Not the *Frick*, which is surrounded by its *own weather* left over from the Scottish Enlightenment and flavored with cold tea and Frigid® brand embalming fluid). No, the museums that make you feel loved! The museums where the pictures love YOU!

Always this coat-room madness; Izzy almost always refused to give up his coat—he thought the attendants rude—he wandered the museums of New York like they were bus stations—not that the Metropolitan resembles anything else—but it is a god and must be placated—you cannot *walk by*. Isidor planned a little progressive dinner of consuming art for them (he believed in eating his enemies)—three courses of his favorite painters—they wouldn't be staying here long, but Mary-Ann always checked her coat because she liked holding the big number in her pocket while she looked at the pictures. —I'll give you a number to hold, said Izzy.

John Sloan painted the very 27 November they had just walked out of—you could almost hear the high note of Santa's bell among the strollers on his crisp day—even HI SANTAAA!, although no one was as badly behaved in 1910—only the *breakthrough* of television has made *that* kid possible. There was the same light reflected from snow secreted on the tops of awnings, and some of the roofs—men and women looked happy enough—happy even—on the street; it looked as though conversations were going on, not just when friend met friend, but that there was a *general conversation*—in which, back then, everyone in town knew they were necessarily engaged—if you were rotting in a back room, diving under the river to build a bridge, hatching an evil plot, sitting in a club behind high windows, you were engaged in the conversation, the exchange which is this our town—even Isidor couldn't avoid it—though when he walked alone he sometimes sought refuge in his own summary pronouncements—*Oh oh, crazy one!*—others heard part of the encyclopediac storm of controversies which consists in I Katz—he talks to himself.

And so do ten or twenty thousand other people in Manhattan—including a guy at the corner under the El in Sloan—his teeth are clearly visible—he's not smiling, he's quietly forming a word—there's no one listening except John Sloan maybe—the word may be SHADDAP—he's talking to himself—*you've got to.* It would be wrong to say Sloan's street looked any friendlier, any more open than it does today (it was Murray Street, near City Hall—oh maybe there were a few more people living around there then—they were only just getting used to the idea that they could fill up Manhattan with masonry—*go ahead, pave and pave and pave me boys, you won't hurt me!*—you *can't* hurt me—just getting the idea that outer space loomed directly above them, uptown) for New York is an open and friendly place. If there were anything different about John Sloan's people it was merely that they had a little more time on their hands—not much—but after the job they'd come out on the street, and the marketing (not the way *you* mean) and the odd drink would be the evening—they'd not to rush back to their apartments to speak on the telephone or watch television or work some more—work was *over*, this was *night*.

—That's the way to live, on Murray Street, said Isidor, who had already collected a ton of not so much Newyorkiana, visual, ephemeral, fictional, intangible, as it was a complicated series of references showing actually and exactly HOW TO LIVE in New York—how other people did it successfully—people of all sorts. Not just Sloan's people who were *extremely tired*, but menus from restaurants long gone, timetables for Fifth Avenue buses in 1928, in 1955—pictures of people in the subway, the skyscraper lithograph in Iz's small living-room uptown, which was blocky, but *examined* the thing, you could see, from the favorite angle of the guy who drew it.

Izzy's collection was his legend to the New York he was building, decision by decision, to live in. MacK liked the hats and Mary-Ann the light reaching out from bar and shop—it made you want to get down to Murray Street right away, *that* Murray Street. Seemingly without having to move their eyes from the canvas across the wall of the museum, the velvet rope, the ticking hydrometer maintaining life in Art's veins like Lenin in his box of jelly, across the guard's stoically uninterested midriff, they went from Murray Street uptown maybe to the fights with George Bellows. Iz stood in front of it a long time, his lips bulging ever so slightly, their need of cigar—smoke circled around the fight, under light much stronger than the bulb at home—Iz contemplated the sweating indoor night of sixty years before for what seemed an hour—the black air above the ring, black as the night building in the lithograph at home—everyone else in the gallery was quieted by the power of Isidor's concentration—he wasn't looking at the painting but was, obviously, *in* it.

### THE CITY SPEAKS:
### OF COURSE WE WILL GIVE YOU ROOM
### FOR YOUR EPIPHANY
### —IF YOU'RE REALLY HAVING ONE

Who knows what correct atmospheres Izzy was storing up; what he could apply to these neighborhoods when he was next there or what mustard-plaster of understanding he could stick to the next prize-fight he attended. —See honey, he suddenly said, taking Mary-Ann's arm, see how that guy is leading? Look at the power in that rotation, how the guy's arm doesn't extend all the way, he's throwing a strong punch there honey, but he's reserving a lot of power in his upper arm still, see? Mary-Ann looked at the fight, through the smoky light of the drawing and through the imaginary cigar smoke with which Izzy had now filled the gallery. —Did ya bring me in heah to show me how to hit? she said. Because I know how to hit ya. Isidor expected his laugh to hurt him—the armagnac—but it did not, thanks to the K.O. of his H.O.—a brilliant discovery—must be the adrenaline, he thought. —Thought you could pick up a few tips, honey, that's all. —Why I oughta . . . —Honey, honey.

Today's museum food was a tiny, cold Thanksgiving in a sandwich, without Badedas, without wine, without armagnac, without the stimulant of debate even, bloated and hung over as everyone in the Metropolitan Museum of Art was. Without the knowledge of the quietly teeming holiday teasing the edges of Manhattan, rolling the city in the light proper to the coming month. Too, 'Mr Ardent' wasn't there. Like all museum food this had a patina to its leading edges, tasted first of oven, then corrugated board, then polyvinyl chloride, smelt of Windex and the warm, coffee-laced shit of slow-thinking businessmen all at the same time. —If you needed *another reason for never leaving your apartment*, said Isidor, so many people come to this great museum that they have to *kill* you so you won't come back. That will be $17.54 apiece. MacK was then all for leaving; Fifth Avenue had ultimately a way of creeping in and *getting* him, even if he were enjoying himself—in other words it suddenly made him feel he was at the very least an entire avenue away from a bar. He usually exited by way of the armory, where his opposition to epic (or what Izzy had long contended was an opposition to it and a perverse will *not* to understand the way the world worked) was temporarily expressed in his love of romance; lots of huge axes to chop heads with and plenty of ornamented helmets to roll them in—this was one part of the museum in which it was harder to find a connection to life outside, on Fifth Avenue—but maybe not. Often there are Japanese tourists in the armory *laughing* at the samurai armor of heavy wicker: why? Izzy said MacK could visit the armory if he wanted to, but that he was going briefly back upstairs (Mary-Ann had gone to Flanders for half an hour). Iz wanted to look at his girls, as he called them—MacK went with him.

Having the same taste in turn-of-the-century girls they both liked spending time in the marriageable company of Charles Dana Gibson's women, whenever they were available—their chestnut hair upswept, their sleeves, collars, hats—their penetratingly intelligent and worldly eyes. —But there is no Gibson Girl today, said Iz. —The guy's a mere illustrator, piped up one of the guards. —Sez you, said Izzy—there's only a few guys allowed to use a pen around here? Rembrandt, Dürer, that's it? Walk down the street, man, take a look.

But there they were in front of a Sargent—a black-haired society bride with the same commanding expression, a pure warm white skin, skin which warmed the pale rose of her dress. —Skin of the rich, said Isidor, you get it from a bottle these days. They'd visited her often enough that MacK hadn't noticed how like Mary-Ann she was (obviously this woman never used the word DON'TCHA—although if it had been invented, why not, this woman could have done *anything*)—and he felt jealous—Izzy had taken a step into one of his old New Yorks—with Mary-Ann, into her and it—he could live in the dark-haired pale-skinned world. Perhaps it sent him out of himself and into Fifth Avenue twilight in 1900—heavy on carpets, floor clocks, carriages passing outside? —What do you think it was like to be in her company? mumbled MacK. Imagine her sweet voice. —Who are you, said Isidor loudly, Edith F***ing Wharton? But these women suggested an honesty in the *conversation of the city*, which was being had more directly then—or so they liked to think. Looking at its boiled front you might think the Metropolitan only a gateway to various heartbreaks of the past, crunched-up stuff from people who gave up, were schmecked, killed—a huge *pain in the ass*—but for Isidor here there were entranceways to the city and his love for it; to Mary-Ann and her love. So was she also part of his collection, part of the clues to New York he was always gathering, filling the shop and their tiny apartment with? Isidor and Mary-Ann fit their little place well—she represented a number of decades, was the women of New York, in the low light of their place in the evenings. —Pretty good-looking broad, huh, said Isidor, as he always did. ——In thinking about the past, said MacK, it's important to decide how noisy it was.

# The Grim Reaper

——How was Flanders, said Iz to Mary-Ann, in the sun on the big steps. ——A little cloudy today, Isidor. The warmth of the afternoon was hard to credit but there was also the spiritual warmth of the chestnut vendors and the warmth of FEAR, fear they might be sucked down Fifth toward 59th and below where the first of twenty-eight days of incredible inhumanity, of reckless and pathetic acquisition, little people being squashed by BIG PEOPLE with more expensive shoes, dirty and tired-looking women weeping silently in front of Gristede's, of Whelan Drug, having lost heart even to hold their hands out——in short, Christmas®——had just begun. ——Times Square, said Isidor, will be just about going about its business today——you can't buy anything there except souvenir belts, fake IDs and condoms that taste like *strawberry shortcake*——you believe that? I saw that in a window. ——You can dump ya god damn kids off to go to the *movies* ya know Isidor, said Mary-Ann. ——Ahh, that's nothin'.

It seemed a reasonable goal.

Assuming you believe in these antiheroes.

The ring had been gnawing at Izzy's subconscious and he took it into his head to visit the bar at Jack Dempsey's. What you want on a semi-holiday: you want something old, beat-up, you want anonymity, you want something stupid, yes you do, to *hide behind*. Dempsey's no longer really smelled of the 1940s but there might have been a slight odor of the city in 1955 or even 1960——something about the tablecloths, the fans, the glasses of ice water?——when Izzy's mother would bring him into town on the bus and walk, painfully disapprovingly, to Herald Square and back to Port-of-Authority, having purchased *one thing*, her rule——a slip, a bird cage,

173

a door mat . . . But in front of the Mutual of New York building Izzy had an attack of defensiveness. —I can't take him to Dempsey's, he said to Mary-Ann as if MacK were not there. Not the Grim Reaper. —Oh Isidor that's so silly, said Mary-Ann, who always leaned forward when in motion, like Miss Clavell, whom she also resembled—but that was only a Catholic connection in MacK's mind maybe? MacK was wounded. —Wait a minute, he said, is Jack Dempsey's so important a spot in your solar system? Surely it is robust? Surely ONE VISIT by me in your *color guard*, cried out the *Reaper* now in the middle of Broadway, the 8 x 10 glossies and clippings and cartoons all nostalgic for the ring and JACK and RUNYON and LARDNER and LIEBLING, surely a MINUTE'S DRINKING THERE, A SEVEN-OUNCE SCHAEFER, WILL NOT CLOSE JACK DEMPSEY'S FOR ALL TIME!?

Isidor had smelled a rat, which if proven to exist had the alarming possibility of robbing him of all he held dear—the past New York, the city of *ago* which he was a-building in his mind—tunneling through New York as if it were a giant cheese—finding his way between only things he admits into *his* New York. *Exempli gratia* technically Isidor wasn't walking, *didn't exist*, once he left, say, the New York Public Library until he arrived at the Wilbur Sisters—because there was nothing he passed going up Fifth to 47th and then over to Madison, which COUNTED . . .

(MacK did this too—his search for the 1940s, the vanished radio world, the smell of hot vacuum tubes, dust on shellac pressings—he discovered a route from the RCA Building to Harvey Radio and then on to several musty theatrical sound houses, and a recording studio on West 47th where a little old guy in a cardigan and brogues was happy to talk to him and show him his collection of microphones, some of which were RCA 77s and GE velocity mikes which he was *still using*—and must, MacK thought, have the *spit* of very famous people in them—the place began as a CBS studio during the war and as it had their good engineering was sold on after—to him, Mr Sweater, as if he was a cat that lived in

174

the joint—guy still makes a living recording *voice only*—Peace Corps promotional programs—Father Nodolny—all the stuff that gets wiped or goes in the trash can in all the radio stations of America, MacK thought.)

. . . But the *rat*—Isidor shifted from one foot to the other and looked MacK up and down, disdainfully, disgustedly, even fearfully—to Isidor MacK had acquired a hooded cloak, a scythe, his hands sloughing flesh . . . —He killed Lundy's, honey, he *killed Lundy's*, said Isidor, suddenly very resistant. There was some humor buried under that—somewhere. A little. But positively father and husband-like: grim. —Aw, he did not, said Mary-Ann, the place was gonna go anyways—ya said so *yaself* after ya had the chowda. But Izzy had begun to notice whenever he came upon a bar, a restaurant, a *space*—for that's what these were, atmospheres which fit into his schema—if he took *MacK* there, within a few months, or even weeks, the place closed, forever. Iz's theory about it was growing—in his mind the visitation of MacK had closed or was going to close the Bavarian Inn, the Dublin House, the Madison Bar, Keene's Chop House, Sweet's, the Gloucester House, Bruno's Pen and Pencil, McSorley's, Gage & Tollner (the evil *influenza* of MacK reaching across the East River), Lundy's, and who knows, even Lindy's; Ratner's, the Gold Lion, the Old Town Bar, Bill's Gay Nineties, the Lambs Club, the White Horse, the Juniper, the Oak Bar at the Plaza, The Oyster Restaurant and Bar, Yonah Schimmel and now Jack Dempsey's itself. Iz's idea of how and why this was happening was *racial*: he persisted in thinking MacK a bringer of a wave of *westerners* to the city—not that MacK worked on Pine Street—but Izzy felt this huge *influx*, wasps, WASPS who knew nothing and would never know nothing about Manhattan. Visiting the ancient eddies of tap room culture they initially revel in them, but on the second or third visit find them dirty; they begin 'upgrading' each neighborhood so as to force something old and not American, as it's defined in California or Kansas, or in the midwest, OUT. But Iz also thought the problem could be what he thought of as MacK's *pathological affability*, an odd combination of ease and demur, morality and carnival, sourness and generosity, which directly came into contact with the waves of feeling, the fights internal and external, the New York sounds embedded in the plaster and wood of the walls of these altars and temples of his—Iz believed in those chaps who show up with lots of dish mikes, flood lamps, wire recorders and bowls of mercury at haunted houses, and extract the wailing emotional history of the building groaning from the wall. —I'm half French, said MacK. —Oh *yeah*, said Isidor. Very French guy.

At the mention of the Lundy Brothers they'd all twitched, a tinily involuntary turning toward Brooklyn—Isidor saw the whole thing, the vaulted ceilings, exotica of the twenties—the stolid, heavily letterpressed menu of unadorned oysters, pan-roasted fish; the millions of small paper cups of tartare sauce, the ice water which smelled of bread, vice versa—vanilla ice cream in a dish—but most of all that Lundy's was obviously a farm, not a fish farm, a fish *waiter* farm, the nursery of the race of New York fish restaurant waiters—bred 'em up here from sprats and sent them in tank trucks of brackish water to Sweet's, the Oyster, Paddy's, Gage's—also a big demand for them in Hoboken—a steamy sheen to their skins after some years, their eyes begin to stare, and are glaucous, they work their mouths, looking for oxygen?—their constant and usual phrases, *What'll it be?—I'll haveta check—No idea, Bud.*

—We can't take him to Dempsey's, said Iz, it'll go OUT OF BUSINESS. —*Isidor*, even supposing it might, said Mary-Ann, what do you cayah? How's it worth saving—witout da *champ*—da champ *in poison!* Isidor gave her a very long look. For here was the voice of a true champeen.

—You may have a point, said Isidor at long last starting across the street—but don't pull anything funny. Don't order stuff they don't have—get a beer or a martini or a highball—*What else would I order?* said MacK—and leave it at that. *You too,* he said warningly to Mary-Ann—if you want wine, ask for '*a wine*', not a glass of Bordeaux. You got me? —Yes Sir.

And they went south and west into Dempsey's, where the huge and ancient maître d' looked at them, this is *Jack Dempsey's,* mind you—1977 AD—like they were so much *air* or popcorn smell blown in from the Square—and followed their slightly unassured progress to the bar with the look of a guy who was going to treat them as *tourists,* or *complete* idiots, or *baboons*—this always drove Isidor crazy—being treated badly as a *tourist*—not badly as a *resident.*

# I Never *Wuz* a Grand Duke

The bartender looked like a barber. Didn't say anything either. —It's creepy—surrounded by people who don't know a thing and this guy treats you like some interloper or hick, said Izzy, remembering the protests of the fellow who'd suddenly pulled in front of him in a new BMW on the *sidewalk* on Second Avenue—Iz tapped the guy's tail-light with his by now well-broken-in brogue—the slick fellow leapt out of the car—wild-eyed with the fear of being in NEW YORK CITY—*I'm not some naïf from Ohio—you know—that you can just do things to!* —But you are, said Isidor, pointing to the license plate—you are from Ohio. I think you *are* someone I can do things to. Guy drove away which was too bad, Iz needed a fight that day.

At the bar. Isidor nervous in Dempsey's. A look between MacK and Mary-Ann. —Gimme a slug a whiskey, said MacK. —Let me have a *pousse-café, s'il vous plait,* said Mary-Ann, demurely outlining the obscenely appropriate glass with her curvy hands—to wind Isidor up. —What!? he yelled, turning red, I'm afraid I *must* intercede for my friends, they're INSANE—which was good Iz talk but not a word you slung around in Jack Dempsey's; for what place stated The Old Mental Capital more certainly? Guy still looking at Iz—You people have a problem? —*No,* absolutely, said Izzy, *flushing* with embarrassment. —*Problem here, Don?* —*I dunno . . .*

How often do you see a red Isidor?

—My *friend* and I will have a martini. Very dry, straight up, olive. My *other* friend will have——? A wine please, said Mary-Ann, twinkling, piercing the brow of this guy who looked like a fisherman now. Not a bad-looking gal you thought he thought—oughta show her the wine list, what's she doin' with these toids?

Let's admit it, the wine list was

## You want Red? Want White?

—How do you get salt-and-sun skin like that, said Isidor, as the guy bent, mixing, the short back of his little jacket of the past riding up, the clip-on suspenders—in Times Square? —Maybe it's workin' with oysters that does it, said Mary-Ann. Isidor was beginning to feel he could, or should, cultivate any bartender, all the bartenders of Manhattan, for that is what you have to do, if especially you are too self-respecting to get shrunk. *Some days you just want to hug every bartender in New York.* But he began to get uneasy, looking at *this* guy, imperturbable, immutable—he sent out an Ozymandian challenge to everyone in the place, or specially them maybe—it dawned on Izzy that the guy was unreachable—he wasn't a sour Manhattan bartender, but a sour *New York* bartender, who came in every day from an outer borough, or maybe beyond, some place that wasn't even in *town*—just to do *this*—no sense of commitment to Manhattan, and if that is what you lack how can you pour a good bottle of beer or make a good martini? The beer will be sloppy, with foam on the sides (though not in the way you might get a foamy beer downtown or in a McAnn's—which historical sloppiness would be OK), it won't be in the right glass—the martini will taste of water—it won't necessarily be watery but it will *taste* of water—the guy'll *saunter* over and refill it from the shaker—like this is supposed to be classy—even though the ice has ruined what's left in there . . . Sling your hook, buddy.

—Ach! spat Isidor suddenly, when I'm Mayor there's going to be a law, you have to live in Manhattan in order to tend bar. I am going to license them like DOGS. One eyebrow must have gone up 3mm on Ramses over there—but truthfully—he could have posed for the Sour New York Bartender postcard had someone been pervert enough to issue one—but even in New York there wasn't—but *if there had*, you could sell a lot of 'em. Isidor felt betrayed here in Jack Dempsey's—he had always thought of it as truly suiting his purposes, a way-station for perambulating the West 40s *of* the Forties, and Fifties—granted in a stupid way—but he had already pierced its supposed patina, who cared if they had a Dumont television over the bar—it was a FRONT for a plain Times Square cynicism Isidor didn't like—it was a souvenir shop—they might as well have been selling falafel? *Falafel?*—he could imagine Ramses saying it. If a place isn't going to be real, it ought to be genuine, or at least nice.


Traffic went by in a perfectly ordinary fashion—you'd never have known Thanksgiving was the day before, that the eclipse and apocalypse of good feeling had begun. There was plastic holly and mistletoe over the bar but it had been there many years. Izzy liked the idea the mistletoe might have been hanging here in 1950. Light came into Dempsey's in an interesting way—the large windows on Eighth Avenue were slightly tinted (the Fifties) and the bar area was hung with venetian blinds. The light came in slightly cleansed and perfectly horizontal—Iz raised his glass and looked through the gin and around the corner of the olive; decided that the drink could actually turn light silver, could add to its strength—made light (and surely this was real light? passing through Dempseian filters) glow with the insistent chilliness of TV in the old days—that perhaps the qualities of light on all the TVs in all the old bars came flowing through gin—boxing, *Requiem for a Heavyweight*, Kennedy vs. Nixon, Walter Cronkite . . . Light from the past, which perhaps you could make in the alembic of your drink—you didn't have to go sit in *Dempsey's*.

But they drank these drinks and everything was unremarkable as pie. Ramses received their dough, including a shaved version of the usual Isidorean tip, as Pharaoh would have noticed you pissing in the Nile. He turned away immediately and his starched jacket stated he was positive he'd never see one of them again. MacK's shadow, though hardly skeletally handling a scythe or anything curved except his own slouch . . . perhaps fell across the façade as they left?

Isidor was disgusted to find a crowd gathered around a Santa on the corner of 49th. But then delighted to see *Santa was in chains* and the crowd enjoying it too! This was a real bonus—the day after Thanksgiving and New York was already giving it to Santa. But then depressed again to find it was a protest—the *I.L.G.W.U.*, 'Santa of the Sweat Shops'. As they walked east Iz fondly remembered the Hunchback of Notre Dame on his little turntable of humilia-tion—had to admit Santa looked awfully good in such a pose—it set him up emotionally for weeks. EXEUNT MIDTOWN OMNES, after Santa is led away.

## What Is To Be Done?

The bus up Madison. Packed. Some people had already had enough of the most enraging day of the year. As they got into the upper 60s and antiques began to appear, MacK saw a shop in which he had complained bitterly to a girl that she was buying a *LALIQUE* box. He was unused to spending money at that time and didn't know anyone who bought *LALIQUE*, therefore he was only a trainee New Yorker—he's lucky they let him stay—they haven't made it very easy for him. Has run up quite a bar tab though, so that'll see him through. Her question, 'What's wrong with *LALIQUE*?' served only to emphasize the Grand Canyon of culture which separated them (MacK firmly staying on the north rim). It wasn't *LALIQUE* at all he objected to—not knowing what it is and still not—but the idea that he might, or ought to know what it is, and worse the idea that he might or ought to feel at home in this expensive shop and with the idea of buying something merely for the pleasure of buying it (not even that of owning it) (it was hideous)—and the idea she might take it home and sadly put it somewhere on her sad family's very clean shelves (they were constantly locking each other up in drying-out clinics and even mental hospitals)—the idea that the poor ugly little $400 box wouldn't stand the ghost of a chance of making anyone happy in her climate-controlled clinicky family.

Could have said to Isidor, *I was once in that shop with her*, but it was already past and it wasn't much of a story: *Once we argued there*. Though a story you seldom forget. Whereas some men will wander the streets looking up at a window here and there, or fondly remembering a tryst in the rest room of a petit resto, even feeling nostalgia for a caress gained in a taxi at a particular corner (let us hear it for 34th and Second. Woo!), MacK's romantic map consisted in the pin points of fights and breakings-off. He'd been summarized *a cold-heart* at 42nd and Fifth (frighteningly central and public) and tremblingly, brimmingly 'let go', for *having different concerns,* all the way up Second, in the 80s, on a block that seemed to have been cleared by the police for her purpose—he couldn't recall why there—oh *immature*, to be sure, but couldn't remember what they were doing up there—fighting, surely.


This bus was full of people who had the fear—they'd seen enough—but it didn't smell like Christmas yet, that mixture of boughs in the open air, snow coming, your coat, sprayed by the women who've no idea who you or they are, who spray you, in department stores, vacantly, with perfume; and soup, alcohol, cigarettes. Valium and Prozac may have smells. Everyone seemed very *vertical* so it was just the usual Friday afternoon skanks—with a few people who'd braved the initial shopping. Everyone up and down in black and grey and dark blue—some of the uptown ladies in dark brown but looking a little self-conscious about it. A hat or two and small fussy brassy brooches. Isidor stood on the rear steps, one step down into the well, having got Mary-Ann a seat, and feeling squeezed.

A tall boring-looking guy, a sort of Mr Reasonable, who looks like he lived around 84th and Madison, one of those kind of joints, he starts *staring* down at Isidor in the well. Not exactly moving toward him as though he has to get out . . . The bus stops, someone gets on at the front, it moves on. The guy's glasses and *hat* strongly suggest that waspie pre-eminence: *I'm a real New Yorker, not you, blah blah blah*—a strange look which looks outer-American in New York (or boring, like the bus is suddenly full of bankers or people who went to *YALE*), totally stuffy Manhattanite if you hit him on the head, put him in a sack and dumped him out in New Jersey or Arizona—which would be a good idea—he'd f***ing *FREAK OUT* but would then start running the local Chamber of Commerce—he keeps staring down at Izzy who has to keep looking away, the guy is so silly-looking—that body, that mien.

—*Excuse me*, the guy says very pointedly, almost theatrically, *I don't think it is a very good idea of yours to stand in front of the door where people will have to exit.* Says this to *Isidor Katz*. Mary-Ann flinches in her seat and MacK stops listening to the guy going on next to him about a work thing—amazing how all these conversations sound the same, it could be Shelby Stein and the guy from Programming, on bus, subway, at lunch, in elevators—*In any case I think Bob should look the figures over before we send them out to the coast*—who has not said this? What the Hell is it about? Everyone *already* work for the same company? But ingeniously Iz immediately matches the guy's volume and tone: —That so? It happens that it's not my intention to block the door, *Sir*—*I'm* prepared to move out of the way at any moment. For your information I am standing here because the bus is very crowded, you notice that at all? I got on this bus at Madison and 48th. I do not know where you got on, but it was certainly after that; *ergo*, I do not believe there is room for

*YOU* and your prissy hat [someone laughed] on this bus and if you're so f***ing [the guy blanches—he knows he's in unfamiliar jungle now if he didn't before—he's never even seen a *movie* with that word in it] concerned about civic proprieties then you, *YOU*, *Sir*, ought to have refrained from getting on this bus, *THAT* would have been the action of a man of *principle*, you could have waited for the next bus and the next and yes the next—but excuse me, you're probably an extremely important person who simply must, *MUST* get uptown—*on the bus!* [General laughter.] *Sir*, I don't propose to interfere with any person's entering or leaving this bus, *or* with their civil liberties [the bus slows as it approaches 79th], unlike yourself, you proprietorial J Press cock-sucking eugenic skunk. [A quite elderly lady who seems to be enjoying what Iz's saying comes over to him in his well—the bus halts and the door opens—Mary-Ann and MacK move up with some others to disembark.] —Now watch me, says Isidor, see what I do, I'm going to *help* these people off the bus—I immediately relinquish my place on the step and I *help them off* as a truly civilized person might do, as he *MUST* do, as he *is doing*, ass hole [he reaches out to the old lady]—May I help you, ma'am? —Oh, thank you, very much, she says, looking around at the others as though she had suddenly found herself on television. —I don't make *summary judgements* about people, they're all my brothers and sisters, let me give you a hand [to a large lady with packages] here, you see? I'm *not* going to stand for your insinuations and I'm *not* going to listen to you run down the people of this city and this nation, says Isidor [climbing down on to the street now, to the guy, whose expression is one of the grimmest imaginable],

## SOCIALISM FOREVER!

shouts Isidor—the doors close and the bus goes on up the avenue, to the strains of the 'Internationale' and not 'Silver Bells' or maybe both if you have the stomach for that kind of imaginary segue—Izzy didn't even need to shake his fist at the bus retreating with the white guy in it—he knew that was a cliché but it was one he loved—and he was pretty good at it too.

Mary-Ann's eyes were bright with admiration for Isidor. The three stood on the sidewalk in contemplation of the resolution of the drama—her cheeks were red in the cold. What a grand girl she was: she'd taken Izzy's performance as gallantry; what's lacking in town. MacK saw she cared deeply for Isidor, and, always grateful for insight, came over a little teary, being hungover. Isidor half-turned to them, but kept an eye on the bus till it was out of sight; then allowed himself only a *You believe that guy?* Mary-Ann took his hand and he walked several blocks with her this wise until coming to himself and becoming annoyed and embarrassed put her hand in her coat for her. —I always knew something like that would happen, he said to MacK, once I moved to the *East Side.* He knew no one in Yorkville—except John, who was *fired.*

# The Day After Thanksgiving Day

MacK associated female warmth with six o'clock, when women dress for the evening, and thought of a rainy day when he watched Rosenthal getting ready for a dinner they had been invited to on the West Side, where—he thought—he would be able to show off this classy dame for the first time in a gracious old apartment with table lamps and sofas (so rather unlike Rosenthal's tea-stained futon and deckchair phone booth in SoHo)—real book-lined city living as he endorsed it—and Rosenthal was brushing her hair, putting on a wool dress; her glasses, the warmth of her skin and eyes, all filled MacK with a feeling of arrival—acceptance—of course these book-owning lamp-burning dickheads didn't *like* Rosenthal at the party—she did keep talking about her spastic colon—but so what? —MacK had never been so warmed than during her dressing, watching her attention to small things. He compared Tumbleson's approach to her garments and herself unfavorably: there were two aspects of it he could not accept. First, Tumbleson was a Debbie. MacK had grown up on a street where everyone was named either Mark or Debbie—even the parents; *Debbie* was a name he early applied to the bright, conversational, yet fundamentally unsympathetic women—built with white bread—of Episcopal America—underneath which there is such a coldness and such a deadness of intellect, and such a willingness to be derailed confused and beguiled, that MacK sometimes thought the only place for them all was Washington DC.

Let us speak plainly. Talking about the Christians and the other Devil-may-care people of our country, completely engulfed by the nation's television imago, who have no culture, who still mentally wear the twinset and pearls of a classical *evil girlfriend*, pleasantly steely and steely pleasant—*one says this through clenched teeth*—people who haven't a thought in the head and don't need to, because if you have a career these days you don't have to think—this is why parties *suck*—the Debbies don't let go. MacK shuddered to think how Tumbleson was acting now she'd found out about Rosenthal—but in contrast to Rosenthal's warmth, evinced in her choice of fabrics, her way of moving and dressing, there were two aspects of cold Tumbleson, one attitude which MacK felt she always used against him, a breezy ease and beauty, especially in the summer. Tumbleson made a point of sleeping past the alarm, even unto 8.45, the point of causing MacK to panic—and then *slipping* out of bed, *slipping* out of her nightgown, *slipping* on a cotton dress, *slipping* into her shoes and *slipping* out the door, having paused at the mirror only to *slip* on her lipstick with a stroke and to shake her hair into its lovely place. *MacK*, who after all had ablutions, to take up half the morning, felt *diseased* compared to this. But there was a more straitened, rigorous Tumbleson, who was raised to embrace, who did embrace, the goal posts and waspie altars, who though she expressed herself happy with MacK was constantly on the lookout at the Yale Club for someone with a legal or Pine Street bulge—a Tumbleson who wore imaginary sweater and pearls under her import shop trousers and her Charlie perfume; a marble girl who professed to be having a good time while she had already determined that the grim future was only the grim family (like hers), a Tumbleson who was, in short, a *miserable f\*\*\*er*, who *would* have been at home among the marketers and marketeers, who seemed to have forgotten most of what she learned (having in fact treated her college like high school, floating across a sea of Schlitz on a raft of 'Marlboro' men)—the people offer as high proof of her coldness Tumbleson's bedtime dramas of chastisement—which MacK had been at first forced to administer, get used to, and to which he was now highly and unfairly addicted—clearly the habit of someone who was having a good time before she stopped smoking and drinking and f\*\*\*ing and would finally at the age of—twenty-eight?—grimly go in search of money, a Debbie of the first water although Debbie was not her name.

The long-suffering tobacconist *Seligman* had had to endure her interrogations at Christmas and on MacK's birthday—*What's the difference between this blend and that one?*—of course he set himself up for this, early—making the fatal mistake of everyone who chooses a business involving many many tiny things and objects and their collision with people who *want* but can't understand them—the madness and doom of stationers and hardware men—but told MacK he couldn't bear to have her in the shop again. —*I felt dizzy, Mr MacKenzie; I couldn't play chess for the rest of the day. I don't like that woman, I'll be honest. Smoke judiciously, Sir.* —I'll be honest too, said MacK, and he had gone out into the snow to again ponder the Rosenthal/Tumbleson jumble.

# Plaza Garibaldi

If you would only allow a sketch of the look of 75th and Second at six o'clock on the evening of the day after Thanksgiving—we don't often get the big vistas in town—so we notice what to others might seem minutiae—the exact color of the bite of sky between one building and the next, the specific quality of dirty ice that makes you slip and fall on your ass on Murray Hill between 36th and 37th and Madison on February 14th 1977 . . . Thank you. The block in which the *Plaza Garibaldi* sat was in one of the neighborhoods wherein dwelt, as MacK thought, many of those who are *unsure* of New York—they may not be staying long—okay!—thanks for coming. There was a peculiar air of REASSURANCE about many of the businesses here, including a comedy club—well, people need to laugh—but they were also being reassured, Isidor said, that they needn't venture into DANGEROUS MIDTOWN for entertainment. The delicatessens have a sterile, foreign quality—the pastrami has no smell—do you get it?—the pastrami has NO SMELL—for people who think they *ought* to like pastrami since they now live in New York—in timid slices out of vacuum 'paks' from the supermarkets of suburb—*Hi, ho, the deli-o, the pastrami has no smell.*

As if to underline the tentative natures of the inhabitants of Second Avenue between 70th and 90th Streets, MacK recalled—in walking across 79th with Mary-Ann and Izzy—the sudden appearance and disappearance here of a girl he'd met on one of his forays out into that god damn country. She had taken a job at ABC—yeah, yeah—and was completely out of her depth—flipping out would be an understatement—could only make herself walk from the apartment she'd rented to the job and back. She began to phone MacK constantly—he didn't know what to do—till one afternoon she invited him over to meet some of her *relatives*, who were to indulge in one of the great nightmares of life in the metropolitan area—*driving a sofa into the city on top of their car*—the poor f***ing bastards. The Hellishness was short-lived—her uncle was quite a parker!—they adjourned for the chef's-salad-and-carafe-of-white-wine in—again—one of these places. A *nautical* motif, with nets, floats, rope, which—technically—is not allowed in New York. The aunt, who'd seemed real, became voluble, then boldly, demonstratively drunk. She disappeared into the ladies and it was full two hours later that the uncle and the proprietor pulled her out into the street by her feet. —*It's just—everything's so—*, she said over and *over* again—of course who has not thought this?—and the unhappy ABC-girl—could have told her—disappeared from New York almost as fast as had the kind, interloping station-wagon—the aunt's legs kicking out of the window—toward the George Washington Bridge.

Second Avenue looked just about right for a dinner between friends on this year's very cold vision of the day after Thanksgiving. —Turkey mole? said MacK. —Forgetaboudit, said Iz in his finest put-on Bensonhurst. —Bet you five bucks.

A small amount of rich grey light left in the sky, and four lamps over the façade of the Plaza Garibaldi. Chilly, but—and perhaps this was the holiday again—the three approached the front door with a warmth—of expectation?—certainly Isidor was fresh from his triumph over Mr Reasonable and was gasping for a margarita—his current favorite drink in his current favorite restaurant. So as Pedro the maître d' always said in taking your coat—*Chili today, hot tamale*, which MacK could not believe, that a person from Mexico thought that was funny.

Rosenthal had just arrived.

Once inside there was always a brief flurry of absurdity, plastic plants and gold and green spotlights, which resolved itself—once Pedro had waddled away under the mound of your wool—into something slightly less hideous but which became pleasant when you got loaded.

GREAT!

The always (to be) uncomfortable beady encounter between Isidor and Rosenthal—who could nonetheless get along for an hour or two, although during a two-hour dinner Izzy's head of steam sometimes built so that by dessert Rosenthal almost had to flee. But tonight the little god of Thanksgiving, Spencer Tracy, blessed the four and brought them together maybe.

—How ya doin? —I'm fine, Isidor, how are YOU? (A slight kindergarten note in this—*And what's YOUR name?* —made MacK sweat a little—but things were to be OK. —Hi, Mary-Ann. Kiss.

—Your glasses look very Protestant tonight, said MacK to Rosenthal, almost Episcopalian. MacK loved Rosenthal's holiday look. Her cheeks were red from the walk to the Far East from the Lex, a long ride from SoHo. There was a little tension as the waiter came over—the usual tension before Isidor discovered what every-one was going to drink, *i.e.* that they *were*. He offered Rosenthal a gin and tonic, staccato fashion; Rosenthal was in one of her millet phases—it has to be said, even though you could point to the Rosenthal of TODAY who partakes of meat and bourbon and has no spastic colon. She replied that she did not like the *taste of alcohol*, at which Iz properly erupted—of course she did, she must, who didn't, and even if she did not, *that was not the point* of alcohol whatsoever.

—Don't you live in New York? he asked—this is your *medicine*; it may be bitter but you must have it, and shall be the better for it. The Isidorean pharos was open, the full candlepower of its arcs trained on poor Rosenthal; so early in the evening. MacK was afraid Izzy had already classed her as a bean-eater. —*No,* said Rosenthal, standing up for herself in a way MacK liked, for who dared, though he too found her resistance to drink baffling—I don't need alcohol to constantly readjust, and sour, my view of life. —*Yes you do*, said Isidor—don't you see how absurd that argument is? You're saying, *Life is good—everything is pretty much OK*. —No! said Rosenthal, hurt by this truth. —Yes you are, said Izzy—life's good and there aren't so many problems with the world, not any you can't address—that's what you're saying. With a clear head you can survive life, its vicissitudes, control it, conquer it, live it, love it—right? —Well, said Rosenthal. —That is so *f\*\*\*ed up*, said Isidor, it's almost beyond me to address it; your point of view denies the existence of crime, corruption, greed, jealousy, poverty,

ignorance, religion, impotence, Nixon, the IRT, insurmountable obsta-
cles, I don't *know* . . . ——How the f*** did you even GET here tonight?
said Iz, this city, in case you didn't know, contains all our moral history
as a nation and living in it constitutes a necessary embrace of our
achievements and failures——what did you *walk past*, may I ask? ALL
THE LOVELY PROBLEMS, said Isidor, that evolved with us, that
EVOLUTION, and nothing else, brought up *with* and *for* us, to suck
us down the drain as soon as it becomes necessary. Don't you see this
means, on a human level, as one human being to another, that I CAN
NEVER TRUST YOU? That I can't *bother* with you since you don't
see what is all around you? ——*Whoa!* said Rosenthal——who had once
spent a *flanneled year in Oregon*——gimme a gin and tonic! She has
comic timing, beamed MacK. The lighthouse shut down, or at least
the foghorn; Isidor was satisfied but watchful like a cat.

They didn't trust each other one bit, even and especially after
that——Izzy realized she had merely *knuckled under*, which pissed him
off. But though he was usually on his guard against the tackier
blandishments of that decade, Isidor warmed under the twinkling
lights in the fake trees by the fake fountain in the fake Plaza
Garibaldi.

## Not Love Just Yet

Rosenthal's reasons for hanging out with MacK remain obscure.
She was intrigued by his working above 14th Street——although she
est née in the suburbs (*dynamite high school French*, MacK thought,
though girls shouting *Crassan, Crassan!* in Bonté could impress him)
she had spent so many years downtown that someone who had regular paid employment was *rara avis*. Rosenthal moved into SoHo
when it was merely a place, practically before it had *gouache*. MacK
and his triangle (meaning the present three points, implying nothing) were odd, to her, and the triangle, especially Izzy-at-the-apex,
thought Rosenthal must be mad to live in that little place——if you

lived uptown you were drowning in boredom and all its excrements but at least you had room. But to MacK, spending time with Rosenthal down there was impossibly romantic (though this has now been commercially catechized FOR you, it may be rehearsed): the little shops, the ginkgo trees, street corners and cobbled streets in the rain, bookstores where they didn't care about you, but about books; the unfamiliar and disgusting foods to which she introduced him (millet in many unsuccessful disguises)—pretending one is in Europe (the mark of someone who hasn't yet embraced town, but fun nonetheless) watching the old fellows at *bocce*. Their romance—his—was fraught, as MacK was slow to discover Rosenthal was a *taster*—with six or seven chaps on the go at once, besides the neurotic painter whom she thought of as the *boyfriend* and who constantly said *She's not my girlfriend* to the world. Ah! *these* days no one like Rosenthal can afford to move onto *Spring Street* and do nothing but live. She was particularly interested in Isidor; none of the people of her suburb—nor those at her nice, friendly college—nor the strutting intellects of SoHo had a *smidgin* of self-hatred; Izzy's lush endowment of it kept her willing to eat with him and MacK—by now she could withstand the accusation of Nice.

Rosenthal!, of tribulation, *the never quite*. They had stood and sat, she and he, in various places, in various poses, for some considerable time. On and off. MacK sometimes saying It, or sometimes something like It, and sometimes not. They had *been around*, had the odd Sicilian late night slice and the dawn taxi cuddle. What had come of it, see for yourself. But on a previous freezing holiday they stood in the Park, at the foot of a formal garden. MacK feigned newfound delight but in truth he was f***ing cold and knew the place well—he had regularly been going there, practicing saying It, as if with Rosenthal, several moons, on any noons he could spare.

The garden made her exclaim—he supposed it was the plan, for all the flowers were asleep or dead. The chill was not merely weather cold; the pergolas were planted with the cooler herbs, the mints, and lemon thyme. Twined and bare a tunnel of twigs stretched before them toward an octagonal-lighted building—the toilets, mused MacK, but good old him: however cold and wet he began to brim with arbor ardor. They looked at the bower and at each other. Rosenthal's glasses fogged. Opportunity was not knocking so MacK went out, so to speak, onto the porch where it cowered and boldly dragged it inside. MacK, or maybe it, licked his chops. —Do you realize, said MacK, we're about to go up the garden path together? —About time Sir, she said. Picture him!, the picture of elation. Up they went, but bear in mind, this is not metaphor, there were two people walking in a garden. Up they went, not touching, it would have been too awful to have to release her gabardine-smooth arm too soon; she always demanded release, in order to run around and exclaim over dead birds or rhapsodize about theatrical posters. At the arbor's terminus were benches damp and green ranged around a fountain, which was drained, as MacK, no—as he longed to be. They stared, at the two copper children of the fountain, diaphanously clothed. MacK began to wonder where the water came out, when it did—Rosenthal was looking too. —Nice-looking kids, she said, boy and girl or boyish girl and girlish boy? Or girlish girl and boyish boy? —Goyische boy and Jewish girl, said MacK. Frightened of the nursery, MacK arose reluctantly and to examine slowly slid down the icy empty fountain bowl. —Now I'm here! he called. He faced these copper children. Mother would call them angelic. Staring at flesh, even rendered in hard metal, could give him to morbid ponderings on his physiological future. The thighs—a hint of musculature—around back—MacK felt sick—he remembered with relief he was standing in the large stone basin. —Do you like him? called Rosenthal. —This is *him*? said MacK, no, I hate him. Although she is all right. He had lost track already that these were copper children—embroiled in the erotism of the ? shared moment—looked again at the thigh-green, the line above where the diaphanous napkin-suits gave way. Soon there would be exciting conflict here if they were not related—again forgetting—then imagining them sickeningly to be friends life long as in English novels who would never try it on with each other—faugh!

In the process of thinking this his diaphragm grew warm and heavy with questioning. —*Does the female every truly desire the male?* he asked, addressing still the flanged copper crotches but, of course, meaning Rosenthal. —What! she said, for she truly couldn't hear. —Even, he went on, in incensed boudoirs, even after romantic monochromatic cinema, even after drinking the optimal glop liqueur? Do they? Lust? You can tell me. You *must* tell me! MacK screamed—she eyed him rather distantly but that had been the story. She whispered lowly—*Yes*—he realized it was vagueness, and not audible proof exactly. —Your tone, he said, it reeks of qualification and emasculating doubt. Rosenthal stared at MacK, evangelical—*I have experienced lust*, she said; his knees shook—the implication, so plain, was that she had, but never when he was in the vicinity—he wanted to fling himself at her feet or onto one of the decorative prongs of the fountain, the boy's toe maybe, extended in the sculptress's attempt at innocence—*Yes*, she said.

Once they sat on the steps of a celebrated mausoleum—despite the solemn air he was trying to breathe of the place, *jugglers* leapt about in front of them—Rosenthal was *exulting* in the sunshine—as if she were in *California*—ye gods! MacK stroked her neck in futile daydream—*Let's go to your place!* she said—her meaning clear. In astonishment and joy MacK tripped over his laces and cut his forehead; they did go to his place but to ransack the medicine chest—the sense of *emergency in the park*, the time of bandaging, the smell of tincture merthiolate iced their blood—the day ended in frankfurters. Sadness of yore.

MacK climbed out of the fountain. Rosenthal was particularly beautiful in the cold grey light. Her mouth hung slightly open as she dwelt, leagues away, on other men. MacK wondered if he could really kiss her on that chill bench—of what value are such damp proofs of love? Even coming there so often middays, turning to empty space and saying it, could he now? He rotated toward her in an earnest twist of his torso—his precisely practiced Currier & Ives Suitor's Body Posture (send 25¢ in coin for complete instructions—no stamps). —Listen, said MacK, oft here at noon—*Nph!*—his prepared oration cut short by the fullness of her lips! —Enough? she said—at least he hoped it was a question. Certainly not!— reaching—. But for what, and on what level of the spirit, of honesty? They embraced. —Your coat's dirty, she said. This is where MacK always fell—in the midst of his passion, they noticed his *flaking details*. —*Yes, yes*, he laughed, so desperate, so nonchalant—they are the same thing. Their heads close by—their hands and arms in a sick panic of nonlocation—they again viewed the fountain— transformed for MacK now from sentimental junk into a jubilant Triumph of the Spirit©—out of a pain in the ass, art—the copper children playing out the great drama. —Let's go far away, said MacK. —He stood, and ran in the direction of Fifth Avenue, flailed his arms to signal the pitifully unexistent European express bus. —Come back! she yelled, come here. MacK approached the bench, regarded once again its low damp feel on his legs and end—so many times he'd sat here, adeptly executing the dentitions and fricatives of bliss.

She looked at him in good humor, too good maybe—she often laughed at him at Just the Wrong Moment. She opened her mouth—her stomach growled—leonine—MacK was excited. —I'm hungry, she said. But without the select tone of romantic double entendre, no suggestion that *MacK* might make the meal, except like the wieners of bandage day. —*Come, let's eat*, he said—turning to disgust himself with the sight of the two oxidized brats, still trenchant in their pose of innocence.

# Lucky Garden

Rosenthal was dreaming of men or the meal to come maybe. Canal Street, teeming with vegetables, whiffs, radios; the slit throats of ducks—MacK persisted in questioning her about lust but would she answer? When the question got over steamy she would stop and root through vegetables, caressing round ones and throwing phallic ones around fitfully, treating them like *dirt*. All around, radio blare and a stifling neon buzz as of summer pond insects—the gantlet of squat ladies and their smelling shopping bags—finally the *Lucky Garden*. The Lucky Garden may be lucky but it is also popular—how could it possibly be lucky?—the luck of their usual table was lacking and MacK and Rosenthal were forced to stand for a time—the proximity of the ladies with lines in their faces and the shopping bags barred MacK from pursuing lust. Instead they two chatted friendly about storm drains and the ponytails of dancers. MacK held they were thicker and shorter until *c.* 1957, the tails, not the drains, with a growing trend toward long wispiness which peaked in 1975. Rosenthal held quite the opposite view.

*HUA*, the waiter—the thick *rubber* menu—sea crow in red eye sauce, shining root with black blubber—thank you. In the booth behind, Hua held this colloquy with people not of these parts:

—What is this pork fried rice? —*Ah, pork fi rice is, ah, rice fi with pork. You want?* —Well—is it any good? —*Yah!* —Okay, well, I guess we'll have some of that—whuddya think, Jane? —Mmm. —*One pork fi rice.* —And, uh, what is this won ton soup? Hua leant over the menu and squinted. —*Ah, wa ta soup is, ah, soup with wa ta! You want?* —Well, I, uh, is it good? —*Yah!* —Okay, well, I guess we'll take some of that. —*One wa ta soup.* —Uh, two please. Sir. —*Two wa ta soup!*

*Ye gods*—but the lubricated iridescence of MacK's and Rosenthal's food pushed him again toward the physical, the carnal—the in his view advisable—the briny slime-play on his plate, the voluptuous rises, the cruel dimples he could make in its heavings with his wooden stick—ah!—the way he could bind the turgidity of the sea crow with white strands of his onion—Rosenthal noticed—fueled by her food she was going on between mouthfuls about the Other Team—but since his first steps MacK had felt only revulsion and pity for the National League and couldn't listen. He took the check from under his water glass, where Hua always put it, and as she babbled and ranted about those poor fools who lack a hitter-designate, who can *never have heroes*, he wrote to her on the back:

*Darling. Even though at this moment you are speaking of the Metropolitans, I really think I have fallen in love with you and all this elliptical hanging is driving me nuts. Nuts do you hear. I know I've never written you before but I thought this might be a way of saying that I'm trying to get you into bed. Why are we being so polite?*—as she was *still* talking about Shea he placed it slyly on her saucer—and by the time MacK stopped thinking dreamily about her discovery of the note and how wonderfully the evening would be bound to go, he found she was talking about trees—he jumped in with his petrified opinions about the craven municipality of liquidambars and the overriding importance and beauty of birches—there was no doubt the food had given them a relaxed but stimulated feeling—perhaps it was that chemical—he hoped it was conducive to lust—she finished vilifying the nation's major arboreta. —Sure the Scotch pine is a dangerous Yule tree, said MacK, but what do you do? —Crusade, she said, and then suddenly *Hua was screaming.* —!*Waaah!* He came over and beat his fists on the table. —What! shouted MacK. —Note! he wailed, O so dirty note—from *Missy!* —wild of gesture he threw the *check* down on the table before MacK could figure out . . . Rosenthal whapped Hua in the face with the rubber menu—*What's the big idea?* she yelled—Hua pointed to the billet doux. She read it. —Enough! said MacK, grabbing Rosenthal's wrist and the rubber menu, Hua, please accept my apology. I am the author of that filth, not she. Missy is innocent. —*Huh!*—Yes, a great wrong, said MacK, caressing her wrist since he—aha!—had it. Hua went away to sulk where the teapots are stacked. Rosenthal read the back of the check again with charming eyes out of the animal world and blushed—something he had never seen. She turned it over and began arithmetic. —I'll get it, she said throatily.

Hua presented her with a minty toothpick on the way out but she refused. —No MSG for you next time Missy.

The lamps over the wet street—MacK bathed in the light of dark promise. On the CC she took his hand—took his *pulse* actually. When she had established the diastole she turned to him demurely and said: —What do you think of a fellow who lets a girl pay the tab so easily? —I thought you said you would pay, you said you wanted to pay, *you paid!* MacK could see passengers worrying about him; he looked at them ferociously and they went back to their newspapers *of lies*. —Getting back to lust, he said. —Getting *back?* —To the *subject* anyway, he said. Damn if he was going to give it up no further away than it usually is. —I just cannot believe, said MacK, that you women, so floral, would ever want a sweaty spotty man on top of you, writhing and croaking—it makes me ill for all of you. —I'm not a 'you women', as it happens, she said angrily. —You mean to say you're the only one who has lusted? —Not at all, they're not *all* sweaty and spotty.

So that was it! They weren't?

She pulled him off the train—one is never lucky in the Lucky Garden to drink enough. —But where? he said, they're all the same around here. She took his arm. —So what *do* you think of a fellow who lets her pay it all? —I don't think about it. Who is he?

In this dump, people sized them up from the unconquerable claims of their booths—every bar a little Klondike—revenge often comes to sit in places like this. —Maybe you've lusted, said MacK—he could say the word loud with luxury in the clatter of this dump—maybe you have—for men—*but what about beer?* They drank—all sin and spite and smile. —It's true, said Rosenthal, that when men have wrassled their lust for beer is when many of us lust after *them*. ——Because, said MacK, that is when we are unaffectedly adorable, poetic and kind. —*No*, it's just man smell, said Rosenthal, beer and cigar and leather. Drives me rather wild. ——Today began, harrumphed MacK, in the loveliest public garden, it began with an earnest dialogue on lust charged with meaning and implication and promise—now we exchange tawdriness even as we breathe the menthol smoke of this Hell hole. ——Yes, said Rosenthal. She took his hand—its wholeness—not the artery.

## Plaza Garibaldi

Race was the circus ground on which Rosenthal and Isidor were never to agree. But out of respect for MacK, or possibly the holiday, they put away the guns of heavy issue.

What Mary-Ann and Rosenthal made of each other was polite, if nothing else—and it may have been nothing else. But when these fellows were together, Mary-Ann and Rosenthal slid abominably—according to everyone—into the roles of guardians, or vestals, or even low, gum-chewing usherettes. Thinking about Our Years in Yorkville, even though he continued to live on the West Side—MacK still gets the taste of Pedro's mother's fresh tortillas and of margaritas in his mouth—still excretes their salt, he thinks. This is the only genuine paean possible, on behalf of these three or four people, to the decade in question, the bright little lights in the trees, the baskets of tortillas and the electrically puréed guacamole, the margaritas in goblets the size of toilets and then the traditional MacK–Iz parting of the ways—Izzy taking the high road of wine to brandy, MacK the low road of beer but arriving in Sot-land afore him. The girls had a good time but felt they had to rein things in, because they wanted to be able to come back to the Plaza Garibaldi and sometimes it was conceivable Izzy and MacK could have too much fun even for Pedro; *arriba*.

There *was* turkey mole and MacK collected $5 from Iz. It struck him this night—the bastard son of Thanksgiving but settling down to the Plaza's own kind of continued nonspecific festival, nondenominational Mexican gaiety—looking at Rosenthal and at Mary-Ann—that what they had here: —What we have here, he said to Isidor and to them, is a couple of Game Girls. —What are you talking about, said Izzy, who was nervous MacK was casting some kind of aspersion on Mary-Ann. —No, said MacK, listen, been thinking all about it—if you don't mind my telling you 'bout this be-YOU-ti-ful goil, he said in a weak imitation of Izzy's stand-up Bensonhurst (he hadn't practiced or thought to use it till now—it was no use at work)—I mean *Game Girls*, in the sense that they're with us; they'd go with us anywhere, wouldn't ya girls? —What do you mean, said Iz, I'm not going anywhere, I'm *not leaving*. Are you talking about going camping again? Because if you are . . . —Camping! beamed Rosenthal—bringing herself down firmly one notch with *everyone* for about twenty minutes (Isidor *camping!*).

MacK had had a vision: World War II and he had to go fight, at least some of the time. —!—said Isidor. —Rosenthal is battling on, you know, said MacK, seeing us through it—it is an old-fashioned chicken farm, out on the Island, the hen houses are dark red. A sunny morning in the winter of war, the ground covered with ice—you drive up in one of those *rounded cars*—she comes out to sell you eggs—they're rationed—she sometimes delivers them in a rounded station-wagon, with *wooden sides* and *dark green fenders*—she's gamely keeping the chickens &c. going because she loves me. Mary-Ann could be doing the same thing, he said, because she looks sincere and wonderful, too—the way they both look when they put their hair up—it would go perfectly with the wood on the sides of the station wagon and the brown eggs in racks, and the sun bright but low in the sky because it's a morning in the war and you're lonely. —Er—what are you talking about? said Isidor. —I think it's sweet, said Mary-Ann, MacK thinks we're beautiful and loyal—that's how he's expressin' it. Here he felt a foot slide up his calf! —That's what you think of me? said Rosenthal, a wartime chicken farmer?

MacK looked from one friend to the other; he said nothing, yet he felt he hadn't told the half of it, the stirring love for and of the Game Girls in their slightly mannish mackinaws—the denims or twills of war, the *trousers of war*—the head scarves but beauty coming through. He gulped, having suddenly had an epiphany: —I apologize, he said, I just realized I've been having an emotional fantasy about *Mrs Harmon*, the lady who used to bring eggs to our house—her Nash Rambler—her hair, I now see with horror, was very like Rosenthal's when in a girlish or old-fashioned design—I even remember the egg lady's *barrette*. —*What*, said Isidor. —It's something Rosenthal favors when we lie around her apartment on Sunday. —When the suburbs, said Isidor, creep into the city and reclaim the hearts of those who are their own? Like some f***ing *monster* movie . . . I hate to interrupt this. —No you don't, said Mary-Ann, you love to interrupt. MacK hated having to explain his affections in this way. —Let's not go into the shrinky side of our bringing eggs, said Rosenthal. A turkey mole was carried past them to another table—MacK collected $5. There was nothing more to be said about chicken or war or, for the moment, the prettiness of the girls, glowing now with the warmth of their chilis and tequila whereas before they had glowed with their inner fires against the cold city. It wasn't mean to them; our town was quite nice to both these girls.

Rosenthal was determined, as always, to get some *personal sweetmeat*. Why go out to eat if people aren't going to talk about themselves? Otherwise you could stay home and read a book. The thought had never occurred to MacK, who usually found himself there for the beer, unless it also involved Izzy, *then* there would be *talk*—that was a reason. Sometimes there was something spicy to go with beer—but MacK was never a respecter of foods, which drove Isidor mad. —How was New Orleans? said Rosenthal. —Oh, we ate *saw* much, said Mary-Ann, Isidor spent almost every day at Galatoire's—I couldn't even get him to take a walk. —We did visit the famous World's Fair, said Iz. —We did not visit it, said Mary-Ann. —Yes we did, said Isidor. Mary-Ann turned her head pointedly toward Rosenthal. —We went up to the *fence*, she said, Isidor was too cheap to go in. —*What!* yelled Isidor and Pedro looked up, though he didn't flinch—he was used to Isidor already, for today. —So we just walked *around* the whole thing, several times, said Mary-Ann, around and around this screwed-up inna city industrial wasteland, just *starin'* *in* at the WORLD'S FAIR. —You have to admit it didn't look too hot, said Izzy. —But to have gone all that way Isidor. —I don't see what you're complaining about, you got your *beignets* and your Picayunes. —Oh, Rosenthal, would you like one? said Mary-Ann, drawing the pack. —Sure! said Rosenthal, which flabbergasted MacK. —I think those lack millet completely you know, he said. Listen, the girl was changing—and for a second here they were again, the two pretty girls on the Home Front.

But was there a better picture to be had of the desires and tendencies of Isidor and Mary-Ann? Walking around the perimeter of the WORLD'S FAIR, which couldn't HURT you—what was he afraid of anyway? Mary-Ann with her New England pluck; the thing certainly couldn't have hurt *her*—and Isidor outside the chicken-wire fence, unable to go in, in some weird way, even for the chance to laugh—*LOUDLY*—at that screwy country. One can only imagine the concrete and plastic bayou, the miniaturized streetcars of desire—because he *didn't* go in—he felt he was being kept out—Iz took all fences personally. There was his fear of America—he was in it enough for his own taste—the WORLD'S FAIR might have been too strong a dose of it. The sight of people having FAKE FUN—he was probably right to avoid it. Instead he took it on himself to single-handedly keep the *French Quarter* in business while everyone else went to the FAIR.

Fake fun is something New York is still low on, thought MacK, though 57th Street has for some undiscoverable reason become simply a conveyor belt to the great engine of the perplexity of the people—and someone is trying the same thing with 42nd; let us all watch our backs. The gods willing, this will fail and the pimps can get off their glueboards on Eighth Avenue.

Late under the little lights in Pedro's tree—Izzy and Mary-Ann reliving the arguments and dinners of New Orleans; MacK and Rosenthal cruising on some wave of collaged nostalgia, but this is what it was like when they were in their twenties—they thought they were growing into, or more secure in their coupledoms—you think, *this is adulthood*—but it isn't. Sitting in a restaurant and having a job is not being an adult; adulthood is precisely the *opposite* of those things. Adulthood itself is what lasts, sometimes grinds; not Mary-Ann and Isidor, MacK and Rosenthal; not the Plaza Garibaldi, not the holiday outside. New York lasts. The awful weight of self-awareness goes; at fifty you never think *I have a job and am sitting in a restaurant*—life becomes a whole, details cease to matter or, it seems, even to exist—everything's a blur. New York lasts.

In a moment Rosenthal would want to go to MacK's—and by the time they got to the subway she wouldn't. She'd want MacK to come downtown and then wouldn't, actually in love with her subway rides *solo* more than anything, still treasuring being a city girl on the—whoop de *do*—IND. Some people lead charmed lives.

Heat—in the friends—Pedro's hand. The blast of the night cold in the spirit-hot face. *Sobering* is the word they have got for it . . . in *Hicksville*. —Bavarian *Inn*, said Isidor. —Oh no ya don't, said Mary-Ann, time to go home. —Wait, said MacK, rocking on his heels in a breeze of reassuring chatter issuing from the comedy club. —No no, said Rosenthal, c'mon and walk me to the subway. MacK had a confused vision of subway tiles, Rosenthal's little place; he really always wanted to sleep near Isidor and Mary-Ann—the nails in the floor—but you're supposed to be *keen,* aren't you. —Let's go, boys, said Mary-Ann, fun's over. —I can't believe we're being *dragged away*, said Isidor . . . —I *know*, said MacK, and now Isidor was . . . gone . . . entirely yanked around the corner by Mary-Ann in the snow.

The warmth of Rosenthal, her overcoat, on the way to the Lex, which if MacK squinted had mackinawish tendencies. —The trouble with you and Isidor, she said, is

**You guys love each other so much
you don't know what to do with it.
SO YOU DRINK.**

—Hey MacK, wheah's ya *hat?* called Edward Kennedy from around the corner. He could hear her struggling with Isidor. —Yes, said Rosenthal, where is your hat?

My *hat*, MacK thought, with a pang. He had been so recently bereaved of it, far away in the f***ing Hamptons. When he had turned from his hat for the last time, his eyes stung and it was not the wind. It was a sentimental hat—that is, MacK was sentimental about it. It was of fearful green stuff, like oiled pork crackling, lined with a large green and white tartan of—another insult to aesthetics—vinyl. Shaped like the Devil's Postpile, with a neat brim. A snug 7⅜—his *HAT*—now subject to the Law of the Sea. MacK at sunset, 4.37 pm—stood, waiting for his hat to be washed ashore—it bobbed merrily. Would the spite of nature end if we left off torturing her? Somehow the sea around his hat (already no longer his) became the color of rain slanting on the stone street where he had bought it. To it he then turned a face impassive, an Easter Island head—for its own dear sake. His hat was a begging-bowl, turned up to the sun in the waves—the sky a bouquet of trout skin spraying like the 4th of July from the crumpled vase of—his hat. A *bird* had come, flying low and skimming—skiddingly perched upon it there in the waves—actually sat on the brim and there and then in the waves, used it as a pot; while MacK watched. He didn't like that bird, it had the whole Atlantic but it had to use his hat. He tried to accept—forgive—he had loved his hat so, the incident was probably inevitable. It was time for the hat's Appointment with the Duke of Edinburgh maybe—MacK had always known of this Appointment—there was a small card pertaining to it sewn inside the sweat band—the Royal arms. He Stood, Waiting for His Hat to be Washed Ashore. He stood on the beach, suffering vague guilty feelings that he was unread on the subject of eternity. It was deep winter, the beaks of the shore birds chattered—not with gossip nor rebuke, but with cold—the sun could not spark the colors of the grasses stooping by the bay—even the red sign, KEEP OUT THIS MEANS YOU!, was cold and alone.

A *tweed* hat of a similar shape had been denounced by Tumbleson—*It makes you look like a pinhead—like an idiot*—but this one had risen above, and taken MacK with it—he was in normality's realm, and protected from the rain. The sea. *This is America,* he had thought. Twice it had come within far wade-reach—if it had not been deep winter! —if only his love for his hat had conquered his deep affection for his shoes and his overcoat, his fears of virus—although he did quite ruin his shoes, allowing the waves to lave them as he watched his hat. It was at Flying Point, not at Sagaponack as was later reported in the *East Hampton Star.* A hat flying like that, he thought, the refractive day, the mighty Atlantic, his vision suddenly framed and made crystal by despair, could be the subject of a great oil—or even acrylic—on the beach you rarely know your location with respect to the particulars of the bay.

The *sou'wester* had not done—even in its limitless American yellowness—the romance was all—the wearing of it chafed MacK's razor-burn and spirit—the sand flowing in low white winds. So had the *beret* failed, alter scalp as it was for him—had become dark and foul in the week of supposed holiday sea-damp, a sink of pneumonias.

*Could you horse-whip a man for not modeling the dynamics of hats he lets loose on the public?*

Lovers ask—unknowingly—*unfeelingly*—that you sacrifice the very personal thing. Time. Thinking. The drink, the cigarette—perhaps these things are all the same thing: you? They are asking you to give up—that's the way it's always been done—give up some of the molecules, the blocks. In the end, most of us won't do this, now—even a few molecules. So: everyone parts, in our century. So Mary-Ann and Isidor—not that night—some time during the next year it was. They'd gone curiously back and forth about mar-riage—one never knows how to put it—sometimes the teeter-totter does seem right—one exhilarated and up there, the other getting an ass-banging, splattered with mud—Isidor ran back and forth like a child at the beach, daring and fleeing Mary-Ann's foamy bridal tide. The months he wanted to get married she didn't. They were both against it, truthfully, but each had periods when they'd consider it, for reasons of the long, though faint, aroma-like fingers of the suburbs.

*It's bullshit! Let's not do it!*

*It's bullshit! Let's DO it!*

MacK *expected* them to marry but would have been surprised if they *had*. But during one of the months they were both against it, the cat who patrolled the back yards died—and blocks and blocks away—the true ecology of this our town—Yorockefeller University (so called by Isidor because he was usually lighting his a.m. cigar at the corner of 66th and York, where this guy usually sitting at the base of the fancy fence usually said *Yo! Rockefeller!*) broke ground on a new white building for thinking very clean and important thoughts in—no, we don't understand them either, but to be civilized is to pretend that we do—and some very highbrow York Avenue rats and mice began looking around Mary-Ann's and Isidor's street. Looking around in their *bedroom*. Can anything convince you that a *change* may be in order quicker than rodents running across you at night? It must have been when the weather was coming warm, and the river does contribute something to the tenor of life in the Far East—and the Nazi must have stopped clearing up after his Hell dogs—they wouldn't blow him maybe—for there were a lot of cockroaches too—but this is synchronicity gone beyond its normally appalling bounds. During one hot exchange Mary-Ann said *I ain't stayin' around this bug house—mouse house*—and it quickly became a talisman of a kind—in a few weeks it propelled her out of Yorkville, out of town. BUGHAUS! MAUSHAUS! This girl left New York.

## The Wilderness of the Shiksas

Isidor had lost something complex—which is a complicated losing—but natural, and he knew it. Here began several years of going in and out of bars, and, like MacK, wandering. —*That's laughs tonight on Wilderness of the Shiksas.*

Mary-Ann's departure seemed to precipitate the end of Yorkville—as they had known it—but while Izzy was still preparing to leave—for a new life downtown, downtown, everybody's got to go *f\*\*\*ing* downtown—the Bavarian Inn closed, suddenly and forever, and was quickly remodeled in one of those heartbreaking transformations which are little shows of the rage of non-New Yorkers making an incursion, a midnight raid on Manhattan—like a businessman from New Haven visiting a prostitute on 11th Avenue—the sting of a little insect from outside. The place was boarded up for a few weeks and then there emerged from it a bar seemingly made of the plywood it had been obscured with. It was hard to tell what motif they were aiming for—*I'd say probably the bull-shit motif*, said Isidor, as he and MacK stood there sheepish with two glasses of watery Michelob dark—well—one gets curious—*one needs to know the bars*. The place matched what was happening to East 86th Street—it could have been a shop selling souvenirs or crap wool hats or socks—it had a vaguely Irish name—it was a PUB only because it said so—it had as little connection to the Irish people of Yorkville as it did to real bars made out of stone, glass and wood. But East 86th Street was empty of Mary-Ann.

A funny thing—the death of the Bavarian Inn was Isidor's mile-stone, the northern mossy side of which read BEER and the dry southern side WINE—as if the Bavarian Inn had been the only fount of true beer in New York—though of course it springs from many taps. Izzy moved south, into the heightened connoisseurship of the Village, where *beer*, Sir, is now the libation of *interlopers*.


MacK was walking across East 86th on a bright afternoon—looking for socks—Izzy was still in the neighborhood but not for long. In front of MacK was this frankly unbelievable character—a real *schtarker*—very dark blow-dried hair in a shag—Jackie O dark glasses—tan in a can—okay so he coulda got it at CLUB MED—big fat hands, bracelets, rings—tasselled shoes—couldn't see the trousers for the enormous fur coat, blown and styled by the same hand as the head—guy was walking in the weird way people walk who have formerly been very fat—they waddle still with their toes pointing out—you could see him—for he had *bully* written all over him—lunging around, terrorizing everyone in the schoolyard—but what he looked like isn't important. As he went along he stripped the cellophane off a pack of 'Ass Hole' (Blue)—dropped it and the cover foil on the pavement—lit one from a book of matches—dropped that—opened a pack of Doublemint—threw down the string and top—all the time waddling, with a *soupçon* of saunter—opened the stick of gum, threw the wrapper and the silver paper over his shoulder—walked on, chewing and smoking. MacK felt he was following a truck shedding its load of depressing furniture—but this must be THE GUY who was changing East 86th Street—*he* obviously owned the plywood bar, the shops of dark glasses and batteries—he picked his nose with his cigarette hand and locked himself into the pages of *Mad*, a woman looking for snot with a fuschia pinky nail, cigarette holder in one hand and a Manhattan in the other; there he was, the *Destroyer of Yorkville*. What had *MacK* done compared to *this* guy?

Occasionally MacK thinks of Yorkville and the *'PLAZA GARIBALDI'* if he's on Second or Third in the 60s or 70s—neither he nor Isidor has been there for years now— it's still up there, he thinks—you might find yourself in one of the coffee shops on York Avenue—those places where you seem to find yourself only on the coldest day of the year—but who has anything to do on York Avenue? F*** York Avenue. Noche Bueno.

## In Nature's Realm

OH we all have to spend time away from this our town—it is a curse of living here. Having taken pains to *establish* yourself you are then sent *away* by the gods to see what you might or might not be missing—pastrami?—with luck you recognize it's *nothing* and pluckily come back as soon as you can, though with a deeper understanding of that god damn country. But those who are exiled or even self-exiled briefly are a bit finer and more honorable, it must be said, than those who live their whole boastful lives on Second Avenue and suddenly fall down *dead* from pastrami.

Sometimes—appallingly—one has to leave town because of *romantic feeling*. Not the odd weekend—MacK and that little stick of dynamite from Production tussling over eggs benedict in the middle of the Catskills—but wholesale *exodus*, for months at a time—even telling yourself that THIS IS IT, true love and it doesn't *matter* where she lives—that New York has done everything for you that it will. *Yes, you're a little tired of life in town—getting on a bit—other parts of the country have something to offer—nice to have a garden* . . . Oh, *brother* what shit you can talk!

These things continue to happen and it's just terrible. Even to Isidor—who is not someone you think of as *bursting* to get out of town. One summer night he was wandering around—not so long after he'd moved to the Village—Mary-Ann was still in the air. Isidor thought he might *eventually* arrive at a point where there was jazz and the attendant clear liquors— although he was not in those days in the habit of making for clear liquors invariably on passing out the portal of the office. He walked back and forth on 8th between Sixth and Broadway, becoming disgusted with himself for being interested in various fashions on display and—this was one of the warm evenings which draw students like bugs out of their filthy dormitories—the proximity of KIDS displaying their fondnesses—licking each other between gulps of *gelato* and pot smoke. Iz had long thought of 8th as a boardwalk, summer or winter—it smelled of popcorn, gum, the sweat of mate-search—and is jammed with Guys in Cars sweeping the pedestriennes with binocular eyes and tongues. Even if you're no longer a Guy in a Car you can become susceptible—the atmosphere of musth—and Isidor was, to his discomfiture—though part of the unpleasantness was that same knowledge—that he was perhaps no longer conceivably—or let us say *reasonably*—a player in this drama—or mightn't immediately be conceived as such by the girls passing in their leotards. The beat beat beat of the martini-intricate jazz—its punctual brushwork—took him along like a wave to his usual club. It was still early but here was a trio and here was a bartender. This bartender Isidor had been training-up—he was coming along nicely but sometimes spotted people's spectacles with a too-sweeping ejection of crushed ice and Boissière from the mixing glass. So as to avoid being dotted this way, no regular was sitting at the bar. But there was this oral surgeon.

Their banter will not be recounted; mating sounds so lame when reproduced. 'I'd say it's more a matter of mood', as Khrushchev said—that is, it's a matter of Her receptivity, not Your cleverness. Things just come together, and so, they did—between Isidor and this oral surgeon of Portland, Oregon. Is the predictability of this too brutal?—it's not meant so—just what is the point of elaborating the conversations which rapidly devolve upon one unenunciated foregone conclusion? HAH?

To Isidor, sex is an urban activity—in fact the only *point* to the sexual act—if there can be said to be one at all—over the centuries has been to *build cities*. All that covered wagon stuff, all that self-sacrificing procreation so hideously *implied* in elementary school textbooks is insane garbage. And so is all the sex life of the jungle, the desert. *Tribes*. Sex is no fun in such places. What can be worse than trying to have a nice walk in the woods with someone whose idea of a nice walk in the woods is *anything but*? Is *perverted beyond belief*? Do you even *know* what tree bark feels like against your bottom? Do you know how many ANIMALS might observe you two, even goaded to the attack by your desperate exercises? Think about what a large mushroom would feel like, accidentally squashed by you or the beloved in congress—and how absurd black stockings look under flannel-lined blue jeans. What about all the mentally ill who now live in the woodlands of our country—Millennialists, Nazis, duck hunters who could converge on your frolic, condemn you, photograph you, shoot the animals who had gathered to watch? You don't need cold air or damp *spores* blown onto your organs while you're trying to express the primitive thought. And all that *beach eroticism* is gull shit. You don't want sand in these sacrosanct pockets and folds, you don't need fish swimming around them nor gulls frappity crapping on your head. You don't! And there's nothing exciting about *patches* of sand—*photographic calendars* notwithstanding—what would you say if the beloved had patches of sand and sea-foam and sea-wrack on himself, herself, in the *Algonquin Hotel?* You pull back the sheets and there, by the beloved's attractive underwear, is a *patch of sand* and some *kelp!* You'd VOMIT.

*No*—it's a clean, urban activity—a thing done along precise *lines*, with striking angles to it—if it is to be satisfactory. Yes it costs money to live in town—because of the equipments. Of course you need a cocktail shaker, a strainer, gin—but perhaps most important is the city itself—the dark pane of your window, the lighted city beyond—what is more erotic? *Asking* you. A machine capable of emitting saxophone, piano and brush-on-drum sounds without distortion. Between music and the lighted city will you find pleasing angles of intersection, an architecture (feh!) and an engine. Far from being a *woodland romp*, or even a plushy boudoirish thing of frills, derrières and pillows, sex requires various girders, railings, turnbuckles, skyscrapers, contrasts, *chiaroscuro*—to guy, as it were, desire. Sharp things, snaps, straps and silk coverings—the parachutes for desire expressed, spent commitment.

Jazz—if used wisely it can warm and enrich our lives—if used foolishly it can damage or even destroy them completely.

What could be more natural to an oral surgeon, even if she *were* from Portland? Their night was vivid, kid you not. Strained and loose, strained and slack—if this were a tale of San Francisco you could liken it to a ride on the California Street line, looking down at the gripman's cues painted on the street: DROP ROPE; TAKE ROPE. On this awful day there was, for some inexplicable reason, a word lacking in the vocabularies of both oral surgeon and book dealer and the word was GOODBYE. Which lack of word led Isidor in a few short weeks to have let his apartment—to *Sidney*, gosh sakes—and to find himself knocking on the pine door of opportunity of the Land of Many Uses, the great Northwest itself.

Still more than an employee but rather less than a partner of Mr Playfair's, Isidor negotiated six months' leave from Bibulo & Schenkler. ——What are you going all the way out there for? said Mr Playfair—how can you think you are in love with a dentist? But when Izzy looked around, walked around the streets he told himself that this was *exactly* the way desire is to be set and lit and consummated in this our town. Told himself that his vivid night, the curve of the slumbering oral surgeon back-lit by his bit of glittering urban cyclorama (a little slice of Union Square at that time), that nothing and no one he could see on any block promised that vividity and therefore he was going to get him some more of that—while he is not a romantic in the street sense—abjuring and rejecting the word love—observe his actions. Besides it doesn't matter—as you know—that one party doesn't express love if the other does. The word is there on the coffee-table. This oral surgeon was shapely, American—the kind of woman you feel you might get to know if you were allowed to watch made-for-television movies—sunwashed suburban interiors and earnest automobiles—things that ought never to be shown in New York along with television altogether maybe—we aren't prepared for it and most of us can't take it—the filth and the lies—and inasmuch as it tempts us to think that there might be a rapprochement possible with the United States and its people.


Cast a cold eye on Portland, on Seattle—these places where all the scaredy-cats of Boston and San Francisco have gone to drink coffee *without black people*—these so-called 'cities'—can they really pretend they sip cappuccino among the perhaps crumbling but certainly light-toned culture of the Old World? If you want to sit and watch a lot of people in funny-shaped suits drink coffee, why not *go* to Milan? Don't stand on ceremony. Leave now. Yes people there have *time* to drink coffee—if that's your idea of a good time—in the Northwest people are *so afraid of Japan* that they've turned the miracle drug of caffeine against themselves—homeopathically—why Seattle is fast becoming an anagram of *lattés*—it makes them work very hard and to worry worry worry about their Eddie Bauer cars and jackets and boots which must always be very clean—Mount Rainier and Mount Hood never get muddy—did you know that?—because all these white people in fleecewear who weigh nothing prance so lightly up and down them.

Isidor found an apartment and quickly associated himself with some book and art dealers in Portland and San Francisco. His card, wistful already:

**ISIDOR KATZ**
**BOOKS & MANUSCRIPTS**
*ASSOCIATE OF BIBULO & SCHENKLER*
*FOURTH AVENUE • NEW YORK*

He quickly found that life in the Northwest is supposed to resemble, or has become, a catalogue—one spends a great deal of one's time having the bedroom closet fitted with intricate shelves—to display one's spectrum of crew neck sweaters—forest green, teal and crimson especially totemic in the brave Northwest—and acquiring such sweaters. Socks and shirts—anything that can be made more interesting than it is intrinsically in *different colors* must be stacked and arranged in the Northwest home—every house a little Federal Reserve of cashmere and argyle—as if in one of the catalogues or the stores that are like catalogues. Isidor just put his socks in a *drawer*, like any other grown-up in New York. This stuff didn't *suit* Isidor—the whole phony casual tenor of the place couldn't suit anybody who reads a *real newspaper*, he thought—even though it costs $25 in Portland. So there he sat dutifully for a few weeks in a slate-grey crew neck and khaki *get-up* that was never really going to let him *in*—with his $10 cappuccino and his $25 *New York Times*—feeling distinctly like a kid and idiot.

This didn't please the oral surgeon, who had already begun to worry that Isidor was not going to *fit in* to the Northwest—what he did was too old-fashioned and he wasn't interested in re-doing his apartment in any way to resemble a catalogue or a store that looked like a catalogue. This oral surgeon was a bore, a sweater collector and someone who saw nothing wrong in the frighteningly inbred appearance of all the fleecy jogging families of the Northwest. You may say the problem is that orthodontics is a bore because someone has to do it, but the answer is *No*, the only place you need orthodontics is in a superficial empty society—the even, fascistic smile all you need to *get that contract*—we get along all right with our own teeth in New York. Isidor concluded this rather rapidly. Of course, *boys,* being rather dull creatures, we only discover these things after making that big move for love. Making the move is our declaration, which proposes to awe and silence the distant-dwelling beloved for months—to be a statement which will endure—so that no aspect of the emotional life need be discussed once we're ON THE SCENE. What awful, predictable folly. What pathetic animals. Dopes!!

In business Isidor did well, immediately, the book and antique shops of the Northwest containing almost archaeologically the literature previous to 1980—for a time he couldn't believe his eyes—what all these hungry young capitalists drawn from all over—supposedly *OUR ONLY HOPE AS A NATION*—had abandoned in favor of trash. But he very quickly decided it would be best to get all the good books the Hell out of there and safely back to New York, which he commenced to do—the dealers went over like ninepins, blitzed on caffeine—while coming to the realization that the *New York Times* does not New York make, and that Portland was not a city just because they said it was. There was no jazz save cool jazz—and that was pretty tepid—because everything in the Northwest has to go with coffee, the colors of sweaters or music or bus timetables. There are no buses.

How long could you really discuss oral surgery and sweaters? —we have exhausted them here—so Isidor made plans to meet MacK on the rocky coast of Northern California. MacK was floundering about in the wilderness of the shiksas *at the same time*. Down Izzy drove on the coast of Oregon—the most puzzlingly empty landscape he'd ever seen—having left the oral surgeon to her appliances after she'd spoken of his *need to male-bond*. At the same time MacK headed west from New Mexico and north from Hollywood, growing more and more uncomfortable with every hour that continued to *be California*—it's a BEHEMOTH. They arrived about the same time late in the day at a holiday home of the type they both preferred—utterly drab with a sturdy refrigerator with a freezer of great promise. Outside: seals, rocks, redwoods, pines, whales

### ET CETERA.

One of the many towns out there still divided by railroad tracks—like the parting on a balding pate—freight has become an infrequent though alarmingly bulky thing when it does occur in nature—there may be one train a week—but it will take three hours to parade before you. In these here parts.

Waiting those three hours in front of the only blinking light in the whole of this vast ruined economy—in the rain—their engine running. The light reminded MacK of the control panel in his safe warm studio back in New York—thousands of miles away—his tired bored brain flew him across the shiksas and deserts—and circled the RCA Building in a way he would have liked—suddenly swooping in an open window—how often he imagined this.

Iz and MacK sitting there. —It seems the whole f***ing country must pass us by, said Isidor, in the form of this train in the rain. Even the Erie Lackawanna of Iz's childhood and the Pacific Fruit Express of MacK's. This *Hell train* rumbled along between them and LIQUOR. Admittedly: pretty aspects of the trees—folding mists, ocean—mountains which raced away on all sides from this town; the grandeur of its clean but very shut lumber mill, an immense graceful presence on the south hill, pale yellow with expansive lettering of pleasing green. But they stared at the side of the train and could

see the word LIQUOR across the tracks—the depressing emporium
where it was dispensed in the gaps between the lumbering slow
box cars. *The arm lifted* and the cars drove over the grade crossing—an unmistakable sound, cars crossing a railway—its wet
boards—in Northwestern rain. You can smell that. —I've an idear,
said MacK, whose jocularism was to say it that way in small clap-
board towns—we pay homage to the great de Voto with his own
special American martini since we're out here in America . . . especially considering the look of this liquor store which will have no gin
*you* ever heard of. —Gee Whizz, said Isidor frightened, don't you
know that he only admitted of two drinks in the entire world? His
rather cloudy though masculine version of the Harvard—beg
pardon—martini—and a shot of bourbon? The guy never admitted
Scotch even. —*Slug*, he called it a slug of whiskey if you don't
mind, said MacK. He was a primitive, but in places like this that may
not be a drawback. —He never even drank *wine*, said Iz, shivering.
—His biographer described his death, said MacK, as a matter of
becoming *electrocardiographically disorganized*. —I'm not surprised,
said Izzy, if all you ever did was bump between gin, bourbon, Lewis
and Clark *you'd* be disorganized.

Take a look at this joint. There was no attempt at window display.
Cases of liquor—ready to go—but who in the shut mill town can
afford them? MacK's idea of de Voto devotion involved, as Isidor
feared, a domestic gin which might be called *G.'s*; this possibly noble
or at least interesting study was taken down more than a notch by
the sole availability of Italian vermouth. Isidor began to mope in the
wine aisle and he wasn't going to get any happier in *there*—MacK
could see from a distance that the labels were an anglo-orthographic
rabble. You know the smell of a lousy liquor store do you not—stale
smoke, spilled beer, aggressive corks, turkey snacks or corn
chips—you can't be sure. A display of dusty corkscrews and stop-
pers tweaked MacK's memory of the child-oriented utensils at the
holiday home. —We need a strainer. Iz flushed and looked around,
ever the realist, thank God. —*You* ask 'em; I'm not gonna; forget it.

—Just these, said MacK, placing the *G.'s* and the vermouth on the counter—his eyes flicked briefly at the ICE MACHINE, for St Bernard's recipe calls for 500 LBS. OF ICE—but remembered the generous freezer in the holiday home—though what had they needed that much ice for in 1950? —It's for frozen vegetables obviously, Izzy had said lugubriously, on checking in. —And I need a bar strainer, said MacK. —A what? said the genuinely grizzled man, old before his time, putting their two bottles in a paper bag *without a cardboard separator*, and looking at their twenty as though he could now sell the place and get out of town. —A cocktail strainer for cocktails, said MacK, feeling the floor opening up as you do out there in that god damn country. —I don't got that, said the grizzled man, pushing the bag toward them hard enough that the portions of his long hair unrestrained by his railroad engineer's cap launched themselves toward MacK in a recriminatory way. And HERE was the mistake: —You know where we can get one? said Isidor. As you might in a lot of places but not here. —We *sure don't*, said the grizzled man, shifting the pronoun so as to draw the population of the town all behind him to stare down MacK and Isidor—torches, rakes—KILL THE MONSTERS—the first time he'd looked either of them in the eye—and at that moment MacK realized the grizzled man had *no idea* why they were buying gin and vermouth at the same time. —Thanks a lot, we'll be seeing you, said MacK in an on-air voice. They went past unused rolls of red corrugated paper—sent to Grizzly Liquors by a distillery—*Hit the juice, it's Christmas!*—out the scuffed Plexiglas door into the rain. —Faggits!

—You hear that? said Isidor, settling on the front seat with the holy infants on his lap. —Yeah, said MacK, you want to take it up with him? —Certainly not, said Isidor, although it disturbs me when I think I could get a kicking from someone like that who's so close to my own age. How can someone who's thirty-five have tattoos and a *dirty railroad hat?*—he's so young . . . Iz was close to tears for some reason.

Too weird of course to ask in there about olives—so another

trip, so many *stops*—at last at the tough-looking *Bev's Strip Mall* a tough-looking little super yielded two tough-looking steaks and a squat jar of the toughest-looking olives—they had taken on the dim quality of BAIT; and so home.

This yellow kitchen must have been preserved by archivists. Well-brought-up fellows, they put their groceries where you're supposed to put 'em—considered the look of the bottle of *G.'s* on the counter of red lino. MacK checked the dusty ice in the freezer; Isidor stared at the two bottles summarizing any past number of decades of American sophistication—they struck him as incongruous or anachronistic here in the archaeological kitchen—red lino—pines, rocks, ocean outside—the street lined with sober shingled houses, in each garage perhaps an older but well kept-up car—the whole little town oddly dream-like—the towns Iz and MacK grew up in transplanted to the edge of the sea for one of those reasons dreams have. —Guy called us faggots, said Isidor. —What he said was fag ITS. —Yeah I know, but *aren't* we acting a little . . . urban? said Isidor—looking at the bottles—ashamed to hear himself say such a thing, and MacK astonished. What they both needed was to be *kicked* back to New York. —And that was just the guy to do it maybe, said Isidor. Brave Engineer O'Booze. Isidor seemed suddenly abashed, chastened in the wholesome kitchen and afraid.

MacK made the de Voto martini, which is quite something —strong enough but perverse in the quantity of vermouth—the non-New York taste of *G.'s*—and a suspect fishiness in the ice—but *that* cannot be laid at St Bernard's feet, they should have made NEW ICE on arrival, what were they thinking of? Isidor entered here on his disquisition—why the martini is an urban drink—the Koh-I-Noor of the sexual tool-box—with the geometry of lights outside, stools, dimmers, high heels, so on—such was the extent of the homosexual panic induced by Engineer O'Booze that he had to

## DEFEND THE MARTINI!

—Name the worst place for drinking a martini you ever were, said Iz—I'll go first—a back yard in Alabama. The humidity first *infected*, then *killed* the martini—even though the guy had decent gin, he was one of those who treat it like punch—a pitcher . . . —Yosemite National Park, said MacK—no way to keep anything cold—and the stupid *scenery* overwhelmed the drink and Red's attention—can you believe that, I *made a martini* and she keeps apostrophizing Bridal Veil Falls. —Ah, Red, said Isidor.

Nevertheless they executed several de Votos—eventually raised their voices in a triumph of camaraderie—good to meet in exile—unhappiness was *total* for them both—and these tough-looking drinks went well with the tough-looking steaks broiled in the white gas range of 1950, tasting headily of plentiful methane, Irma Rombauer and Marion Rombauer Becker. —Bernard de Voto must have had a regular *Mississippi* of hangovers, said Isidor upon arising, and it is all the fault of *G.'s*. —Italian vermouth does not help our cause, remarked MacK from the toilet.


These boys had determined to drive south a few miles the next day. —Field trips suck, said Isidor—but he couldn't accept lingering in the holiday home—stack of firewood, stack of board games—the atavistic kitchen threatening him all day. Iz in driving south from Portland and MacK North from Hollywood had been equally annoyed every few miles by small circular signs announcing the Trees of Misery—'*Only 375 miles* . . .'—a grove of hideously deformed *Sequoia sempervirens* belonging to a cruel megalomaniac. The regular appearance of these harping signs had driven them both wild with disgust—finding they were only ten miles from this grove it became their objective.

Isidor behind the wheel of his car—the coast highway took them rapidly away from the town—through big vegetation—here the sea tears at California assiduously and often manages to crack and flood it—it was true that the groves were '*cathedrallike*', as the brochure had it—but worship seemed a doubtful idea and one felt that outside this cathedral were only grim, enveloping elk—Portland and Los Angeles seemed imaginary.

Sometimes the most comfortable, even cozy road is deadly—in a dark grove, the road submerged and lined with boulders, Isidor strayed—admiring nature, his enemy—the left lane—and immediately had to contemplate the dull insistent face of an oncoming motor home—*Say!* said MacK—swerved to the right and onto a run of boulders, *Where there ought to be a shoulder*, said Iz bouncing—then back into the lane. —I have to tell you that is all drink and your buddy de Voto, said Isidor—my liver is generous but it's not a member of the Justice League of America. MacK slapped Iz like Abbott slaps Costello. —*Quit your fooling now!* —*Waaa!* said Isidor, *I was just tryna* . . .

MacK was truly shaken by this, the closest he'd ever come to death—they both disliked the ignominy of an automotive end—he continued to feel a gag-reflex of revulsion for days to come. But also found himself thinking *Not so bad to get knocked off with him*.

Sad enough perhaps to have *bought* these sickly trees—think of struggling to make this purchase in the Depression—but to have *named* them for whatever feeble associations the original proprietor's mind made of their deformities—to think *that* is what draws people—and it does. The Heidi Tree. The Giant Squid Tree. The El Greco Tree. The Walter Scott Limping Around with his Cane Tree. —The Hitler Tree, said Isidor, walking dispiritedly about, looking at one bent and looming over a lot of little succulents. —Jackson Pollock Tree, said MacK, pointing at one despairing, completely ill. Despite its insertion of the signs into the alimentary canal of Highway 1, the Trees of Misery had actually lost track of what it was supposed to be. However moronic it was to visit these trees, all gloom was banished upon entering the gift shop, a most fabulous example of such a place—it had everything—a *complete* range of cedar ware rubber-stamped 'Trees of Misery'—rubber tomahawks—all kinds of totem poles—plastic donkeys which shat out cigarettes—battalions of shot glasses, coffee mugs and thousands of embarrassing postcards covering not only the Trees of Misery and California's north coast but Seattle and San Francisco and Hollywood and BREASTS—o you can tell yourself you are buying this stuff with a self-aware love of the history of crap but you ARE standing in line buying it, ya jerk—along with the guy saying to his ice-cream smirched kid *Suck up to yer momma if you want her to buy you that, go on, suck up to yer momma!* Ah, gods. Isidor went for a revolting painting of a huge-breasted squaw; MacK key chains, refrigerator magnets and cedar desk implements. —This is *my* idea of squaw-candy, said Isidor.

Toward the holiday home, in brighter weather. Stopped to buy crabs—Izzy was pooped and made to argue taxonomy with the fisherman—who retreated *immediately* behind a sham of mental retardation—Iz's epicureanism was taking a beating in Portland, despite their white walls and posters of roasted peppers—he still flared up occasionally. —*But this man did catch this crab*, MacK intervened.

The introduction of sunlight, two species of seafood here on the edge, after all, imparted a sense of reason, the hope of solving their lives logically. But at table Isidor made further wry comments about his liver, which MacK received in much the same spirit, finding himself in his own miserable woman-chased woman-found Hell—he took it Iz was worried. —You going to drink all of that? —I'm resigned to it. MacK found in Isidor and in himself a new recognition of mortality and was surprised—instead of *resolutely abusing themselves*, they recognized they could feel better without *all* of these liquids; perhaps *some* of these liquids. *Which realization living a complete lie* will bring you to, as MacK well knew. Isidor seemed timid, daily underpinned by fear of death—sobered. Of course you have your frightened moments, but never doubt it or cease to believe it is final. He couldn't have actually said that Isidor felt the same, at that miserable time—not that it came out directly—but we're aging at exactly the same pace, thought MacK. Out to the garage to smoke, preserving the illusion of American health-n-wealth in the holiday home, not to sully please with the bitter odors of the corruptions of cities, as the rules on the back of the kitchen door more or less suggested.

—I used to want to live in the garage, said MacK, but my father wouldn't hear of it. —Male preserve, said Isidor. —More than that, I liked the rafters, the unfinished walls, the high roof where you can hear the rain, said MacK. —What rain, beach boy? —We had some rain, wise guy—where did you get these cigars? —A lucky find in Portland, said Iz—the morality there, the schizophrenia—you wouldn't believe it. HOKAY so everyone jogs during the day in their matching outfits, then they go home and you ought to see 'em eat—cholesterol city followed by these huge childish desserts. In the morning she—I mean *they*—eat this cereal with so many gizmos in it it's like a patisserie. And *I'm* supposed to feel bad for having a CIGAR. Non-fattening. Compact. And they give discomfort to our enemies. —*She*, hah? said MacK, are we going to discuss oral surgeons? Iz's face fell. —Well I've got to give the whole thing up, don't I? It's ridiculous, I can't be part of all this racism . . . it's nationalistic in a weird way, all these *catalogues*, these *designer beers*. —What about business? —I have neatly vacuumed Oregon of its modern firsts, I assure you. Quote—there is nothing left for me here—unquote. —What about her? —Well—here he focused at the ideal reflective distance, MacK thought, and Izzy's eyes and moustache looked rather like his own father's. So this is the warm, Jungian paragraph. —I just have to leave her to this profound emptiness, which she *will fill*—with sweaters. —Wow. —Yeah. I meet her at a club, take her to bed, she's *visiting* New York, I don't know she's practically *hemorrhaging* from sweater withdrawal—I think she's excited about *me*—I go to her brother's birthday *luau*, I'm the only guy wearing a shirt with *buttons*. —!— —So that's the story. And you? What about you, Sir, and the vaunted Southwest?

—Well we have fared much the same out here in this god damn

222

country, said MacK. I can take you through the whole miserable business in five minutes should you wish it. —Why leave New York? said Isidor, I mean, I more or less had to—I thought—but you? —You glom on to these women, said MacK, they glom on to you—and you convince yourself there is life out there, or out here rather, that you can both live—and it's *so* untrue. —What about NBC? said Isidor. —*Accumulated vacation*, said MacK, it swelled and it throbbed—they said if I didn't take it all right away they'd excise it. A holidectomy. —Nice. —And Red had to go to the desert to make this movie—an expedition to the *vaunted Southwest* with this woman who seems to like me . . . —That's the thing, said Isidor, that '*seems*'.

Now they're going to Have a Cigar and Discuss Women?—so this is the warm, Homeric paragraph?—as they sit and look out the open garage door at the dark sea. —So we get out there, said MacK, there we were in the vast Region of Guns and Christianity—there was the desert, huge and haunting—in fact *really deserted*, deserted in the mind of man. Well you can go out and shoot things but the only place where life occurs in the vaunted Southwest is on television. —Shouldn't bother you, said Iz, media man after all. —What I do in my little room is *futile*, said MacK, but damn if I am not going back there and get all my meals and drinks sent up from Hurley's—see if I don't. But their television is revealing, brother—mainly advertisements for trade schools—a sign that culture has failed completely—the only way you can make a living is by fixing TVs—the thing that ruined your brain in the first place—along with the heat. So we drive across two square states and in Albuquerque she points out this big bookstore. —Really? said Iz. —And a news-stand and she smiles at me coquettishly and giggles '*Last chance!*' So it dawns on me what she's saying—where we're going there's NO NOTHING. No books no music no movies except pornography and *elk-murder*, no selection of gins no single malt no beer except you-know-what no cigars no pipe tobacco. And then we go up and up to this trailer camp in the sky where they're making the movie. —Who's in it? —No idea. I did say I was going to read all of Stendhal one day so I have these *paperbacks* from the *thrift store*. —*Y-e-e-e-c-c-c-h!* said Isidor rising off his bench. —This terrible, empty routine has developed, said MacK, and I say this in *full realization* of the naïveté and dullness of my routine in New York—but somehow there is little drudgery in walking to work from 50th Street. —Well the No. 1 is the people's train, said Isidor, they express themselves there, you get some variety . . . I suppose. —She has to get up at 3.30 every morning and drive down the mountain to the 'location', she comes back late every night, pissed off and half stoned, film people are all the same. We haven't made love since we got there —we suffered from the altitude for a week and she hates me for my constant complaining—there's no this, no that—but damn it; it's *factual complaining*—there really is no this and no that.

—So it's *attitude sickness*, said Isidor. —Once in a while I drive to Albuquerque, which now seems like a cultural OASIS, to get the *Times*. —You!? said Isidor. —Yeah, said MacK. Turns out they only order three copies for the whole state. —What about Santa Fe? —It's banned in Santa Fe. So this is how I'm living. I get up every day and look in the mirror and say *This is how I am living*. I started cutting tiny pictures of pretty women out of mail order catalogues—*Catalogues!* moaned Isidor—yes and the local paper said MacK and this being the vaunted Southwest they are merely gardening or posing in front of new kinds of sinks. I make up stories about them. That's all I do all day. There's this kick-ass bar but you can go in the afternoon and *not* get your ass kicked. After a month the bartender said *What's happenin'?* I said, I bet you I am the only guy in here wearing Clinique® Turnaround Cream. —Gee *Whizz*, said Isidor.

—When I'm overwhelmingly *ultra* miserable I drive over to the next town. It's got a big PINEY LODGE—stone fireplace, antlers, bottles of beer, club sandwiches. It's a desperate scene, man, I put too many *longings* into it. I need it to be New York, just for a moment or two. Clatter. Service. I *can't love Red*, not without bookstores, bars, people in diverse clothing shouting, the sound of breaking glass . . . —So? said Isidor.

—So I asked the waitress out. Out into the woods. —I'm impressed, said Isidor, who nonetheless looked pale. —There's this picturesque rocky *stream*, said MacK, in our town Burger King is a natural feature. We walked along, didn't talk of much, she was from the place—kind of Fifties hairstyle. Then we had one of these thunder showers which come every afternoon. So we ran under the trees—soaked to the skin—and—! There was this penetrating *smell of ozone*.

—I don't . . . said Isidor, shifting in his seat, nauseated by the idea of relations out of doors, picturing MacK and some kind of girl in pigtails, a *tree*, mit *burls*—

—*I'm sorry*, said MacK so anyway the storm ended—we ended—(*Isidor groaned again*)—and we went and sat by the stream. Then at almost the same moment we both got up and started gathering stones from the stream. Large stones like they made the lodge fireplace from. —Yes? said Isidor, looking at his watch. —We waded out in the stream and piled them into cairns. We were each making a little shrine. Shrines, what the f*** are you, said Isidor, do you know it's nearly bedtime? —I get your disintegration, you get mine, said MacK. My cairn was of light grey stone, a taller middle section and shorter piles on the sides. Hers was circular, black pebbles. She put two feathers from a blue-jay inside it, and they turned as the water flowed through it. —Yes, *AND*? said Isidor. He was about to explode. —She said, *what's your shrine to?* And I said, this is a shrine to the RCA Building. *Where's that?* she said. It's in New York, I said, 49 West 49th Street, no 50 West 50th Street. I work there. *Oh*, she said, *cool*. What's yours to? I said. She smiled and said *Mine's to love*.

—So you make a *replica of the RCA Building* in the middle of the woods? said Isidor, you think that's healthy?—It simply appeared under my hands, said MacK. It pointed the way home. —So? —I drove her to her place. The car regularly aquaplaned at fifty miles an hour just like it says in all the textbooks. I got back to the house and Red was there fuming, on the phone to her sister—a woman who for some reason is a constant and willing receptacle of Red's mistrust and disappointment and venom about show business and me—in front of her on the table were all my little pictures—the redheads with the new kitchens, blondes riding lawnmowers, brunettes luxuriating on leather sofas in their socks—and she accused me of having affairs with them! —What! said Iz. —*You've been seeing these women while I have to work!* She practically threw me out. *Ai yi yi.*

But after all, one's crazy 'bout one's baby.

Isidor maybe saw his future as irretrievably lonely and tortured—but at least he was *going back to town*. You can't make life happen; nobody can make anything happen. But you can surely be lazy and self-deluded and lonely. The idea that they'd be parting in the morning was already palpable in the smoke, up in the rafters and canoes of the garage. They got off a few loud jokes over coffee in the morning and then it went flat and Isidor made haste to leave. MacK dreadfully sad. He and Isidor always went around thinking they saw enough of each other—or that they could do without it, which really wasn't true.

### SO YOU SEE WHAT TROUBLE YOU CAN GET INTO? IF YOU SET ONE FOOT, ONE *TOE* OUTSIDE NEW YORK?

## Iz On His Own

Toward MacK and The Hour at day's end—walking in his very serious shoes, which he is one of a dwindling band of men in New York to have regularly re-soled, and half of *them* are Yalies—as he'd said to MacK the very day he'd bought them, back in Our Years in Yorkville—*These are shoes for a guy who WALKS*—and walked all of this our town in them. Up and down from his abodes to the Battery, across all of lower Manhattan, way WAY up to the Cloisters. For years and years. Even after he acquired the shop from Mr Playfair, he often left in the afternoon, rain or no, supposedly 'buying'—bullshit. Out, away from books, the cigarred office. Stopping soon for a cup of joe, of java, mud—the whole old New York thesaurus of coffee—but *no* espresso, *screw Portland*, he said, out loud, too often. Miss Plein would look after the shop. Even though Miss Plein is from Queens and sounds it, THAT doesn't put off his customers because they are the true democrats born of this our town.

When he got Bibulo & Schenkler, half inherited, half purchased, Isidor had had ideas it could become one of the midtown East Side firms—a few very levant titles in a draped window with some Georgian furniture—one of your really discreet side streets—say East 56th? That's a little far north maybe but *you* know. But he quickly decided, after being tortured by some of the *incunabula hounds*, that he didn't give a damn about incunabula, f***ing Gutenberg, or even fine binding. Who gives a damn? *Swaddling clothes, what are we, f***ing Egyptians? I should change my name to Moishe maybe. They'll be asking for papyri next. I sell books, not botched attempts at books!* he shouted in the shop on the day he decided this. He liked smoky old books and that was it. It was funny, but he found he couldn't apply his capable, statistical, finicky brain to the minutiae of very fine books—in the course of several weeks he packed up all the very rarest stuff and sent it up to auction, where it fetched boring, enormous prices. *Screw it*, he thought—East 56th sort of thing would never have suited the history of the shop. It wasn't right to do that to Mr Playfair; why pay gobs of rent, and *be obliged to cultivate an English accent*. So Bibulo & Schenkler, he had decided long ago, would remain a downtown book business in location and character—the shop would always smell from his modest Montecruz use. Big cinema section, lots of *handled* but interesting firsts—a ton of books on the city.

Poetry he took advice on—*one thing about Isidor Katz*, he thought to himself, *I don't issue opinions on stuff I know nothing about, that's for sure*. His own interests, spicy meats, hangmen, Sing Sing, vanished restaurants and bars, the Fulton markets, Robert Fulton, and Fulton J. Sheen, he amassed with a vigor in buying which often left some of the other dealers open-mouthed. These holies were kept in the shelves around the entrance to his office. Yet—unlike some of our great downtown booksellers—he was willing to sell them. It made him happy to find someone who *liked* the Fulton Fish Market, and—this is unthinkable in the unwritten portion of the constitution of the Antiquarian Booksellers Association (founded 1906)—he liked to talk to people about the books they bought or wanted to buy, can you imagine? But this was the legacy of Mr Playfair, who'd run Bibulo & Schenkler, since *he'd* half bought and half inherited it, in 1940, like an affable professor with liberal office hours.

But forget the shop—you like the sound of it, *you* visit it—Fourth Avenue—you'll see it—he's determined to stay on Fourth Avenue, which has always threatened evanescence, because, Isidor thought now, walking up through Chelsea, particularly *now* I'm determined to stay on Fourth because of how much time MacK and I spent there—why we spent most of our spare cash in college right at the Peacock, and Bibulo & Schenkler—he knew this yet had never thought it much—about his days as a customer in a shop he'd never have dreamt to own. Worried about MacK.

The mud left a dark scum at the back of Isidor's throat; which he liked, whether from java or pipe or cigar or flu or bile rising because something on the street annoyed Hell out of him—always just a little something rising back there was good. *When rises Katz so does the bile*. He'd been walking Manhattan for thirty years, nearly—which shocked him—this was a day for shocks maybe—cleared his larynx of the mud. —*Scum*, he said, out loud, as he passed a news stand.

BLIND PROPRIETOR: F*** you, man.

—Nah, nah, said Izzy—still more than half to himself—the scum put him in mind of a visit to Seligman the tobacconist—walk needs a focus after all—it was time to kick Seligman's ass. And now not just about the whole nasty saga of cigars in the last few years in Manhattan, f***ing-A disgraceful. You start off discovering something of value, from the previous culture, said Isidor, like these shoes for one thing, shoes for a guy who *WALKS*—granted the real property of old Yale farts who can't wait to get 'em off and run barefoot through the deep pile in their club every lunchtime—or cigars—no one gave a f*** about *cigars* in *1978*—except Isidor and Mr Playfair—maybe Jackie Onassis, who knows—they were just for puffy-faced old guys with an irritated drooly lip and an egg-cream eye—then all these *Pine Street* guys come along—they have the salaries—and they buy all the good cigars in New York! —*They even give them to their girlfriends*, said Isidor out loud at the corner of 35th and Seventh. And all the good cigars in New York was a SHIT LOAD of cigars. Sidelong glance from a woman in a very old-fashioned hat. So then you have New York, *New York*, mark you, where everyone really does deserve the best stuff, devoid of cigars! New York, which has always been the most *loyal* to cigars. Screw Chicago—what do they got? They got NOTHING.

# Chez Iz

What is *happening* to *Chelsea*, said Isidor, look at all this arty garbage, man, I tell you—almost as if to MacK, as if MacK was there—it is INtolerable. Where there was recently a perfectly, respectably, *miserable* coffee shop, with a perfect cup of miserable mud—Iz went there sometimes—there was now a yellow-painted GALLERY offering artifacts native to the Gilbert Islands. In the yellow frame of the window a large *tapa* cloth, bark beaten to the merry rhythm of the hydrogen bombs, thought Isidor—but he stopped and contemplated its pattern, as that morning he'd stared at the remarkably similar one graven on Sylvie's back. —Only book dealer currently in Manhattan with a girlfriend with Maori tattoos *after all*, out loud in front of the gallery. Stick that in your Roxburghe and bind it, said Isidor.

But who was going to *recognize* 'the book dealer Isidor Katz' in a man talking to himself in front of a yellow gallery in Chelsea? No danger. Clean white shirt—not a cop in the city'd lay a paw on you, man—say what you want.

After he lost Mary-Ann and drifted, or fled, downtown, *head-long*, and threw in his lot with Mr Playfair, Isidor hadn't known what to do about the *horn*—you get out of practice. Can't go solo—it was an out-of-body experience for Iz anyway—always *saw himself doing it*, so absurd, too pathetic silly and human. Afraid too he'd clock out during it one day. Who isn't? Along with the shop Iz inherited, in a legal-size filing cabinet, a collection of Mr Playfair's leisure time reading from the late 1940s and early 50s—the most absurd magazines ever essayed. But Izzy's casual perusal of them—*What Babes Really Want*—*Cowgirl Roundup*—*Untamed Fury* (girl in a leopard-print tank suit threatening a stuffed ocelot with what was not so much a whip as the handlebar grip from a tricycle with plastic streamers)—*Beautiful But Rough*—*The Big-Opportunity Field Of Custom Upholstery*—*Hitler's Women*—*Bevy Of Brawling Beauts*—*Dish Of Delightful Dreaming*—*Fish Bite Every Day*—never let himself think about *Mr Playfair* leafing through this madness between the Sherwood Anderson first and the *Shepherd's Calendar*—for all Izzy knew the stuff might have come in with some library or other—lot of funny people about. Miss Plein bought a library last year from a *Bronx midget*, who collected everything on miniature railways he could find and also, oddly, a lot of George Eliot—and in practically every book she found a twenty dollar bill.

But once Izzy had secured a pad, he began constructing its ethic. Whereas his place in the Far East had reflected the old booky, homely New York values—the life he and MacK were forever *glimpsing* in windows they passed—and never quite achieved—guy moves to the *Village*, go nuts, right? He found some black lamps which matched his japanned martini shaker. Kind of thing.

This place, in a pre-war tower off Fifth Avenue, had a sunken living-room, bordered by a wrought-iron railing. It seemed to MacK that for a time Izzy sank, along with his living-room. He moved in a pile of the silly magazines—he wouldn't have books at home, for a time, couldn't stand them—even though he was now a partner in the business and life had improved, he was without Mary-Ann, and he'd *decided* to dive—sunk in gloom in his sunken living-room—into a few adventures suggested by this lurid old crap. So there was a succession of jungle babes and vines, cowgirls and lariats, girls with black hair and red shoes who might have been Mary-Ann but clearly weren't.

**Just a nutty little period!**

# Sylvie

One day Isidor came across Sylvie, as you do discover people in town—almost as if they're on a shelf you haven't looked at for a time. She was working at Peacock, where he'd gone to ask about World War II pictorials to fill out a collection of journalism he'd just bought. She turned away from him to the card file and here were these remarkable, combed, *spiced* patterns on her back. Had to ask her out of course, that was obvious, marks on the back. Turned out she was—wait for it—a *second-generation anthropologist blue blood who shared a turret* with her father at the American Museum of Natural History—this father'd 'given' her a going-over by a south seas tattooer for her 21st birthday. So she *had* to be a jungle girl, Gee Whizz, she really was a jungle girl. And she knew all about Isidor's jungle. Sylvie was beyond smart, beyond passionate, and in several weeks she was living in Iz's tower. Things that had been sunken rose up. *As the Katz rises so shall the living-room.* Izzy felt more like himself and reintroduced his books to the place. Oh there was still a jungle aspect—Sylvie liked the bachelor pad lamps and the cocktail shaker particularly—the patterns on her back fit right in with Isidor's design for living.

KATZ PREDICTS! Very few men and women will find them-selves settled together in this our town any more—rubbernecking is one of the genetically programmed habits here—if you both assert you're happy together, married even!, you're still looking for the finer thing. But fineness has a limit; fineness is a *finite* quality—and no one can recognize that in New York because you are trained by this our beloved town to salivate after the *infinite*—that is what your guy and gal on the street imagine to be HAVING IT ALL. But some-thing drives you to *act normal* and see what happens. What the hell is it! Act like people and see where it gets you? Wears you down is what it does. You walk the streets and you feel your nest is—not exactly soiled—but perhaps that this wrong person—no judge-ments, just wrong—is *turning your own apartment against you*. If that is possible.

Martinis get bigger and Bigger and BIGGER—there *is* a bloody limit—disagreements longer, along with the evenings and the heat. You're willing to admit to trust in the beginning maybe, even though you both know this is just an extended bonk, *extruded* even. Plenty people can live with the wrong person but NOBODY can live with the *idea* of the wrong person. The city itself becomes wrong—you cease to be able to see yourself in it—being drained, you lack the vital inch of courage you need to open the damn door and put your foot out.

Don't you see that everyone has that courage here? Except the oldies and the Yalies? They're all BRAVE. That's what it takes to live here—this is why New York whups any other dam' town—it's BRAVE. We continue to live rather than to watch TELEVISION.

But Isidor and Sylvie were of the luckiest—with their intellectual compatibility and mutual style and fondness for games out of very bad mummy or sarong-and-torch movies—as you might imagine —they found each other and did not have to leave town.

Isidor became more like his own customers—this was when he began collecting New York, on paper, in earnest. He also bought furiously for the shop, expanding the Old New York section into an entire aisle on the second floor. *Sunlight and Shadow in Old New York. Brooklyn Waterfront.* Maps, menus, even ephemera, which Mr Playfair had scorned: bus tickets, boxing programs—his apartment and the shop began doing duty *as* New York for Isidor—he lost interest in going out into it. He lost himself contentedly and endlessly in *patterns,* New York's and Sylvie's. On Jungle Night! There was the shop—his tower—and Sylvie, who became—quite simply—his nurse and his muse—*My NUSE*, as Isidor put it—which MacK firstly heard as *NOOSE*—quickly and violently disabused.

When Chelsea turns into Times Square you never know—it's always when you're not paying attention. There's the question of the Garment District—an iffy thing to identify these days—and even the older idea of the Fur and Flower District—which somehow floated, ethereally, a little up and over from the Garment District. You're walking along—north—you can already feel or smell Times Square's hot motor—and you get NOTIONS, window acres of machine lace, buttons, edges, elastic—which have never given you any notions other than that you'd better get out of there before someone sews a pink bunny from Hong Kong onto your jacket—nominally Times Square is much more a district for notions than the *notion portion* of the Garment District.

But it's stupid to talk of *districts*—that is for HICKS—every cross-street is different.

Isidor slowed—the thick leather brakes of his shoes doing this job admirably—as he passed a window rather theatrically displaying theatrical footwear. He recalled his one attempt at Seventies style, a pair of lime green platform-soled oxfords with wing-tip sewing, bought the day after he'd got completely rubbished on mushrooms. Whatever explosive insights to a whole new LIFE STYLE these shoes had been a part of had completely worn off by the time he got them back to his dormitory, though he left them on the shelf next to his beloved *Beowulf* and *Cid*, holding up the *Cid*, for the rest of the year—they cost eighty 1973 dollars. In the present window were some black shoes with ankle straps—Izzy blinked a little, kept moving, and thought about Miss Plein teetering about the shop in such a—but *Sylvie*, jungle night might be edifyingly augmented with—a blast of hot stale DISCO woke him up to the irritating realities of 42nd and Seventh. Across the street he noticed an Orthodox guy—a big one—coming out of a topless bar. Sweating, adjusting his incredibly boring hat—where do they get them so *generically shaped*, mumbled Isidor, you never see these hats in shops—you'd think Ben Gazzara was buried in the last one. But big Orthodox guy? Topless bar? —What'd he think about in there, said Iz. Felt bad for speculating on Miss Plein's sex life and wandered Times Square in disconsolation—over MacK—the end seemed to have been kicked out of his errands, his entrails—thought about going to the tobacconist and *kicking his ass* for killing his friend. Seligman would deny everything: *This is my fault? I've always recommended very moderate smoking*, he'd say that, said Izzy, but it isn't true—all through the Seventies he sat in his f***ing shop with his silent mop-head partner and smoked—they must have got through half a pound of latakia a day—playing chess or pretending to. —Not so arrogant now, are we? said Isidor aloud and got a look from a suburban couple in front of 'Cats'—they're killing the guy, they've killed him, is all, said Iz. The couple obviously came to the theater often enough that they didn't want to *flee* Isidor, but you could tell they wished there wasn't A MAN TALKING TO HIMSELF right in front of 'Cats' so early in the day. They'd thought to buy their tickets early so as to AVOID ISIDOR.

# Naga Mouris

Awful fellow for curry, Isidor—*I'll bhuna you under the table*—always been that way.

When the red dawn of Szechuan first hit New York, Isidor announced to a table of MacK, Mary-Ann and *Sidney* he was going to crunch up, as he put it, an entire Chinese pepper. Black, uncertain eating like a big bug. Bets were placed—he did so—and struggled to show little reaction. —How was it? said Sidney, who had the most money riding on it. —Not so bad, husked Isidor, who picked up his chopsticks and continued his dinner. The conversation resumed and several minutes later MacK reached for the water pitcher—he then saw Izzy had pushed his chair into the *corner* and was drinking directly from the pitcher with both hands. Later, when they were walking across the park, a staggering, crimson Isidor suddenly rushed for an embankment and stuck his head deep into the snow. [Hissing noise.] —That'll be twenty bucks, said Sidney.

Hotter, hotter, hotter—during his year at Oxford he studied little but bitter beer, and started a curry club—bested the Fellows at their own game—Izzy figured his tongue had a lot of Hunan and Mexican training in New York, whereas the Brits had grown up eating *jam*. In the spring he was trying to save his scholarship by characterizing Spinoza's ascending grades of knowledge as the Curry of Opinion, the Bhuna of Reason, and the *Vindaloo of Intuition*—which did little for Spinoza, Balliol, or Isidor. On the last day of term the owner of the 'Mumtaz', where he'd spent all the time he wasn't in the 'Mitre', told him there *was* something hotter than vindaloo, Ceylon, *phal,* and *thal:* NAGA. —*But you will not be finding it with ease, Dr Isidor.* —You shouldn't call me that yet.

Iz came back to New York—his many adventures—the shop—but since 1975 he's been in a kind of cloud—beneath everything Isidor does he's really doing only one thing—like those religionists for whom a conscious chant becomes a relentless, unconscious prayer—he has been thinking about NAGA.

Wandered in and out of Indian groceries and spice shops around 6th Street, or up Lexington, asking for naga. *Asked* these guys, who were just trying to run their businesses—and don't need to have anything to do with obsessed people—though that is always part of business in this our town—in beseeching and pathetic tones, for naga. Instantly they knew they were dealing with a madman. —*You will not find naga*, they all said with charming and nervous smiles, *no no no*. MacK had the feeling Isidor had approached some of these people a *number of times*. Iz would take him into a shop and look around for something that might be naga—without asking. Maybe this is it, Iz said once, picking up a big green thing—the pods in *Invasion of the Body Snatchers*. —*Oh ho ho ho no, that is not naga*, said the shopkeeper, shooing them out onto First Avenue.

One day five years ago there had been a glimmer of hope, Iz thought, in the person of *Sani*. He came out of the back of one of the Indian groceries after Izzy had dispiritedly asked for naga and became tearful upon the answer—came toward him on a cane—a young man on a cane, smoking a *bidi*. He reeked of romantic suffering and turmeric. —*Naga?* said Sani, *it is possible that I could find you naga*. Isidor's compact body flattened and then lengthened—*doyoinnnggg!* —a pointer dog in a duck-hunting cartoon. —*Do you know anything about naga?* Sani asked, coming closer, surrounding Iz with smoke and spice. —*It is not a thing that people . . . cultivate*, said Sani. *It grows only wild, in the hills of Assam. And there, in only one department really, in Sylhet. Call me Friday evening. After we make deliveries I am usually here in the shop, smoking and having coffee with friends. Perhaps I will have news for you*. Like a scene in a Charles Boyer movie, Isidor took the phone number of the shop and went out, up the steps to the street, in the rain.

But come Friday Sani had mysteriously disappeared. Izzy phoned several times only to be told *He's out, he's out*. The third time things got sinister. *There is no Sani here. There has never been a Sani. Leave us alone. Stop bothering us, or things will go badly for you*.

It took Iz weeks to recover. You can't really get everything in New York—it's just something people *SAY*.

Now wandered into a news-stand. Casually perused *Leg Action, Leg Display, Leg Scene, Leg Quarterly, Leg Geographic, Leg Literary Supplement, Popular Leg, Leg Modeler, Leg & Garden, Inside Leg, Leg Frontier, Leg Theory, Leg & Bass Fisherman, Leg Times-Picayune, Tri-Leg Quarterly, P.M.L.A., Leg Diggity, Leg-A-Rama, Leg Aroma, Leg Neurosis, Leg Mania, Leg Psychosis, Leg Embolism, Leg Aneurysm, Leg Freakout, Leg Nam, Leg Thorazine, Leg Flashback,* and *Knee Joint Action* with his usual *savoir-faire.* Presiding was a man from the subcontinent. With the usual casual indolence Iz asked: —Where are you from? —I am from Bangladesh, Sir, said the man, if it is any of your business (displaying a certain residential period in New York). —*Naga?* Iz asked, not even explaining, he no longer had the heart but carried on the search on a zombie level, the reflex of sadness rather than of hope. Without the hesitation of a second: —*Go to the Madhuban restaurant in Jackson Heights. They will give you naga.*

Out to the street and put up his hand for a cab. Was almost frightened he'd found it—frightened he was going to have to eat it immediately. No time to phone—let anyone *know*; MacK or Sylvie. In the car he wondered aloud if he oughtn't to have taken the BMT. —Is it unseemly, searching for a treasure of the developing world by *private car?* —What is the matter with you man? said the driver. —Naga.

The waiter asked Isidor if he wanted the lunch buffet, steamy and deep-colored in chafing dishes in the window along Roosevelt Avenue. —I want *naga.* The waiter opened his mouth, shut it, and *ran away,* to the kitchen. There was telephony. The owner of the Madhuban, Mr M M Narwal, suddenly hurried in wearing a *spy coat.* He smiled down at Isidor, reached in his pocket, and brought out two soft pods of orange-pink. —I suggest that I can make you a lamb vindaloo with this naga, said Narwal, also perhaps a shad fish curry. Narwal pronounced it *sad.* —Sad! said Isidor. —Shad. A man grows these in his own house. I put the tiniest bit on my rice at home

237

last night and my wife said, what is that you have got there, I can smell it over here. This is the naga, I said to her and O gosh is it hot. Narwal pronounced it *hardt*.

Before the naga, a deep red carpet of somosas, pakora, achingly tender pieces of chicken from Narwal's tandoor; a sobbingly wonderful chana bhaji—Isidor BLIND TO IT.

Now the waiters gathered around Isidor's table, the guy from Manhattan who was going to eat naga. He was afraid now—afraid his eyes would puff up, that he would have to apply lotions, tourniquets and scrapers to his soft tissues. That it would be like the *Vindaloo of Intuition* that once forced him out into the streets of Edinburgh, spasmodically waving his arms, where he was nearly run over by a taxi.

But the naga didn't taste like *capsicum* at all—more like perfume—it didn't blister the tongue—it filled Isidor's head with hardt exotic humors. —I'm feeling a little panicky, said Isidor, to no one in particular—I'm hallucinating. Colors plunged that were not in the wallpaper of the Madhuban—a *policeman* on his lunch hour moved toward the chafing dishes with a spoon which, for a moment, became *stupendous in size*.

Now here was Narwal, pulling up a chair. The table was littered with perspired napkins, cups of spice tea, gulab jamun. —Do you know anything about naga? said Narwal, are you all right, Mr—Isidor? My friend has to grow them in Long Island City because of course it is not legal to bring produce into this country. Isidor hunched himself into his jacket. —I didn't know SPICINESS was a thing controlled by governments. —*Oh* yes. Do you know anything about Bangladesh? said Narwal. If only we could become politically stabilized, it could be one of the world's most wonderfully productive countries. We have everything: forests, petroleum, minerals. —And naga, said Isidor, banging his fist on the table, don't forget. —Yes, said Narwal, of course in Bangladesh we still have great problems of the natural world which plague us. Tornadoes, earthquakes, tidal waves, floods . . . —But do these really affect the *naga?* said Isidor—you listen to me—naga could play a big role in redevelopment. *With naga you could rule the world.* —Thank you sir, thank you very much, said Narwal—your bill; I leave you. So he too found Isidor deranged—starry—especially after he'd *got* the stuff.

So often there is no talking to them.

Flagged a gypsy cab, admiring its battle-scarred gun grey body—thought it would do, being blown around in the battle between the monster foods at the end of the world. —Back to Manhattan, said Isidor. —'Back'? said the driver. Cruelly. —Hey guess what, Iz said to the guy, I've been thinking for months that I need medical attention. —So? the guy said. —But what I needed was *Madhuban* attention.


Horizontal light and sound of the glimmering river and bridge world—mid-afternoon sun on struts, trains, the water. A real division, thought Isidor, between Manhattan and America—*tenks gut!* —so what Queens has crazy restaurants with naga?—it's still the other place really. Some grandeur (?) along the FDR—homeyness (?) of the small coffee shops of Second. The guy is still hallucinating, is what.

—Here, here, says Iz, off here. Fine. Great. Here's fine—anywhere right around here—*STOP!!!* The driver twitches like a cat and pulls over.

Isidor always felt things were made dark by the Citicorp Center. Ostensibly reflective, it nevertheless seems to draw all life, all light toward it, from blocks around, to suck energy, simply to suck. —Rather like myself, he said—and laughed. Got a look from a curious cop—this was *Lexington Avenue* after all. —Stayin' out of trouble? said the cop, unexpectedly, curiously, *sweetly*. —You bet! said Izzy—taken aback, felt he was recognized in some way—suddenly *existed*, oh dear, instead of being a flying, incisive consciousness, a narrator of the city—they're on to me? Started sassing the cop when he was a block away—more looks. —Trouble with the mouth, that's what it is, said Iz. —I'll stop yer mouth, said a guy in a doorway. —Mouth trouble, said Iz to himself—thinking of MacK and the . . . tumors. —Trouble is, MacK's never used his mouth *enough*, said Isidor at the corner of 58th and Lexington, it's like Sidney always said—his grotesque lack of movement or gesture.

Sidney had once proposed to MacK that he open an *Œconomy of Movement Center*, and he said you had to spell it that way—where those who worried about such things could lose the elaborate gesticulations of the Old World, and become as stiff and still as MacK! *Make a million bucks*, Sidney'd said—*deductible too*. Sidney was the only guy they knew who regularly used the word 'deductible'—to go through life, thought Isidor, with that point of—but here the Citicorp Center. The overhangs, the blue-green corners stealing light—*you steal light from the city?* —Sunlight and shadow in *new* New York, Iz said. Under the overhangs, and in the arcades surrounding the thing—OUT OF WHICH GLASS MAY FLY AT ANY MOMENT—thanks a lot—don't care what they say—there are dark pools, places where the light of commerce doesn't penetrate—where the glutinous hagfish from the executive floors descend to gape and exude their slime—the cyclostomata (*'one of the lowest orders of vertebrates'*—ENCYCLOPAEDIA BRITANNICA) of banking attach, bore into an exotic dancer or two . . . Isidor felt something rising in his blood—fired by the naga—a fight, a fight, the FIGHT he'd always wanted to have with the tobacconist. He'd fight for MacK—why not? Raise a real stink and give up the f***ing stuff *today*, right in front of the guy.

Naga and this brush with one of his possible selves—Isidor suddenly remembered the cop *singling him out*—f***'s sake, you *believe* that? he said. —I'll believe anything, *now*, said a guy also waiting for the light at Madison and 53rd. Up there in the Fairchild Building MacK had been kissed by Olive just an hour or two before.

# The RCA Building

Iz really wished powerfully he could shut up, but there was a tinge of trip surrounding him, and he felt powerless to rein himself in—a little afraid now that his mouth trouble really was getting worse—right there on the street—as he walked. —Is there anything worse than to feel something *inside you* is *getting worse* when you're on the street, said Iz, no wonder everyone's got these f***ing *phones* now, call the mama soon as anything goes wrong. *Mom, I'm having a heart attack on the street. I just wanted to say . . .* Questioned why his steps were westward and remembered he'd got to pick a fight, immediately, with the tobacconist. —Perfect time, after all, go defend the guy, kick that little runt's ass.

Fifth Avenue, seen down the side street, seemed to be an unrolling, inviting carpet, beckoning Izzy toward the tobacconist's— the slightly hallucinating bookseller—he went over. —Gee Whizz this naga is really hanging on, he said. Decided to wander a bit—no hurry after all—the tobacconist's runty ass is always there for kicking until 5.30. Walked down to 51st and turned into Rockefeller Plaza. —Go past MacK's place, he said. The big metal guys on the AP Building still trying to get out that edition—just another dope on the phone, said Izzy, crossing the street and gazing down into the skating rink—Prometheus, his shell, like a phone in his hand—he's on the shellphone, said Isidor, he's talking to the *News* guy about his massive forearm . . . *Atlas is over on Fifth at the moment, whadda you expect, he's going to put the f***ing WORLD down? For YOUR call?* A gay little family of tourists gathered at the edge of the rink, hoping they might find Isidor's talk informative. Across it, leaning placidly his hands on the stone ledge, a security guard, his visor down low over his dark glasses. But obviously looking at me, thought Isidor. —I see ya, ya big palooka. But what were they talking about, Prometheus and the burly reporter from the nearly defunct Associated Press? —About MacK, obviously, said Izzy on the move—*this* was the phone call he was dreading maybe, I was dreading, that's where he works, worked—what'm I *saying?* Guy's not dead and hasn't even told me he's *going* to be dead, definitely, said Isidor. The gay little family slipped away. Isidor gazed into the lobby of the RCA Building from under the awning outside—some *tan* guy standing around smoking—limousines purring in the little street. He thought, sentimentally, of MacK's studio up there—where he'd never been—but thought—the guy's had his hands on some knobs up there—there's some biochemical, some *genetic vestige* of MacK in the microphone, or at least in the screen, said Iz, who knew his stuff—he'd sold a big collection on radio a few years back—and dismissed such a thought.

But whatever news was passing from—let's call him Bud—to Prometheus was definitely *dread, dread news*, thought Iz—and found himself walking over to Sixth, by Hurley's, past all that dreary Irishry where MacK used to meet his . . . *fancy women*, I can say that if I wanna, said Isidor. Hurley's, MacK's martini local—though Isidor appreciated the atmosphere in the little place which had cocked its snook at John D Jr and his play bulldozer—was very hard to take; all those NBC veeps in their suits. Still, something about it, said Izzy. The dread news—found himself wondering if MacK's obit would be in the *Times*—maybe NBC would put it in—last chance to be in the paper, said Isidor wistfully of his friend—he wasn't aware that MacK's name had been in the *New York Times* the day he assumed his job. But it appeared only because of Shelby Stein's promotion to television—the *New York Times* doesn't know or care anything about radio—*running as they do one of the worst radio stations in history themselves*, said Iz heatedly—inserting *actual slices of cheese* between movements of Beethoven. Your Beethoven and cheese station. Pictured the announcer pushing a slice of gouda into the cd deck—those horses' asses in their tartan trousers, their *view of culture*, you don't even see guys at the *Times* dressed like that. Can you imagine asking the Mayor questions in Black Watch pants? He glanced up 47th, its heaving mass of black clothing—oh and there the little wise men in their boat of books—a place he and MacK haunted before Iz was even in the business.

The sweat was back—the naga kept making things a little too vivid—or perhaps it's the DAZZLE OF MIDTOWN, said Iz, its CHARM, to which I've obviously become impervious—and turned west onto 46th. He felt two things, besides the naga's haloes—a slight saliva at the thought of the tobacconist's cigars and large jars of latakia—and a mob rustling in his blood because he was going to have it finally OUT with the guy—the *squirt*, said Isidor, passing the Universal-Brasil Restaurant, Inc., where a little placard beamed in the window, as they might have placed there forty years before, in the movies maybe, though he'd smelled it before his eye met the yellowed card—

## FEIJOADA TODAY

—and because he'd lunched to the hallucinogenic limit at the Madhuban, Izzy felt his various dark systems bubble like the *feijoada completa* in the vats of the U.B. Rest.

As it always referred to itself: 'U.B. REST. CANNOT ASSUME RESPONSIBILITY FOR COATS OR HATS ESP.'—'NOTICE: GRATUITIES ARE THE RESPONSIBILITY OF THE CUST. AND NOT U.B. REST.!!.' What an odd hotbed of responsibility and doom, he thought, for a lot of Brazilians, was the U.B. Rest., Inc., though maybe these guys got kicked out of Brazil for being too Portuguese. It was nothing less than a black, hot mood—and he got the tobacconist's sign in his sights. *Man* he was going to enjoy this, more than naga or feijoada. Saw himself suddenly tall as the Citicorp Center, battling an equally titanic tobacconist—designed by Philip Johnson—who therefore had a hole in his head.

# The Epicure Pipe Shop

West 46th was always a street of our hemisphere—which always amused Isidor: the Brazilian places boiling their feijoada; the moccasin company across the street boiling the feet of Yalies—the tobacconist's had been the first intrusion of anything stylish, so far as anything in 1970 can be said to have been stylish. —But he was a brave arty guy, said Isidor, he had long hair and a SWEATER. Painted the whole place black—displayed the tobacco in white *Japanese bowls* in the window, as if you could pour milk on it and eat it with a spoon. And he'd had some heady blends, 'Owl', Iz's favorite, so stuffed with latakia and yenidje it was like imbibing all the bonfires of youth; reliving every piquant dish or afternoon . . . 'Forest', MacK's—a strange quality of the past, of corks, of wood. Light on leaves, veins of the natural world—with a little *salt*, of adventure, of Stevenson? The incense of several days on which you fell in love. Then there'd been a problem about it ten years ago, suddenly stopped making it, MacK reported to Iz one Saturday—Izzy flew into a rage and *took a cab* there and demanded to know why his friend's favorite tobacco should have been withdrawn—course he should be smoking 'Owl' anyway—but yelling mit scrimming at the poor guy, who still saw himself as doing a *service to all mankind* (though this was to transmute to something quite other)—Izzy had him backed into a corner behind his antique cash register, the motherf***ing *chess set*—when the little guy let out with the incongruity *Most of the people who smoke 'Forest' are no longer with us!* —Gee Whizz said Iz, maybe this is MacK's problem too, though you don't expect to find yourself among the bills of mortality of your favorite tobacconist's. What I mean, you'd be still standing there, hearing about it. Or would you. There was a customer in there on Saturday mornings in the 1970s who had no larynx, but when you're in your twenties you just think—*weird*. And when you're in the West 40s.

## The Epicure Pipe Shop

The tobacconist *Seligman* was never quite happy to see Isidor enter his premises—though he could never quite remember why—at least without his friend, the one with the glasses. The one who used to go on and on and *on* about the yellowing pictures of radio stars in black frames in the Wilbur Sisters, those insane old bitches. *F\*\*\* Madison Avenue*, thought Seligman, why I have ten times the panache they do. Or, did. Wait, I have panache still, *I have panache* he was saying to himself as Isidor came in and up to the counter. Couldn't quite remember why this man—*Good afternoon, Sir*—big smile.

But Isidor found himself capable only of *glowering* for the nonce, glowering at the jars, the pipes *in their little holders*—everything's so *dusted* here, so f\*\*\*ing funereal, he . . . *said*—! —Our customers like a clean shop Sir, smiled Seligman—as to *funereal* I'm sure I don't know what you mean. Issey Miyake and all the Japanese designers use black extensively. How can I help you today? —Yeah, said Izzy, narrowing his eyes and pursing his lips ever so slightly before he could help it in a horrifyingly exact *impersonation of Seligman*—let me have eight ounces of 'Forest'. —!— Seligman remembered Iz now to be sure—and was torn between feigning ignorance of their past, the long past he shared with this customer of his—and saying *I thought I told you*—. —'Forest'! shouted Izzy—make with it! —We don't get much call for that particular blend any more, *Sir*, said Seligman, deciding to stonewall. —How about you make me up a batch special? said Iz—and then smoke it yourself? —I'm afraid I don't—what? said Seligman, who'd been threatened, aside from all the people on the BMT, who he felt hated him, only by one stray unsure robber, who'd got away with $50 and a jar of perique, which Seligman found returned on the doorstep of the shop the next morning—a note:

## TOO STRONG!

Iz was again glowering at the rows of pipes, lurching and looming threateningly over the small glass case of meerschaums and calabashes—and sat down suddenly in the black director's chair where Seligman had used to play chess. —Listen, are you all right? said Seligman, can I get you . . .? —He's dead, or almost, said Iz. —With the *glasses!?* said Seligman—the man with the glasses had been his only protection against *this* man, whose name he . . . —He smoked 'Forest', said Izzy. That is, until you took it off the market. He phoned me this morning. —I'm very sorry, said Seligman, in a tone which, even though prissy, Isidor remarked in his distress as the first *genuine thing* Seligman had ever said. —Perhaps there's time for good news yet? —*Nah*, snapped Iz, leaning his head on the glass case which I have done with Windex just this *minute*, thought Seligman—but restrained himself. Customer in trouble.

Of course many have died—not all from my tabacs, thought Seligman—some quit, some left, some had HEART DISEASE FROM BIRTH—for this he steadfastly refused to take any blame—cancer was more than enough fuel for his sleepless nights with that damnable WQXR and the *Oxford Book of Chess*, he thought. —You're not intoxicated, are you? he said suddenly—he hated drunks, and this man . . . —Not in the way you mean, said Isidor, suddenly raising his head from the glass surface, where, Seligman noted, there was a MARK. —You ever hear of naga? —I don't believe so, said Seligman—was this to be a calm conversation, suddenly, he thought—is it an African tobacco? —It's not tobacco, said Isidor—*it* smokes *you*, pal. —You're on this? —Forget about it, said Iz. —Coffee? —!

These two were sad. They were sad and would be drawn together today through the various sadnesses of tobacco. (Together they make quite an emotional pair—Seligman and Katz—it sounds almost like a plausible business—the demonstrative, intuitive Katz, the prissy, exacting Seligman. But they never would have agreed on what to sell, not pipes, not *books*, Seligman couldn't even *spell*.)

There are *obvious* sadnesses to tobacco and some which aren't so—sitting there in the shop the whole kaboodle of them ran parallel through Seligman and Iz—they sipped at black bitter coffee—what else would the tobacconist brew on his dirty hotplate behind the case of jars?—coffee black as the placards he'd had made describing his *philosophy*—thanks a lot—THIS IS THE KIND OF PIPE I WILL NOT SELL—*okay*—blah blah blah—black as his turtlenecks of yore, his droopy *moustache* of yore—black and oily as the latakia squinting at them from the jar of 'Owl', as the *feijoada completa* three doors down—it was black.

—People can't smoke as much as they once could, opened Seligman. —Oh? Noticed that have you? —Well I mean, the air is dirtier than it once was . . . Mr? . . . —Iz. —Than it still is? —No, *Iz*—for Isidor. —Isidor. There's also a lot more background radiation. —So? —So everyone gets cancer more easily—that's what's put a dent in our business. —A *dent?*—in your—? —If everything else was clean like it was a hundred years ago you could smoke all the time and nothing would happen—it's my theory.

The long ribbon-cut leaf of sadness running through Seligman and Izzy at the moment was the *nostalgie nicotine*—even though both had grown up in New Jersey they ashamedly longed for the Edwardian era, gas-lit obsequiousness, the beginnings of the idea of *infinite choice*—a blend for every moment—all this masculine bullshit which later went *completely haywire*. A thousand elegant pipe shops, cigar emporia—Gibson girls in basements rolling Egyptian cigarettes, kissing them closed—for long hours.

Isidor burst out: —What I want to know is, what is this f***ing plant doing on earth if it is not for our delectation? It's no good for anything else. The flowers are pale, though they do look good in line drawings—I've sold some plates. Why the f*** is it here?

—They make an insecticide from it, said Seligman, who had absorbed the usual knowledge. —F*** bugs, said Iz—here's what's funny—I've been doing some thinking about it—every single *commodity* that's half way wonderful, by which I mean, FOREIGN TO

HONKIES, who, let's face it, have *nothing*, went through more or less the same thing: a guy SAILS somewhere, he finds NATIVES, they're USING SOMETHING, it's coconut, it's pepper, it's sugar, mace, tea, tobacco—the guy says THIS IS GREAT!!! He BRINGS IT BACK TO HONKYLAND. Jumps off the boat and rushes over to the castle to show it to the KING. King tries it out, thinks GREAT!!! —kings like everything—you imagine that? What a great thing it truly is to be a *King*, people bringing you amazing stuff all the time? —I number several Dukes among my customers, said Seligman. —That's *buying*, said Iz, I'm talking about the amount of *stuff* you get every day, in *vans*, when you're a KING. So anyway the *thing* it becomes a fashion, then a *rage*—everyone's using it—they're trying it out for *everything*—there were people brushing their *teeth* with tobacco at the French court. They start using what-you-may-call-it for medicine, too—but then they go CRAZY, it starts to create an economic hole, besides destroying the poor little place where they grow it—the grey eminences think it's a BAD THING, we have to *regulate*—and then they *tax* it, that is how they show their revulsion—it becomes an *outlaw thing*, a ROGUE COMMODITY—look what happened to sugar—simple enough—when you and I were kids. Look at pepper—you have to go to 6th Street, skulk around, I had to *leave Manhattan* today to get my soft tissues properly insulted. —What? said Seligman. —*Coffee,* said Isidor—*bad* for you now, no, can't have *that*—so in the end we're to be left with what our race—*Broadly speaking*, cut in Seligman—yeah, what our race had in the beginning: beer, and *bere*—and matzobrei—all stuff made from stupid *grains*, stuff around the Iron Age farmyard—it's enough to make you *weep*—we tried everything, said Isidor, throughout history, to get a little zip in our mouths, our lives—but no. I'll tell you this for nothing: we all die. I'd rather die having had a decent cigar and a curry than have had my taste buds smothered by the BIG MATZOBREI since birth. —What do you mean, *matzobrei?* said Seligman. —I've had enough shit sitting on my face, said Isidor, if you know what I mean.

—Possibly, said Seligman, who was squeamish.

—On the other hand, said Iz with hostility, MY FRIEND IS GOING TO DIE FROM SMOKING. So the court physicians in their wigs have the last laugh, think of it—those *frogs* in their *brocades*? How can *they* be right about anything? What are *you* doing, Seligman? Isidor glowered at the racks and jars. Why are you doing this? How do you feel about killing your customers?—it'd bother me.

(Door opened and a guy in a suit came in. Seligman gave him his usual conversation—while he measured the guy's 6 oz. of 'Nostalgie'—an odd concoction of obsequious enquiry and shared smugness, as though he'd run into this guy *later*—as if anyone even thinks much about what they smoke—aside from Seligman and Iz—they're just doing it, aren't they?—the tobacconist doggedly saw his customer to the door.)

—All your customers like that? said Iz, who was hardly ever in the shop with others—how few there were, really. —Most of them, said Seligman—once they get all that snow white hair, I just think, *whew.* Izzy opened his mouth at this. —I'll tell *you* something, though, said Seligman, this whole city has gone to the dogs. —What! said Isidor—*really?* —Don't act so astonished, said the tobacconist. —I'm not, you *ass.* —Oh. Well, let me finish. Do you *know* why the city has gone to the dogs? —No, said Iz impatiently. —It's because of *that man*, who was just in here, said Seligman. —So-o-o, said Izzy, that's him? *That's* the guy who ruined New York. —Not him in particular, Sir, Mr—*Izz*, said Seligman—I mean them. All of them. THEM! —*Who?* —The Yalies, said Seligman—all these *men* who walk around in suits all day and treat me like some kind of person from New Jersey—*Which*, interrupted Iz, *you very deeply are*—Yes, said Seligman, though I am not from New Jersey in that *way*—I mean all these . . . *men* . . . who *take the train.* —You're being incoherent, said Isidor. —I can't be any plainer about it, said the tobacconist—Yalies who live in Connecticut and take the train in here and make too much money and who switched to cigars from their pipes ten years ago. —So that's it, said Izzy. —You think this isn't a tough business? said Seligman. —I think it's always tough being a JIVE-ASS MOTHERF***ER, said Iz. —Listen, you like coming in here to buy my things, said Seligman, let me tell you. —So? —Those cock-sucking Wilbur Sisters almost put me out of business ten years ago. —I won't stand for this, said Isidor, those sweet old . . . —Sweet my eye, said Seligman, they teamed up with that fellow Nachtkapp, from *Vermont*.

(The name of *Vermont* strikes terror and nausea into all the retailers of this our town—its inextinguishable *cachet*, the fact that anything from *Vermont* can be sold in New York for over $3,000, the citizenry's idea that you can get in your car and shoot up the Taconic and acquire wood and wool products uniquely manipulated, books never seen or even whispered in the catalogues of the Public Library or Columbia.)

Iz remembered Nachtkapp, a hulking round-shouldered invader, a guy from *Vermont* who as a woodworker was inventive maybe but who could not shake the hippie dust off himself, the aroma of sandals and soap and candles and BRATTLEBORO out of his clothing and hair and beard. (MacK and Iz examining his wares: *Ponytail alert*, MacK had breathed.) He set up a shop off Fifth Avenue with his Hobbitish pipes and a range of undistinguished wholesale blends, until he cemented a deal with the Wilbur Sisters. —Probably had to *sleep* with them to get those recipes, brooded Seligman, up at his window regarding the passers by on West 46th hungrily. Obviously the whole thing had upset Seligman, who'd made a bid to be the pre-eminent, even the only modern pipe designer in North America—he'd gone out into the woods—*Seligman in the woods!*—how deeply troubling it was too, Pennsylvania somewhere, to find a couple of biddable brother cretins, woodturners out of *Grimm's* who might do what he wanted—the whole project took on Ruskinian overtones—and then this enormous hippie blows into town in his hippie van and somehow got a plushier little shop and all this—boo hoo—attention. There'd been no course but retaliation, Seligman telling his customers that Nachtkapp's pipes were—'not *fine*'—as only Seligman and the legion of purveyors of the exclusive in New York can pronounce the word.

To see Seligman's eye crinkle and sneer when he uses the word *fine*. In fact a customer of his once suffered a very *fine* testicular injury when one of Nachtkapp's Tolkienesque creations suddenly burst and precipitated a firefall of 'Balkan Sobranie' onto his lap. Seligman visited the burnt fellow in the hospital, bringing him tobacco and grapes, and then started telling the story around—*one of my better customers was emasculated by a Nachtkapp pipe.*

—I had to *fight* 'im, *I had to get 'im good*, said Seligman, looking out the window, sounding more Jersey than previously. —How'd you—?
—Oh, I don't know, *specials*, that's the main thing, said Seligman.
—*Specials!?* —Yeah, sales and things—you know. —Oh *very* ruthless, said Isidor, remembering how he'd been prevented from buying any books upstate for months by a dealer who'd spread the word all around Dutchess County that Izzy had *leprosy*. But Seligman had really been able to cancel out Nachtkapp's *claims to fineness*, just by word of mouth, among the smokers left in New York. *Mouth trouble*. He bruited the word *fine* around so much that it became his own; the Wilbur Sisters had never thought of using it, running a *country store* as they essentially did; Nachtkapp was caught with his tie-dyed pants down using the word *distinguished* which sounds like something the *luggage* trade might use; the Dunhills were off in their upholstered humidor doing god knows what. (MacK had once drawn a chilly parallel, Iz remembered, between the Dunhill humidor, Steinway Hall and the Frank E Campbell Funeral Home. Isidor had insisted it was merely a mahogany problem.)

—Nachtkapp got very nervous at his drill-press perhaps, but within a year a lot of his bowls had burnt through, if you take my meaning, said Seligman. —Where'd he go? said Izzy. —*Vermont*, said Seligman, suddenly hooting with laughter as if it were the funniest answer on earth. —No listen, he said, there's no business in this any more. But I got mad, mad at myself partly, but mad—like I said I got to feeling everyone's hair turn white, and then all the people smoking 'Forest' started to croak, and all these gentlemen who were coming to me got more and more money and they were meaner and meaner. —*Mean* to you? said Iz. —*Yes*, said Seligman—so I thought, you ass *holes*, I'm going to hang in here and see you out. I'm going to keep selling you this stuff and if it kills you so much the better. I'm going to *taper off*, myself, and I'm going to advise moderation in such a way that it will fire them to smoke more and more, and I'm going to rid the streets of Yalies. —Listen, said Isidor, my friend is not a *Yalie*. You've killed your own tovarich. What is all this Yale anyways? —It's just my *name* for them, said Seligman, Yale doesn't produce quite enough people to cause all this *wanton destruction* of the city. But they started it. —Have you ever *seen* New Haven? said Izzy. —God no, said Seligman.

# The Epicure Pipe Shop

Let me tell you something, Mr—? —Katz, said Isidor. —Katz, said Seligman, that reminds me I have to feed . . . —But *Iz*. —Anyway, it's the triumph of the rentiers, *Iz*, said Seligman, all over again. —What! said Isidor—you're a Marxist? —Certainly, Sir. —*A Marxist tobacconist*. —Yes (in the precise tone which had ruined Nachtkapp). —Gee *Whizz* there aren't even any Marxists in the *book* business any more—I can't believe I'm hearing this, the *rentiers*. —I came to New York in 1964, said Seligman—you ought to have seen it. —I went to the Fair, said Izzy. —Ah, the Fair—what a riot of capitalist waste matter—great—but the whole town was just bursting with fun, said Seligman. —Marxist fun? —*All* kinds (severely). But you know who ruined New York besides the thousands of faceless Yalie rentiers, was the *Presidents*—Carter started in on the credit cards, shaming people out of their very necessary lunchtime martinis . . . —You're defending martinis? —*Yes.* No one out *there* understands the pressures on a New York businessman. —You're a martini Marxist. —Yes—of course Ford, drop dead, all that, then you wind up with Reagan, the *one man* in the whole country who was *totally unqualified* to be President, and his calabash—excuse me, *cabal*—of industrialists and spooks up the wazoo—Seligman was beginning to smolder with his theme like a pipeful of 'Nostalgie'—and then Bush who took Eisenhower's *warning* about the Military-Industrial complex and said *Listen, this sounds kinda good, we're going to go with this.* And of course, said Seligman, it benefited no one in New York, most of that corrupt Republican economy is conducted and coffered out in the god damned *West*, Texas, California—*Florida*—he lost heart for a moment—anyway Mr Katz I have perhaps said too much. —You left out Nixon, said Isidor, Nixon didn't do the city any good. —*No!*, said Seligman, won't hear a word against Nixon. Practiced law for a long time in New York—he *contributed*. A marvelous pipe man, Sir—he came in here once out of curiosity. He used to play the piano. —What piano? said Iz . . . well at least you had a hand in doing him in. Alger Hiss used to buy a lot of sickly Cavendish from that guy on Fourth Avenue but that doesn't mean . . .

—*Yes,* who knows, said Seligman. The mutual embarrassment of a protracted political discussion descended. —Look around, said Seligman—it's all class war now. I can't walk down the street without getting yelled at—it wasn't like that in 1964. —Maybe the moustache, said Isidor suddenly—I've never liked it. —Ha, said Seligman, what do you . . . really? Isidor was getting a little steamed now, thinking again how much 'Forest' this idiotically-moustachio'd *Marxist* for God's sake had pushed across the counter into MacK's tissues. —I've always had the same moustache, said Seligman, since I moved into the same apartment—always had the same wife. We got married when we were in design school. I used to sit with her in the kitchen window, looking out. I used to say to her, *I love this city*—before I meant it. It was part of trying to love her. Then I came really to love her, and really to love the city, and then you stop having to look out at the lights and say that. —Very moving, said Iz—your wife a Marxist too? —No, said the tobacconist (the equivalent of the pointed little *yes*, being pronounced *neau*) *neau,* she's a craftsperson. She makes latkes.

—That's handy, said Isidor.

—She'd like me at home now—it seems odd to be looking at retirement when you're in this kind of business—you tend to think of yourself as a little institution of some kind. But for now, Mr Katz, I'm going to keep opening the shop—the word!—my *father* kept a shop—and looking through the obits for my customers. Listen, I want to say that I am very sorry about your friend—but that was 'Forest' trouble and there's nothing I can do about it. Do you think your friend's obituary will be in the *Times?* —Why do you ask me that, said Izzy—how the f*** do I know, you're the *second* guy who's—

The sun came in now at a low angle, just the way it does to show all the shopkeepers of midtown, at least the ones on the north side of the cross streets, that they might go home. It came across the bowls of yenidje and latakia and Virginia and across Seligman's handsome proclamations. WHO TOLD YOU TO SMOKE ALL DAY? —Is there anything I can do for you, Mr Katz? *Autonomically*, it later developed, Izzy asked for 4 oz of 'Owl' and while Seligman fussed with the jar and the scales in the way he'd been doing since 1968, with some slightly loopy, theatrical flourishes he'd convinced himself were Dickensian or *Dunhilllike* Isidor selected a straight-grain billiard from the wall, and picked out a new pipe tool.

—Hey, here's my *American Express*, said Isidor pointedly—guess you don't have a problem with that. —None what so *ever*, said Seligman. He put everything in one of his large grey envelopes (as a Marxist Seligman had always abjured little shopping bags with handles), the shop's trademark—he also used them for mailing latkes to relatives—and dropped in a box of matches—the *staggering largesse* of the guy, thought Isidor, he hasn't given me matches for *ten years*—but it was a sign Seligman had enjoyed talking to Isidor for the first time *ever*. —How'd you know I needed those? said Izzy. Seligman smiled sarcastically. —Sir, it is my business to know these things. Izzy didn't know what to say. Took his big grey envelope which is awkward to carry and won't fit in one's briefcase either and heading toward the door ejaculated an !OKAY!, the friendliness of which startled both of them. The door—its fussy little shopkeeper's bell rang—perhaps for the last time—after all, he'd never have a conversation like that again with *Seligman*. The Unabomber of midtown!

—Smoke judiciously, Mr Katz, said Seligman.


## On the Avenue

Passed the U.B. Rest. now without registering any insinuations of *feijoada*—the avenue ahead was bright and loud and looked appealing—the minutes he'd spent in Seligman's shop seemed like a dark return to some large struggle of the past—like he'd gone and sat in a scene from a very old movie, a painting maybe—or gone to sit in a small family mausoleum, thinking things over, yes. Seligman's *Yes*. A dark scene in a dark shop from a dark movie.

In truth: visiting Seligman—whatever mood the tobacconist was in—always depressed Izzy because he caught an unpleasant breeze of possibility from his own life. Isidor's father kept still a small haberdashery—Isidor could not dissociate his father's shop—its *shopness*—from other shops—which is one reason why he often said something rude, loud, funny, or provocative as soon as he entered a shop of any kind—MAKE A NOISE. It hadn't worked so well at Lord and Taylor last Christmas—rather hard to be entering there through all the umbrella'd throng from Fifth—they didn't know Isidor of course—they didn't take his point—just thought he was a nut who'd got stuck in the vestibule like all the others—he *staggered*—toward the Clinique—threw him out and now he can't even walk on the same side of the *street* as Lord and Taylor. Isidor feared he might wake up one day and find himself the proprietor of the haberdashery, struggling with steam and enamel, the Old World—nothing so airy and light as his book shop, with its upright, individually priced *palpable thoughts*, which can bear him away to anything at any moment—a guy who is wanting to adjust his scarf, turn up the collar of his overcoat as it were, in the chill of a little life he had escaped.

Turned right on Fifth and found himself in a small whirl of associations with MacK—Isidor could feel the RCA Building pulling at his back—MacK's electric office in there somewhere, radiating—felt a pull to the left, to the McAnn's toward Vanderbilt, where you go way downstairs—Vanderbilt!, Gee Whizz—at that moment MacK and Tumbleson were—but after all. Went to head more or less downtown now, get the news, *f\*\*\*!* he exclaimed aloud. Nearly at 42nd now, busy and benign today in a Vincent Youmans kind of way—Izzy stopped to take a look in the window of Nat Sherman, in a kind of knee-jerk of smoking desire, or familiarity—but conscious that Seligman didn't even admit Nat into the *pantheon nicotea*—brightly colored cigarettes, some pretty ugly pipes, accessories that would ream-n-kleen Alfred Dunhill in his grave—*what a f\*\*\*ing tragedy*, Isidor said, aloud, shaking his head, then rushing across 42nd.

The Seligman problems hung over Izzy and the only place he could escape the breath of haberdashery or keeping a shop where claustrophobia is sold in small amounts was to hurry up the steps to the library. *Need books.* Entered as he always did exactly under the name TILDEN, the only one he liked, and scurried across the huge marble lobby before it could be filled with roaring torrents of deep green water—his frequent nightmare.

## Books and Manuscripts

It is Isidor noticing the various stains of the Berg Collection. Mr Playfair had never dealt in mss, being *physically afraid of them*—one reason why Bibulo & Schenkler wasn't an all-rounder of antiquarianship. Mr Playfair thought books much healthier, as they were white things in general, including lots of nice antiseptic ink—he used to fill his bedroom with paperbacks when he had influenza—the idea that in handling a ms you might touch some tobacco ash of Hammett or the vomity spittle of Fitzgerald, however dried, gave him palpitations.

—This is a good thing to do after lunch in New York, said Isidor, aloud—the guard in the middle of the Berg Room immediately caught his eye—Iz held it and continued—perpetuate someone else's neurosis. And smiled—this somehow seemed an acceptable comment to the guard—as if addressed to him—and he let go Isidor's eyeballs with an Official Warning.

The stains recalled the whole trial of literary effort in a particularly awful way—what the words didn't say the residues of coffee, wine and tobacco told—on blue air-mail tissues, the corners pinholed. There was lots of violet ink, violent scrawl and stink: Kerouac's rainbow pads from the corner markets of the road, Auden's economic ledger sheets . . . —Really it's all business here, said Isidor, that's what *I* think. *Sending the third draft of—don't know if you can use—Dear Mr Moss—can't be in America for a year or two.* News print and yellow news print banged and harangued on: Delmore Schwartz apparently had a problem with his ribbon. Red invaded black and built his sorrow. —This was the Golden Age of Typewriting, said Isidor, and of I Will Gladly Pay You Tomorrow—the guard again—wasn't it? A question in the guy's eyes and again an almost imperceptible acknowledgment that he was not going to caution or exclude Isidor, who went out into the big hall now, muttering. —You notice how all those guys wrote their letters on one side? They knew their shit would be pinned up in here like butterflies.

Quickly down the hall to one of the better places to howl while you piss in midtown; but it's no place to make a phone call. Iz decided to let Miss Plein prove herself this afternoon. —What emergencies, after all, crop up in my profession? A chapped morocco binding cries out for 'Fortificuir?' Man at the door with a delivery of silverfish?

# On the Avenue

Isidor headed in his natural direction, down Fifth, moving south-ward—pausing at the corners only as sensibly as anyone else—diminishing rapidly and becoming an ant along with the rest of them by the time he shouldered by Empire—which looked rather upright, stiff and presentable today, not *drooping* like it sometimes does. You couldn't have seen much of what Izzy was thinking now, but as he walked under the canopy—when is this f***ing thing going to get fixed, *finally fixed?*—and wondered as usual why the EMPIRE STATE BUILDING has *discount drug stores* in its clay feet—he noticed a certain aluminum gleam to Empire's sides which seemed like modern light-weight coffins. Now he had to go down and see MacK—he didn't like feeling that head-ing downtown had anything to do with death—but perhaps it was just looking at the poets' letters—thought suddenly with a pain that MacK was in the habit of wearing lots of *dead people's clothes*—from Mrs Leninsky's family—his own uncle even—and he fretted that MacK had caught something from a garment like that. —But, said Isidor at the corner of 29th, as he hurried toward the all-important corner, you don't just throw away a *Pendleton shirt*.

# The Hour

Dim street lights and shaded lamps in apartments in the Village. Steadiness filtered from the modest lighting of old; lamps which have comforted MacK for many years. Soft lighting of the stair in Grant's Tomb, the cloakroom of the Music Hall, the gently coffered, mortuary ceiling of the *old* lobby of the Museum of Modern Art—architects have got to go—like the underbelly of the RCA Building's canopy which mothers MacK from rain and snow when he arrives at work.

There was a soothing city once, MacK thought—a courtly city—lobbies and foyers, though Granolithic, used to welcome you before they became sterile and official and ignored—the vast lobby of The Wynd had since the 1950s acquired all the warmth of the Staten Island Ferry Terminal—he often expected the Last Boat gong to sound when crossing it at night.

Incredibly, a truly comfortable and unknowingly welcoming bar has survived in this our town—or it has been nudged back into comfortability, down here around . . . such-and-such a street. No further triangulation—this can't be shared with you.

Somehow this soft thing managed to survive, like a pretty kitten with a red ribbon fallen onto the tracks of the IRT. You don't want to know *how*. You just worry how long it will be before it is splattered all over the News. You just stand there worrying.

So I have not yet done for The Hour, thought the *Grim Reaper*. Its doorway is set slyly into a stocky building of the 1920s, which, upperly, attempts grace, and flanked by two round lamps glowing like portholes. I have not cursed and closed this place, thought the Grim Reaper, because Isidor and I tend to drink at Isidor's when here in Isidor's neighborhood; I have saved this place for the odd occasion when Isidor feels a need to flee his tower; when he has been thrown out by his *Nuse*; hounded out by the cat.

The exchange, thought MacK the Reaper, the Big Talk, to happen in this soft place, in just a little while. Almost like talking about it at one of the aforementioned tombs, or in the Pillow Bank. But The Hour was not open yet—who IS it that decides when the public needs a drink? HAH?—and anyway MacK was early and anyway it would have been—not sacrilege, but at least disrespectful in the ordinary way—to enter without Isidor. So MacK took a spin around several surrounding blocks, wishing to empty his skull so that the time in The Hour would be

## THE MOST MEANINGFUL MARTINI
## IN THE WORLD.

Memorable—at least to Isidor, who it seemed would be staying alive in order to remember things.

Up the street, a flicker of the Seventies—a brick and tile façade behind which had lived a pair of art students, best friends of his college girl, the one who left him confused for many years about the meaning of himself. Prevented from becoming this or that socially useful item, MacK thought, I became *the most well-known useless person in America*. Discovering his true vocation had been denied him by his carousel of distractions and ladies, none of whom except the beautiful possible Olive would have had it in her to accept any kind of self-discovery once the bales of NBC cash were a permanent part of the landscape of his apartment. But this is no way to clear the head.

Some years ago MacK would blunder through the Village, unaware of its treasures, after the *Mary Murray* bundled him safely back on to Manhattan. He would seek the horizontal copper lights of the midtown evening, and Tumbleson, play at that futile error.

Walked past the worst deli in the world, so bad that this is the exact spot where his argument about having food prepared for you falls down dead. Isidor always refused to acquire a sandwich here before stepping on a subway for the Yankees. —You have to be very careful about mayonnaise, he would say. —A whole sandwich could go off in half an hour? said MacK, knowing it was no use. But Isidor's *countermeasure* was to buy a sandwich *near* the Yankees, in one of those places that sell corn popped in Indianapolis—more than once he left the sunny stands after one of these subs and a paper pail of beer to puke and puke in the stadium's bowel. —Do you really think the Yankees themselves clean all the food preparation surfaces in the neighborhood? said MacK. —Well yes I do, said Isidor. —There's something more at work here than mayonnaise.

MacK lurched at the thought of food, imagining that soon all he would be able to swallow would be some kind of foamy pink fodder.

He was surprised that so much had happened to him in the Village. Time piles and piles things up. He was annoyed at anything that had not to do with Isidor.

Here was the dry cleaner who had offered to clean and hand-press a shirt for MacK, in a leaving-town agony once before an affiliates meeting. Two hours later the man proudly showed his handiwork. The shirt was in a glory. There wasn't a wrinkle on it nor anywhere *near* it. Noble on its hanger, sporting a little ascot of tissue paper which puffed up its throat like a proud bird's. What is more, it seemed no wrinkle *could* be put in the shirt. MacK wore it indelibly for three days through the entire meeting and then on to fishing in the Sand Counties with Red, who was bug bit and testy. In a fairy tale moment, a fish MacK caught gaped and swallowed at him, in his hands, as if pregnant with MESSAGE and then whipped MacK in the chest with its tail and died. From that moment the charm the dry cleaner had put on the shirt evanesced—the shirt became stained, wrinkled, odorous; it displayed suddenly everything that had happened to it in five days of conventioneering, wading and being unfaithful with a bait shop girl while Red slept petulant.

Now of course you could always walk up 8th for a guilty, quick—NO A PERFECTLY INNOCENT AND CITIZENLY, INNOCENT PARTY STARE in a certain shop-window of interest. So he did so. The meek passing by were *unaware of the torrents of filth raging in the famous yet modestly dressed man,* he thought. Guy has a right to look in a shop-window. Could be anybody. Could be for any of a hundred reasons after all, although always disgusted at the idea of being taken for a she-male, yuck-*O*. Afraid always of a repeat of the Pine Street bulless who happened by here several summers ago, saw MacK gazing at the sexy little things and made a peevish, dramatic *show* of staring at him and then at the shoes, at him and then at the shoes, whirling with her elbows raised in fury and outrage, somebody call the cops, a man is looking at a shoe in a window. But of course as the shrink blessedly said, *that's about HER fears, isn't it?* O clever shrink. Some nice ones here, red calf with dainty ankle straps, about six inches—but as he admired, with all the practiced nonchalance he could summon, MacK felt a small funeral within. It was the funeral of TINSEL. Found himself profoundly shocked at how NEEDLESS it would be to have to lever someone like the beautiful possible Olive into these; if one were in a position to *ask* this, one would obviously have love, *really love*, and what would be the need? MacK breathed out to see if it was the season of locomotive steam yet. Not quite. Breathed in to see if it were the season of crackling. No. And there in the distance was Isidor.

This moment was always one out of books, a romantic moment to MacK; he couldn't say if it were epic to Iz. The feeling that things will be all right with the world for the next few hours. The Republicans can go hang; you're safe, or if they do press a Button at least you will die in good company. Don't want to die in Macy's or even the RCA Building, thought MacK.

MacK looked back at the window—finding it always unbearable, the last thirty yards to be closed between Isidor and himself—a black pair with extreme louis heels—one or the other usually had a witticism or an observation at the ready.

MacK was once standing in front of a cinema, attending an unusually slow approach of Isidor from Sixth—a hot day—and became aware of something like a puppy tugging or clawing at the tail of his jacket. Discovered a neatly dressed but laughably tiny woman of sixty. —Who is that coming? she said. Who are you waiting for? —Ah, nobody, I mean—what? said MacK. —Is he famous? said the little lady, is he *appearing* here? —Well, yes, appearing, said MacK, but not for, you know. Not for money. It's just someone. *Arriving* really.

—Oh, said the lady, but you looked so expectant, as though you were to greet him . . . *officially*. —Ho ho, said Isidor, rolling up, who's this? —Your biggest fan, said MacK, relinquishing all to the control of the God of Sidewalk Encounters. —I'm very pleased to meet you, to have this moment with you, said Isidor to the tiny, almost *invisible* lady. —I'm a great admirer of yours, said the lady. —Oh? Have you been to my shop? said Isidor. —Shop? said the lady, I don't understand you.

It tailed off into confusion and even bitterness, Iz getting ratty with the lady. The two MEAN MEN fled into the cinema and watched a brutal movie from the 1950s, where the crew-cutted hero *abraded* his way through a lot of dishonesty which smelt of 'Kent' cigarette smoke, and women wearing dress-shields, with his head. He wallowed and thrashed through the heartbreaking seediness mother tried to steer you from in train-stations.


Isidor was closing the last few yards, clocking MacK's position in front of the window. MacK hadn't known what to expect from himself at this moment and panicked, as if Isidor might be snatched from him now. Izzy was attempting to look ironic. So MacK could see there was to be a determination to keep things on the old keel. Which was a relief and infuriating. MacK was suddenly afraid of the evening, having today not thought much about what it would be like. He found himself thinking within a new column for his ledger: women who had given him cigarettes but not themselves.

—I recommend red, said Isidor, pulling up in front of the window. I view this as a positive amenity of my neighborhood. —I'm sure I don't know what you're talking about, said MacK. —How ya doin'? —Do you remember the woman *Vicola?* blurted out MacK. —Sure, said Isidor, What-is-his-name's sister-in-law. You cad. —I spent a very hot summer with that woman, said MacK, *sans* AC or even a refrigerator. We went out to this bar on Broadway every night which had this enormous *fan*. We smoked all their free cigarettes (Isidor's eyes widened at this bold mention of the dirty little engines) night after night, said MacK. She got me going, that was one of my periods. And all that smoking *amounts* to sex, really—there's something streamlining, skeleton-fluorescing about it but we would go home for a grope out of *school*. —Why tell me? said Isidor looking nonplussed. —She was completely mad, said MacK, and rather well-endowed. —Takes one to know one, said Isidor, I mean, ah, the mad . . . what are you saying, it's all *her* fault? And immediately Isidor looked stricken; this was to jump the gun. —No no, said MacK, turning away at last from the pricey *talons*—you just think Why Not? What else is all this about? He felt bad about Isidor and the gun.

So *this* is the guy with the random anecdote, thought Isidor. The footing has yet to be found here. —We could go in and buy a pair each, said Isidor. —She'll think *we* wear them, said MacK—forgetting his stance of ignorance on the subject—that's out. Do you subscribe to the idea that they are a missing snatch or wi-wi? —At *$120 a pair?* said Isidor I think not, Sir. No. —Then what? —I think, Sir, said Isidor, staring off perhaps by chance in the direction of New Jersey, at fourteen one is clammy. I think one is pocked. One is unworthy of meeting the gaze of girls, but still one has simply the need of admiring them, and one finds one can look down, at their choice of adornments there, which one thereafter associates with their charming personalities and little affectations. Their own ideas of beauty or provocation to be found there. And one looks down and down forever. Think about it: the height of your sexual powers is the lowest point of your existence. —Oh.

They then walked in unexpected silence to the closed door of The Hour. Shadows moved upon the blinds. Promise but as yet no cigar. —They open at six? said Iz. So, this is defusing something, he thought. Possibly for the better. They looked at each other, MacK angry at himself for being a little mired still in a useless part of the past. —We could always get a pre-martini beer, said Isidor in his

Joisey accent. We could do whatever the f*** we wanna. We don't gotta wait around for these jerkoffs. —Okay, said MacK, in some irritation, feeling in fact a distinct *Lack o' Wanna*, having desired The Hour to be open now, he and Iz to be the first customers, friendly-welcomed, everything in readiness. So they would have to circle the neighborhood as well as the subject.

But the subject won't *wear* a street corner, or a 'forced march', in Isidor's phrase, even though it is an angry thing, and you do see people arguing about it on corners; their mission is to defeat it, at least for the night, give it a lethal injection. That's legal in this state. That is the method preferred by most of the condemned.

But not so easy—where the hell are they going to go? Isn't *everyone* you see in the streets around this time of the evening looking for a place to say something important? Isidor said: —Since the unfortunate death of Bradley's, indeed of Bradley himself, one feels little beck in this quarter. MacK felt a breeze as he turned to look at the near avenue. —We could walk to the Juniper, he said.

Mutual, stony, sickening awareness. Turned and walked together toward the problematic place. —I wouldn't worry, it's entirely possible, said Isidor, that we will be too early for all the asses that infest the Juniper. People like that, even though they're going to spend the whole night there, are so confident of their infestation, like insects and their globalization, that they don't observe the rituals of opening. Indeed, these asses are impervious to pleasure and don't have any idea of the importance of being the first foot in an expectant and ordered bar. —It can almost be the little death, said MacK. —Huh, said Isidor. They crossed the avenue and pushed through the acclaimed, soiled door of the Juniper—shabby, considering who-all the *Juniper* said had pushed in before you.

—But oh the asses are here, said MacK. Waiting to fan out to all the *other* bars, perhaps even into The Hour. —Gee *Whizz*, said Isidor. Like they had shouldered their way into a smoked beehive, or a cool cave which they were revolted to find lined with bats.

We don't do ourselves any favors, we men, by smoking, by sneering while we drink, nor by scratching ourselves and chewing gum while giving our opinion on an article in the paper to the bartender. It would be well to remember that the bartender reads the paper every day with more attention than you do, which is why he says only

—yuh—

while you kick up the dregs of stupidity; why he stares down at the filling glass. He can't believe YOU'RE here again.

We don't do ourselves any favors by burping and farting and spitting next to each other in the GENTS, in fact they ought to take that sign down. And as for trying to start the *same* tit-bit of conversation with the ureter adjacent—. The Juniper, in all its glory. Don't mean to pick on, of course. Two pints.

*Beer*, on a cool night which anticipated the velvet of gin—Iz and MacK both dead and confined to this *roadside hut on the way to paradise*—if like so many you imagine it as the Taconic Parkway. So the thing closed in, darted at them maybe. Isidor said: —These drinks don't count ya know, simply do not count.

Don't need to tell you they left the Juniper two bubbled furies—floated through the door of The Hour soon after, indeed the first to arrive and in better spirits instanter.


# Martini I

The Hour is a place you almost can't believe in—you sit at the bar with your eyelids flickering, you think someone is about to fling something at you or strike you; someone outside the window is going to shoot you. Isn't this place as softly lit as the cupola of Lenin's Tomb, isn't it about to be invaded by loud people, their music, their ideology? But no.

So they are at last here, considering the spectrum of bar-light, a comforting halo of old-movie and places you have inherited, per-

haps where your parents used to go when they were in love. MacK
and Isidor said nothing for a few minutes. Things go back and forth
between two men while gin settles in. Things *fly* back and forth.
The conversation to come lights up in each like a distant town.
—Can't you give us some nuts or something, said Isidor, here we're
paying twelve bucks apiece for these drinks you know GOOD
HEAVENS. Isidor thought The Hour approached perfection, if
not the sublime, but found the staff over familiar—and weirdly
reluctant with the snacks. And in the weeks since the *thing* is in
some certainty bruited upon MacK—knowing, really—this is the
first moment the idea

### *HEAVEN*

comes to him and he thinks he really has to pick which one it is to
be, for as the poet laureate said you will go to the paradise which you
*believe* awaits. You can pick it YES YOU CAN.

   —I'm going to have blond wood furniture and grey carpeting,
said Isidor, intuiting all from MacK's absent expression, and showing that he could speak very naturally on the subject. It's going to be
on the upper East Side. Heaven has an exact address. —That's
not far, said MacK; he had never considered a *convenient* next life.
—Commuting is for asses, said Iz. There's this indirect lighting.
—I'll bet, said MacK, thinking that the only source of light in the
heaven of Isidor would be from the fire of Hell; that he would have
*planned* it that way. —It's a large round salon, straight out of Fred
Astaire's bigger hangovers. There are comfortable sofas and next to
each sofa is a tall stool, and that's where the waitress sits so you can
admire her legs. When she's not bringing you your drink. —Oh?
said MacK, feeling Isidor had stolen into his head one night with a
flashlight and mask. —Or, said Iz, there are stools they used to
have in shoe stores and you sit on the top part and the waitress
sits across from you with her feet up on the slanted part and you
admire her legs and shoes. You can even tie and untie her ankles. It
doesn't matter. The food is all shellfish and Spanish sausages, but it

doesn't kill you and there are steamed vegetables for when the saints come around to make sure you're eating healthy and enjoying yourself. MacK considered the scenario and apart from wondering at the idea that Isidor's heaven had authoritarian saints, and if it were quite a good idea to be so specific, he experimented by putting G de B, from American history class in 1967, in it. Boing! Like a charm it worked. —This seems a little decadent, said MacK. —They're not strippers or anything, said Isidor, they're wearing *suits*. —Well it seems okay for a while said MacK but you'd tire of it (thinking he wouldn't.)—No I wouldn't, said Isidor. —Yes you would, said MacK. —No I wouldn't. —Yes you would. —No I wouldn't. —You would too. —No I would not. —HEY! Mr Katz! This from a man who looked totally out of place, ye gods he looked like a *student* or worse. What was he doing in The Hour? Ordering *beer!?* Bah! Iz turned aghast on his stool, you'd think it'd been the voice of his mother. —HEY Mr Katz. How are you? Isidor took in a lot of oxygen in a hurry, a shame. —*I'm fine thank you very much for asking me BUT WE DON'T NEED ANY POEMS TODAY!* And followed this up with a frighteningly piercing gaze MacK didn't think he had ever seen before. Shrivelling of young fellow. —Oh. Oh okay. Okay sorry. He retreated into a semicircular portion of the bar lit with blue lights. It was the children's area.

—You mean this instep thing—you see I do not mince words—to remain your pre-eminent concern for *eternity?* said MacK. —Yes. —Overriding our deep and mutual ministrations to this very drink here—to the bars and restaurants of old—to the mystical smokes? —That's the way it is, said Isidor. He didn't seem very sure. This pissed off MacK and he decided that since this was supposed to be *the* evening in which things, nay, every thing, was had out, he would try for higher ground.

—I go for the intangible, said MacK, it seems safer. I think there must be a heaven only of smokes. —I had a fog one in mind for a while, said Isidor. —Same thing in a way, said MacK, conciliatory, but he went on: one will just be suspended, a taste bud as it were, in the volumes of memory in smoked and smoky things; the world is about to go up in smoke anyway . . . what could be more natural? —This is a little depressing, said Iz. —Not just smoke, said MacK, but extraordinary smoke, smoke that is smoked. Opening a tin of latakia on the first day of October. Every day would be the first day of October. That is a heavenly moment—the oak paneled library where we used to—*You can't smoke there any more*, interjected Isidor, *I checked*—Anyway, said MacK, I could float in that for eternity, or let us say a long time, in the Wordsworth and Chaucer and Keats that latakia smoke contains. —Keats, said Isidor, I don't know . . . —Better than hanging around with a lot of *fetishists*, said MacK. When I am thirsty the trout-brown angels bring me lacquer bowls of lapsang souchong. There is a hint of cigar leaf some days as in the old Sobranie No. 10. —The yellow tin, said Isidor. Puked once after but it was classy. —And when I am hungry, said MacK, they bring me the salmons of Argyll smoked over peat of the Hebrides, and a glass of Laphroaig. And anyway you are *always* puking, so . . . —Hey, I got smoked salmon in *my* heaven, said Iz, *plus* you get girls. Goils mit legs!

Laphroaig, latakia, lapsang . . . all the beautiful possible Ls! thought MacK. Suddenly. One might snuggle, even settle down with Olive before a fire of birch logs, their impossibly white smoke, in some mountain cabin forever away from All This (*this perpetual, annoying belief in escape of those not born in New York*):

When sunlight manages in, it is dappled, our red house, standing in cool churchly dark, alone—we're out days. The wooden furniture cools. The beautiful possible Olive makes flanken and I just sit on my ass. The darkness of the forest here, this elbow in the redwood road, can't be penetrated with my reading lamp. Things over-arch our path home. The dark muscles courage from the fog and the smoke of our fires. The brightest thing is *Schlitz* beaming from the tavern window. Folks are nice to us there. We don't stay late. Weekends we tell stories and watch each other bathe. She feels safe when I build a fire . . . it's cool enough to do so every day. She dries her pretty hair by the hearth, sometimes wafting the smoke my way. Smoke fires me when I take her in my arms. I'm a bear. She thumps. And maleishly not contented with love, I have to spook her. —*O no, I've left the ax outside : on the woodpile : in the dark.*

Smoke and girls, they thought now, gin doing what gin telepathically, clairvoyantically does to two people, could be invited into the idea of a third heaven, the heaven of the restaurants. —This telepathy is really . . . said MacK. —Whew, said Isidor, it's . . .

## Martini II

But here and now in the red aorta of The Hour, their friendship seemed weighted down in the prow by what they were not discussing. Not so much as on the deck of *Titanic,* trying to keep your toes from being sliced by violin strings and your ass out of tubas, but things were canted and MacK and Isidor knew that. Isidor looked out beyond the red lit area toward the blue, where the poet sat all indigo in his surplus jacket with cigarette. —How can anyone drink their beer over there, said Isidor, look what color the foam is. I find that rather lurid. —He's a poet, isn't he? said MacK.

The martinis in The Hour were not of the Caracalla size favored by the bulls of Pine Street, but they weren't of the old Restaurant size either. —What about this, said Isidor, do you realize they have 'smalls'? The boys were insulted to notice a small elegant glass displayed behind the bar, DEMI MARTINI. —If I tip my head like this, said Izzy, things feel better and that glass makes sense. I think I might slow down.

This sitting here should not be ruined by any plunges, MacK thought, I'm not here for an orgy but for quiet love of things. And just enough neck oil. —*Deux demis*, said Isidor to the pup in the white jacket, who was a craftsman without a haircut, as it turned out.

MacK felt a sting of guilt, but it was not a time to suffer this and so he spoke. —I have something to reveal, he said. Isidor started, his eyes widened and he looked ahead at himself in the mirror. —You mean . . .? —No, it's not that, ah gods not yet, said MacK, who'd forgotten for a *second* why they were here. It's that I already had a martini today. Isidor turned to stare at him as if World War II had begun again. —Really, he said. I never heard of anyone doing that ever before. —Well, it *was* in midtown, said MacK, and it *was* the lunch hour and it *was* . . . the Yale Club. —I see. So you're flying, is that it? said Iz. What a place to spend your . . . he didn't finish. —Don't worry, said MacK, it's been . . . sucked out of me. —Good, said Iz.

—Can we get back to heaven for a moment? said MacK. —Where do you think it is that you are? said Iz. —I think really, don't you want to make sure the food is good? said MacK—the delight of leggy company and the comfort of smoke aside, don't we really think it will be a sort of restaurant? Heaven might be a *regular table* and you sit there day upon day. —It's not about gluttony, said Isidor quickly. —Not at all, said MacK, it's about a comfortable seat and a table in front of you for eternity. —See, you always have to have this *table*, said Isidor, you know that? You're always squirming and sweaty when there's nothing to *hide your lap*. —I guess so, said MacK, ignoring this aggression, after all, one will have to eat, drink, smoke and write postcards. For a long time. He thought of his studio in the RCA Building, the comfortable chair, the neat piles of Things to Say, the clock and the controls slanted toward him, *To Network, To Key Stations, Master Control, Standby, Announce, Flag Announce, Telephones 1 2 3 4 5 6 7 8 9, Network News, Presentation Only*, the Neumann microphones in their suspensory which floated so easily into any position. Maybe he could take it with him as a drinks holder? —It's not that, said Isidor, it's that sometimes in your life you have to stand up, use your legs, proclaim your midriff to the world, be seen in total. —Really? said MacK, it hardly seems requisite now. Isidor blushed. —Yeah.

Silence.

—You may well be right, resumed Isidor, the white cloths would seem true to judeochristian iconography; the vessels. —We can construct heaven, said MacK boldly. After all, everyone else has. This guy was talking to me on the bus—he started complaining about Scientology, EST, the Forum, B'Hai, the Mormons . . . —Complaining? —Yeah, he said he didn't like 'made-up' religions. And I said *Oh! You think THOSE are the 'made-up' ones?* —What'd he say? —He got off, said MacK. —You silenced him. —He got off, that's all I know, said MacK. —Where? —Church Street. —*HE GOT OFF AT CHURCH STREET!?* shrieked Isidor, who sometimes believed MacK never thought anything out. —Oh.

—So let's *make* with the heavens, said Iz. —I nominate the waiters, the long bar, paneling and chowder from the Tadich Grill in San Francisco, said MacK. —Yes to paneling, said Isidor, but I do not want to spend eternity with those guys. I want the waiters from Gage & Tollner. —Well of course we don't want waiters with *wings*, that is for sure, said MacK. Don't you find it revolting, in religious painting, when you see an angel's back, *where the wings come out?* —Don't get me started, said Isidor. An angel may be a waiter but that doesn't make a waiter an . . . They looked at each other and then simultaneously said: *Paddy's Clam House*. —And why not, said Iz, they're already there, maybe. A Fish Restaurant the model for heaven. —You'd better let me pick the wine, he said nervously. —So? —Sherry-Lehmann's catalogue of 1963, he sighed. —And the cigars? —What are you *talking* about! Isidor barked. THEY'LL HAVE CIGARS!

Then Isidor pictured Seligman wandering marbled halls, wringing his hands and checking on all his killed little businessmen.

—You pick the sunlight, said Isidor. —From Paris. —Done.

This was very embarrassing because here was the thing now almost out in the open. Practically *on the bar*, with the nuts and the stack of napkins. The bar, whereon the man in all the jokes comes in and plumps a strange machine, or an octopus, or a set of ladies' under-garments, or a little duck on a fruitcake tin.

So, MacK : —Look it's curtains, really. The guy said. He knows I don't want to do anything about it, he's pissed off—so that must be why he was—*brusque*.

(A choke-making word.)

—What he said was that he had to give up and stop counting the *nodules*. I hate that word. And that was that, as far as *he* was concerned, even though *I* need to've had many, many more women and less to smoke, possibly that would have been good, said MacK, in a disorganized way. Was he beginning to feel electrocardiographically disorganized? —Here I'm going to die without having had enough sex, said MacK. What everyone dreads.

Isidor glared at his martini. He asked that its best silveriness emerge now and bless MacK and himself with the most important quality of the martinis they'd had in Jack Dempsey's, years and years ago: namely to exist in the past, at least for one moment. Please. That old-television silveriness that always stopped time. Before. But of course if you're saying there is a Before, then it never did stop it, Isidor thought. Very ruefully.

MacK and Isidor had both raised themselves and turned straight-on to the mirror behind the bar. For the next while they addressed each other's reflections in the mirror, for face each other they could not.

—Aren't you angry at the smokeables? said Iz, after all, they've done you in. —My pipe never hurt me, said MacK, it was cigarettes. One, to be exact. Isidor's eyes bulged out. —One!? he said, his indignation rising on a number of fronts, *which* one? —I'm not sure. —Those 'Gauloises' didn't do you a pack of good, said Isidor. —*Au contraire*, said MacK, they do you just about a pack of good. —If I were you I'd be completely pissed off, said Izzy, I'd punch out every smoker and doctor in town. They collude. I'd want to kill and kill and kill. —*No time*, said MacK. Which silenced Isidor. —There's literally *no point* in being angry, I find, because I've lived here. Known you. There have been many rounds of pleasing drinks. We VOTED together. And I've had a really good microphone at work for the past fifteen years. —What! said Isidor. —You know, the Neumann. —I can't believe I'm hearing this. And MacK felt an awareness of how many times he'd denied things to Isidor, days when they weren't in sync. But these were not many.

—But, see, I'm not going to let you get away with this, said Iz, and he immediately felt like crap again, because he had to; MacK *would* get away. —Hey, man, these little drinks have *reduced the scope of the discussion*, said Izzy.

## Martini III

Brought by the bright boy. —Thank you, bright boy, said Isidor, who meant only to cherish, but felt rude. Let's get to the bottom of this. —Why? said MacK. —So we can *move on*, of course, said Iz. We don't want to talk about this *all night*. Do you want to talk about it all night? MacK felt something askew. He had imagined that after he and Isidor sat down in The Hour that there would quickly come nothing more to be said. He realized he had imagined nothing, no life beyond *his ass* on *this seat*. How stupid. No more talk and therefore no more Isidor, no more Isidor, no more world. As if *Isidor* was going to die. And of course this was all a bit hasty; his carcinomas were obviously not in the business of doing him any favors, but why ought they to kill him in a comfortable bar with his favorite drink and man? No, no, they are far too obtuse for that. So: —No, said MacK, I don't want to talk about it all night.

—*Good*, said Isidor, I just wanted to know how you *feel*, I mean, these things are sent to comfort us, and we embrace them, we embrace them with enthusiasm because they are godsends. And it turns out that months or even years ago these *things*, these compounds *rounded* on you, and now you're—. Think of all that travelling we did on the IRT, *going* to Seligman, *going* to the Wilburs.

I mean, what I want to know is, WHAT IS THIS PLANT FOR? Does *everything* we like have to *kill* us? Loving something, and knowing that love, causes your death? Inevitably? Because time passes and you feel things. Maybe that's the way we all die, thrusting ourselves into the perfect drink, the girl with the highest heels, the best job, the best book. Think about it, said Isidor, you eventually find the best book to read and it *kills you*. You have to *insure that time will pass* by chasing the gods that offer the most. Otherwise you can't be sure that time is going by, and while death will come, he will come merely to throw a blanket over your head and hit you with a frying pan—*Dunnng!* MacK reflected on this. —You never liked the Wilbur girls, he said. —That's not exactly true, said Isidor. I disliked all the pictures. Their famous dead customers. I'm not going to smoke a pipe from some dump just because *Herbert Hoover* did. What does Herbert Hoover know about smoking? —What does he know about *anything?* said MacK. —Metallurgy, said Isidor, since you ask me.

—No—what I have to say to you, said Isidor suddenly, is this. He rose. *O no*, thought MacK. Isidor held up the nobler-sized drink and squinted through it, first at MacK, then with some blurring at the rest of the world. Saw his silver wish come true.

—I always believed, said Isidor, that when our mutual, clownish attempts at quote normal unquote life, I mean our attempts *to mate* had failed, and failed ultimately, that when all the women we have courted and chased all over town totally and finally rejected us *forever*, that we would end up together, I mean sharing a place. That we'd live that long. Of course I have Sylvie now, and the shop. And a cat. But without being superstitious, or disloyal to Sylvie, and to the cat, to my future with them, I still always believed that I would end up on my way to the Battery with you, or McSorley's, or Seligman's. Or I thought we'd finally leave the city *successfully*—don't stop me please I know this is *pure* fantasy—and live on an island in Maine or maybe even become retired FLORIDA GUYS, stranger things have happened. Just two old *guys* who pretend to think. Who carry on with culture. I read the *New York Times* and you drive me crazy with television, and all the stuff you personally *remember* from television. These two cynical old skunks who religiously observe the cocktail hour and you could hear them cackling for hours if you walk by their house on a warm evening. We end up talking like Abbott & Costello. In the local store we're very polite but often giggle. Occasionally some very pretty women come to visit us. Women who like us but can't stand us for more than a WEEK a YEAR.

—There's always lots of bottles, said MacK, but we keep the place up. —That's right, said Isidor, still looking through his drink with one eye. We grow a lot of coriander, capsicum, and hops. —Fag its, said MacK.

Here Isidor caught himself.

—What I want to say is that this STINKS. I reject the idea that LIFE could come to an end just as a simple sum, so many cigarettes, martinis, taxi rides, books, laughs. Nights. I mean to say: if we really are ORGANISMS, then we ought to DIE IN THE FOREST. Biodegrade. We ought to quietly become leaves and granite. Just slough away in soggy blue shreds from the tide pool.

—I thought, said Isidor slowly, the city would save us.

MacK turned away.

The inward movements of friendship.

The world had tipped toward them for an hour.

—So what I'm *saying* is, said Isidor—he reached out toward MacK with his drink—is that this is your cure. *I'm telling you*, you get this down you, you walk out of here no problem. Think about the *Lenni Lenape*, man, I know, I know, Lenny Who? said Iz, heading MacK off at the pass. You know what they used to do when they got poison ivy? —No. —They used to *eat* it. No kidding—they break out in a rash, they don't go for *calamine lotion*, they f***ing CHOMP DOWN on the stuff, they swallow fistfuls of it and Boom. So I say: more to the more. Me and this martini sez you're going nowhere. You're CURED.

Izzy stopped looking at MacK through his martini and took That Sip of it.

MacK turned back to the bar and looked at the olive in its trian-
gular silver cloud. —I'm *cured*, he said. Cured. I'm cured. And off
he went to the gents.

—Gee Whizz, said Isidor in a whisper. I get *naga* and the guy *dies*.


—Do you know that in all our fair heavens, said MacK, who looked
a little wet on his return, and spoke a little bravely, we included
nothing from Sevilla? The boys realized they had included nothing
from Sevilla, which does have many heavenly Restaurant and
Manhattan qualities.

*The waitering is done in short jackets.*

*There is ice water which tastes like New York.*

*The clams are dirt cheap.*

*There is Tabasco for the steaks.*

*There is Roberto, student of Isidor, beloved of the gods.*

*It is located at the corner of Bedford and Charles.*

You sort out your heaven, but of course it is not here. And they
were not men to drink all night any longer, they are reasonably
sober, sober reasonable men. One is ill. That Day had come down to
This. —What you wanna do? said Isidor, wanna eat? MacK
contemplated the pink foam of the future. —Perhaps. —Want to go
to Sevilla? —Sure. Or, maybe . . . They both felt the heavy weight
of the medical. Felt it here. And here. —It's not so hard, said Iz,
just when we finish up here we could walk, you know, right over
to Seventh, and then down to Bedford, and boom. MacK flared
after staring at a map he was trying to form in his mind with the
grid of bottles behind the bar. —Why *Bedford*, he said, you just
walk over to Charles and then *down* to Bedford, avoiding Sheridan
Square like a good fellow. —Bedford and Charles don't intersect,
said Isidor in his most challenging matter-of-fact. —It's located at
Bedford and Charles, said MacK. —What are you talking about?
said Isidor, there is no such corner. —Look on the matchbook,
said MacK, it *says* Bedford *at* Charles. —That's *IMPOSSIBLE, YOU*

*ASS HOLE*, said Isidor loudly and he couldn't believe he said that and neither could the bartender, young Matt, who though lacking intrinsic presence was still the bartender and as such his startled glance at Isidor carried some small authority. Isidor waved at him—Sorry—and burped. *Waaap*. MacK looked at the illuminated bottles. —I didn't come here to be insulted, he said. —I don't think you can be too sure about that, said Isidor apologetically.

Inside: Isidor was angry and bereft. MacK was desolate but it was too at Bedford and Charles.

—It's not 'located' there said Iz. Softly: I'm telling you. After this pause, of anguish, Isidor said: Look at us. We're having our *last fight*.

Got their coats, which had only just shed the cool air of their earlier walk through the neighborhood, and took them through the red and blue areas of cocktail out into the cold. MacK thought: if we go to Sevilla, there will be all that, and this will not be it. But then after Sevilla it will be it, and perhaps that will not be so good as it is freezing and who knows if I will be full of bonhomie as usual after Sevilla or maybe tonight it will just be *the aftermath of beef* and that would be intolerable, that *that* would be it.

—It was a 'Marlboro', said MacK, from that stupid idiot in McAnn's. Or one of the god damn Brits and their god damn 'Silk Cuts', I've almost decided. Isidor looked at him. —Of course it couldn't be one that you *enjoyed*, he said, that would never do, would it?

—No, said MacK. Listen, I don't think Sevilla tonight, he said, looking uptown. —Not hungry? said Isidor quickly, I understand. —It's not that, said MacK, I'm not sure that it *exists* any longer. —Sure it does, said Isidor, looking down. —I'll just go, said MacK. —We could go tomorrow, said Isidor, feeling around in his coat for—? He pulled out a mashed instance of the grey envelope by which

## SELIGMAN

is known in midtown and the various suburbs, and handed it to MacK. —Oh, said MacK looking rather delighted. Inside was a pipe of his favorite billiard shape and a four-ounce pouch of 'Owl'. —The cure, said the shaman Isidor. Neither MacK nor Isidor were *thinking* what this *meant*; it was their old exchange. Because of this, now far from tears, MacK filled the pipe and stood on the curb looking like an overly friendly lamp post. They regarded each other. MacK breathed in, a setting-off-uptown intake. The air in his nose was cold. —Have you ever, he asked Isidor, had a certain, exact hair? A special one that you coddle, a TOY HAIR? That you let grow maybe, while exterminating all the others, on your eyebrow, or ear, or maybe even in your nose? In the morning you can't wait to get out of bed to see how it's doing? And test its springiness?

Isidor looked up and down the street. —Gedaddahere, you crazy nut, he said. He took a few steps away. MacK's smile began to wane and so did his color. Suddenly this was intolerable, they were being pulled apart by two hateful little gods, right there on the street, yanked apart with twice the decisiveness of Mary-Ann and Rosenthal—but half the strength. Isidor turned and walked toward the south. He didn't look back. *These are shoes for a guy who walks*.

MacK stood looking after him. He lighted his pipe—'Owl' never burns very well until it has been breathing New York itself for a few days. He lighted the pipe and, like Early Man bearing fire, carried the flavorful embers of the Old World, of *Isidor*, uptown.